PS: I Hate You

PS:
I Hate
You

LAUREN CONNOLLY

BERKLEY ROMANCE
NEW YORK

BERKLEY ROMANCE
Published by Berkley
An imprint of Penguin Random House LLC
penguinrandomhouse.com

Book design by George Towne

Library of Congress Cataloging-in-Publication Data

Names: Connolly, Lauren, author.
Title: PS: I hate you / Lauren Connolly.
Description: First edition. | New York : Berkley Romance, 2024.
Identifiers: LCCN 2024006153 | ISBN 9780593815663 (trade paperback) |
ISBN 9780593815670 (ebook)
Subjects: LCGFT: Romance fiction. | Novels.
Classification: LCC PS3603.O547256 P7 2024 | DDC 813/.6—dc23/eng/20240223
LC record available at https://lccn.loc.gov/2024006153

First Edition: December 2024

Printed in the United States of America
1st Printing

To Brave Joe and Debra

AUTHOR'S NOTE

This book deals with emotionally difficult topics, including child neglect, verbal and physical abuse, a car accident, suicidal thoughts, miscarriage, loss of a loved one, anxiety, and potentially unhealthy relationships with food. Any readers who believe that such content may upset them or trigger traumatic memories are encouraged to consider their emotional well-being when deciding whether to continue reading this book.

Winter

CHAPTER

One

In between muttering curses at the funeral home's abysmal Wi-Fi, I consider if hiding in a supply closet to work during my brother's wake makes me a terrible sister.

"Well, you didn't want a funeral anyway, did you?" I whisper to the shelves of cleaning products, as if Josh is a ghost, invisibly sitting next to the bottles of lemon-scented floor polish. "You wanted us to rent a booze cruise and smash piñatas with your face on them."

My brother couldn't stand somberness. He was the funny one. A natural comedian who could take the darkest moment and make a joke that would have you laughing while the world around you was a shit show.

Like right now. If only he was here.

But if Josh was here, then there'd be no need for an over-the-top mourning ritual he never asked for.

If there is an afterlife where he's floating around, Josh is dying all over again, but this time from laughter, watching me sit on a half-empty box of toilet paper rolls as I try to put out a digital fire at work, all while wearing itchy tights I scratched so hard that I tore a hole in the left ass cheek.

"You're welcome," I say to my laptop as my updated report finally sends, not sure if I'm talking to my boss on the other side of the country or to the specter of my brother. Probably both.

And just when I'm sure I've gotten away with my sneaky errand and can rejoin the crowd of mourners filling the building, the closet door opens.

I squeak in surprise at the sudden intrusion and lean back, which is a mistake because that puts my butt on the empty half of the box. The cardboard lid collapses inward, taking me with it. I fold at the waist, laptop smashing against my chest, pantyhose-covered legs shooting straight up in the air.

This day got worse. I didn't think that was possible.

"Shit. Maddie." A deep voice says my name with too much familiarity. "Are you okay?"

No. No, I am not okay.

There is an endless list of reasons why I am the furthest possible thing from okay.

Top of the list: my brother, the person I love—loved—most in the world, is gone only three months before his thirtieth birthday.

But the reason I'm not okay in *this* particular moment is because the person asking after my well-being is the man who did an impressively thorough job of breaking my heart.

Dominic Perry.

Josh's best friend, and someone I was hoping to avoid for the rest of my life.

But that's hard to do when the man steps in close, reaching out his hands to help me unwedge myself from my bath tissue prison.

And of course, he looks like a heartthrob in shining armor as he comes to my aid. Dom has been devastatingly handsome ever since his face caught up with the long slope of his nose. Chiseled jaw, warm brown eyes that trick naive nerdy girls into trusting him, and black hair that swoops in an infuriatingly perfect wave over his pale forehead and around ears that stick out just far enough to be charming.

Today, he's dressed in a black suit that hugs his body.

Shouldn't funeral suits be ill-fitting? My theory is grief is supposed to make your clothes sag and bunch in all the wrong places. That's the excuse I'm using for the blockish, weirdly clinging dress I found in the back of my closet.

"I'm lovely. Seriously. Living the dream down here." I attempt to lift myself with the sheer strength of my embarrassment.

Doesn't work. All I manage to do is flip my hair into my face, reminding me that I spent all morning heating and spraying it to get my brown strands to curl half as well as Dom's do naturally. But I could comb super glue into the shoulder-length mass and still end the day with only a half-hearted wave left.

"Here." Strong hands grasp my elbows and pull me to stand with ease.

When I have my feet under me, I shove my hair out of my eyes and shuffle to the side, away from his broad chest and the scent of some mystery cologne that has me thinking of frosty cedar-filled forests where men in flannel go to chop wood just for the hell of it.

I could sell tickets to a place like that. Retire at the ripe age of twenty-six.

Breathing through my mouth, I search for the black heels I kicked off the moment I was alone, because they pinch my toes the way grief shoes should.

"What are you doing in here?" Dom asks, his voice a raspy rumble that gives me chills.

"Plotting world domination, obviously. Josh was supposed to handle the foreign policy, but now he's left me with double the workload. Rude of him. I plan on filing a complaint."

Did I mention inappropriately timed humor runs in the family?

Arguably, hiding myself in a closet is in everyone's best interest. These strangers want to watch me cry prettily. (But is that even physically possible? Who can have saltwater leaking out of their eyes and not look like a flushed, snotty mess?) No one came to this depression parade to hear my morbid sarcasm about my dead brother.

This whole funeral was my mother's requirement. Cecilia Sanderson needed the pomp and circumstance of tradition to mourn the son she never spent much time loving while he was alive. Some of the throng outside this closet are Josh's friends, but most people are here because of her and the articles she's been writing and posts she's been curating about her son's inspiring yearlong battle against cancer. His death tripled her followers.

Somehow, I've ended up alone in a closet with the only person I want to avoid more than my selfie-obsessed mother.

"Noted," Dom says, taking my ridiculous statement in stride. He looms over me. "I was looking for—"

"For some toilet paper?" I cut him off. "You found the right place. Don't be ashamed. I hear grief often causes diarrhea. I'll let everyone know you're indisposed." Taunting him is the best way to distract myself from how my body reacts to his proximity. Going hot, then cold, then tingly and tight.

Like getting a disease. Dom is infectious.

He's also immune to me and my verbal barbs.

"Thanks for that," he deadpans, then his voice softens. "How are you doing?" Dom crosses his arms as he stares down at me. I can see his chin tilt and feel the weight of his eyes on my face. There's an air of demand in his posture, as if he expects me to answer with a thorough outline of my emotional state.

Dominic Perry is used to taking control of a situation.

This room—which was too tiny before he shoved his way in—now feels like his more than mine. The space is claustrophobic enough for my fingers to stretch for my inhaler. I shimmy around him, needing out. Needing to breathe air that's not infused with his essence.

"Spectacular. Like I'm the only survivor at the end of a slasher movie." In an effort to ignore the overpowering man, I check my laptop, making sure nothing got damaged on my short trip into the toilet paper box. Everything seems in working order. I close the computer, slip it into the padded pocket of my bag, and sling the strap over my shoulder as I reach the door.

All the while, Dom turns with me, tracking my every movement.

"I know it's been a while, but I'm here for you." His voice rasps over my nerves, leaving me raw and my fingers cold as they grasp the doorknob. "You can talk to me."

Been a while.

That's one way to refer to the night we spent together, and the day after where he . . .

Don't think about that.

I might finally start crying if I do. And if any tears come out of my eyes today, they better be for Josh and not some asshole who regretted me.

"That's so sweet of you, but I'm good." I shove out of the suffocating closet. "Got a few other one-night stands I like to call for deep, emotional conversations. You're low on the list."

Leaving him, I stalk down the hallway, toward the sounds of a gathering I do not want to join. But uncomfortable chatter with strangers is better than spending another minute in an enclosed space with bad memories personified.

If anyone at my day job heard the way I just spoke to Dom, they'd think I got bit by a bitchy zombie. But I don't care. No way in hell or any other dimension will I ever be vulnerable for that man again.

Younger Maddie had a different mindset.

There was a time I would've done anything to claim the smallest sliver of Dominic Perry's attention. He was the star of all my teenage fantasies. The guy I imagined would someday see me as more than his best friend's kid sister.

When I was nineteen, my dream came true.

But it quickly turned into a nightmare that sent me packing, escaping to the other side of the country just so I never had to see his handsome, heartbreaking face again.

Avoiding the thick crowd of unfamiliar attendees, I slow at a table covered in framed photos of my brother. There's so many. A few are of him and me. But a lot are of Josh with friends. Josh in beautiful locations. Josh on adventures. Josh traveling. Always smiling.

Always leaving.

The table is like a fun-house mirror of all the times he went so far and I didn't see him for so long.

I left, too. The absences weren't all his fault.

Now I'll never see him again.

"Maddie."

Dom followed me, and I hate how good my name sounds in his rumbling voice.

"Dominic." I pitch my voice low, mocking his deep delivery. There's no need to turn and face him when he casts a heavy gloom around me like I've stepped into the shadow of a mountain. "I told you, I'm peachy. Go pretend to care about someone else."

"I'm the executor of Josh's will."

The words take a moment to register. Mainly because I don't know what an executor is.

"What?" Unable to fight the urge, I glare up at the unfortunately tall bane of my existence.

"He named me executor," Dom repeats, and I still don't know what that means, which infuriates me. "There are items he wanted given to family"—he waves at me like maybe I forgot Josh was my blood—"and close friends. Since we're all here, I reserved a small room for everyone to meet. I'll distribute everything."

"Wait," I snap. "Wait wait wait." My hands wave in the air as I try to shut him up before he says more things that piss me off. "That's supposed to be, like, a lawyer's job."

Dom watches me, expression revealing nothing. "Executors don't have to be lawyers. You can assign anyone."

From his tone, I get a silent—judgmental—question. *You don't have all your affairs perfectly in order for the day that you die, Maddie?*

No, I don't. Because I'm a normal fucking twenty-six-year-old.

"And Josh chose . . . you."

My brother chose Dominic Perry, Mr. Responsible Asshole, for this special postdeath job over *me*.

His sister.

Are you kidding me, Josh?

We weren't some estranged siblings that barely knew each other. We were close. We talked on the phone every week, even if he was on the opposite side of the world from me. We had enough inside jokes to fill a small-town public library.

When Josh told me about his diagnosis, he cried, and I cried, and we hugged and lied to each other that he would kick cancer's ass.

But when he needed a fancy official *executor*, Josh chose Dom.

I glare at the cluster of Joshes framed on the table, imagining my brother laughing at my frustration.

"I have something for you. From him." Dom steps back as he says the words, knowing the siren song he's singing to me.

Something from Josh. Even if my brother left it in the care of the man I hate most in the world, I must have the mystery item. I'm tempted to snarl *Give it!* and make grabby hands, but I have some sense of pride.

Just a little bit.

"Fine," I snap. "I'll come to your special *executor* room."

The man nods and leads the way. At least this gets me far from the crush of strangers again.

Although, if I'm going to a room with family, that must mean—

"Madeline!" My mother's voice sounds the moment I step through the doorway. "Oh, Madeline. There you are." She strolls up to me, looking red-carpet ready in her all-black suit and heels. In an effortless move, she scoops me up into a hug. Almost as if she's been doing it my whole life.

She hasn't. I can count the times Cecilia Sanderson hugged me on my fingers and still have a few left over.

"Mom." After an awkward pat on her back, I let my arms drop.

She sets me down and smooths her hands over my hair. "Here, we need to remember moments like this."

Before I realize what she's doing, Mom has her phone up, my head clutched against her breast, and the camera clicking. There's no time to say this is a day I hope I forget through an overindulgence in gin tonight.

Mom releases me so suddenly that I stumble back a step. Not that she notices, too focused on her screen, working on some social post or another about the grieving mother and the surviving daughter she loves oh so much.

A firm press on my lower back steadies me. Glancing to the side, I realize Dom has braced me, but before I can hiss at him, he steps away and strides past without a word.

"Black is not your color," Cecilia murmurs, distracting me.

Would you believe that's only mildly hurtful compared to other comments she's doled out over the course of my life?

"Thanks, Mom. Appreciate the feedback." I could put in the effort to say, *Hey, Mom, maybe don't insult your daughter when she's only wearing black to mourn her dead brother.*

But then I would get an eye roll followed by the claim that I'm being dramatic, which would then lead to a useless back-and-forth that would change nothing about the way she talks to me. If Josh dying wasn't enough to have Cecilia reevaluating how she treats her remaining kid, what hope do I have?

Another woman strolls up to us, sipping from a martini glass. I welcome her appearance only because I now know there is a bar somewhere.

"Hi, Aunt Florence," I greet her. She's not actually my aunt. Florence is Cecilia's mother, my grandmother, and the woman who technically raised me, though there wasn't a lot of child-rearing going on at the time. Mainly, she made rules, and if she caught Josh or me not following them, we got locked out of the house until we shouted enough apologies through the window to earn reentry.

"Madeline. How is Seattle?" Florence narrows her eyes, studying my face. "I know it's rainy, but do you ever go out in the sun? You'll never find a man with you looking so washed out."

Shot number two for the day. Three if we count Dom finding me floundering in a box of paper products.

"You know, I think we do get some sun. I'll have to look into that. Wouldn't want people thinking *I'm* the corpse." No point in arguing that they're both as pale as me and that we have the kind of skin that burns rather than tans—when I go outside, I wear hats and a thick coat of sunscreen.

She grimaces at my comparison.

Luckily, when I glance past my two blood relatives, I discover a collection of welcome faces. I dodge around my mother, straight into the embrace of the woman I wish had given birth to me.

"Maddie! Oh, Maddie. I'm sorry." Emilia Perry, Dom's mom, pulls me in for a tight hug. This embrace has every bit of generous caring that my mother's lacked. "I can't even . . . I don't know what to say." She holds me close, her arms strong, body soft, ink-colored hair smelling of vanilla.

"That's okay." I'm not normally a hugger, but I hold Emilia close, feeling a pressure behind my eyes, but no corresponding wetness.

What's wrong with me? Why haven't I cried?

It's been a week since the doctors pronounced Josh as dead, but I haven't shed a tear.

Maybe I'm as cold as my mother and grandmother. I always thought I was different from them. That I broke away from their mold.

But maybe I've been fooling myself.

"Oh goodness. Look at me." Emilia releases her hold and tugs a tissue from her pocket to dab her cheeks. "Mr. Perry wanted to be here, but he was called in for an emergency surgery. He sends his love."

Nathanial Perry works as a neurologist at the local hospital, while Emilia is the outreach director for a green-energy nonprofit. Or at least, that's what they used to do. It's been a while since we talked.

"Anything you need," she continues. "Just say the word. Josh was family. You're family."

Am I?

An ache in my chest has me rubbing my sternum.

"Thank you," I murmur.

"You're *like* family," a cheerful voice clarifies, and I glance over to meet a set of playful brown eyes in a face that looks similar to—but not exactly the same as—the man I hate. "Keep in mind that we're not actually related. So . . . like . . . dating wouldn't be weird. You know?" The guy gives me a wide, devastating grin.

Adam Perry. Standing next to his equally handsome twin brother, Carter. Dom's younger siblings—who I remember last as two scrawny thirteen-year-olds—tower over me and their mother, both looking like they belong on an Olympic swim team next to the likes of Michael Phelps.

"Last time I saw you, you couldn't drive," I remind him.

"Yeah, but I'm all grown-up now. I can take you anywhere you wanna go." He waggles his eyebrows, and Carter snorts.

"Are you hitting on me at my brother's funeral?"

Adam's flirty smirk falls away. "Oh shit. Sorry. That was insensitive."

"No. It's okay." I reach out and pat his chest. The guy put on a lot of muscle in the last seven years. "You were doing great. Keep going."

His face lights up like the time I gave him all the Kit Kats from my Halloween candy haul. "Really? Okay. You remember that purple bikini you wore—"

"No." The word, spoken in a deep, unrelenting voice, cuts off Adam's flattery.

I almost forgot Dom was in the room. Okay . . . that's a lie. But when he wasn't talking, I found it easier to pretend.

Adam pouts, staring over my shoulder. "What? I was going to compliment Maddie."

"Not like that," Dom growls from behind me, and I suppress a shudder, hating that every cell in my being wants to turn and examine the expression on his face.

I keep my attention on Adam.

"I want to hear the compliment," I say. Would be nice to get a confidence boost after the mom and grandma treatment.

Adam's smile returns, pairing with a too-innocent expression. "Thank you, Maddie. I was very respectfully going to say that the purple bikini"—he pauses, waiting for his older brother to cut him off again. Dom stays silent, so Adam continues, speaking fast—"had your tits looking fantastic and played a starring role in my teenage spank bank."

"Adam!" Mrs. Perry gasps while Carter coughs into his fist and Dom lets out a snarl, his body coming into view on my left side as he charges for his brother.

But I make it there first.

I fling my arms around Adam's neck, and the big man lifts me up in a crushing embrace.

"Thank you," I mutter into his neck. "I needed that."

"Anytime." He lowers his voice to match mine. "If you need to relax, come find me. I got some pot I can share. High-quality stuff. Only the best for Maddie Sanderson."

When he sets me on the ground, I find myself doing something I did not expect to do today.

I laugh.

The idea that Dom has tried his hardest to exert control over his wayward brothers—a task he's had since he was nine—but one still managed to sneak weed into a funeral brings me an immense amount of joy.

"You really know how to woo a lady." I chuckle. "Thanks for the *generous* offer."

Dom scowls between the two of us, unaware of what, exactly, his little brother just whispered in my ear.

Well, isn't he lucky to have a living brother to be pissed at. The thought reminds me of my own anger, my loss, and the reason I let Dom drag me to this room.

"You said something about executing," I prompt him, trying not to let my fury at his role show in my voice.

Dom lingers a moment more before striding over to a table and picking up an accordion folder. He undoes the tie, keeping the flap closed as he speaks to the small gathering. "Josh's will stated there are letters in here for everyone in this room."

A letter. My palms sweat and my heart races and I envision my brother's specter again, ready to chat with me postmortem. That's all I want. More time with him.

Dom pulls out envelopes one by one, reading out the names. "Cecilia Sanderson. Florence Sanderson. Mom—looks like this is for you and Dad. Carter. Adam."

Me me me. Say my name. Give me the letter!

"Rosaline."

I flinch and jerk my chin to the side in time to see the woman step forward and accept her piece of my brother. With her bronze curls pinned in a high bun away from her cheeks, I have a clear view of the tears cascading from her thick-lashed eyes. *Well, there's someone who cries pretty.* Rosaline even makes grief look beautiful.

I didn't realize she was in the room, but I should've known.

Of course Dom's wife would be here.

Dominic and Rosaline Perry. The picture-perfect couple, and Josh's two best friends.

Another time, I would fall into a painful spiral of comparing myself to the gorgeous woman Dom chose over me. But today I have something more important to focus on.

My letter.

Give me my letter.

"There's only one more," Dom murmurs, and I can't help an evil smirk.

Mr. Responsible Asshole got to execute the will but didn't warrant a bonus note.

Who does Josh love the most now, huh? I bite my lip to stifle the taunt, wanting to keep from revealing the bitchy zombie in my soul to the Perry family members I like.

Dom pulls out the thickest so far, one of those legal-sized envelopes that need an extra metal clasp to keep the flap shut.

"Hand it over." I reach for the parcel, rabid for whatever bit of Josh is contained within.

"It's not yours." Dom stares at the final parcel, his thick brows scrunching.

"What?" My single-word question spears through the room, sharp and cold as an icicle flung like a dagger. Everyone pauses in the act of tearing open their envelopes.

I couldn't have heard him right.

No. No no no.

Josh loved playing games, but never cruel ones. My brother wouldn't leave last words for everyone but me.

Dom's eyes meet mine, his gone wide with a surprise he rarely allows on his stoic face.

What could have rattled Mr. Responsible Asshole?

"It's ours," he says.

Dom turns the envelope to show the devastatingly familiar penmanship. Josh wrote those letters with his own hand. He might as well have been writing a horror novel once I comprehend what the thick Sharpie scrawl says.

Maddie & Dom

CHAPTER

Two

He turned me into a combo deal? What am I, a side of French fries to Dominic's burger?

I stalk across the room, eyes adhered to the two names, side by side, that have never and will never belong together.

Maddie & Dom

Me and Mr. Responsible Asshole.

My mother and grandmother got separate messages. The twins got their own envelopes. Even Dom's wife warranted her own individual letter. And sure, I know Josh was friends with Rosaline, too, but come on.

They're the married couple.

I'm his goddamn sister.

My fingers brush the stiff envelope as I go to snatch the offending missive. But I miss.

I miss because Dom holds it out of my reach. Easy for him to do when he has a good foot on me.

"If you ever want to use your testicles for anything other than reminiscing about the good old days when they weren't smashed by my fist, you will *give me my envelope*." I hiss the threat, and despite the indignity, I jump and make a futile grab, missing once again by a large margin. My toe-pinching grief heels don't help.

"It's mine, too." Dom keeps it high above my head. "I want to know what he wrote before you run off with it."

"I wasn't going to run off with it."

I was *totally* going to run off with it.

"Liar," he mutters, but lowers his arm.

"Takes one to know one," I return, that bitchy zombie virus pumping strong through my veins. I snatch the letter from his hands but stay put. Mainly because something in Dom's intense stare conveys he'll grab *me* if I try to escape.

"This is a joke!" My grandmother's shout distracts me, and I glance over to find her face flushed, drink forgotten on a side table. "One of Josh's strange jokes I don't get." Florence has a single folded piece of paper in her hand. She flips it back and forth, as if searching for something. "All it says is"—she holds it up, her mouth twisted in a haughty grimace—"*Thanks for the years of therapy.*"

Oh my god. For a brief, shining moment of awe, I find a way to love my brother more than ever before. Of course Josh Sanderson would have the ghostly nerve to hold a grudge into the grave.

"I never paid for therapy," she huffs, oblivious. "What I *did* pay for is clothes, and food, and housing for that arrogant boy. He had money from all those pictures. Where is the check? Where is the money I'm owed?" She glares at Dom, as if he's guarding the treasure chest of Josh's wealth.

What you're owed is exactly what he gave you, I want to shout in her face. But years of living in the cold shadow of Florence's disdain trained me to keep my opinions to myself.

"He had medical bills," Rosaline snaps, never cowed by my judgmental grandmother. "Did you only come here for a payout? If so, you can leave." Dom's wife points to the door while her other hand presses her unopened letter against her chest, acknowledging the precious nature of the correspondence.

Florence sputters, and if I weren't such a petty person, I'd applaud Rosaline.

But I refuse to clap, holding a grudge almost as well as my brother. Whether or not she meant to screw me out of my teenage dream, Rosaline will always be the girl that Dom chose over me. And even if I only hate him now—no longer pining for a taken man—I can't seem to move on from my resentment toward her.

It's not that I hate Rosaline, exactly.

What I hate is who I am, and always was, around her. All through my younger years, I watched as Rosaline formed a tight friendship with Josh and Dom—before romance with the latter was even a consideration. And with the talented, charming girl as a constant presence in our lives, my mother—when she was around—often compared the two of us. Rosaline became a form of measurement that Cecilia used to emphasize the many ways I was lacking. Wasn't long before I internalized her comments and became an even worse version of myself. A greedy, jealous gremlin of a person who could never hope to measure up to Rosaline's beauty and poise and ability to flip off my grandmother. When I'm next to her, I might as well be two inches tall and built of childish insecurities.

So I avoid her, too.

"I never—" Florence starts.

"Maybe," Mrs. Perry speaks over my grandmother, using a more diplomatic tone than her daughter-in-law, "we should all take our notes from Josh and open them in our own time. And then—after this sad day reserved for grieving—you can ask Dom clarifying questions about Josh's will." Her voice hardens on that final sentence as she stares at my grandmother, then flicks her eyes to my mother.

The warning clear.

You two might not care for and defend your children, but Mrs. Perry sure as hell will.

My mom gives a short nod and tucks her letter into a designer purse, probably concerned the contents are as dismissive as Aunt

Florence's. I watch as she pulls on her grieving-mother expression—a small, trembling smile meant to convey strength through devastation—the moment before she strolls out the door into the throngs of her adoring followers. Florence scoops up her martini glass and struts after her, making no effort to clear the scowl from her face.

Good riddance.

"Do you want to wait?" Dom's deep voice recaptures my attention and takes another shivering trip over my nerve endings. I clench my jaw as I force away the reaction.

"I can't."

Josh is in this envelope.

Besides, waiting means putting up with more Dom.

"How about we give you two the room?" Emilia comes to the rescue again, spreading her arms wide almost like a hug, and uses the gesture to guide the twins and Rosaline toward the door. Everyone goes willingly, and even though I don't want to, I watch Rosaline leave.

Her shoulders bow with obvious grief, but that isn't the odd part. What I find strange is how she doesn't say a single word of comfort to Dom before she goes. Not even a glance over her shoulder.

Are the two of them fighting?

I shake my head and snort in self-disgust. Back in my hometown for a week and I'm already falling into my old habits. Namely, creepily observing Dom and Rosaline's relationship.

The two of them started dating in high school, and because of the massive crush I had on my brother's best friend, I became self-destructively fascinated with the girl who had Dom's heart. As if knowing every nuance of their relationship would somehow make him want me.

I thought I got over the habit when I left for college, but here I am, yet again trying to work out the meaning behind their interactions.

Stop it, you weirdo. There are more important things.

Like the letter in my hands.

"Do you want to read—"

"Yes," I cut Dom off. "I will read *my* letter." And do my best to pretend Josh left these words for me, and only me.

With twitchy fingers, I carefully tear along the edge of the seal, finding comfort in the pressure needed to break through the sturdier paper of this legal envelope. The thing is hardy, equipped to hold a large letter. Maybe more.

More of Josh.

I see a slip of white and tug that out first, finding a handwritten note from my brother on a nice piece of parchment with a tiny compass emblem at the top. Josh *would* go fancy for his last words. He was always the type to buy a beautiful journal and use it, while I would purchase one, carefully arrange it on my shelf, and wait for the day when I had something special to write down in the pages. Something worthy of the exterior.

Those days never seemed to come.

Josh knew how to take advantage of beautiful things while he had the time.

"What does it say?" Dom asks, the tension in his voice shoving me out of my memory of my brother where, for a brief breath, my mind was relaxed enough to forget he's gone.

But now the fact blares like oncoming headlights in a pitch-black night, blinding me and setting off a pounding headache.

Gritting my teeth, I breathe through my nose until my aggravation dims to a manageable level.

"Dear Maddie," I read, "my beloved sister, and Mr. Responsible Asshole—"

"That's not what it says." The man leans closer, over my shoulder as if he's going to bypass me entirely.

"I'm the one reading." I turn away from him, pressing the letter against my chest and glaring into a set of brown eyes that are too soft for the hard man behind them.

"If you don't read it right, I'm gonna take it from you."

And because he can follow through on that threat, I stop editing the letter and decide to read it as my brother wrote it.

"Fine." I clear my throat and begin again.

Dear Maddie, my beloved sister, and Dom, my best friend,

I'm not ready to say goodbye.

My voice catches, grief a tripping hazard for my words. But I swallow and carry on.

I think that if I had died fifty years from now, I still would have felt like there were adventures left for me in the world. But time is running out. I'm writing to you from a bed I can't leave anymore. Still, the urge stays with me. To get up and go and see more. To see everything.

Once again, I pause and breathe and try not to drown in hatred at the unfairness of the world. That a man like my brother, who wanted to live so badly, didn't get even half the life that most do. I continue.

I'm not ready to say goodbye, but I know I have to. I have to say it to the world, and I have to say it to you two. But I don't have to say it yet.

My eyes snap up to the door, as if Josh will step through and smile and tell me he's not gone. Not yet. We don't have to say good-bye today.

The door stays closed.

"Maddie . . ." Dom moves closer, his broad body looming over mine, and I don't know if he's about to snatch the letter from me, annoyed that I'm reading too slow.

Panicked at the thought, I press on.

This isn't a goodbye letter. There's one in here. Sorry, there has to be. But it's not this one. This is the starting point. I want you two to do something for me, and luckily, since I'm dead, you can't argue.

I glare at the paper while feeling a tingle of warmth at Josh's familiar morbid humor.

I didn't see everything I wanted to, so you two will have to take some adventures for me. But don't worry, I'll come with you. In fact, I insist on accompanying you. If you would be so kind, Magpie.

The nickname threatens to break me, but I keep going.

Pack up my ashes and spread a handful in the states I've listed at the end of this letter. The ones I never visited. Take me to the places I missed. There is an envelope for each one. Dom, make sure Maddie gets where she needs to go. Some of the places are more exerting than walking to the closest coffee shop. I made good money off my pictures, and I willed most of it to you both. It's yours to use how you want, but I hope you spend some to travel where I never did. Have fun for me. Please do this. It's the last . . .

I stumble over that word, the shock of it a punch straight to the heart.

It's the last thing I'm asking of you. Also, very important: wait until you get to the destinations to open the envelopes.

    Love, Josh

PS: I think this quality time together will be good for you both. Don't hate me.

Beneath his signature is the list he promised. With growing dread, I count.

One . . . two . . . three . . . four . . . five . . . six . . . seven . . . eight. Eight.

My brother wants his ashes spread in *eight* different states.

He wants me to spread his ashes in eight different states with *Dominic Perry.*

"He—" Dom starts, but I don't stay to hear him finish.

I sprint out the door.

"Maddie!" His bellow follows me as I weave through strangers dressed in black, my eyes desperately seeking an exit. I need out. I need air.

I need my brother.

I *hate* my brother.

The words of his letter cycle through my mind as I desperately search for another meaning. How could this be his final ask? Didn't he realize losing him would be hard enough? Now he's demanding I spend however long touring the country with the man I most want to avoid?

And Josh doesn't even have the decency to be here to argue with!

The large envelope crinkles in my grasping fingers as I shoulder my way into the bright midday sun, the mild winter weather refusing to match the dark clouds in my mind and soul.

Even free of the stifling building, I have the urge to keep moving. To escape until I'm far enough to pretend those words I read were fiction. My laptop bag slaps the back of my legs as I stumble through a jog in my heels.

The funeral home's door bursts open behind me.

"Maddie! Don't run away from me!"

But that's what I've been doing since I was nineteen years old, and I see no reason to stop now. My eyes catch on an open gate and my feet propel me forward faster despite the pain in my toes.

Go go go, my brain shouts. *Go as far as you can and never look back!*

"Don't follow me!" If only Dom would leave me alone, then maybe I could forget all this heartache.

"Don't make me chase you through a graveyard." The command of his voice and the pound of his footsteps urge me faster.

"I could never make you do anything!"

I sprint away from Dom, dodging between stone slabs with the names of people who might exist in the same realm that my brother does. They've all left behind people like me. Did any of them set impossible tasks for their loved ones?

The breath in my lungs burns, struggling to leave and struggling to return. The wheezing turns high-pitched, a siren of warning that I've pushed myself too far and am about to face the consequences. I stumble to a stop next to a particularly large headstone and brace my hands on my knees as the air labors from my throat.

I shouldn't have run.

I hate when Dom is right.

"Maddie?" The man looms over me once again. He's good at that. Looming. Hopefully his massive form and judgmental eyes aren't the last things I see before I pass out. "Damn it. Where is your inhaler?"

I pat my bag, attempting to find the little container of medication. A strong hand brushes mine aside and sneaks into the side pocket, as if he knows exactly where I keep the device. Dom tugs it out, checks the mouthpiece for obstructions, then presses the inhaler into my palm.

While my mind goes into desperate survival mode at the loss of oxygen, I shake the device, then try to remember to time my inhale with the puff of my medicine, so the drugs make their way into my lungs. Best practice involves using a spacer—a tube-like attachment—with the inhaler, but the thing is so bulky that I never bother to carry it with me. Not when I usually go months without a flare-up. Sounding like an inner tube with a leak, I squeak through a few more breaths, roughly guessing when another minute has passed, then spray a second round that'll hopefully make it the rest of the way into my lungs to calm the damn things down and open passageways that don't want to comply.

When I was a kid, my asthma attacks would pop up all the time. I think the only reason Florence took me to get my prescriptions filled was so she'd stop getting calls from the school nurse that I was on my way to the hospital.

As I've grown, things have gotten better, and I'll go long stretches without an incident.

But the combination of grief, anger, and running was too much for my sensitive airways to handle.

As the minutes tick past slowly, breathing becomes less of a strain. At some point, I realize I'm sitting on a bench, and I wonder if I made this move or if the man standing in front of me, blocking out the sun with his broad shoulders, guided me here.

That would be a very Dom thing to do.

"Did you"—I wince and wheeze, working around the tightness in my throat—"call an ambulance?"

"No." He kneels in front of me, staring into my face. "I've seen enough of your attacks to know when to drive you to the hospital."

"When I turn blue," I offer. That was the joke Josh would say.

When you look like a smurf, we know things are bad.

Dom's lips tighten, and I remind myself to keep my eyes far away from his mouth.

"Do you want to go to the hospital?" he asks.

I shake my head.

No. Hell no.

Last time I was in the hospital I was holding Josh's hand, his skin cold and chapped as his body tried to conserve energy to survive.

Dom nods, but he stays crouched on his haunches in front of me.

I scowl. "Stop staring at me. I'll be fine in a minute." Probably. At least I can talk now, with only a few gasps at the end of each sentence.

Dom's eyes narrow, but he straightens and paces away from me. My brief hope that he's on his way out, leaving me alone to my misery, evaporates when I watch him bend over to pick up something in the grass.

The envelope.

In my frantic attempts to breathe, I must have dropped it. He spreads the opening, then tips it over. A cascade of smaller envelopes slides into his large palm. Dom shuffles through them, and my fingers curl against my stiff skirt, wanting to snatch them away.

"Eight," he says.

"One for each state." Just like Josh said in his letter.

That damn letter.

Dom slips them back into the large envelope, then turns to face me.

"How are you doing?"

The second time he's asked that today. At least now it's to do with my physical well-being. "I can breathe. So, better than a few minutes ago." I'm still lightheaded, and every part of me inside and out feels raw.

But I'm alive, so there's that.

"Look," he says, "I know you don't want to do this—"

"You're right. I don't."

"This was Josh's last wish."

If I had the strength to get up and shove him, I would. "You don't need to tell me that. And I don't need you to make an argument on his behalf. I loved him more than you ever could have. Of course I'm gonna do this bullshit task. He's *gone*. It's all I have of him, isn't it?"

The berating costs me, and after a string of coughs, I take another puff of my inhaler.

Dom strides up to me, his stare holding mine, emotions flickering to life in his eyes, then disappearing faster than I can interpret them even if I wanted to try.

"We're doing this?" he asks once my breathing evens out again.

"Yes." I grind my teeth before forcing out, "We're doing this."

Dom passes me the envelope, and I hug the piece of my brother to my chest because it's the only comfort I can accept. As he retracts his hand, I spy a flash on his wrist.

A watch. Josh's watch.

Did my brother will him that, too? Or was it a gift before the end?

During the final few days in the hospital, my brother had people with him almost every moment. For months I'd tried to visit so it was just him and me, but there came a time when I had to share my brother, most often with his two best friends.

Does Rosaline have another important piece of Josh, too?

Maybe if I hadn't spent so much effort trying to ignore her and Dom, I would know.

Dom's eyes raise to the sky, squinting at the sun as if he just realized it was daytime.

"Alright. We need to make a plan."

Planning with Dom. Traveling with Dom. Saying goodbye to my brother over, and over, and over, all in front of this man who showed me early on in life he's perfectly fine emotionally devastating me.

Once again, I reach for my inhaler.

Three

The funeral home had no problem incinerating my brother's body, but they drew the line at dividing his remains into eight equal parts.

Apparently, that's not part of their "Your Dearly Beloved Is Dead" package.

Which leaves me with this little scoop meant for flour, this glass container meant for leftovers, and this scale meant for arrogant chefs to measure out their ingredients to a decimal of an ounce, sorting all that's left of Josh into even sections like some corpse drug dealer in the kitchen of Dom's childhood home.

My next shovel is slightly more aggressive.

"Careful," a deep voice murmurs.

My body locks up, every joint frozen with offense.

"This is not the time to micromanage me." I glare across the kitchen table into a set of unyielding brown eyes.

After our graveyard spat, I can't even manage sarcasm. There's too much fury coursing through me.

Eight states with Dominic Perry at my side.

Damn you, Josh Sanderson. Why must you torture me even from the afterlife?

Dom drops his gaze to the container he's carefully applying a lid to before writing a state name across the red top. We bought the high-quality Rubbermaid on our way here. Only the best reusable storage containers for my brother.

Dom, who has shucked off the jacket of his funeral suit and rolled up the sleeves on his dress shirt, is currently handling the part of Josh that's going to Kansas.

Kansas. What the hell are we going to do in Kansas?

I guess we'll find out when we get to the cryptic coordinates on the envelope. It's not enough for us to just step over the state line and toss my brother into the wind. He left specific instructions.

This is so Josh: making a game out of his final wishes. And if it were any other situation, and my partner any other person, I would be intrigued by the process of following clues and discovering the answers to his puzzles. Josh used to create scavenger hunts for me on random holidays. Valentine's Day . . . St. Patrick's Day . . . National Hot Dog Day . . .

"To get you out of the house," he said. Admittedly, I was a homebody growing up, always worried too much pollen would set off an asthma attack. Instead of taking the risk, I would retreat to my bedroom, where Florence could easily forget I existed. There I'd curl up in my window seat with a book, reading about someone else's adventures. Josh wanted me to have a few of my own, even if it only meant I ended up at the local Wawa where he'd be waiting with a bag of sour-cream-and-onion chips and a Dr Pepper.

I can imagine my brother sketching this all out, seeing it as another series of quests for his introverted sister.

Did Josh not trust me to go on my own? Did he think I needed Dom spurring me on to finish this final task?

I'm not *that* travel-averse. Josh took me on a few trips over the years. And I have a list of places I'd like to visit. Someday. In the future, when the timing makes sense.

I have the luxury of time, unlike my brother. Guilt rubs against my skin like sandpaper on a sunburn.

Josh already visited a lot of the huge tourist states like New York and California and Louisiana. But he focused most of his traveling internationally, which is why there is still a collection of states he never touched. There are a few interesting ones on the list, but others I'm not looking forward to.

Oh, wait. That's right. I'm not looking forward to any *of them.*

Because at every single destination, I'll have Mr. Responsible Asshole by my side.

"Maddie—"

"Why do you need to say my name?" I cut Dom off. "I'm the only person in this room. Who else would you be talking to? Just say what you want to say." I'm being petty and argumentative, I know. But his face brings it out of me.

After achieving the spectacular feat of making this day even worse, Dom informed me that Josh's ashes were at his parents' house. Apparently, my brother arranged to have himself shipped to the Perry family rather than my mother.

Good choice.

Cecilia probably would have made Josh into diamonds or something weird she could wear in photos.

Dom said my mother never asked for them, so he didn't feel the need to give Josh to her.

Plus, the will specified *I* was to spread the remains.

Me . . . and Dom.

Hell, I hate even thinking about us together, much less physically sitting in the same space as him.

But we need to converse to figure out next steps.

Travel plans. Traveling together.

I want this over with. I was ready to fly back to Seattle and say goodbye to the East Coast and my past forever. Too many people on this side of the country have left me. Now I'm the one determined to do the leaving.

But turns out I'm not done here yet, so instead of hiding in my hotel room with a bottle of gin until my flight tomorrow, I let Dom talk me into coming here, our old neighborhood, where his mom and my grandmother still have houses. We're at the former because I would forever like to avoid the latter.

This kitchen holds mostly good memories. Gorging on Mrs. Perry's pancakes every Sunday morning. Putting together LEGO sets with the twins on rainy days. Josh making us grilled cheese sandwiches as an after-school snack while Dom helped me with my homework on the days when Aunt Florence kicked us out of the house.

I shove that last recollection away. Sure, Dom was nice to me at one point in my life, back when treating me like a kid was fine.

But I grew up, and I guess that confused his cold robot brain.

His jaw tenses, then relaxes. "Fine. I think we should start with Delaware."

"Delaware? That's one of the states? But it's like . . . next door." We lived in Pennsylvania our whole childhood. How did Josh never pop over to Delaware? I've even made it down there.

Dom sets one of the envelopes between us.

Delaware
38°42'55.868" N
75°4'54.433" W

My brother's handwriting is clear. He wants a piece of himself dropped off in the First State.

"This is Rehoboth." Dom taps the longitude and latitude. "On the beach."

"Isn't looking up the coordinates cheating?"

He narrows his eyes. "How else are we supposed to find our way there?"

"Use a compass and a map?" I shrug, my eyes on the scale as I measure out another 13.25 ounces of ashes. Josh, previously an average-sized guy, now only weighs six pounds, ten ounces. Divided eight ways, that gives us roughly 13.25.

There's nothing in his letter that stipulates his ashes be spread evenly in each state, but if this is the last task I'm going to complete for my brother, I'm not going to half-ass it.

"We'd be roaming around Alaska for the rest of our lives that way." Dom holds up another envelope.

Alaska
62°44'9.406" N
151°16'42.517" W

The creamy parchment has an extra note the others don't.

Save me for last.

"But if you want to use a compass," Dom keeps speaking, "spend weeks wandering around a state with me—"

"Google works." I cut him off and pass over the seventh section of Josh. "Rehoboth is only a couple of hours from here." A glance toward the window shows the warm glow of early afternoon. We still have daylight, and I never made it to the funeral bar, which means I'm completely sober. "I agree. Let's do it first. Let's do it now."

His hand pauses in the middle of writing, leaving the lid reading *North Dak-*.

"You want to go now." Dom does this infuriating thing where he says something that should be a question, but his tone makes the phrase sound like a statement. Like a demand. Like he came up with the idea first.

Or like what you just said was so ridiculous he needs to repeat it back for you so you can hear the nonsense of your own words.

I don't know which this is. It's been almost a decade since I spent every moment mooning over the subtle fluctuations of Dom's voice, picking out the thoughts hiding behind his stern gaze.

Now I don't bother trying.

"Yes," I deadpan. "I want to go now." The sooner we get to those coordinates, the sooner I hear from my brother again. I agreed to play Josh's game, but my fingers twitch knowing that his voice—even if it's just in writing—is inches from me in the collection of envelopes.

And this way I only have to see Dom seven more times.

Less if we can lump a few states together, which I plan to.

The man watches me, and I try not to fidget under his silent scrutiny. And when I do fidget, I blame my scratchy tights and not the fact that my body always seems to want to lean toward and away from him at the same time.

Dom doesn't answer right away, quietly finishing the process of portioning my brother. Only when we have the Rubbermaid containers stacked in a box, the table cleared, and I'm hovering by my bag, ready to escape his presence, does he finally speak.

"Okay. Let's go now." Dom grabs his keys, picks up the box with all that's left of Josh, and heads toward the front door.

We're really doing this. We're really going to play Josh's postmortem game.

After my mind fully grasped the wildness of the task, I half expected the responsible, no-nonsense accountant to say there was no reason to follow it to the letter. That the outlandish request was extreme, and we could find a practical solution.

When we were teenagers, Dom was always the reasonable voice in the face of Josh's outrageous antics. He couldn't always talk my brother down, but sometimes he managed it.

Then there were the times Josh was more persuasive, and Dom ended up playing sidekick in a senseless activity he never would've chosen himself.

This is one of those times.

My brother's death must have been the ultimate debate winner because Dom is acting like Josh's wishes make perfect sense. Here he is, ready to drive a state over to spread only a fraction of my brother's remains with a woman who hates him.

Hell, maybe he hates me, too.

Most likely I just annoy him while also making him feel guilty, which somehow hurts worse.

Part of me is furious that Josh foisted this task on me without my say-so. That he's using my grief to make me go along with one of his tricks.

But then there's another open, bleeding wound in my heart that wants to do anything possible to connect with my brother again, even if it means playing his silly game.

When we get to the beach, we can open the envelope. I can read another thing he wrote.

Will the message be for me? For Dom? For both of us?

But Dom and I aren't an *us*.

Maybe for a few weeks—years ago—we were.

A silly, naive bundle of days that meant too much to me and nothing to him.

While I've always hated the idea of being Dom's dirty secret, I am glad that Josh never knew what happened between his best friend and me, and that he never had to choose sides. I'm not sure how I would have survived if Josh had picked someone else over me. Not after Dom already had.

Which reminds me . . .

As much as the words twist in my throat on their way out, I manage to ask the question that's been quietly nagging me since the moment Dom slipped into his car at the same time as me in the funeral parking lot. When he drove away from the wake alone.

"Don't you need to check in with Rosaline?" Even if the two are fighting or whatever, the guy should at least send her a text. "We'll be getting back late. The missus might worry."

But if you say your wife is coming with us on this errand, I'm out, I silently vow.

I tried to avoid them both in the weeks leading up to Josh's death, dodging them in the hospital hallways and ducking out of my brother's room to go work whenever one of them showed up for a visit. I thought of it as trading shifts so Josh was never alone. But really, I was being a coward, hiding from the reminders of how I wasn't good enough.

Josh is gone now, and his final request only demanded I spend time with Dom. I refuse to suffer through this alongside the happy couple.

Dom pauses in the kitchen doorway, then slowly turns, and I watch his thick brows drop low, his expression confused.

"Didn't anyone tell you?" His tone has a touch of incredulity.

There's something big. Something I should know that I don't.

Something everyone else knows.

I cross my arms over my chest and glare, not liking that I'm in the dark, even though I firmly put myself here by never wanting to hear anything about Dom when I talked to Josh.

His gaze flicks down to my brother's ashes, and I brace for what comes out of his mouth next.

"Rosaline and I are divorced."

CHAPTER

Four

Two hours alone in a car was not enough time to come to terms with the fact that Dom is divorced. When he offered to carpool, I immediately shot him down because no way did I want to be in an enclosed space with the guy. But also, I needed the entire drive to work through the new information in my head like an equation.

How is it that the perfect couple are no longer together?

Dom and Rosaline were the model high school couple: the handsome straight A captain of the baseball team with the gorgeous debate captain and valedictorian. Homecoming King and Queen. They would have been Prom King and Queen, too, if Josh hadn't convinced half the senior class to vote for him instead as a joke on his best friend. My brother wore the same suit as Dom and a black wig and insisted his queen waltz with him before he returned Rosaline to her exasperated—yet clearly amused—boyfriend. The summer Dom and Rosaline broke up—the one where he kissed and touched me and I convinced my hopeful heart there was a chance with Dominic Perry—was merely a blip of a mistake on their spotless record.

Once they got back together, they got married in a beautiful ceremony that both their families attended. Dom got a job at an accounting firm, and Rosaline eventually enrolled in law school.

All this info was fed to me through Josh, who relayed his friends' lives like they were on a hot-air balloon ride to perfection. No bumps or unsteady breezes. Just a constant upward trajectory.

And now they're divorced.

"What the fuck?" I mutter to myself, not for the first or even the tenth time.

I can't make sense of it. If I want to understand what went down, I'll have to ask Dom.

Not going to happen.

If Josh were here, I could have gotten the details from him.

Or . . . maybe not.

After pulling my car into an open spot on the street that leads to the Rehoboth boardwalk, I consider the timeline. Dom said they're divorced. That doesn't happen in a week. This has been in the works for a while, and there's no way they'd be able to keep news of it from their best friend.

Which means that Josh knew before he died and made no mention of it to me.

Why wouldn't he say anything? Am I truly this cut off from what's going on with the people from my childhood?

Isn't this what I wanted?

There's a knock on my window, and I yelp in shock.

Dom waits outside my car, standing by the door with an unreadable expression. I'm tempted to stay here and make him hover there like a creep until I get my whirling thoughts in order.

But then he holds up an envelope.

Delaware

The need to know what my brother wrote overwhelms everything else.

He's not gone yet. There's a piece of him in that envelope as well as the glass container I pluck from my passenger seat.

Yes, Josh rode shotgun.

Yes, I may have had a few one-sided conversations on the way down here with my dead brother.

I pop the door open, almost whacking Dom in the leg with it, but the asshole moves out of the way too fast.

"Let's go." He walks ahead of me and I follow behind, trying not to grimace at the renewed pinching of my heels. I should've insisted that we swing by my hotel before heading down here so I could change, but I was too distracted by that word bouncing around in my brain.

Divorced.

Finally, I push it away, coming to terms with the fact that I *cannot* come to terms with the new info about Dom at this moment. Too much has been thrown at me today. All that I have the mental capacity for is this ash-spreading ridiculousness.

When we reach a path to the beach, I immediately kick my heels off and groan as the cold sand cradles my aching feet.

At the sound I made, Dom turns around, taking in all of me. "What's wrong?"

Good to know my pleasure noise sounds like I'm in pain. "Your face."

Boom. Zinger. To be fair, I'm hungry, and I should've been drunk hours ago, so my comedic skills aren't at full capacity.

Dom huffs an annoyed breath and faces forward, somehow managing to walk on the sand in dress shoes and not look like a stork on ice skates. Fuck him very much.

The sun is low in the sky at our backs. On the West Coast, this would be a beautiful beach sunset. But I don't want some picturesque setting. If it was, there'd probably be more people congregated here. As it is, there's a fisherman a little ways down, someone bundled up and sitting on a blanket with a book, and a jogger who passes us as Dom heads in the opposite direction, away from the potential spectators. When he comes to a stop, I sidle up close, but not too close to him.

"Are you ready?" He holds up the letter, the salt-scented wind attempting to pluck the thin envelope from his fingers.

But nothing as silly as a beach breeze could overcome the force that is Dominic Perry.

"Open it." I hug Josh against my chest, staring down at him through the glass, trying to conjure his voice to overlay the man who's reading some of his final words.

Dear Maddie & Dom,

Welcome to Delaware!

Dom is terrible at reading exclamation points, but I suspect that there is one. Josh liked to infuse energy into his messages.

So close, and yet I never stepped over the state line. Thank you both for bringing me here. I love the ocean. How the water stretches on and on, seemingly endless. Every coast I've visited reminds me how small I am in the world, but also how lucky I am to take in a view that always inspires awe.

Sorry if I'm getting too sentimental, but I figure these letters are the best place to get a little sappy.

I want you to take me for a swim. Yes, I know you both are pool people, but I want you to wade into the wild. Let the waves tug at you. Let the waves take away some of my ashes.

Then, once I'm gone, find the closest bar with any of the Dogfish Head beers on tap and raise a toast. To me, of course!

Take a picture and try to smile for me.

Love,
Josh

Dom folds up the paper slowly, then returns it to its envelope and carefully tucks the missive into the lapel of his suit jacket. All the while he gazes out over the water.

I glance down at my outfit. Under my wool peacoat I still have on the ill-fitting black dress and hellish tights that I now realize have a hole in the toe, too.

I want them gone. Even in the chilly air of winter, I want to strip these clothes off, throw them into the ocean, and never see them again.

But all my other clothes are back at the hotel in Pennsylvania, and I'm not about to drive hours in nothing but my matching green bra and underwear set. There are at least two tollbooths between here and my hotel where I'd give the workers a show.

Still, I can get rid of this depressing uniform for a moment. Divest myself of the itchy, stiff funeral trappings.

"Okay, Josh. Time to go for a swim." I set the container of his ashes at my feet next to my heels, slip off my jacket, and reach for the hem of my dress.

"What are you doing?" I can feel Dom's eyes on me, but I ignore the weight of his gaze as I pull my dress over my head in one swift move.

"I'm being a good sister, obviously." I drag my tights down my legs, shivering as the winter breeze against my bare skin raises goose bumps. The temperature hasn't dropped below freezing yet, but the air isn't balmy, either.

"The letter doesn't say to skinny-dip." There's something in Dom's words, a strain of his vocal cords. Like he's pissed off, maybe.

Who cares? He's seen all this before.

And decided I wasn't worth his time.

I flick my hair over my shoulder in a dismissive move, then grab Josh off the ground. "I'm not getting naked, perv. But I'm also not going to sit in a bar in a wet dress. So, makeshift bathing suit it is. Come or don't. Preferably, don't."

"We could come back in the summer."

Meet up with Dom more than I have to? Not likely.

"Do what you want." Without another glance his way, I stroll with purpose toward the gentle waves.

I want to sprint into the water. A quick, daring submersion that I can't back away from. But if I do that, my lungs will probably seize up, I'll have my second attack for the day, and I'll end up drowning myself in the process.

Then Dom would have to give me CPR.

I don't linger on how that thought has my nipples tightening and my skin growing overly warm. Those are obviously reactions of disgust.

So, with my finicky lungs in mind, I ease myself into the frigid surf. Toes, feet, ankles, calves. Each meeting with the icy water, prickling to an almost painful degree, and yet still somehow making me giggle.

The water has a cleansing sensation. Numbing the discomfort of the day. Washing away the sticky residue of half-hearted sympathy.

The ocean spreads far in front of me, darkening with the setting sun. A vast inky expanse I imagine myself slipping into.

Is this what death feels like?

I hope so. I hope Josh didn't hurt at the end. Didn't fear.

I hope he saw it as his next adventure.

"Don't go too deep." The commanding voice tears me out of my peaceful contemplation and water splashes behind me, sending sharp pricks of cold scattering along the bare skin of my thighs where they haven't been immersed yet. A result of Dom's approach.

He doesn't ease in like I did. He charges. And when I turn to snap at him about telling me what to do, I choke on my words.

I forgot. Over the years, an occasional dream has plagued me where I'm back in Dom's arms, his body against mine, something I thought was love in his eyes. All born from the memory of the night we were together.

As much as I hated him, I thought I'd never forget.

But I did. I realize now that his form was only a hazy recollection paired with a tangle of emotions.

Now he stands in the fading twilight, solid and unavoidable.

And dressed only in briefs.

But they aren't black. Or gray. Or green. Or some other solid, responsible, boring color like I would have guessed if asked.

"What is that?" I point to his crotch with the hand I'm not using to clutch my brother's remains to my chest.

Dom glowers, setting his hands on hips that taper too nicely. My eyes fixate on the tight skin just above his waistband. He doesn't have the sculpted six-pack he did seven years ago, but his abdomen is solid and defined and . . .

Not what I should be focusing on.

"Do you need a lesson in male anatomy?" he asks.

"You're wearing colorful panties!" my voice squeaks out, the pitch sent high from incredulity and freezing water.

His scowl deepens. "I'm wearing boxer briefs made for men, purchased in the men's section of the store. I assume."

"You assume?"

"Josh gave them to me."

Of course he did. My brother *would* gift his perpetually black-wearing friend a pair of pink briefs covered in pineapples.

Not only did Dom keep the underwear, but he wore them to my brother's funeral.

I don't want to dig into the emotions brought up by that fact. So instead, I attempt to be the responsible one in this duo.

"What's the procedure here? Any more directions?"

Dom doesn't answer right away. He stands knee-deep in the ocean, immobile as waves pound his shins, and he stares at me, his hands still resting on that small stretch of skin that looks tight yet soft and might taste like salt now that the ocean air clings to him . . .

Wanting more of the numb, cleansing feeling that comes with the ocean water, I wade out farther. The waves push and pull at me, as if they want me to keep going. As if this ocean wants me to be a part of it.

This will be one of the places that Josh lays to rest.

It makes sense that it is an ever-moving mass. My brother didn't rest in life—why would he pause for even a moment after death?

I dip my hand into the water swirling around my thighs and bring a finger up to my lips, spreading the salty liquid on the seam of my mouth. I sneak my tongue out, knowing that this isn't sanitary but needing to take some of this ocean into me. Testing it as if I am assessing its safety, when really I am only trying to remember everything about this place. Using all of my senses to drill this memory into my mind so I will never forget where Josh is.

"Whenever you're ready," Dom says, sounding close again.

I don't want his voice to be part of this memory. He's going to be here—next to me—for every one of these goodbyes. Every final moment with my brother will have the shade of Dom.

Why couldn't this have been my task alone? Didn't you trust me to follow through?

I could've done it. I would've done it for Josh.

"Stand here." I point to my right side. "I'm going to just . . . let him go."

Let him go. If only it were that easy.

Dom doesn't argue as he comes to stand beside me, the heat of him radiating off his body in stark contrast to the numb sensation of my lower limbs. I pry the lid off the Rubbermaid, and the wind of the ocean already starts to stir the leavings of Josh.

"I will miss you." Dom's voice is steady while my hands shake.

I take note of the direction the wind is blowing and turn so Josh will fly with the breeze instead of back on us. I hold the container just above the water and let him spill out into the gentle waves, ready to watch the particles of my brother become one with the majestic ocean.

But the jackass floats.

"You've got to be kidding me," I mutter.

What I imagined was going to be a beautiful weaving of sparkling dust motes with saltwater waves instead looks like some sewage muck hanging out on the surface.

"This was supposed to be beautiful, Josh," I rail at my brother. "I was supposed to start sobbing. Can't you just fucking join with the ocean like you wanted?"

"He'll mix in with time," Dom mutters.

"Or he'll wash up onshore and become a litter box for a seagull. Sink, you asshole!" With my hands, I press the remains of my brother into the water swirling around us. I don't know if this is something that I should be grossed out by, but this day is weird enough as it is that I don't have a measure anymore. My normal compass is broken. If I ever had one. If I did, I doubt I'll be able to fix it.

"I thought this was a group activity," I snap at the stoic man beside me. "Are you going to help me mix him in with the ocean? Or are you gonna stand there in your rainbow underpants and watch me do all the hard work?"

Dom hesitates a moment longer. Then his big hands join mine, pressing the ashes under the surface.

"Thank you." My tone is all sarcasm.

If Josh wanted me to maintain an air of poise and loving sadness, then he shouldn't have paired me with a jerk and asked me to dump his remains in the ocean when he was just gonna float his ashy ass around.

After enough swirling and pushing that the remains of Josh finally fully merge with the frigid water around us, my hands are numb, my nerves are fried, and I need a drink.

Good thing that was part of his request. It's as if he knew that the first activity would require the second. I straighten and wade toward the shore, barely feeling my legs as I move.

"Let's go find a bar."

There are plenty of bars in Rehoboth, but a lot of them close for the winter. We finally find a restaurant/bar combo near a cluster of hotels.

"Do you have Dogfish Head on tap?" I ask the bartender as I claim a stool covered in faux leather. The material squeaks as I situate myself, the butt of my dress damp from underwear that was never intended to be a bathing suit. This is the unsexy version of soaked panties.

"Of course." The middle-aged white man pouring drinks attempts to appear interested in our arrival, but I can spy the boredom in his eyes. "Which one do you want?" He points to a chalkboard behind him, and I realize there's three beers from the Delaware brewery to choose from.

Dom situates his long-limbed body on the stool next to mine, grimacing as he takes a seat. He's got on a dark pair of pants, but I can still see the water saturating them.

How the material clings to certain areas . . .

I shake my head to rid myself of the thought and wave him toward the drink display.

"You first."

Dom considers the board, and I consider if the bartender will kick us out if I start shoving cocktail napkins down the neck of my dress to soak up excess moisture.

"Ninety Minute IPA," Dom says.

"I'll take that, too." And I decide to hold off on the napkin plan until another customer distracts our server. He pours us two glasses of the dark, hoppy drink, setting them on Dogfish Head coasters with their little shark logo.

Once the drinks sit in front of us, the bartender wanders off, leaving us to hesitate over the first swallow.

Time for the toast.

That's what Josh demanded in his letter.

Problem is, I don't have any words. They're all lodged deep in my chest where I can't think of them, much less speak them.

Dom wraps his fingers around his glass, then pushes mine toward me. Stiffly, I pick up the cold beer, wishing I were clutching a cup of hot tea instead.

Or a glass of gin.

Dom clears his throat, then raises his IPA high. "To Josh. A good friend. And a good brother."

"That's it?" I scoff. If I'd known how basic the toast could be, I'd have done it myself. "I can do better than that." Glaring into Dom's dark eyes, I finally force some loving words out without fracturing to pieces. "To Josh. The *best* friend. The *best* brother."

If I'm not mistaken, something like a smile tugs at the corner of Dom's mouth. But next I know, he's tapping his glass against mine and taking a sip. I follow suit, tipping back the beer and downing one large gulp, trying not to gag as the bitter taste hits my tongue.

Done. Letter requirement fulfilled.

I set the glass down hard on the bar top and slide it Dom's way. "That's yours now." I wave the bartender over and order a gin and tonic. When he turns his back to pour my drink, I glance to the side in time to find Dom watching me. "What?"

His brows are drawn together. "Why did you order a beer if you didn't want it?"

"Because the note said to. And I'm not about to lose on a technicality."

"Lose?"

"Yeah, lose. Break the rules. Whatever." I flick my fingers toward the jacket he draped over the stool next to him. The jacket that has Josh's Delaware letter. "I told you I'm doing the tasks, so I'm doing them. Which reminds me . . ."

The bartender sets a glass of clear bubbling alcohol in front of me, and I hold out my hand before he can wander away again.

"Could you take a quick picture of us?" I offer the man my phone. He shrugs and accepts it.

"Smile, asshole," I mutter to Dom the second before I slap on a false happy expression and the flash goes off. I thank the bartender as he passes my phone back, and I consider why I felt the need to even pretend happiness in the photo. It's not like anyone is going to see it. There's no photo essay I have to turn in.

Josh isn't going to peek his head out of the afterlife to review our performance.

Trying to get my mind away from more reminders of my brother's death, I drink my cocktail with relish, savoring the piney taste on my tongue.

"I wouldn't have called you out," Dom says in response to my earlier comment. "I don't see this as a competition."

"Hmm" is all I give him back. Of course he doesn't.

He sees this as a responsibility. That's how Dom views everything in life. A series of tasks to successfully check off his never-ending to-do list.

How did divorce end up on there?

I spent the whole car ride pondering it and still couldn't come up with an answer. My brain could not put "Dom" and "divorce" into the same sentence and make it make sense. He's too much of a fixer to let something as monumental as his relationship break. The Dom I knew would do everything in his power to find the solution to whatever marital problems arose.

Maybe he's not the Dom I knew anymore.

Unlikely. Today has shown me he's still the overbearing rule follower he always has been.

Then why did he get divorced?

The thought won't leave me alone, and the gin loosens my tongue.

"So, you and Rosaline are calling it quits."

Not the smoothest topic change, but I doubt Dom expects much from me.

"Yes." The single word answer is all he offers, choosing instead to sip his first glass of beer and stare at the colorful bottles arranged behind the bartender.

"She get tired of you refusing to let her peg you because you already have a stick up your ass?"

Dom chokes on his swallow of beer and pounds a fist on the bar top as he struggles to get the liquid down his throat rather than his lungs. "Maddie!" He gasps finally.

"What?" I hide an evil grin behind the rim of my gin and tonic. "I was just asking a question."

He growls something under his breath that sounds a lot like a curse, and I'm proud of my ability to get Dom to use irresponsible language.

That's what he called it growing up. *Irresponsible language.*

Dom was always calling Josh and me out whenever we cursed in front of the twins, saying he didn't want them to learn irresponsible language. Josh would laugh, I would apologize, and when Dom turned his back, we would silently mouth swear words at each other while Adam and Carter watched and giggled.

Rosaline never got a reprimand, because she never used expletives.

Once the red flush of almost choking to death on an IPA clears from Dom's cheeks, he turns on his stool to face me. His legs are so long that his knees bump into my seat, making me wobble and spill gin on my hand.

"Sorry." He doesn't sound sorry.

I scowl at him and lick the alcohol off my skin, not about to waste the substance that's going to numb my hurt for the night.

His eyes track the movement of my tongue, probably judging me for my cavewoman behavior when there's a napkin at my elbow. But that bad boy is going in my bra once I finish this drink.

"Tell me, then." I lean forward, putting the spotlight back on Dom and his screwups. "Why are the perfect Perrys parting ways?" To aggravate him, I make sure to pop my *p*'s on the alliteration.

Dom studies me as he takes another—careful—sip of his drink. Once he's swallowed, the man finally responds.

"Sometimes something big happens. And it makes you look at your life. And you realize you've been living it wrong," he says, holding my eyes. "That you let something go on longer than it should have."

"Wait. Wait wait wait." I wave a hand in front of his annoying face, trying to get his intense gaze to focus elsewhere. "You're telling me you got divorced when Josh *died*? Like, last week, you signed the papers?"

Dom shakes his head slowly. "We signed them months ago. His diagnosis was the big thing. That's what had us realizing it needed to happen."

My mind absorbs this information about as well as my underwear sopped up seawater. I take it in but have trouble grasping it.

I wave at the bartender until the guy pockets his phone and notices me pointing to my empty glass and holding up two fingers. Once I know more gin is on the way, I let myself refocus on Dom's confession.

"You're telling me it wasn't some big betrayal? You two just decided, 'Eh, not working for us anymore'?" I keep my voice careful on the question, making sure I don't display any particular emotion preemptively. Before I even know what I'm feeling.

"Something like that." Dom lifts a single massive shoulder, then lets it drop before picking up his beer for a deep pull.

So casual. So easy, the way he shrugs off a years-long relationship. A relationship that devastated nineteen-year-old me and left a shadow of self-disgust that lingers to this day.

"The end of an era," I mutter, not mournful in the least.

How can I be when the largest stain on that era was me?

A single night when Dominic Perry felt so grateful—or maybe so bad—for little, desperate Maddie Sanderson that he gave her a mind-melting orgasm. My first orgasm. A sexual experience that altered my universe and was apparently so unappealing, Dom felt the need to propose to a different woman the next day.

The ultimate pity finger bang.

Was it so bad that I drove him into a loveless marriage?

The bartender sets my two G&Ts in front of me, and I immediately down the first, then reach for the next one.

Dom's only response is to drink more of his beer. The last of it, in fact.

I expect him to push the one I'd foisted on him aside and request a water. That's what a responsible person would do, knowing after this we need to drive however many hours back to Pennsylvania.

Instead, Dom scoops up the IPA I barely touched and takes a swig. An evil urge has me raising my hand for the bartender to return.

Looks like I'm getting drunk with Dominic Perry.

We drink too much to drive. The bartender seems unconcerned about overserving us, and I put too much stock into Mr. Responsible Asshole eventually cutting me off. I was sure Dom would turn down the first shot I ordered for him.

If not the first, then definitely the second.

No way would he throw back the third . . .

The only thing that stops the steady flow of beer, gin, and tequila is closing time.

We stumble our way to a motel that was obviously meant to serve summer beach guests rather than winter funeral attendees. Everything is painted aqua blue and covered in seashells and draped in fishing nets.

For a brief moment, my alcohol-soaked brain panics at the thought of sharing a room with Dom. Then he asks the front desk worker for two rooms, and I realize we're not at a roadside inn in some historical romance novel, so of course there's going to be multiple rooms available.

When the young guy glances between the two of us with a skeptical expression as he hands over our key cards, I can tell what's going on in his mind.

Why are these two wasted people springing for an extra room when they're obviously going to hook up?

I have too much gin in me to let him continue thinking such an incorrect thought.

Leaning an elbow on the desk, I extend my body over the surface and get ready to blow his mind.

"He's divorced." I jab a finger Dom's way. "I'm single." I point to my chest. "But we're not going to sleep together or have sex. Because I hate him, and his face, and his pineapple boxers. Boxers, I might add, that my *brother* gave him. But in, like, a totally platonic way. I think. Holy shit." I smack a palm against Dom's massive chest. "Did you hook up with Josh?"

Dom's hand covers mine, holding it captive as he stares at the ceiling and exhales a deep breath that sounds suspiciously like *What the fuck?*

Ha! Irresponsible language. A point for me.

"No, Maddie. Josh and I never hooked up. We were just friends."

The guy sounds entirely too sober for someone who had four beers, three shots, and no food.

"Well, good. Only one Sanderson stain to your name." I tug my hand free of his, the maneuver surprisingly difficult, then snatch my room key card.

"Maddie." Dom's voice sounds growly. He's probably just mad that I'm airing his dirty laundry—his one mistake—in front of this random motel worker.

"Dominic," I mock with a deep tone as I stroll out of the office. At least, I attempt to stroll, but the ground keeps rocking beneath my feet, so I do more of a swaying walk with the occasional dance move thrown in, so no one knows how unsteady I actually am.

Outside, a chill breeze pushes humid, salty air through my damp dress, and I look forward to peeling off every piece of clothing I have on and standing in a hot shower for a good hour.

"You missed your room." The gruff voice coaxes me to turn

around, and I find Dom not far behind me, his focus on a vending machine.

"How do you know? You're not even looking at me."

Which is good. I don't want him to look at me.

"Because our rooms are that way." He points to a stretch of doors on the other side of the office.

"You could've told me sooner," I mutter, retracing my not-so-straight steps. "I hate hotels. And motels. Every room is the same. A copy you can't tell apart. They're all lifeless."

On my way to my door, I veer off course and intentionally stumble into Dom, shoulder to shoulder, so I can stare through the glass at the snacks, too. The colorful wrappers inform me that I'm hungry, but when I pull out my credit card, ready to blow my life savings on gummy worms, I realize that the machine doesn't have a card reader.

"This is bullshit." Gesturing toward the dollar bill slot, I glance up to include Dom in my commiserating and maybe enjoy one of his disappointed frowns. Instead, I watch as he opens a leather wallet to pull out some crisp dollar bills.

"You carry cash? Are you kidding me? Who carries cash anymore? Are you ninety? Do you pay for your groceries with a check? You had exact change for the tollbooths, didn't you?"

Dom lets me rant as he inserts his archaic money into the machine. He presses a series of buttons, and when I see what falls I let out a groan.

"Peanuts? You've got to be fucking kidding me!" One advantage I have on the six-foot, however-many-unnecessary-inches man is that I can get low faster than he can. I drop to my knees, plunge my hand into the food dispenser, and steal his legumes.

"Maddie." His voice holds a warning I refuse to heed.

"Dominic Dickbag Perry. You've got rows of delicious candy and chips and the cash to buy it all and you pick *peanuts*. Like some serial killer."

"Peanuts have protein."

"Try again," I demand, poking an aggressive finger against the glass.

"Give me my peanuts." He makes to grab them, but I step back fast, out of his reach.

"No!"

Seeing his intent to try again, I shove the bag down the neckline of my dress with a triumphant "*Hah!*"

Mr. Responsible Asshole would never violate the sanctity of my clothes without my permission.

Unfortunately, my alcohol-infused brain temporarily forgot exactly how dresses work, so almost immediately, the peanuts fall out the bottom of my skirt as if I'm a giant bird popping out eggs on the sidewalk.

After a beat of hesitation, I drop down, sitting cross-legged on my newly laid peanut bag.

"You're sitting on my food," Dom says.

"You get them back when you pick a proper snack from the machine." I point to the collection of deliciousness he blatantly ignored on his first go. "This is a cognitive ability test."

Dom watches me for a stretch of time that seems too long. Probably because my ass doesn't like conforming to the shape of hard, cold concrete and a lumpy nut bag.

Finally, he turns and rests his head on the glass of the vending machine again, contemplating the array of options.

"If you pick a granola bar," I warn him, "I will call the police and tell them that you've violated that vending machine multiple times without an ounce of remorse."

Dom flicks me a side-eye glare, then inserts more money and presses a series of numbers. I hear the heavy *thunk* as his selection drops. When the man squats to retrieve the food, my eyes accidentally find their way to the perfect shape of his ass encased in those formfitting dress pants. Not an imperfect grief crease to be seen.

Definitely not proper funeral attire.

"Here. This pass muster?" Dom straightens and tosses a neon green bag into my lap.

The familiar snack sparks a nostalgic flame in my heart, warming me from the inside.

"Sour Patch Kids! These are my favorite."

I hug the bag against my chest like it's a teddy bear.

"I know," Dom says, and his confidence grates.

"Fuck you. You did not."

He slips his hands into his pockets, staring down at me with an unreadable expression. "You like to pretend they're pirates and you're the kraken and that you've demolished their ship and are eating them alive."

"Well, that woman—whoever you're talking about—sounds incredibly creative." I tear the bag open, pluck out a little red guy, and hold him up between us. "Arg! Please spare me, matey! I'll give ye all my buried treasure!"

Then I chomp down on him whole, shivering in delight at the sour tang on my tongue.

Dom watches me, his lips pressed in a tight line.

"Try it." I hold out one of my precious treats. But only one of the orange ones. Dom doesn't deserve a red or green or yellow.

I expect him to sigh, or scold me, or ask for his peanuts again. Instead, Dom crouches in front of me until our faces are unnervingly close together. Then he opens his mouth in an invitation.

Scared of losing a finger, I cautiously place the candy on his broad tongue, then yank my hand away. Dom holds my eyes as he chews slowly and swallows. Then—not an ounce of inflection in his voice—he speaks.

"Arg, matey."

Damn him.

A laugh bursts out of me, drunken giggles quaking through my body at the ever-serious Dom Perry's terrible pirate impression.

As I crumble under my hilarity, the man's face slowly transforms. A small tick at first, in the corner of his mouth. Then both corners.

Suddenly, he's smiling.

Dominic Perry grins at me, wide and devastating. And so unexpected that my body moves before I know what I'm doing.

I kiss his smile, greedy for the memory. Aching for the time when his smiles were mine.

Craving the time when he kissed me and I believed he meant it.

Desperate to return to a moment when I was happy.

When Dom's mouth is on mine, I don't care that my ass is freezing from the cold ground, and my brain is whirling from too much gin, and my chest is in tatters because my brother is gone.

When I taste Dom's warm mouth, feel the silky tangle of his hair fisted in my fingers, hear his deep groan as the noise vibrates down my throat and through my body, I'm nineteen and hopeful again. The world is only a little bit shitty in a way I'm used to. And there's a lovely bright spot that is this man who has his arms wrapped around me, my body pulled in tight to his broad chest.

The moment disappears as quick as sugar on my tongue, with Dom prying us apart, his unyielding hands on my shoulders to hold me at bay.

"Maddie," he rasps. "We can't."

But that's a lie.

We can. Easily.

He's divorced. I'm single. And my brother—who may or may not have lodged a protest against his best friend hooking up with his sister—is gone.

We can.

Dom should've been honest and said the words he actually meant.

Maddie. I don't want you. I never did.

Silly me forgot. The alcohol eased my protective shields, but a sober wave brought on by rejection helps them slam back into place.

"Obviously. We're not going to do anything." I swat Dom's hands away, realizing he pulled me to my feet during the lip lock.

Good. That'll make it easier to get away. I dodge around him and power walk toward my room—I can read the number clearly now.

"Maddie, wait." His heavy footsteps follow me, but I don't look back.

Instead, I focus on properly swiping my key card as my mouth goes on defense. "Did you think that meant something?" I force a laugh that comes out too sharp. "No. See, I just realized I've never tossed anyone's salad before. Wanted to know what it was like to kiss an asshole." The door pops open, and I tilt my head over my shoulder, managing a smirk as I meet his dark eyes. "Learned my lesson. It's shit."

Then I slam the door in Dom's face. Lock it. Throw the dead bolt.

I ignore the knocking and him calling my name as I rush to the bathroom. My knees hit the tiles hard, and I barely manage to get the seat cover raised before I throw up every trace of the night.

All the gin I downed. The swallow of IPA in a toast to my brother. My one measly piece of candy. The drop of seawater I brought to my lips. The little butterflies that tried to struggle to life when Dom smiled at me.

All of it comes spilling out my throat in a sickly yellow bile revealing the truth of today.

Nothing about these last few hours was beautiful or life-changing.

This was just a new version of the same old disappointment.

CHAPTER

Seven

I leave the motel at three a.m., when I'm sober and Dom is asleep, making sure that by the time he wakes up I'll be long gone. I'm back in Pennsylvania before the sun rises, and that's the least amount of distance I need from him after last night.

I manage to pack up my things, drive my rental to the airport, and board a plane to Washington without further fucking up my life, and I think that's something to be proud of.

Back in Seattle, I vow not to think about Dominic Perry until our next ash-spreading excursion. Unfortunately, there's a picture of us on my phone that my fingers insist upon opening multiple times a day.

Maybe Josh is haunting my hands, and he's bored, and he's decided to torture me. Like right now, two days after the funeral and beach disaster, I could be on an animal shelter website contemplating how many abandoned cats I need to adopt to fill the hole my brother left in my heart. Instead, I'm lying on the floor of my apartment, staring at the awkward photo of Dom and me in Delaware.

My smile is terrible. All toothy and strained and fake. More of a grimace than anything.

Dom isn't even trying to fake it. He's not even looking at the camera. No, the man is staring at me, probably wondering why I'm going through the trouble of getting a picture taken.

I should delete it. I don't need it.

When we're done, I tell myself. *When all the trips are over, I'll scroll through the pictures, then I'll get rid of them. Another way to say goodbye.*

A pounding on my condo's front door interrupts my melancholy musings.

I ignore the familiar knocking pattern and swipe my phone off. Then I stare at the ceiling of my condo and try to remember how old Florence is.

My grandmother and mother are both terrified of aging and regularly lie about the years they were born. Still, I know Cecilia was twenty-two when she had me, and I think Florence once mentioned being pregnant when she was twenty while she was lamenting my inability to find a boyfriend in high school.

Florence is forty-two years older than me.

If I live as long as she does, that means I'll have to live forty-two years without Josh.

Probably more.

I know these aren't healthy thoughts to be having. They certainly aren't comforting. But my brain continues to cycle through different ways to define the time stretching out in front of me without my brother.

Forty-two years.

Unless my life ends early. Like his did.

The knock repeats itself, this time followed by a demanding shout. "Maddie, let me in!"

I roll over onto my stomach, smashing my face into the plush carpet, wondering if I just need gravity to force the tears out of my ducts. There's a part of me that wonders if my grief is worse because I can't physically expel it from my body with heart-wrenching sobs and flooded eyes.

Even after the Motel Mistake, as I've dubbed it in my brain, I still haven't cried.

Sure, I curled up in a miserable ball on the bottom of the slightly sandy bathtub and begged Josh to reach a hand through the veil and drag me into the afterlife with him.

But I didn't cry.

I did come up with creative new ways to curse my brother for insisting I spend more time around his best friend when drinking was involved. Turns out drunk Maddie easily forgives and forgets how Dom dropped me like a hot potato.

"Maddie!" The muffled voice holds a scolding note. "Don't even try to pretend you're not home. I can smell your cinnamon candle through the door!"

With a groan, I push myself up to my knees and contemplate crossing the distance to the entrance of my condo. I wouldn't need to travel far. My place is small, and normally I consider the compact condo cozy. I've filled my living space with a cushy green couch, a massive coffee table, and lots of meditation pillows. Not that I meditate. Spending too much time in my own mind seems like a bad idea, especially lately. The pillows are for extra comfort when sitting on the floor.

No, it isn't the square footage that keeps my limbs from moving forward.

I'm just not sure I'm ready to face the other side of that door. Not sure I'm ready to let them in.

There's an audible huff and another hard tap of knuckles. "I'm not above using my spare key! You better not make me go all the way back to my place to get it just because you're in reclusive sloth mode."

He won't go away.

With a grunt, I heave myself to my feet and maneuver around the butcher block island that designates where both my kitchen and entryway start. There's no point in glancing through the peephole. I know who's on the other side.

When I swing the door wide, I come face-to-face with my ex-boyfriend—and current best friend—Jeremy Hassan.

Jeremy is the most handsome man I have ever encountered in my life. And I am including every single picture of every single celebrity in that designation. Jeremy is hotter. It's an undeniable fact. He is tall, golden-skinned, with heavy-lidded dark eyes that gaze into your soul like you're his salvation. It was unfathomable to me that this deity come to earth would want to go out with *me*.

And I'm not saying that I think I am a horrendous troll destined to live alone under a bridge. Most days—now that I live a country away from Cecilia and Florence's nitpicking—I like my face. Sometimes my hair does what I want it to. And I look adorable in a sweater.

Which is good because the majority of the items in my closet are sweaters.

Still, I am *not* on Jeremy's level.

But we did it. Two years ago we went out. Then we kept going out. For *months*. I took pictures as proof, just to make sure.

But the most mind-blowing part of the situation? The moment I realized I wasn't into him that way.

How does *that* work?

Jeremy is so hot, I used to apply sunscreen before hanging out with him. If I could get sunburn from a person, it would be him. And worse than that? He has a great personality. Funny, smart, and kind.

Truly, it's not fair a man like him exists in the world.

But we were sitting on my couch one day, and I looked over at his face of perfection, and I thought, *All I wanna do with this man is continue watching our marathon of* Charmed *and never sleep with him again.*

We had slept together, multiple times, and it was . . . fine.

It had to be my fault that it was only fine. Jeremy is too gorgeous and giving for sex to only be fine. There are people who are so good-looking that they don't try in bed. But Jeremy made sure I orgasmed before he did. Every time.

But those orgasms were simply . . . fine. A pleasant clenching rather than a full body wave of pleasure.

Still, I didn't end things. Because I loved Jeremy even if I wasn't *in* love with him, and I was terrified a breakup meant he'd walk out of my life. He mentioned being in a relationship before me, but other than saying his ex was a guy, he never spoke about him. Jeremy had cut the man out of his life entirely, and I was sure he would do the same to me if I admitted my feelings were platonic rather than romantic.

The idea of being honest with him started to give me asthma attacks when I thought about it too deeply.

Then one day Jeremy showed up at my door with my favorite lavender latte and a croissant.

"We haven't had sex in a month," he said.

I'd gaped at him.

"And I have a crush on the guy who moved into Unit 2F." His smile was apologetic while his eyes were wide and hopeful. "Will you hate me if I ask to be your best friend instead of your boyfriend? And by ask, I mean insist, because I don't want to give you up, Maddie Sanderson."

It was the sweetest friend proposal I'd ever received. And for the first time in months, I felt like I could breathe.

"I can't believe you broke up with me before I broke up with you." I'd worn an exaggerated pout while pretending I would've had the courage to end things. Then I assembled a charcuterie board of my favorite snacks for us while he told me about 2F—and I tried not to be nervous about a new person in his life potentially pushing me out of it. But Jeremy claimed he knew we were soulmates the day we met, when he strolled into our building lobby and heard me shout "Not my cheeses!" when the strap on one of my grocery bags snapped. My utter devotion to dairy products thoroughly charmed him and gained his immediate respect.

Sometimes, it turns out, soulmates are meant to be friends.

Now I can't escape him. Which is a problem because Jeremy is too kind to handle the rage that simmers under the suffocating weight of my grief.

Jeremy Hassan befriended a quiet, playful introvert.

Not this toxic, defensive version of myself seeping from a wound in my soul that refuses to heal.

But maybe I can manage banter. Something like what I threw at Dom, but without all the sharp edges. Then I can convince Jeremy I'm fine, and he'll go back downstairs, and I can lie on the floor and contemplate mortality for a few more weeks.

Jeremy's eyes soften when they find mine. "Maddie," he sighs.

"You're here for Brie, right?" I hear the panic in my voice. This reaction is not his normal show-up-to-my-place-and-scrounge-for-food smirk.

"No." Jeremy spreads a long pair of arms. "I'm wearing my baggiest sweatshirt and Carlisle's cologne. I'm here to hug you, Maddie Sanderson."

I'm not a hugger. Can't remember a time that I was. I prefer the unemotional touch of a doctor during my yearly check-up to a spur-of-the-moment embrace from a friend. I know it's strange. It's not that I'm repulsed by the touch of someone else. I hugged Mrs. Perry because I knew that she liked hugs and uses them to say hello. I hugged Adam to shield him from his brother's wrath.

But they don't comfort me. I have no instinctual urge to press my body against another's. And when I'm prompted to, the act feels like . . . an act.

The exception: sweatshirts.

There's something about the soft material that I love having pressed against my cheek as I'm enfolded in sweatshirt-covered arms.

But again, it's not about the *person* in the sweatshirt. It's the piece of clothing itself that I find comforting.

I'm a sweatshirt slut.

A hoodie whore.

And Jeremy knows it. Knows that this isn't him giving me a hug. It's his deliciously smelling piece of loungewear. Maybe I can only truly be comforted by the idea of an animated blanket.

"Come on. I smell really good." He coaxes, arms wide as he steps into my home and kicks the door shut behind him.

Cautiously, I shuffle into his hold and allow myself to be engulfed.

And damn, Carlisle knows how to pick a cologne. I bury my head against the soft material over Jeremy's chest, suck in a deep breath, and imagine a heated comforter transformed itself into my personal hugging machine.

"We would've come. You know that, right?" Jeremy murmurs the words against my hair, breaking the illusion.

Guilt condenses in my gut as I sigh and step back. He doesn't fight me, letting his arms drop to his sides.

"You didn't need to." I don't know what I would've done if Jeremy and my other best friend, Tula, had shown up and tried to coddle me. Maybe I would have broken and finally shed some tears. Or maybe I would have watched their faces crease in concerned confusion as I hid and snarked and never cried.

At the time, I didn't understand what Josh's death was doing to me.

I still don't.

And I'm not doing any of the things normal grieving sisters are supposed to do. In fact, the only times I've felt relief, brief as it was, were the moments I berated Dom.

Hell, it felt so good to tear into that immovable man. To spew my inappropriate humor all over him and only receive his stoic responses in return.

I could never treat Jeremy and Tula like punching bags. They've done zero to deserve that, and I'm terrified my messed-up grief will drive them away.

"I know I didn't need to," Jeremy says, reaching out to gently tug a strand of hair that's fallen out of my messy bun. "But I would have come. For you. So you didn't have to be alone. Especially at the funeral."

"There were plenty of people there . . . Wait. How did you . . ." I trail off as my face flushes with mortification.

The day after Josh passed away, I texted Jeremy and Tula with the news and told them I'd be gone for a few days. But I didn't tell them about the funeral. If I had, I *knew* they both would've come.

"I looked up your mom's blog," he says, grimace twisting his handsome face. "I wanted to make sure she wasn't dragging you into her influencer bullshit."

As I walk into my kitchen area, I can feel his frown like a press against my shoulder blades. "I kept my distance. And I didn't stay at the funeral long. Just went to say hi to some old friends." Adam and Carter pop into my mind, and I smile at thoughts of the twins. I found them on Instagram, DMed them both for their phone numbers, and now we have a group chat set up. Adam is the most active one on it, mainly sending GIFs and random videos updating us on his life.

"What did you do after the funeral?"

I fumble with a jar of jam, almost dropping the glass container, but manage to catch it at the last second. "Nothing much. Went to a bar. Toasted Josh. Spent the night in my hotel room."

No need to mention who was at the bar with me and how I ended up at a random hotel after repeating past mistakes.

Jeremy settles on my couch. "You look gorgeous, by the way."

I'm makeup-less with my hair in a messy bun, wearing my normal at-home uniform of leggings and an engulfing fisherman sweater that I pretend Chris Evans gave me from his personal closet. Not red-carpet ready or even done up for a night out on the town.

But Jeremy knows how much I love my sweaters. He would never disparage them. This is his attempt at making me feel better.

"I'm only baking the Brie. Not giving you all my cheese," I warn him instead of responding to the compliment. What do I say anyway?

Grief combined with embarrassment does wonders for my pores, apparently.

"Baked Brie is all anyone needs in the world." Jeremy leans over my coffee table, studying my latest puzzle in progress. He picks up a random piece and tries to notch it into place, failing.

"That should go there," he mutters.

I pinch my lips together to keep my smile at bay. Jeremy is wonderful at running marathons, singing karaoke, and managing the media relations of the largest university in the city. But he's horrible at puzzles.

And being in a romantic relationship with me. But I was bad at being in one with him, too, so fair is fair.

Having him as one of my best friends is better, especially since falling for the sexy dentist in 2F hasn't stopped him from wandering up to my apartment to demand the elaborate charcuterie boards Carlisle refuses to make for him. I can always be counted on to have an array of cheese.

I set a baking sheet on the counter and line it with parchment paper.

"Full wheel or half?" I ask.

"Full. Tula should be here soon."

My hand pauses on the fridge handle.

Tula comes by almost as often as Jeremy, despite living a few blocks away. But the fact that Jeremy knows she's coming is a hint. A reason to be worried. They don't plan visits. They just show up.

As if summoned by her name, there's a quick knock on my door before it swings wide.

"I brought margaritas." Tula strolls into my kitchen, plops down a massive travel thermos on my counter, then pulls out limes and salt from her bag. Her dark hair and tan skin are damp from the light rain I spy out the window. Even though she lives in a city with almost constant precipitation, Tula barely ever bothers with an umbrella, claiming they slow her down. I've only seen her use one on our bookstore outings, and that's more about protecting the precious pages than staying dry herself.

Tula moves around my condo with the ease of familiarity, unearthing the margarita glasses she gifted me on my birthday—mainly so they'd be on hand when she comes over for an impromptu happy hour, where she pays me with citrusy alcohol to listen to her rant about the men at her company that think they're better engineers than her while they screw shit up that she has to fix. I enjoy gossip and drama that has nothing to do with me, so I happily sip my drink and share in her outrage.

When all the fixings are on the table, my friend halts and stares at me, claiming my eyes with hers as they soften with love and sadness. "How are you doing?"

This is the moment. The one where I should break down in sobs, crumpling inward on the gaping pit in my chest. My two best friends are here, ready to support me.

Instead, I feel something like anger.

Not at them. I'm grateful for them. They're here for me, and that means more than I could ever express.

But the slow, low simmer of fury still heats my skin until the soft cotton of my sweater itches like cheap wool. Reining in my unexplained temper, I turn away from her probing stare.

"I'm baking Brie, and you brought drinks, so I'm better than ten minutes ago." Searching the plethora of dairy options in my refrigerator is a good excuse to not meet her eyes.

"How was the funeral?" Tula ventures.

"Look," I snap, then breathe and calm my voice. "I didn't want you all coming because it wasn't *his* funeral. Not really." Instead of slamming the cheese on the counter, I take special care to place the Brie down gently. "It was a room full of my mom's followers and people I didn't know."

Except for the Perrys.

Except for Dom.

Don't think about him.

Don't think about his judgmental eyes.

Don't think about the taut skin of his hips disappearing under the waistband of pineapple underwear.

Don't think about how he growled out a pirate impression that was so serious you had to taste the sour candy on his stern mouth.

Don't think about how he pushed you away. Again.

Maybe I should've invited Jeremy and Tula. They never would have let me make such a fool of myself.

"That's exactly why we should've been there." Tula takes the jar of fig jam from me after listening to me mutter a string of curses while trying to open it. She pops the lid with one turn. "You would've known *us*. And we could have held your hand, and gotten you drinks, and mocked strangers with you."

And guarded the janitor's closet so Dom never found me floundering in toilet paper.

Maybe it would've been nice to have them there.

"It was on the other side of the country." I shrug and focus on situating the Brie in the exact center of the baking sheet.

"We would've gone to the other side of the world for you," Jeremy says.

See? This is a perfect time to cry.

But my tear ducts are dry.

They deserve a better friend than me. Someone who fully appreciates the level of love they have to offer.

"Fine," I mutter. "I'll let you know about the next funeral."

Tula huffs. "Just don't shut us out. We're here for you."

"And not just because of your snacks," Jeremy adds. "Though that is why I first fell in love with you."

"What's that?" Tula points to the coffee table, and the only corner where puzzle pieces don't lay claim.

"My laptop?"

"Yes, obviously it's your laptop. But what's that open on it? And it better not be what I think it is."

"I don't know what you think it is." The heat of the oven brushes my cheeks as I open the door and slide the tray in.

"Maddie." Tula tries to catch my eye. "Please don't tell me you have your work email open during your bereavement leave."

I can't tell her that. Because I do.

"I'm not *actively* working." My voice sounds surly with defensiveness as I straighten. "Just running some reports. And making myself available in case any fires pop up. It's not like I'm doing anything else with my time off."

"You are *grieving*." Tula grasps my shoulders, all but forcing me to meet her gaze. "That is something. A huge thing. You need to close your email and really take some time off for yourself. Redford can survive without you."

That might be true at most jobs, but mine, not so much. Over the years, I've become an integral part of the makeup of The Redford Team, an accounting firm that serves clients nationwide and needs their only logistics associate on call most working days. My boss has a general idea of what I do and how I achieve it, but she's distanced herself from the particulars. Without me, systems would start crumbling within a week. Maybe sooner.

If I tell Tula that, she'll start badgering me about work-life balance.

The thing is, I *like* how imperative I am to the company. How they rely on me and how all my coworkers know I can be trusted to keep the ship floating.

"Yeah, well, maybe if grieving came with clearly laid out tasks that definitively took up time, I'd take work off. But I'm just reading and putting puzzles together and falling in love with Nam Do San. Plenty of time to get some work done."

"Oh! You're watching *Start-Up*?" Jeremy shares my K-Drama

obsession. "I'm with you. Do San is dreamy. I would do very bad things to him if I could."

"Good. Yes. Binge emotional TV. Do puzzles. Schedule an appointment with a therapist," Tula says. "But *don't* pretend like nothing in your life has changed. If you stuff everything down, you'll explode. You can't ignore this."

"I'm not ignoring it. Josh made that impossible." When I press the buttons on my oven timer, I shove them a touch too hard, and the display beeps a warning at me.

Don't get mad at your friends, I scold myself. *They care about you.*

I didn't expect to have to fight my temper so much. A few times this past year I contemplated a world post-Josh and figured it would involve a lot of public crying.

But I'm not even doing that privately.

"What do you mean?" Tula gives me space by leaning back on the island, but she continues to study me. "What did Josh make impossible?"

"Did he leave you something?" Jeremy abandons the puzzle and gives me his entire focus. "Like the letter he left your mom?"

Guess she did share that with her followers. I wonder if they saw the real correspondence or if Cecilia made up whatever her son supposedly wrote to her.

I suck in a deep breath, let it out slow. "Josh wants me to spread his ashes. In eight different states. The ones he never visited."

And that's where I stop. With half of the truth. Because I'm a bad friend.

I've shared almost every part of myself with these two. They know about my shitty parents and neglectful grandmother. They know Josh was the one who showed me how families should love each other. They know one time a boy broke my heart, so I decided to start somewhere new. Tula was the internet friend I met freshman year of college in an online fandom group for a fantasy romance series. She's the one who waxed poetic about her university in Washington. She's the reason I ran here when I ran away.

But I've never spoken Dominic Perry's name to either of them.

And I don't plan to start now.

I can't do it. Can't pick apart the weird, unending relationship that leaves me vulnerable time and time again. Can't admit to them that I'm still gutted by a boy who hurt me when I was nineteen. I don't need them to tell me he shouldn't still affect me this way. I already know that. And I refuse to give Dom any more power over me. As far as I'm concerned, I'm the one making these trips, and he's only tagging along.

And as far as Jeremy and Tula are concerned, I'd rather let them think I'm spreading the ashes on my own.

"Shit," Jeremy mutters. "That's a lot of places. How do you feel about it?"

I shrug. "Not sure. Having something to do, something for him, I think I like that part. But it's a lot. A bunch of goodbyes. And that first one was hard enough."

Tula frowns in concern. "People can make requests in their will, but you're not legally bound to follow through."

"I know that. But . . . it's Josh."

It's my brother. It's the last thing he asked me to do.

The last piece I have of him.

Well, pieces. I've got the seven remaining Rubbermaid containers tucked in the high cabinet I don't normally use because I need a step stool to reach it. I was briefly terrified that TSA would confiscate him, but they let me through no problem.

"If you want company, I can come. We can come." Jeremy tilts his head toward Tula, and she nods without hesitation.

They are better friends than I deserve. I should tell them about Dom, but I can't find the words in me. I don't trust myself to talk about him.

And I don't trust myself not to drive away these two people I love more than anyone in the world now that Josh is gone.

"Thank you," I say. "Really. Thank you. But I think I have to do this on my own." Looking for a way to hide my lie with a change of subject, I point to the fourth glass Tula set out. "Is Carlisle coming?"

"No," she says, unscrewing her thermos to pour our drinks. She hands each of us a glass, then clinks hers against the rim of the remaining one. "A drink for Josh. He will be missed."

I remember the last time my brother came to visit me. Josh and Jeremy teamed up, convincing us to go barhopping and end the night at a karaoke spot. We sang and laughed, tipsy on life and friendship.

The next morning, when it was just the two of us, Josh told me about his diagnosis.

I think that night was the last time I was happy.

"To Josh." Jeremy holds up his margarita. "The best drunken duet partner a man could ask for." He tries to keep his voice light, but I can hear the tightening of his vocal cords.

They knew my brother. Cared about him. They probably even cried for him when they got my text.

And I didn't invite them to his funeral because I couldn't handle my current life colliding with my past one. I press the guilt away, vowing to never let the toxic mess in my chest spill out onto either of them.

"To Josh." I hold up my drink and try not to think about the last toast I gave for him and who I was toasting with. "And to a few more trips with him." *He's not gone yet.* Trying to lighten the somber mood, I attempt a smirk at my friends. "I'll bring you back some souvenirs."

CHAPTER

Eight

Rain drips off my jacket as I step into the lobby of a downtown high-rise. Luckily, this is Seattle, so they know the likelihood of someone walking in here wet. The smooth tiled floors sport absorbent mats for the first ten feet or so, and I don't feel bad about giving myself a little shake to disperse the excess moisture.

As I swipe through the security station, the guard on duty, Simon, smiles and offers me a wave.

"Haven't seen you around lately." He's just making polite conversation, and I'm not about to do a deep dive into how I was working on the other side of the country during my brother's last two weeks of life, then came back and acted out a half-assed bereavement leave at home, especially not with a guy I've only had a few casual chats with.

With an ease developed early in life, I let a smile curve my mouth despite the gaping hole of pain and anger and sadness in my chest. "Went home for a long visit. And Pamela has been fine with me working more remote hours. Hard to convince me to change out of sweatpants if I don't have to."

Simon chuckles. "I'm with you there. Have a good day."

"You, too!" I inject cheer into my voice and face as I wave and head for the elevators.

Pamela requested I come in the next three days in a row, when normally I'm only in the office once or twice a week. When I get off the elevator, I stride through the open workspace my company prefers, aiming for a cubicle in the back corner where I can get a semblance of privacy and therefore focus enough to work. I barely set my bag down before Pamela, director of logistics, is at my elbow, looking both regal and harried.

"Maddie. You're here. Thank god. The deployment mix-up is a nightmare, the numbers aren't matching the report, and we're meeting in ten minutes with the heads of the Northwest team."

I offer my frantic boss an understanding smile I've honed over years of working with her whirlwind personality. Everything seems like life or death when it comes out of her mouth, even if it's something as simple as forgetting to water the plant in her office for a week.

"Let me take a look. I reviewed everything last night, and I'm sure we can get it straightened out."

"You are a lifesaver. I don't know what I would do without you. This entire company would collapse." As dire as that statement sounds, it's not entirely an overexaggeration. As the sole logistics associate, I do deployments and project processing—along with a collection of other data-driven tasks—that keep operations running smoothly.

If I were to disappear off the face of the earth, The Redford Team would have a hell of a time filling the void left in my absence. Hence why I was working at my brother's funeral. It's not that Pamela was disregarding my personal time. It's just that there was an emergency and literally no one else was equipped to deal with it.

Also, I might have kept the fact that I was at my brother's memorial to myself. Pamela knew that Josh was sick. She's known for a year and hasn't batted an eye about my trips to the East Coast to check in on him. As long as I got my work done, there was no reason for her to worry. And as long as I got my work done, there was no reason for me to ask Pamela for time off. My job is largely portable.

And, once again, imperative for the company to keep functioning smoothly.

As I settle in at my cubicle, I ignore the guilt that pricks at my stomach, the little voice in the back of my head that says a good employee would be proactive about training a backup. About pushing to have another on call to fill my shoes if they ever become empty.

But whenever I decide I'm going to bring it up with Pamela, something more pressing comes up.

Besides, I don't mind being a necessary cog in the Redford machine. I like knowing that Pamela trusts and relies on me. That I'm her problem-solver. That everyone in the company knows who I am and how integral I am to our success, even if I'm not one of the rockstar accountants who brings in the big money.

Odd as it may seem to the people who mocked math nerds in high school, at Redford, the accountants are the applauded celebrities. The hotshot bad boys. The "work hard, play hard" crew.

My mind flits away from The Redford Team to another accountant I know.

Dominic Perry.

He's of the "work hard, then work harder" mentality. I doubt he'd fit well at our firm.

Although, I've found people tend to like the taciturn asshole for some reason. Like his hot face makes up for his domineering personality.

I don't get it.

Seemed like you got it when you tried to kiss him.

I shake my head, trying to shut up the part of my brain that enjoys replaying all my past mistakes on a loop whenever I let my guard down.

Focusing on work keeps me busy enough to drive away all unwanted thoughts about things I left on the other side of the country. The day goes by at a normal pace with multiple morning meetings, and the rest of my time is filled with digging through datasets, processing accountant deployments, and doing a hundred other little tasks.

When lunch rolls around, I check the windows and smile to see the rain has paused. I love the gray clouds and thunderstorms when I can stay inside all day watching how droplets spill down the glass panes. But when I want to walk the block to my favorite falafel shop, I'd prefer to stay dry on the excursion. As I finish wrapping a thick scarf around my neck to fight off the Seattle winter chill, I do a quick check of my personal email on my phone.

I freeze at the sight of a familiar name.

Sender: Dominic Perry
Subject: Travel Plans

Maddie,

You didn't give me your phone number. Please do so.

We still need to spread Josh's ashes in Alabama, Alaska, Arizona, Idaho, Kansas, North Dakota, and South Dakota. Provide me with dates you are available, and I will begin making travel arrangements. I can cover the initial cost until Josh's assets are released.

My phone number is (215) 555-6055.

Dom

"You've got to be fucking kidding me," I mutter, glaring at my phone screen.

Did he get a robot to write this?

No, I remind myself. This is Dom through and through. Demand the pertinent details, and don't mess around with anything silly like emotions.

Not that I want him to bring up feelings that I may or may not have toward him. But after the motel, I just thought there'd be . . . something.

Frustrated with myself and Dom and the universe, I exit my inbox, shove my phone in my pocket, and vow not to look at or even think about the message until I get home tonight. Maybe not even then.

Dom can wait.

Luckily, I don't have any afternoon meetings, so I'm able to squirrel myself away in my cubicle after I get back with my spicy falafel wrap and stew in my cranky mood. I'd have trouble pasting on my helpful work smile with Dom's cold message rattling around in my brain.

At the end of the workday, I'm still irritated. I stow my laptop in my bag, put on my rain gear, and stomp the entire three blocks back to my condo. Back in my home, I shuck off my rain jacket, then start pacing. Without work as a distraction, all my mind can focus on is the email. As my agitated feet pound a steady rhythm back and forth, I mentally plot my response to Mr. Responsible Asshole.

Fuck off.

No, that's too simple and makes it sound like I'm backing out of Josh's wishes. Which I'm not, as much as I want to never see Dominic Perry's face again. If it weren't for Dom's involvement, I'd be on a plane tomorrow, heading to a new Josh destination. I want more of my brother's words *now*.

But I'm worried if we meet up too soon, I'll make the same bumbling mistake I did in Delaware. That my grief will manifest in bad choices.

Then there's also my job. Pamela was flexible this past year with me working remotely because of Josh's illness. But I'm not sure these ash-spreading trips would be met with the same understanding.

With these two concerns in my mind, I force past my needy urge to tell Dom to pack a bag by tomorrow. Eventually I come up with a message as devoid of emotion as his was.

Sender: Maddie Sanderson
Subject: RE: Travel Plans

I can meet you in Alabama any weekend in April. Give me the coordinates. I'll make my own travel arrangements.

-M

There. I completely ignore his request for my phone number, because I see no reason for him to have it, and I suggest just over two months from now so I can utilize the weeks to reconstruct my Dominic defenses. We're still too close to Josh's . . .

What do I call it?

Death day?

Whatever. All I know is I'm not okay yet and being around Dom has me doing terrible things.

Like kissing him.

I need to not kiss him ever again, which means I need to not be emotionally vulnerable near him.

My laptop dings, and I realize there's already a response to my email. Was the guy hovering over his inbox like a hawk? Ready to swoop in and make more demands on me?

Sender: Dominic Perry
Subject: RE: RE: Travel Plans

The first weekend. It's more efficient for me to make both bookings at the same time. And I'll text you the coordinates when you message me.

-Dom

"You pushy asshole," I mutter while typing.

Sender: Maddie Sanderson
Subject: RE: RE: RE: Travel Plans

It's more efficient for you to type the coordinates into the means of communication we're already using.

. . . .

Sender: Dominic Perry
Subject: RE: RE: RE: RE: Travel plans

Texting and phone calls are a more immediate means of communication.

. . . .

Sender: Maddie Sanderson
Subject: Control Freak

Dear Ass,

Stop holding the coordinates hostage. The only way I'm showing up in Alabama with Josh's ashes is if you tell me where to go. I will get there on my own.

Sincerely,
Don't Fuck With Me

The response to my no-longer-playing-nice email takes longer, no doubt as he weighs his options.

I want to do the Josh tasks, if only to open those envelopes and read more of my brother's words. But Dom is the one who reached out first. I can hold out longer than him, I know it. I may have agreed to follow Josh's rules, but that doesn't mean letting Dom boss me around the whole time.

My email dings.

Sender: Dominic Perry
Subject: RE: Control Freak

Dear Don't Fuck With Me,

34°19'38.00" N
87°46'57.00" W
   Send me your flight plans when you have them. Please. And I would appreciate it if you at least let me book our accommodations.

-Dom

In this message, I can read Dom actively learning the error of his ways. His domineering tone is slightly diminished. He'll soon accept that I only take orders from my boss, and that's because Pamela pays me well and appreciates my work.

A childhood that consisted of zero control over my life makes it almost impossible for me to allow someone else to dictate my choices now. One more reason to be pissed off at Josh for this postdeath dance he's making me do.

But I'll follow the steps because I love him and each one gives me a sliver of the brother I no longer have.

Sender: Maddie Sanderson
Subject: RE: RE: Control Freak

Fine

I won. Kind of.

Now I have until April to mentally prepare for another Dom encounter.

Spring

I never considered coming to Alabama. Really, none of the southern states hold much appeal for me. I'm a cold-weather person. I want sweaters, hot drinks, and stormy skies that randomly expel torrential downpours that give me endless excuses for not leaving my home.

But Josh's envelope said Alabama, so here I am at an airport in Birmingham.

Step one: pick up my rental car.

Step two: stop at the first drugstore I spy and buy a bottle of sunscreen too large to have been allowed in my carry-on.

Step three: find the hotel address Dom emailed me last week.

Yes, I still refuse to give him my number.

Partly because I don't like the idea that his name could pop up on my phone screen whenever he feels like it.

But mostly because I know not having it gives Mr. Must Maintain Control At All Times a hefty dose of heartburn.

After I complete step two, slathering my upper body in SPF 75— you can get burned through the car window, FYI—I pull up my email and find a message waiting for me.

Sender: Dominic Perry
Subject: Alabama Trip

Maddie,

Let me know when you've landed and you're on your way. Text me using the number I gave you.

Sincerely,
Dom

I smirk, imagining him popping antacids to deal with me.

Sender: Maddie Sanderson
Subject: RE: Alabama Trip

Dear Control Freak,

On my way.

Sincerely,
I Don't Use Phones Because That's How The Aliens Find You

Somewhere in the world, he's angrily growling my name, and that brings me an immense amount of satisfaction.

Flipping back through our email exchange, I find the address he sent me. The vindictive goblin that lives in my soul wanted to wrestle all control of these trips away from Dom. But I found myself letting him take the lead on booking our stay for this first excursion. An oppressive weight bore down on my brain whenever I tried to think about the logistics of each of these trips.

Planning another goodbye to my brother.

So when Dom pressed for me to let him handle reserving rooms for our stay, I folded. But I booked my own flight, refusing to allow him that much control over my movements.

Turns out, not taking control was a mistake. I discover this the moment my GPS announces I have arrived at my destination.

There was supposed to be a hotel.

Instead, I pull up to a cabin.

Like, in the woods. Outside of civilization.

"What the fuck?" I mutter, parking on the gravel drive.

When I pull out my phone and double-check everything, it's clear I have the right place. I even google the address, and this cabin comes up on a rental website.

I swipe over to my email and realize I overlooked a sentence when reading Dom's message.

Code is the last four digits of my number.

Hotels don't need codes. Houses with automatic locks do.

It's not outlandish that I missed the directive. My eyes took in the address and dismissed all other words he wrote, avoiding as much of Dom as I could.

With a frustrated huff, I shove out of my car and stomp to the front door. As instructed, I type in the four-digit code from the phone number I refuse to use in any other context.

The lock clicks, and I storm into the cabin.

It's empty.

And damn him . . .

The place is incredible.

Everything is wood, and dark metal fixtures, and warm lighting, and soft furniture. Fuzzy blankets lay draped over the backs of the sofas, and a massive stone fireplace begs to be set aflame. The open floor plan shows a kitchen and small dining table in addition to the cozy sitting area.

Trying to ignore the lumberjack wet dream, I sulk across the thick, woven rug toward a hallway that—thank the universe—reveals doors to two bedrooms and a bathroom.

"What is this nonsense?" I hiss to the beautiful, empty hideaway.

"What's wrong?"

I guess not so empty after all.

Dom looms in the entrance, taking up the whole doorway with his broad shoulders.

My eyes wander over those shoulders that are covered in soft flannel, as if he dressed to match our accommodations. My traitorous gaze takes in the rest of him, searching for some flaw. But there's nothing—other than the man as a whole.

Because he hurt me, and my body still wants him.

"What's wrong," I grit, reminding myself of my fury, "is you booking us a teeny tiny house to stay in. Together. What the hell?"

Dom closes his eyes, draws in a deep breath that sounds a lot like *I'm on the verge of strangling this ungrateful brat.*

"It has good ratings," he responds after his meditative breathing. "And it's close to the coordinates."

"I'm sure hotels are around here, too. You know, places where we don't share a bathroom." I throw a thumb toward the only toilet I see in this place.

I can't poop for the next twenty-four hours. The irrational thought blares in my head. No matter that everybody poops, and I've done so plenty of times in Dom's parents' house when I was growing up.

Suddenly, as if my intestines heard my vow to give up normal digestive practices, I need to use the facilities.

Urgently.

Unaware of the turmoil in my mind and abdomen, Dom fully enters the cabin and shuts the door behind him.

"You don't like hotels," he says.

The comment, quiet as it was, reverberates in the air between us. Bringing up *that* night.

The night we will never, *ever* discuss.

We were both sloppy drunk. He wasn't supposed to remember anything. Not me lamenting my distaste for hotels. And certainly not me kissing his candy-coated lips.

My stomach roils again, and I realize that I'm going to break my silent vow within a minute of making it. Without a word to Dom, I charge into the bathroom, slamming the door behind me, latching it tight, and whimpering in relief when I see a bottle of air freshener on the shelf and a small window that slides open easily.

A few minutes later, I exit the bathroom, pretending like it wasn't weird for me to have turned on the shower yet have my hair completely dry.

"Well, come on then." I stroll past where Dom's leaning his too-tall body against the kitchen counter. "Let's go."

"Not yet. We have a reservation."

My feet slow. "What do you mean? How could we have a reservation? Josh didn't know when we were going to places."

"I made it."

Fury threatens to freeze the blood in my veins. Or turn it to lava. "You opened the letter without me?"

Dom gives me a look like I spoke to him in a foreign language.

"Of course not. I searched the coordinates. When I found the destination, I looked up the website and saw you needed to make a reservation. It's the Dismals Canyon. You're supposed to go at night. I figured we'd eat, then go."

I swallow my anger and pause my plan to fill Dom's socks with shaving cream.

"Fine. We'll get dinner. But only because you're entirely unbearable to be around when I'm hungry. And especially when *you're* hungry."

Dom frowns. "What's that supposed to mean?"

I roll my eyes. "Don't pretend like you don't know. You're infamous for getting hangry." Giving Dom shit for potentially being in a bad mood is hypocritical, seeing as how I am a perpetual bitch around him now. But there's this deep-seated craving in me to get a rise out of him. To rattle his calm demeanor the way he does mine by just existing in my vicinity.

"I don't get hangry."

"Yeah, you do. Why do you think Josh, and the twins,"—and Rosaline—"and I always had snacks on hand for you?"

Now he's the one rolling his eyes. "I don't think chucking bags of Cheez-Its at my head and telling me to stop being 'Dom the Dick' qualified as *having snacks on hand for me.*"

I shrug. "You secretly love Cheez-Its. And you always ate them."

He grumbles something I can't hear. Probably some irresponsible words, which I count as a success.

"Look at that," I taunt. "You're already pissy. Time to eat dinner." I stride past him and out the door, breathing easier in the late afternoon air that doesn't hint at his cedar cologne.

The idea of carpooling is too much for me, so we drive separately to a nearby diner. When we sit down at a booth, I fish Josh out of my bag and place him next to me, on the tabletop.

"He's eating with us?" Dom's eyes flick from the Rubbermaid of ashes to me.

"Do you have a problem with that?"

Dom opens his mouth to answer, but I cut him off with a raised finger.

"What's that, Josh?" I tilt my head toward the remains. "You think Dominic Perry should keep his opinions on his side of the booth? What a good point. I agree."

Dom frowns.

"Oh, sorry." I bend even closer, until my ear is pressed against the airtight lid. "Could you say that again? I'm having trouble hearing you over the pulsating vein in Dominic's forehead." I barely suppress a smile when the man smooths his fingers over his temple. "Ah, you were saying that Dom must keep buying underwear a size too small to give him that constantly pinched expression? Well, I wouldn't know, but it's a good theory."

Dom stops massaging his brow, dropping his hand to the table and tapping out an annoying rhythm.

"Is this going to be a regular thing?" he asks, voice dry.

Me talking to my brother and pretending he responds? Probably. I've found myself conversing with Josh a lot when I'm alone in my apartment these past few months. I don't know why I do it. Florence didn't impart any kind of religion on Josh and me, and I've never put much stock in an afterlife. The idea of ghosts mildly intrigues me, but I can't definitively say I believe they exist.

Still, there's something about talking to my brother—or ranting at him, which I'm more likely to do—that does something for me. The act doesn't make me happy, exactly.

But it briefly distracts me from the fact that he's dead. That moment before a response is required, I can imagine one will come.

Maybe this is a creative and healthy coping mechanism.

Or maybe I'm losing my mind because I can't cry, and I'm not grieving properly.

To avoid answering Dom, I snap open my menu, glad the list of food items is tall enough to block out his face.

We make it through the meal without further insults, mainly because we don't speak. A few times Dom opens his mouth as if he's going to say something, and I tense for him to bring up the way I drunkenly mauled him after our first ash-spreading adventure. But then he closes his lips and refocuses on his food.

When the bill is paid—I insist on a split check—I break the silence.

"When's the reservation? Can we go now?"

"Yes," Dom says on a sigh. "We can go."

The drive takes us on winding roads through rural areas, but we eventually come upon a large stone-supported sign announcing we've found ourselves at the Dismals Canyon. I follow Dom's tail-lights up a short drive to a small parking lot. Nothing about the place reveals why we'd need a reservation.

"Now what?" I ask once I meet Dom outside of his car.

He nods toward a sign that points the way to registration. Gritting my teeth, I continue to follow him down an incline where we come upon an outdoor sitting area and a souvenir shop.

"We're here for the night tour," Dom tells the woman behind the counter. "Dominic Perry and Madeline Sanderson."

My shoulders go up to my ears at the sound of my full name in his voice. My mom, Florence, and workers at the DMV are the only ones who call me Madeline. Even though Dom is on my bad side, too, I don't want him Madeline-ing me.

The woman checks our names on a list, then directs us to wait in the shop or in the outside sitting area until the tour—whatever that is—begins.

Without the need for discussion, we head outside, where there's a semblance of privacy.

The evening is cool, and I hug Josh's remains close to my chest while glaring over the railing toward the sound of falling water. I have to use sound because in the dying light it's impossible to see much past the deck we're on.

"I don't see why we needed to make a reservation for a night hike. And why would we hike at night? You can't see anything."

Dom doesn't respond, which only infuriates me more. Maybe I can push him off the trail and he'll get lost in the woods and I'll never have to see his annoying, handsome face again.

But then he distracts me from aggressive thoughts by pulling out an envelope and holding it up so I can read the handwriting.

Alabama
34°19'38.00" N
87°46'57.00" W

Josh. He's in that envelope. He's also in my arms. Just like on the beach in Delaware, I can *feel* my brother beside me in this moment. Can pretend that he's alive for a little while longer.

"Do you want to read this one?" Dom asks.

"Yes." I thrust out my hand. But Dom doesn't immediately pass the letter over. Instead, he holds out his empty palm as well.

A trade.

For a second, I clutch Josh closer, loath to let go of even this small portion.

"I'll give him back." Dom's voice is surprisingly gentle, and I jerk my gaze up in time to catch some unreadable emotion flicker across his face. "You need two hands to open the letter."

Damn his logic.

With gritted teeth, I loosen my white-knuckle grip on the Rubbermaid container, passing off one eighth of my brother. Then I clutch the stiff envelope, and despite my greed for his words, I'm careful when I tear the flap.

A thought comes to me then, one I can't believe I didn't think to ask before. "What did you do with the Delaware letter?" Panic pinches my gut. "You didn't throw it away, did you?"

Dom frowns. "No. I'd never do that. I put it back with the rest. And they're all in a fireproof safe in my town house."

"Oh." Still, I hesitate. "What's the combination?"

Dom glares down at me. "Why? Are you planning on sneaking in and taking them?"

I scowl. "Are you planning on holding them hostage from me?"

"Maddie—"

"Dominic," I snap back. "What if something happens to you? They're all I have—" My breath stutters and my anger heats, and I'm so furious at this man for witnessing my vulnerability over and over again. And I'm pissed at my brother for being the puppet master behind it all. "They're all I have left of him," I grind out. The letters and the ashes.

Dom stands utterly still in front of me, the hand that's not holding my brother braced on his hip, head bowed enough that I can't see his expression. Not that I could interpret it. I've officially lost my ability to decipher the hidden thoughts of Dominic Perry.

But I refuse to mourn the loss. Maybe I never had the ability. Believing I understood Dom only led me to heartache.

"I'll change it when I get home," he says. "And text you the new combination."

What kind of bullshit offer is that? "No. You'll tell me the current combination *now*. And anytime you change it from this day forward, you'll email the new combo to me," I counter, confused why he's making this harder than it has to be.

Though one could argue me hoarding my phone number contributes to the difficulty, but I refuse to linger on that thought.

The muscle in Dom's jaw clenches so hard it stands out in perfect definition. Finally, he grits out a "Fine." Then he stares toward the sound of falling water. "The combination is—"

"Don't even think about lying to me," I cut him off, suspecting the eye contact avoidance is his deception tell. "I'll call Adam and ask him to check for me. I bet he'd love to snoop through your stuff."

Dom hits me with a glare. "I'm not about to give you his number when you haven't even given me yours."

"I don't need you to," I taunt. "I have it. We text. He's got good GIF game. He keeps me up to date on the hip lingo." Never thought twenty-six was old, but when it comes to social media jargon, I'm practically ancient.

"Adam has your number?" Dom's voice is so cold the nearby stream threatens to freeze over.

"Yep. Carter does, too." And I don't worry in the slightest that they'll give it to Dom. I've got a friendship with the twins that supersedes their brother. Still, I make a mental note to text them a warning not to share my digits under pain of death. "We're buddies.

And as my buddy, Adam will let me know if you're lying. So, give me the combo. The real one."

Dom reaches up to scratch the back of his neck, attention focused on the wooden boards at our feet. Then he mutters a curse and meets my eyes.

"Zero, seven, one, eight."

"That's . . ." My brain trips over the familiar numbers. *It can't be.* "You're fucking with me."

He shrugs and waves toward the envelope in my hand. "I thought you wanted to read it. Or I can." Dom reaches for the letter.

Quickly, I turn, blocking him with my shoulder.

"I'll read it." And then I'll text Adam and get him to prove Dom's a liar.

I slip the piece of paper out and step closer to a hanging lantern to read, swatting away the small bugs that also congregate around the light.

Dear Maddie & Dom,

Welcome to Alabama!
 Never thought you'd explore the south, huh, Maddie? But there's beauty everywhere, and I'm determined for you to find it. Even in the darkest of places.
 You should be in Dismals Canyon right about now. Book yourself a night tour—

Dom huffs a noise that I interpret as "Told you so."

—and get ready for something that's fucking cool. Got to see a similar sight in New Zealand, and I always thought I'd get another chance to admire them closer to home. Now it's your turn.

Buy a souvenir I would have liked and take a picture—when you're not in the dark—for my sake.

Then leave a piece of me in the glow.

Love,
Josh

Before I can ask Dom what Josh means, the door to the shop opens and a white man with an impressive gray mustache and welcoming grin strides onto the deck, eyes sparking with excitement when he spots us.

"Who wants to see some glow worms?"

CHAPTER

Ten

The dismalites glow on the canyon walls like stars in the night sky. Each one appears to flicker, but our guide tells us they give off a steady light. Their minuscule movements trick our eyes.

"This next part has lots of roots and stones in the path, so best to use your lights. Red, if you have 'em," our guide calls out in his thick southern accent. He's a fount of knowledge and clearly passionate about this hidden wonder in Alabama. I could hear the anger and sadness in his voice when he pointed out a dark section of the canyon wall where not a single glowing body could be spotted. In the daylight, he told us, we'd be able to see how the space is covered in graffiti.

Fucking teenagers.

As we make our way through a series of connected caverns at a meandering pace, I'm relieved at how nonstrenuous the trek is. Knowing my brother, I wouldn't be surprised if the coordinates of one or more of his letters send us on a hike that would have me struggling to catch my breath.

Josh knew about and respected the severity of my asthma, but he also would point out how avoiding physical activity altogether wouldn't help my lungs. We got into plenty of bickering matches about it. Eventually, Josh figured out the best way to get me to step out of my comfort zone was with bribery.

And what's a better bribe than his final words?

I'll climb a mountain for one of those envelopes.

Note to self: Get in touch with a breathing specialist. Just in case.

I used to see one regularly when I first moved to Seattle. The change in environment seemed to aggravate my airways until I was using my inhaler multiple times a day. But she prescribed me a new medication and talked me through some breathing exercises that helped. After college, I let my appointments and exercises trail off. Now, with the possibility of more outdoor adventures, I should start thinking about how to keep breathing through them.

But that's a problem to deal with when I get home. For now, I can take advantage of the easy pace, only worrying about an occasional tripping hazard.

In the darkness of the cavern, I can still see the broad silhouette of Dom's shoulders. That doesn't stop me from flinching and almost fumbling Josh when a warm pair of hands covers mine.

"Here." Dom's fingers guide mine to a button on the flashlight he handed me before we started the tour. "This'll turn on the red light."

I should've known that not only would Dom come prepared with flashlights for the both of us, but they'd be equipped with the red lights that don't affect our night vision and don't bother the worms as much.

Larva, I correct myself. Our guide explained that the little glowing creatures covering these walls are actually fly larva. True glow worms are found in New Zealand and Australia. But the guy's cheerful explanation gave me the sense that he didn't mind the incorrect label as long as people were still interested in seeing the beauty of them.

I flick on the red light and detangle my hands from Dom's. He lets me go, turning on his own light and waving for me to walk ahead of him.

Noise doesn't bother the dismalites, and other voices chatter around us as we all file forward. The tour group includes a family of five and a couple. There's a teenage girl with the family and when we all first gathered, she gaped at Dom like he was the personification of Taylor Swift tickets. The sight reminded me so much of my younger self that I was tempted to laugh. But my humor faded quickly into irritation when I remembered exactly how the man treated my awe in the past.

Some girls who hook up with their crush and get dropped the next day might feel used. But I don't even have the option of adding that to his sins.

No, that night, after weeks of us spending almost every minute of the day together, Dom didn't use me. He only gave. Gave me kisses. Gave me hot touches. Hell, the guy even gave me my first orgasm.

Dom took his time, asked me what felt good, cradled me against his body, and stroked my clit until he figured out how to make me fall apart. He taught *me* what my body wanted. Meanwhile, he asked for nothing in return.

At first, I thought that made him a good man. Someone to trust and give my heart to and pin my pathetic hopes on.

But even at nineteen, I should've known better. I'd already learned that the only person I could trust to not toss me aside was my brother.

All those beautiful things Dom gave me? They didn't mean anything.

Because that night was only a favor.

A *thank-you* for helping his family out.

A *I know you've had a crush on me for your entire life, so here, I'll touch you once before I lock down the woman I actually want to be with.*

To him, I was a responsibility. A charity case. A box on a to-do list to check off.

Well, he *did* me, and I hate him for it.

And I hate that my body can't seem to get on board the hating train with my brain. My body would like to be added to his to-do list again, with a few extra check boxes next to the task.

The skin on my hands buzzes and tingles where his palms pressed moments ago. Flexing my fingers to disperse the sensation, I point my red-tinted flashlight at the ground in front of my feet and shuffle forward.

I try to forget Dom is behind me as I listen to our guide and follow the group through the twists and turns. Some of the canyon stretches high above us, and other parts press in close until we have to shimmy through claustrophobic spaces.

It's just after pressing my body through one of these that I'm forced to come to a stop. The kid in front of me acts as a cork in the bottleneck as he bends over and blocks my way. The teenager tries to take a picture with a cell phone camera that is not equipped to pick up the subtle glow of a larva.

Josh would have a camera that could. My brother captured the most gorgeous wildlife photos, and I'm not just saying that because I'm his sister. Josh won awards. He got hired by big name publications and companies that flew him all over the world. His success can be gleaned simply from the large number that was left to Dom and me in his will to fund these ash-spreading excursions.

But what I loved most about my brother's photos was the way he'd send them to me. Whenever Josh took a shot he was particularly proud of, he'd commission a puzzle made out of it and mail the pieces to me in a bag. I wouldn't know what the shot was until I pieced everything together.

The walls of my condo are covered in framed finished puzzles of his work.

"Come on," the teen mutters to himself, pinching his fingers on the screen as if zooming in all the way will help.

There's a grunt behind me, and I angle my light back to see what's up.

Dom, who was following close behind me, is bent at a weird angle to get his large body through the thin opening in the canyon walls. Now he's stuck there because we can't move forward with the amateur photographer holding up the line.

Dom tries to hide the grimace on his face, but even in the dim light, I see the discomfort twisting his lips.

I turn back to the kid. "Those are brighter," I lie, pointing to a wall farther on that's scattered with little glowing larva. "You'll have better luck there."

He glances at me, straightens real fast, and pockets his phone. "Oh. Cool. Thanks." Then he scurries away, clearing the path forward. I make to follow but pause when I don't hear Dom's bothersome footsteps behind me. Turning, I realize the man is in the same spot I left him.

"Come on, you massive pain in my ass." I pat my leg like I'm calling a dog to heel.

Dom grunts again. "I'm stuck."

"Are you kidding me?" I run my light over all the places his body touches rock. "I don't have any butter on hand to grease you up." The space didn't seem *that* small when I went through it. But he does have a handful of inches and a lot more bulk than I do. "Use those vanity muscles of yours and pop yourself free."

Dom's scowl deepens in the red glow of my flashlight. "They're not vanity. I play on two rec baseball leagues."

"Ooo. *Two.* So impressive. I'm swooning." In high school, I totally did. Watching Dom play wearing those tight pants, swinging that bat, melted my hormonal brain. But now I'm over all that. The idea of him sprinting around bases and sliding through the dirt as it sticks to his sweaty skin does nothing for me.

Nothing.

As I taunt Dom, I move in closer to get a better look at his predicament. "Did they give you letterman jackets?"

He doesn't respond, and his silence is telling.

"Oh my god. They did, didn't they?" I cackle at the mental image of grown men trying to relive their high school glory days. "What do they even say on them?"

"It was a company gift. It's got the company name. Now can you *please*"—he grits the word out—"help me. I think it's my belt loop, but I can't reach at this angle." His long arm tries to touch his lower back, but the stone outcropping is in the way.

Tilting my head, I consider this man who I've resented for the past seven years. "I should leave you here."

"Maddie," he growls. And damn him for the way that makes my nipples perk up. My areolas are so happy, I bet they've started glowing like the larva. Damn bioluminescent nipples!

"Fine." Coming to the rescue is an easier decision than I expected. And maybe the role reversal is why. Because *I'm* the hero in this situation. The one giving Dom help. The opposite version of this dynamic emotionally devastated me, but if I can keep the power in my corner, maybe I can stand to be around Dom for the next six trips without wanting to smother him in his sleep. "Here. Hold Josh." This time when I hand off my brother, I find it surprisingly easy. Probably because Dom is trapped and at my mercy.

But there's also something about how Dom's hand fully engulfs the small Rubbermaid container that has me feeling like my brother is safe.

I don't bother using my flashlight, instead relying on feel. The denim of Dom's jeans is warmer than the humid air of this cavern, but I ignore that fact as I drag my touch along his waistband in search of the misbehaving belt loop. This close, Dom's breathing sounds overly loud and a tad ragged. When my thumb brushes the skin of his lower back, I hear a catch in his inhale.

Part of me wants to torture him by taking my time, but another part, the one that remembers endless incidents of Dom knocking his head on low ledges, and stuffing himself into too-small desk chairs, and bruising his elbows in bathroom stalls, can't stand the idea of him suffering any longer. Plus, that cedar scent of his is too strong, overwhelming my senses and tempting my body to lean in closer and breathe in deeper.

As I'm forcing myself to focus on my task, my fingertips encounter the stiff protrusion of what feels like a root—Dom was right about his belt loop getting caught. I tug and press and slide until the root gives up its hold.

When I step back, Dom watches my retreat.

"You should be good," I tell him.

He presses off the rock, and his body slides through.

"Thank you, Maddie."

There he goes again, saying my name unnecessarily.

"Try not to let any more trees fondle you." I extend my hand for Josh.

Dom stares at my palm for a stretch, then he reaches out with his, lacing his long fingers with mine.

Holding my hand.

I'm too stunned to do anything other than gape at the way we're connected. The way we're *touching*.

Eventually, I find my voice.

"What are you doing?" And why is my tone so light? It's supposed to be sharp and reprimanding.

His thick brows dip. "You held out your hand."

"For Josh."

Those brows pop straight back up, and he drops his eyes to his other hand that cradles my brother's remains. "Right."

"Yeah." Remembering myself, I yank out of Dom's grip.

He clears his throat as his now-free hand drops to his side and fists. He offers Josh to me, and I take him, turning without meeting Dom's stare again.

Luckily, the group hasn't gotten too far ahead of us while I helped free Dom from the rock passage. When I rejoin the gathering, our guide is giving a lesson about the dismalites.

"Now in this larva state, they're focused on eating. Getting as many nutrients stored up as possible. Because when they're flies, they're only alive for one day. And that day they're focused on one thing."

"Yeah. Fucking," I hear the teenager who was trying to take a photo earlier mutter, then snicker at his own joke.

But he's not wrong. Our guide explains how that single day of life is how we get more dismalites, *wink wink*.

My mind sticks on that fact.

One day.

And I thought Josh's life was short.

What would I do if I only had one day?

My eyes flick over to Dom. He's caught up to the group, the shadowy form of him looming behind me. He has his head tilted up, gazing at the dots of light higher on the canyon walls, the strong column of his neck illuminated by the gentle glow of the moon sneaking through a crack in the ceiling.

I jerk my head away and give it a shake.

What I would do in a single day doesn't matter. I have plenty of days. So many I would have been happy to divide them and give my brother a few. More than a few.

If I could have given Josh half my remaining lifetime, I would have.

Our group moves on, and I hear the pound of water falling over a cliffside.

"You all have been a great bunch! I hope you come back for a day hike to see a different version of the canyon," the guide calls back to us.

Wait, we're at the end?

I stop abruptly, and a large force knocks into my back, then grabs my shoulders to steady me.

"Maddie?"

I turn, feeling time and opportunity slipping away. "The tour is done. We need to spread the ashes."

In the glow of my flashlight, I see Dom's jaw firm and he gives a quick nod of his head.

Between our bodies, I pop the lid off the container. Then I click off my light, and Dom does the same. Darkness overwhelms us, but only at first.

Little pinpricks of light grow brighter as our eyes adjust. It feels like the stars are within arm's reach.

"He said to leave him in the glow," I whisper, not sure what else to say.

Dom offers a small grunt of agreement. "He'll like it here. He's a night owl."

"True." I'm thankful for the dark when my hands start to shake. And as much as I resent him, I'm also thankful for Dom in this moment. The way he just spoke about Josh existing in the present. In the future.

As if he believes my brother isn't truly gone.

"Goodbye, Josh." I tilt the container and let the particles of my brother spill onto the canyon floor.

Dom stays quiet, keeping vigil during one more of my goodbyes.

ADAM: It opened! 0718. Want me to
steal some stuff?
ADAM: Jk
ADAM: Or am I . . . ?
ADAM: Wait
ADAM: Isn't your bday July 18?

I sit in my car, staring at Adam's last text.

He's got a good memory.

Why would Dom use my birthday as the combination to his safe?

During the trip through the canyon, I'd pushed this to the back
of my mind. But now, with the proof from Adam, I can't ignore it
anymore.

But what does this mean?

It makes no sense.

*Maybe . . . maybe it was for the same reason I wanted the combina-
tion. In case something happened to him.*

But if Dom disappeared and I had to open the safe without his
guidance, I never would have guessed *my* birthday as the combo. I
would have tried Dom's. Then the twins'. Rosaline's, because he
might have set it before their divorce. His parents'.

Josh's would've made sense.

Mine . . . doesn't.

A tap on my window makes me jump, and I glance through the glass to see the confusing, infuriating man frown at me.

"What?" I shout, not ready to open my door, and not wanting to turn my car on in order to roll down the window.

Dom steps back, crosses his arms over his chest, and tilts his head toward the house. He should look like a dork, wearing the Dismals Canyon baseball hat he bought to match mine and fulfill Josh's letter request. But he still looks hot, fuck him very much.

Come inside, his body says.

The silent command brings out my petty bitch. I shoo him with my hand, then turn back to my phone and bring up my Redford email. I can't keep spiraling over the safe-combination mystery when he's staring at me. Might as well catch up on some work until he leaves me be.

A moment later, my car gives a slight rock. I glance up to spy the side of his torso out of the corner of my eye. Dom leans his broad body against the passenger door of my car.

Waiting for me.

Muttering a string of curses, I shut my phone off, unbuckle my seat belt, and fling the door open.

"What are you doing?" I snap.

"It's dark."

"Your observation skills astound me. Truly. I thought it was a sunny afternoon."

Dom watches me with an unreadable face. "You should come inside."

"Inside is literally thirty feet from my car." I snatch my pack—lighter now that Josh is gone—and the plastic bag of souvenirs for Jeremy and Tula from the passenger seat before climbing out and slamming the door shut. "What part of this trek did you think I'd struggle with, even in the dark?"

Dom doesn't answer, only pushes himself off my car and strides toward the door.

He's the one in danger. He'll be lucky if I don't sneak into his room in the middle of the night and smother him.

Once we're inside the cabin, Dom doesn't try to dictate any more of my actions. Maybe he does have some sense of preservation.

If I were even slightly tired, I'd lock myself in my bedroom and try to sleep. But it's like the glow of the worms was pure electricity, and now I'm supercharged. If I shut myself in my room, I'll just pace and overanalyze the birthday combination mystery. I need to reconnect with my comfort zone.

Luckily, a cozy cabin is the perfect place to do that. Ducking into my bedroom, I shut the door to gain brief privacy while I change out of my hiking clothes and into well-worn flannel pants and the massive hoodie Josh sent me from Florida a few years ago because he thought the crocodile and alligator high-fiving on the front of it was funny. The hoodie is so baggy, and the material so thick, and my boobs so small, that I don't see the point of a bra. After rifling through my bag, I find my noise-canceling headphones. I slip them on before leaving my room.

Easier to ignore Dom this way.

With my latest audiobook playing, I let my mind sink into the soothing story of a princess in a fantasy kingdom taking bloody revenge on her enemies while trying not to fall for the ruthless vampire warlord who rules the neighboring kingdom as I wander around the living area, searching for what I know in my bones *must* exist in this cabin. I discover my treasure in the cabinet under the TV.

A puzzle.

Most rentals tend to have one. And I love seeking them out.

Despite my largely hermitic lifestyle, I have gone on a few trips over the years. Josh could usually convince me to meet him somewhere, most often by sending me descriptions of a cool coffee shop or weird attraction. But my brother knew I could only handle so much high-energy fun, so at some point during an excursion he would go off on his own to explore while I would stay back, recharge my introvert batteries, and work on the random puzzle at the rental.

This one is promising. A collage of classic national park posters. I glance at the top of the box once, then flip it over, not to be referenced again. I'll complete the puzzle if I want to earn the picture.

A large coffee table made of worn wood provides the perfect surface to work on. I can tell in a glance that the dimensions are large enough to fit the puzzle. With one of the throw pillows from the couch, I settle in a cross-legged seat on the floor and rifle through the soft cardboard pieces, searching for the edges and setting them out one by one.

All the while, I ignore the man coexisting in this space with me. If I'm lucky, he'll go to bed soon, and I can puzzle in peace.

Apparently, my luck is still at zero because Dom decides to linger.

No. "Linger" isn't the right word. If he simply lingered, I might be able to ignore him.

But Dom, always in need of a purpose, fills the periphery of my vision with his room-circling. As I try to focus on my audio story and colorful pieces, he stops every few feet to pick up objects, fiddle with them, and put them back down.

The air of determination surrounding him bothers my brain like pollen irritates my airways.

When he fully pulls a large clock off the wall, I can't handle his self-important fidgeting anymore.

"What the hell are you doing?" I snap, tapping the side of my headphones to pause my book before pushing them off so I can hear myself berate my unwanted roommate. "Searching for recording devices? Casing the place? Stop touching all the stuff!"

Dom doesn't look at me as he turns a knob on the back of the clock.

"There are more than ten clocks in this place," he says. "And they're all set to the incorrect time."

I snort, then scan the room, realizing every item he's messed with is a time-telling device of some kind. Of course that would frustrate Mr. I'm Never Late If I Aim to Be Ten Minutes Early.

"They're just decoration." Most of the old-fashioned-looking devices fit the lived-in vibe of the cabin. Not that Dom would care. His place is probably all chrome and straight edges and fit for a robot. *Ugh, I bet he's a minimalist.* "Knickknacks can be aesthetically pleasing."

"Clocks serve a purpose," he mutters. "Wrong clocks are aesthetically aggravating."

His agitated movements are making it impossible to focus on my puzzle.

"Can't you use your phone to check the time like a normal person? Or, I don't know, my brother's watch?"

Damn. I was trying to be aloof, but resentment creeps into my tone on that last bit.

Every time I see Dom wearing the watch, it's a reminder that Josh isn't.

Because he's gone.

Dom pauses in the act of hanging the clock back on the wall, glancing my way. I weld my eyes to the jumble of pieces on the coffee table, ignoring the glimpse of vulnerability I allowed him.

Next I know, he's crouched at my side, clock abandoned as his fingers fiddle with the leather strap around his wrist. My breath catches when Dom slips the timepiece off and holds it out to me.

"If you want it, it's yours."

I stare at the familiar accessory. Josh only took the watch off at night to sleep. I can't remember a time when he didn't have it with him. One day the watch appeared on his wrist, and it became a part of him like the calluses on his fingers and the scar on his forehead from the time he fell out of the apple tree in the Perrys' backyard.

For a moment, I imagine accepting the offer, slipping this piece of my brother on and holding him with me forever.

But I know myself. Know that I can't stand bracelets or even hairbands around my wrists. As much as I'd love and cherish the device, I'd eventually take the watch off. Then I would put it down somewhere, and it would disappear one day, mixed in with my clutter.

Another piece of Josh would vanish.

I grit my teeth and close my eyes.

Dom would never be so careless. He probably has a custom-made watch stand by his bedside and cleaning supplies to make sure the glass face doesn't smudge.

"Keep it," I grind out. "He left it to you."

"Maddie—"

"Leave me alone. I'm puzzling." I put my headphones back on, restart my book, and command my eyes to only look at the pieces in front of me.

Still, I can sense when Dom stands and moves away. He stays in the main area for a stretch, moving around the kitchen. Probably correcting the microwave and oven clocks. Eventually, he disappears down the short hallway to the bedrooms.

I think I hear his voice attempting to penetrate the noise cancellation of my headphones, but I can't be sure, and I don't bother to check.

The puzzle lulls me into a meditative state. When I finally press the last piece into place, I realize a good amount of time must have gone by, because my shoulders and back ache and my headphones feel welded to my skin. When I peel them off, the quiet cabin seems loud, but it's just my ears readjusting to the fresh airflow. Glancing at the wall clock, I find it's well past midnight. A fact I can trust because of Dom's Father Time efforts.

I stand, my joints creaking with the movement, and I bite back a groan as I stretch my arms high over my head. Multiple cracks sound off in my body, and I sigh in relief.

Then I wander around the room, picking up each clock I find, fiddling with the dials at random, and setting them back in place before heading to bed.

Dom needs to learn there's things in life you can't control.

And I'm one of them.

CHAPTER

Twelve

Ever since returning home from Alabama, whenever I try to sit and read a book, or wait in line at the grocery store, or attempt to fall asleep at night, my mind uses the moment of relaxation to unearth memories of a time I thought I'd left behind me forever.

Memories of *that* summer. The one after my first year of college.

That summer was all kinds of perfect.

Until it wasn't.

I blame these frequent trips into the past on too much Dom exposure combined with the casual communication I've reestablished with the twins.

At the start of that June, I wasn't looking forward to the warm months. Josh had an internship in New York, Dom was set to work full-time, and I expected he would spend his free hours with Rosaline. My mom had disappeared on some excursion she claimed would revitalize her aura. I wanted to be back in school, away from Florence, who always seemed to blame me for her own daughter's absence, rather than the woman who kept leaving me behind.

Dom's mom's accident changed everything—a car crash that landed Mrs. Perry in the hospital followed by months of limited mobility and physical therapy.

I never wanted her hurting, but with their family in need, I finally got to start paying the Perrys back for years of care. No longer was I the quiet neighbor girl who struggled to breathe and lived with a mother and a grandmother who wouldn't mind if I disappeared. That summer I became the responsible young woman who looked out for the twins and picked up groceries and dried dishes while Dom washed them after dinner every night. A dinner I was eagerly invited to stay for by every member of the family.

We got into a comfortable routine, where I arrived in the morning to drive Adam and Carter to swim practice. While they did laps, I swung by the library to find a book for the day. Then I'd arrive back at the pool in time for it to open to the public. Situated under an umbrella and wearing a thick coating of sunscreen, I'd read for most of the day in a lounge chair, using my finger as a bookmark when Adam would break off from his teenage friend group and ask me to rate his cannonball skills. At lunch, the boys would pile into the back seat of my old Honda Civic, filling the hot car with the scent of chlorine and sunscreen—which I insisted they both regularly apply despite their not having vampire skin like mine—and we'd debate over which fast-food drive-through to visit for the day. Mr. Perry always gave me cash in the morning when I picked them up. I think he considered it payment for babysitting. But I didn't want their money.

I wanted their family.

Especially with Josh states away all summer.

Without the Perrys, it would've just been Florence and me until the semester started again. My mom's cleansing retreat in California was set to last months. Leaving on some random trip was her MO my entire childhood. It's not that I missed my self-involved mother. Only, when she left, Florence would remind me that my mother had to escape her life so often because she was miserable. Miserable because her husband was gone. Miserable because her son didn't show his mother or Florence the proper respect. Miserable because I was her daughter, and who would want that?

So, while plenty of nineteen-year-olds would've hated committing their summer months to looking after two thirteen-year-olds, I loved it. I loved how Adam passionately argued for Taco Bell every single day, and how Carter would share an eye roll with me whenever we gave in and let the smooth talker get his way. I loved how the twins wore matching grins when I pulled my old car into their driveway every morning. I loved how Adam would tell corny jokes and Carter would sing along to show tunes with me. I loved how when I brought them home after the pool closed, Mrs. Perry would open her arms to hug the twins from her seat on the couch and say, "There's my little monsters and the monster tamer."

But most of all, I loved how Dom would set aside his laptop, stand from his seat with a spine crack and a groan, then stride across the room and hug me.

I loved how he'd lift me off my feet, until his lips were near my ear, and in a voice low enough that only I could hear, he'd murmur, "Thank fuck for Maddie Sanderson."

And as I recovered from the affection and irresponsible word usage, Adam would scowl at his older brother and demand Dom set me down before he broke me in half while Carter made not-at-all-subtle kissing noises.

It was a little play we did most days, and I lived for it. Because it never felt like acting.

I became addicted. I dreaded the conclusion of summer. Especially when I realized the end was coming sooner than I planned.

The twins had summer camp in August. Two weeks of them gone. No more need for me to pick them up and spend my day with them. No more fast-food dates and silly singing and bad jokes.

No more thank-you hugs from Dom.

Back then, I had no trouble crying, and I spent a lot of that last day at the pool wearing my extra-large sunglasses, holding a book in front of my face, and pressing a towel to my cheeks so no one would notice how tears were streaming from my eyes in a continuous flow.

Adam and Carter were more quiet than normal on our final lunch run, and I didn't even ask before pulling into the Taco Bell drive-through. Not that I tasted the chicken quesadilla even after dousing it in hot sauce.

We were back at the pool, me hiding my face again, when my lounge chair dipped. I dropped my book to find Adam had settled himself by my feet, a surly expression on his face.

"I don't want to go to camp," the kid declared, conveniently forgetting how a few weeks ago he wouldn't shut up about all the adventurous activities he couldn't wait for.

Camping! Hiking! Building fires! Swimming across the lake and back to impress the lifeguards!

"It'll be fun," I said with as much conviction as I could muster despite not wanting our summer to end, either, and knowing that if I had to attend an adventure camp, I would dread every minute of the experience.

Maddie Sanderson and her delicate lungs did not—and still do not—belong in the outdoors.

Adam didn't respond, just frowned hard at the concrete beneath his feet and gave a surly shrug of his bony shoulders.

In that moment, I knew I had to tuck away my misery and be the responsible one. Adam refusing to go to camp at the last minute would be a major stressor on the Perry family, and my goal was to make their lives easier.

"Hey." I'd extended my leg and poked him with my toe. "You know I can't really do camp stuff, right? Because of my asthma." Even if I could, I still wasn't a camp girl, but Adam didn't need to hear that.

He gave me a small nod, pool water from his hair dripping onto my towel.

"Well," I continued in a wheedling tone, "I was looking forward to you going and telling me about it."

Adam stared at me with those big brown eyes surrounded by

dark lashes all the Perrys have. The teen looked like an adorable, hopeful puppy in that moment.

"Yeah?"

"Yeah." I poked him with my toe again, earning a reluctant smile. "I'm going to live vicariously through you, Adam Perry. Go have adventures. As many as you can. Then come home and tell me about them."

His grin, the slow spread of it, was a beautiful thing. "Okay. I can do that."

Then he stood, bent over me, and shook his head like a dog, showering me in pool water. Adam laughed almost as deep as his older brother when I squealed and threw my bottle of sunscreen at him. Then he ran off to rejoin his friends, his good humor restored.

Carter watched our exchange from across the pool deck, smile sad. That said it all.

I dropped my sunglasses enough so the quiet twin could see me roll my eyes. He chuckled and turned back to his friends.

The next day, I went with Dom and Mrs. Perry—who was finally walking on her own—to drop the twins off at the bus they were going to ride to camp. The boys hugged their mom and their brother. Then they each hugged me, and I could still smell chlorine in their hair and was shocked to realize sometime during the summer they'd both grown to my height.

Didn't stop me from babying them by shoving extra bottles of sunscreen in their duffle bags as they pretended to groan. But neither of them had been locked outside by their grandmother when they were ten at the height of summer and gotten so sunburned on their arms and shoulders that their skin blistered and seeped puss for weeks.

No, they had people who loved and cared for them. And I was one of those people.

That was the last time I saw them before Josh's funeral.

After we sent the twins off to camp, there was no reason for me to go to the pool anymore. I figured I'd spend the rest of my summer in the library, as per my original plan. But when we pulled into the Perrys' driveway, Dom invited me inside. Emilia gave me a hug, then disappeared into the office she'd been using during the summer to keep up with paperwork—not even a life-threatening accident kept her away from her job for long.

Still in a sad daze of missing the twins, I didn't realize at first that Dom had led me to the screened porch on the back of their house. I'd always adored the sitting space with its thick-cushioned seats, shaded from the direct glare of the sun and kept cool with lazy ceiling fans.

"Guess you're glad to have more free time now," Dom said, staring out at the backyard, his hands tucked deep in his pockets.

I tried for a smile but couldn't manage more than a grimace. "I'm an evil mastermind who just lost two high-quality minions. 'Glad' isn't the right word."

His stoic mask broke with a twitch at the corner of his mouth. "Ah. So you're the one who corrupted my brothers."

"Of course." My smirk came easy. "They were two perfect little angels before they met me."

That earned me a snort, and I bit my lips to keep from smiling. For most of my life I struggled to form words around Dom. He was a brooding force of intimidation, and I wanted him to like me so much but had no idea how to make that happen. The only way I figured I could manage it was by not bothering him with chatter and continuing to be his best friend's little sister. Maybe then, some of the love he felt for Josh would rub off on me.

But as we stood on that porch, I realized the dynamic between us had shifted in some indiscernible way. That how I felt around the man had changed. Maybe it was the maturity I'd cultivated in leaving home and attending a year of college. Maybe it was the fact that I'd helped his family over the summer instead of living off the Perrys' charity.

Or maybe it was the embarrassing stories Adam liked to tell about Dom when he was in a feisty mood.

Whatever the cause, I no longer saw Dom as some mythical god.

Of course, I still had my massive crush on the guy and wanted him to like me. But the urge to bow down in his presence was gone.

"What are you going to do without your minions?" His tone was light and teasing when he asked, but the reality hit me once again. I turned my head away, blinking fast to get rid of the tears forming from missing them.

"I'm not sure. I've still got a few weeks until the semester starts. I guess I'll just hang out." Not at my house, though, where Florence would pick and scold and berate me for things I couldn't change.

Dom cleared his throat.

"Adam says you read all day." He waved toward the far end of the porch. "You could read here. If you want. You like the swinging bench, right?"

More than most other places in the world. But my eyes tracked over his shoulder to a card table arranged next to an outdoor outlet. A laptop sat on the surface along with folders and stacks of papers held down by a paperweight.

Dom's makeshift office.

"You're working out here." I pointed to the setup.

Dom didn't bother to glance at the arrangement. "So?"

"So, wouldn't I distract you?"

He continued to hold my gaze. "You'll just be reading. You don't read out loud, do you?"

A smile tugged at my lips. "I can. Make different voices for the characters. Put on a whole performance."

His teeth tugged on his bottom lip and humor sparked in his eyes. "Maybe on my lunch break."

Lunch. My mind returned to Adam and Carter. "I could grab us food. If I read here, that is. Get some takeout."

He wrinkled his nose, and the expression was surprisingly adorable on the devastatingly handsome man. "Not Taco Bell."

At that, I burst out laughing. It was either that or cry.

"Okay." I wiped a tear from the corner of my eye, still giggling. "I don't think I could betray Adam like that anyway."

Dom's lips tightened, and I continued chuckling as I wandered over to the swinging bench and pulled my latest paperback from my bag. The yellowed pages were a soothing soft brush against my fingers and the spine let out a comforting creak that melded with the squeak of the sturdy chains holding the padded bench suspended from the porch ceiling. It was one of those large swinging benches, almost the size of the mattress in my dorm room, and covered in throw pillows.

I'd sat on it hundreds of times through my life, but that day felt different.

Because it was just Dom and me.

Now I don't think I could stand to look at that bench. Not after what happened two weeks later.

Not when Dom lay beside me on it, held me tight to his body, kissed me like breathing didn't matter, and touched me like I was precious.

Not when I came upon him sitting on the same bench beside Rosaline the next morning and heard the words that destroyed me.

"Let's get married," he'd said to her.

I hadn't believed it. Hadn't been able to move. So, I saw her raise a beautiful tear-stained face to gaze into Dom's.

"Really?" she'd whispered, though I'd still heard.

"Yes." His strong hands—the same hands that had touched me the night before—stroked her hair. "I want to marry you."

Then he'd kissed her forehead.

It was amazing, really, how that gentle gesture had such a violent reaction on my body.

How his loving words tore into my heart until I couldn't breathe.

Literally. I stumbled around the side of the house, wheezing and fumbling for my emergency inhaler, silently begging that no one discovered me.

The chime of a new email has me blinking my eyes and pulling me back to reality.

I'm not nineteen having an asthma flare-up outside of the Perrys' house in Pennsylvania. I'm lying on my couch in my Seattle condo. My safe place.

And I'm in the middle of a workday, processing accountant deployments.

Heaving myself into a seated position, I drag my laptop off the coffee table and settle it in my lap. And that's when I realize the email that pinged was my personal, not my work.

A familiar name sets me to grinding my teeth, with the sting of that summer fresh in my mind.

Still, I open it.

Sender: Dominic Perry
Subject: Next trip

When can you take some time off work next? How do you feel about Kansas?

Sincerely,
Dom

My gaze slips toward the wooden chest I found at a thrift store and bought because it looked like something a pirate would bury their treasure in. I previously used it to store blankets.

Now it holds six Rubbermaid containers full of my dead brother's ashes.

Josh did always think his booty was priceless.

My heart aches for the chance to hear one more of his ridiculous, groan-worthy jokes. He was like a dorky dad half the time, and I miss his laugh so much my stomach hurts. With an arm wrapped around my middle—as if that'll stave off the pain—I type a reply one-handed.

Sender: Maddie Sanderson
Subject: RE: Next trip

June. Yes to Kansas.

Summer

"We should have combined this with another state."

Those are the first words I speak to Dom when I find him waiting on a sidewalk in Topeka, Kansas. I have to say something to distract myself from how good he looks standing there in his white T-shirt and dove gray shorts that struggle to contain his thigh muscles. The slight breeze rustles his hair, and Dom has the audacity to finger-comb the dark, silky waves off his forehead.

It's been two months since our Alabama trip, and Dom's attractiveness has not dimmed in the slightest.

Damn him.

The fact that I keep noticing his handsomeness drives home the importance of getting through these trips faster. The less time in his presence, the better.

Why? I silently rail at my lovingly evil brother. *Why did you have to stick me with this loathsome panty-melting man?*

But Josh is not here to answer for his crimes. Still, I can hear his teasing voice as if he were standing next to me.

Time to get you out of your comfort zone, Magpie.

Well, he'd succeeded. Being around Dom is the most uncomfortable zone I could be in.

Dom frowns down at me. "Combined them?"

I mentally bring up a map. "Aren't South Dakota and North Dakota just north of here? We could've knocked three out in one go."

Dom's lips tighten, but he doesn't disagree.

I want him to argue with me. Whenever I think about how he held my hand for that brief moment in the canyon and used my birthday as a safe combination and found a cozy cabin to stay in because I hate hotels, my thoughts crash and collide in a jumble I can't sort through. I need the simplicity of animosity.

"Are you ready for the letter?" Dom changes the subject by pulling an envelope from his shoulder bag.

Kansas is scrawled across the creamy paper followed by a set of coordinates that led us here, to the street outside this old theater. I glance up at the marquee to see they have the latest Tom Cruise action movie out but also are running a classic.

Jurassic Park.

Good choice, I silently say to Josh, almost smiling. I wonder if he somehow knew the theater would be playing one of our go-to movies, or if this was a lucky turn of fate. When Dom told me the destination, I was grateful the task would only involve sitting in a dark theater where we don't have to talk to each other. I just hope Josh doesn't expect us to sprinkle his ashes in the popcorn maker or something.

"I'm ready," I say.

Dom hands the missive to me, and I ignore the spike of awareness that prickles across my nerves when our fingers brush. Gently, I tear the flap open and slip out the words from my brother.

Another piece of him.

Dear Maddie & Dom,

Welcome to Kansas!
This is a trip I truly regret missing, especially now that I know you two are taking it in my place.

On my travels, I met all kinds of people, and sometimes those chance encounters had unexpected results. I took a picture one time, and that single shot earned me a favor I never got to cash in. But I called, explained my situation, and asked that the debt be transferred to you.

Reggie and Carmen were happy to oblige.

If you followed my coordinates correctly, you should see a shop called Ink Ever After.

I pause reading, surprised that he named somewhere other than the theater.

Did we get the coordinates wrong?

"Hell, Josh," Dom mutters.

I follow his stare across the street and immediately see what caught his eye. There, sitting tucked between a dry cleaner and a florist, is a shop with colorful designs painted on the window and a sign above the door that says: **INK EVER AFTER**.

And beneath the name . . . **CUSTOM TATTOOS**.

"This is a joke!" When my shrill exclamation reminds me of Aunt Florence at the funeral, I cringe, but quickly get over it and press on. "Josh isn't expecting us to get one, is he? I mean, I want to get a tattoo. Eventually. When I decide on the right thing. And thoroughly vet the artist."

Dom is silent as I pace on the sidewalk and rant about the injustice. I stop to drag in a few deep breaths, worried that just the thought of what this letter is asking will bring on an asthma attack. Dom reaches out to pluck the paper from my lax fingers.

Then the unaffected asshole keeps reading.

If you can't tell from the outside, it's a tattoo shop.

Calm down, Maddie. I can hear you panicking beyond the grave.

I let out a strangled shriek. After raising his eyes for a quick scan of my body, Dom goes back to reading.

You've wanted a tattoo since you were sixteen. It's time to commit, Magpie. Your life is only so long.

Dom clears his throat, and the hint of emotion on his part slows my descent into complete panic. He continues.

Dom, I know you think tattoos are a permanent, often unsightly mistake . . .

I choke on a surprised laugh because, damn, I've heard the man say exactly that.

Josh knows us both. Too well.

. . . but you're going to get one. Because I'm asking you to. Hear that, Maddie? Dom's getting one.

Are you going to let him show you up?

"Fuck you, Josh!" I shout at the paper in Dom's hands.

And I swear I spy a twitch at the corner of my companion's mouth. Like the bastard wants to smirk at me.

Does he think I'll back out, too?

Once you have your ink, take a pic for me. Then ask Reggie where to spread my ashes.

Oh yeah. That's the other thing. He's sworn not to reveal the location until his needle has touched your skin.

You kids have fun! Take lots of pictures!

Love,
Josh

"I honestly didn't think he could piss me off anymore," I growl. "But this?" I wave a frantic hand across the street at the waiting tattoo shop with its green neon **OPEN** sign bright even in the midday light.

Dom carefully folds the letter, tucks it into his back pocket, and steps up to the curb, ready to cross the street.

"You're doing it. You're getting a tattoo." They aren't questions, merely snarled accusations I lob at him.

He glances over his shoulder, one black brow curving upward. "Gonna let me show you up?"

Then the devil smiles before glancing both ways and jogging across the empty street.

Anger seethes in my chest as I follow him.

Of course I follow.

Josh knows me.

Despite hurrying on ahead, Dom waits for me outside the shop, and he holds the door open when I reach his side. With another glare, I stalk into the space and bite down on my gasp.

It's just so . . . cool.

The floor is a dark polished wood covered in intricately patterned rugs. The walls are a collage of colorful art pieces, framed and hung in an attractive disarray. A waiting area full of wingback chairs sits off to the left, beside two floor-to-ceiling shelves filled with worn books.

A slim white man with ink designs crawling up his neck sits behind a high counter, and over his shoulder I spy a Black woman with just as many illustrations on her skin bent over a buff bearded man's shoulder. Her hands hold a buzzing tattoo gun as she sketches a flaming skull into the man's tan skin.

"Welcome to Ink Ever After," the guy at the desk says with an easy smile. "How can I help you?"

All my righteous fury fizzles in the face of reality, and I glance to Dom for guidance. Then immediately chide myself for relying on him in any way.

Still, Dom takes the lead. "Does the name Josh Sanderson mean anything to you?"

The whir of the tattoo gun cuts off, and silence overtakes the shop. The man who greeted us loses his smile and runs wide eyes over us, taking Dom and me in as if we're both fascinating and concerning.

I shift on my feet, wondering exactly what favor my brother did for this man.

"Are you Maddie and Dom?" he asks after a prolonged pause.

I nod, then feel the heat of a hand on my lower back.

"We are," Dom says.

I'm about to elbow him and step away when the tattoo guy's next words distract me.

"So, Josh is gone, then."

CHAPTER
Fourteen

Gone.

The word reverberates through me, a sharp clattering that threatens to shred my insides.

He's not gone yet. There's a piece of him in my bag. And more notes in Dom's safe.

Josh is still here.

Just not . . . like he was.

"He passed away in January." When Dom speaks, there's no hint of the grief and rage I'm fighting against. He's his normal steady-voiced self. "You knew him?"

The man straightens off his stool and the woman comes up beside him, leaning her body into his as he wraps an arm around her shoulders. The two of them join together as they speak to us.

"We met him in Oregon. I'm Reggie, and this is Carmen. We were at Multnomah Falls, I proposed, and Josh happened to be there. He took that." Reggie gestures toward the wall, where a framed photo of a kissing couple surrounded by glittering mist hangs. "It was perfect. He offered to send it to us, no charge. I told him to come through town sometime, and I'd tattoo him. On the house. We kept in touch but . . ." When Reggie trails off, eyes going cloudy, all of us know what he's having trouble voicing.

Josh got too sick to come here and claim his tattoo.

Reggie shares a wobbling smile between us. "He called last year. Told us the situation. Asked if he could pass off his freebie. To his sister and his best friend."

"We said yes. Of course we said yes." Carmen's eyes shimmer now, the hint of tears gathering at the base of her lashes.

She can cry for my brother. This woman who only knew a little of him.

Why can't I?

"Thank you," Dom says. "Did Josh also say what type of tattoo we'd be getting?"

Carmen chuckles and Reggie grins wider.

"No." A dimple appears in the man's cheek as he beams at us. "Josh said you'd never go through with it if he got that high-handed. Whatever you get is up to you."

Carmen slips out from under her partner's arm and goes back to her customer. Meanwhile Reggie pulls out some binders and settles them on the counter.

"Take a look. Take your time. I'm happy to draw up a custom piece if you have any ideas. Whatever you want."

What if I don't want a tattoo? I almost mutter petulantly. But I keep the ungrateful words to myself.

Because they're a lie.

Josh was telling the truth in his letter. I've dreamed about getting a tattoo forever. Of having an artist sketch a beautiful, meaningful design into my skin. But just like all of the pages of those pretty journals I bought for myself, my skin has remained blank.

I was waiting for something significant to occur in my life. Something to immortalize with a permanent symbol.

But do I want to immortalize the death of my brother?

While these thoughts ricochet through my mind, Dom uses the hand that's still on my lower back to guide me toward the counter. He opens the first binder and slowly flips through the pages.

None of the images register. I'm sure they're gorgeous and fashioned with skill.

But they were made for someone else. Not for me.

Not for Josh.

I almost wish he'd left specific instructions on what to get, because I don't know how I'm supposed to pick something that matters.

Better yet, I wish he were here to bicker with and push back against. He would try to coax, then berate, then charm me into getting a tattoo.

Would he win? Would I?

But now it's just me versus words on a piece of paper.

"What are you thinking?" Dom asks, quietly so only I can hear. His warm breath brushes my ear, making me shiver, which in turn makes me scowl.

"I'm thinking Josh is a lot harder to argue with now."

There's a rich sound. A soothing set of notes I belatedly realize is Dom's chuckle.

"I meant about what tattoo you want to get. Assuming you'll go through with it."

I glare up at him and find his eyes already on me. Our gazes lock and hold.

"I'm getting one." My voice lacks the hard edge I tried equipping it with. Instead, I sound almost breathy. "But it has to matter."

Dom firms his mouth and offers a small nod, his stare never leaving mine. "Like a jar of peanut butter on your butt?"

His delivery—stone-cold serious—is what gets me. That, and the memory of a hungover Josh stumbling into my fourteen-year-old bedroom muttering that he made a mistake.

All the angry grief drains from my body as I snort. Then giggle. Then dissolve into stomach-cramping laughter.

To commemorate his eighteenth birthday, my older brother got drunk on cheap vodka and found a less reputable tattoo studio willing to ink a wasted teenager's ass with a nonsensical idea. Josh had tugged down his shorts and pulled the bandage back enough for me to see a beautifully detailed jar of open peanut butter and a realistic slice of bread spread with brown goo.

"*Peanut BUTTer,*" he'd explained to me.

"I am *not* getting that," I force out through my hilarity, then try to suck a few calming breaths in through my nose so I don't have to use my inhaler. Chuckles continue to sneak out despite my efforts. "But I did think it was extra embarrassing how he only got half done."

Dom, wearing his own smile, lifts a single brow. "Half done?"

"Yeah. Half the sandwich." I hold out my hands as if they're slices of bread. "A PB and J. He needed a jelly jar on the other cheek." God, that would've been perfect. A PB and J ass.

Then something amazing happens. A light flush comes to Dom's cheeks. A subtle pink that quickly deepens to an impossible-to-ignore red.

Is he embarrassed? About what . . . ?

A ludicrous suspicion hits me and I take a step back, studying the rule-following man at my side, wondering if I'm about to find out that miracles do exist in the world.

"Dominic Perry." My voice is tight with disbelief and passionate hope. "Do you . . . have a jar of jelly tattooed on your ass?"

He straightens to his full six-foot-three height, crosses his arms over his chest, firms his jaw . . .

Then gives me a curt nod.

My world explodes.

Time has no meaning.

I think I faint but somehow stay standing.

It is very possible that slight dip of Dom's head will be the simplest thing to set off an asthma attack in my life. But I manage to keep breathing while I wheeze out a single question.

"How?"

Dom narrows his eyes, but I would bet my favorite puzzle he's trying not to smile.

"Vodka." He lifts a shoulder and drops it back into place. "And it was his birthday."

"I think I might cry." Or I would if my tear ducts were functioning properly. But that is how overjoyed I am to discover that Mr. Responsible Asshole has a goofy picture forever inked onto his derrière.

It's too beautiful of a thought to believe.

"I *need* to see it."

Dom's head jerks back, eyes widening. "What?"

I don't know why, but in this moment, there is nothing I want more in the world than to see that tattoo. "Moon me. Right now. I demand proof."

Both of Dom's brows raise this time. "You can't be serious."

I rub my hands together with an evil grin, then cup them around my mouth. "Show us the goods!"

There's a chortle to my right, and that's when I remember there's more than just Dom and me in the shop. Glancing over, I realize that Reggie is sitting on a low stool near a set of tattooing tools, watching our back-and-forth with a grin on his face.

"We've got a bathroom down the hall if you want some privacy." He throws a thumb over his shoulder.

I don't give Dom an opportunity to decline. I press my hands into his lower back and use every ounce of my not-very-much strength to force him toward the restroom. When his feet shuffle forward, I know I've won, because if Dom didn't want me to move him, then he wouldn't move.

We reach the bathroom, which is plenty large enough to fit us both, and I shut the door behind us. Closing us in.

"Show me." I cross my arms and hit Dom with a demanding glare even as I fight off eager giggles.

This can't be real. Dominic Perry cannot *have a tattoo on his butt.*

The man meets me stare for stare. Then his fingers go to his fly and heat explodes across my cheeks when I realize exactly what is about to happen.

Dom is going to strip for me.

When we dunked ourselves in the frigid ocean, he kept his underwear on. Even on the night of the ill-fated pity finger bang, Dom never got fully naked. Not that he's getting naked now, either. But I'm going to lay my eyes on a new part of him.

The sound of his zipper is loud in the suddenly too-quiet bathroom.

He turns his back toward me, and I catch my breath. He hikes up his shirt, and my pulse thrums. He hooks a thumb in his waistband, and I bite hard into my lower lip.

Then Dom bares his right ass cheek to me.

Briefly, all I can register is how tight and perfectly formed the partial globe is. But in the next second, all I can see is the image embedded in his skin.

It's the same style, thick lines and bold colors. The same arrangement of an open jar and a slice of bread covered in goo. Only Dom's is a jelly jar with grapes on the label and purple coloring.

The other half of the PB and J.

For a fabulous moment, I live in the joy of familiarity. I know the brother of this tattoo.

But then reality crashes hard into my chest. So hard that I stumble back and gasp for a breath. I bury my face in my hands to hide the way my expression twists with horrible realization.

I'm never going to see Josh's ridiculous tattoo again.

Not that I saw it a lot. Only when my brother felt extra goofy and wore a Speedo swimming rather than a full set of trunks. In the tiny getup, his pale ass was on full display along with his eighteen-year-old mistake.

But what feels like a butter knife straight to the sternum is the realization that Josh's tattoo doesn't even exist anymore.

That piece of my brother, along with the rest of him, is ashes.

Dom's jelly is all on its own.

"Maddie?"

I don't remove my hands from my face. A massive pressure behind my eyes demands I cry under the devastating weight of this moment. But instead of leaking tears onto my face, I only feel the start of a sharp pain in my temple. My grief is a drill, digging into my sensitive brain matter.

Then a firm pair of arms enfolds me, pulling me against a hard chest wearing soft cotton.

"I'm sorry," Dom mutters, his breath warm against my hair, seeping through my skull and soothing the ache. "I thought it would make you laugh."

My next inhale shudders with unshed tears, but I manage to peel my hands away from my face. Then, because the fight has temporarily left me, I let my forehead drop and rest against Dom's shoulder.

We stand like that—him holding me up, me leaning on him—for an indeterminate amount of time, and my traitorous mind points out this hug isn't so meaningless. This doesn't feel like an act.

This feels like relief.

Which means I must break the moment before it starts to mean too much.

"It's very embarrassing," I mutter into his cedar-scented shirt.

He huffs a short laugh but doesn't say anything.

"Do you regret it?"

After a pause, where Dom's fingers spread wide as if attempting to cover more of my back, he gives me an answer. "I used to. But not anymore. Now I think it might be the best part of me."

My heart squeezes tight, and I suck in a deep inhale at the new rush of emotion.

Determination presses away the painful confusion from a moment ago, and I realize how vulnerable I allowed myself to be in this bathroom with Dom.

Why do I keep letting my walls fall when he's around?

Knowing this path will only lead to more pain, I step out of his embrace and avert my eyes. Putting as much distance between us as I can.

"Pull your pants up." My voice is steady now. "It's time to do something we won't regret."

I don't wait for him, striding out of the bathroom and back to the front of the shop, passing Carmen as she sketches orange flames into her customer's skin. Dom doesn't waste any time appearing at my side, and we resume our spots at the counter. Time to make a decision.

My eyes move to the binders but immediately slide away. There's nothing in those pages for me. Unbidden, my attention finds its way to Dom's ass, but not because I want a jar of jelly. A flap of paper sticks out of his back pocket, and I realize it's Josh's letter.

I reach out, slip it free, and unfold the sheet. Dom watches me, face unreadable.

With the tips of my fingers, I trace the message written in my brother's hand, and when I reach the last two words, I know without a doubt what I want immortalized on my body. What I want to dig deep into my skin with ink.

"Can you tattoo this on me? Exactly as he wrote it?" I hold the precious letter out to Reggie and point to the signature.

Love,
Josh

The artist smiles at me, the expression soft. Understanding.

"Of course, Maddie. I would be honored." With obvious care, he accepts the sheet of paper to examine the writing closely. "Where would you like it?"

"My wrist," I say without hesitation. "Where I can always see it."

There's a looming presence behind me, and I realize Dom has

stepped in close. I brace for him to suggest I get it in a place that can be covered up if need be. A responsible location.

"I want the same thing."

I scowl over my shoulder, up at him. "Are you stealing my idea?"

He holds my gaze, an unreadable emotion in his brown eyes. "It's a good idea."

Before I can decide if I want to fight more with Dom about his choice to get a matching tattoo with me, Reggie ushers me to a chair, then copies Josh's signature onto some special tracing paper that he's then able to press against my skin and leave the design behind. Even seeing the script on me in the temporary purple ink, I know I've made the right decision.

For the rest of my life, a piece of my brother will be on my wrist. Wherever I go, he'll be there in this tiny way.

The needle stings something fierce, a sharp, burning pain. I grit my teeth and stare at the wall of designs, distracting myself by visually tracing the lines of other pieces of work.

"Done," Reggie announces sooner than I anticipated, though I'm glad the pain is over.

When I glance down, words clog up in my throat. But I'm not sure if I regained speech that I could articulate how much the sight of *Love, Josh* on my wrist means to me.

"It looks great," a deep voice murmurs, and I turn to meet Dom's eyes.

"You better like it, seeing as how you're getting the same one." I mean to affect a mocking tone, but my words come out almost breathless. Not that I'm unused to that state.

I lose my breath a lot. It just seems to happen more often around Dom.

A smile twitches the corner of his mouth, and he watches as Reggie cleans the tattoo, then covers it with a clear protective wrap.

"Your turn, big guy."

I climb off my seat, switching spots with Dom.

Reggie cleans his station, changes out his needles, and prints a new tracing of the design.

"Which wrist?"

Dom glances down at his hands, then he reaches to unbuckle Josh's watch. "Hold this for me?" He extends the timepiece for me to take.

Unlike in the cabin, I accept it, cradling the accessory gently. While Reggie preps Dom for his tattoo, I fiddle with the device. As I hold the watch, my thumb rubs over the wristband, warm from contact with Dom's skin. The metal backing of the watch holds the heat of his body, too, and I pause when I feel an indent in the otherwise smooth surface.

Tearing my eyes away from the man in the chair, I examine the underside of the watch and realize there's an inscription. A simple message.

Brothers, always. -D

D for "Dom."

Dom gave this watch to Josh.

My brother gave it back in the end.

Fifteen

Reggie sends us to the Topeka lavender fields.

Acres full of purple bushes stretch every which way, almost as colorful as the sunset painting the clouds in the sky. We've arrived just in time, it turns out. Harvest comes soon. We could have shown up to barren fields.

Wouldn't that have been ironic? Bring my dead brother's remains to the lavender he missed in life, only to find ourselves a little too late for it, too.

I wander down a row of the flowering bushes and let my hands brush against the fragrant stalks as I ponder timing and the trickster that is my brother.

"Do you think he meant for us to come back?" The question is out of my mouth before I consider if it was a good idea to articulate it.

Dom follows along behind me, so massively tall that even with a few feet between us I can still feel his presence looming.

"What do you mean?"

I stop my aimless wandering and turn to face him, trying not to admire the way the dying light of the day makes it appear as though there are random golden strands in his dark hair. "I mean, the beach in the middle of winter. The glow worms. Larva. Whatever. You can't see them year-round. And here." I sweep my hand over the purple expanse, glad the other sightseers are a distance off so the only one who can hear this conversation is the man staring at me with an unfathomable expression. "Lavender only blooms in certain months. We just happened onto this in the right time of year. Pure luck." I let my arm drop. "But what if we weren't lucky? What if we showed up and the fields were harvested? What if we showed up to Ink Ever After and they were closed for the day? Or the week?"

"You think Josh wanted us to make these trips more than once." Dom's jaw firms and relaxes as he lets my observation sink in.

I huff a laugh. "I think he would have thought it was funny if we had to. We're talking about Josh. The traveling man. The guy who would never tell me exactly where he was, only a general time zone and a hint or two." Sometimes he could be so infuriating that I refused to play. Other times I'd spend a half hour researching what a maned wolf was and what waterfall it might drink from just so I could understand where in the world my brother was. "I bet he thought about putting more info on the outside of the letters but didn't. He wouldn't see doubling back as a hassle. He left us more than enough money to cover these trips twice over."

Two weeks ago, whatever postmortem process for distributing the willed money finished, and I received the funds my brother wanted me to use for these trips. I opened a second checking account, put all the money in there, and named the account "Evil World Domination Fund." Hopefully that makes someone at my online bank laugh rather than report me to the FBI.

Do you think I have the time to constantly get on a plane and fly across the country? I silently rail at Josh. Guilt quickly follows the selfish thought.

Can I hold this against Josh, when he didn't even get to come

here once? Am I complaining that I might have to scent this delicious lavender multiple times in my life?

What a torturous existence.

"Forget I said anything," I mutter, blushing with frustration and
shame.

Dom doesn't respond, which I'm grateful for. This day has been
too weird and raw, my wrist throbs, and this scene is so beautiful it
makes my heart ache. I don't know if I want to run away or stay here
forever. But as the light fades from the sky, I know it's time to do the
task we came for.

As I reach into my bag, my wrist protests the movement, a reminder of the words sketched into it.

Love, Josh

What a perfect metaphor, because damn, does that love hurt
right now, too.

"I guess this isn't a bad place to rest," I muse, holding the Rubbermaid up so Josh can watch the sun sink and the sky turn a darker
shade than the plants around us. "You'll get to be somewhere that
smells nice."

Dom grunts a noise that sounds like disagreement to my ears.

A spark of temper lights off in my chest. My melancholy eases,
replaced with irritation.

"You've got a problem with lavender?"

He stares over the plants, his face in that familiar, frustrating,
stoic mask. "It's fine."

"Fine?" I hug Josh to my chest, offended on his behalf and on
behalf of these fragrant plants surrounding us. "Lavender is an
amazing scent. Light and fresh and an earthy kind of flowery. Soothing and not overpowering. Lavender is divine. Have you ever had a
lavender latte? They're delicious. That's right, this scent is so good

you can *drink* it. If good dreams have a smell, it's lavender. If angels exist, you better believe they're taking showers in lavender water and scrubbing their asses with lavender soap."

As I rant about the glory that is lavender, Dom focuses on me, his brows raising with each of my fervent, completely factual arguments.

"I have it on good authority that people who like lavender are physically, mentally, and emotionally superior. Meanwhile, people who don't like lavender are soulless robots who want to suck all the happiness from the world. Isn't that right, Josh?" Holding up the container of ashes, I press my ear to the lid. "He says I'm right and that Dom should get his nose out of his not-lavender-scented ass."

Dom crosses his arms over his chest and goes back to staring over the fields. "Rosaline used to wear lavender perfume." He shrugs. "I always thought it was fine. Just fine. Guess that's the robot in me."

The rest of my snarky arguments dry up as his words register.

Great. I just spent the last five minutes inadvertently rambling about how amazing his ex smells. And damn it, she probably smells like lavender naturally and he just thought it was a perfume. That's how amazing Rosaline always was.

And now I'm questioning my love of lavender. Did I come by the preference on my own, or was the scent something I *told* myself I liked because when I was younger, I wanted to emulate Rosaline in all things?

Gritting my teeth, I turn my back on Dom so I can pull in a few calming breaths and remind myself that I was going to try not biting his head off every time I see him.

What happened between us was years ago, and I never plan to give him that power over me again. For these few short trips, I can pretend to be a mature woman. Possibly.

When I've got my temper under control, I ease the lid off the Rubbermaid and face toward the west, where the sun has disappeared beneath the horizon, but some of its light still remains.

"I hope *you* enjoy the scent," I say to my brother, then glance at Dom, giving him the chance to say something, too.

His eyes are on my hands as I cradle the container. "I think he did," Dom murmurs. "And now he always will."

Josh's ashes spill out and mix into the lavender breeze.

I try to keep communication with Cecilia Sanderson to a minimum. It's the same policy she had with me during my entire childhood, so you could say that I learned it from her. She continued the practice up until recently. But this past week, I have had five missed calls from my mother. When my phone starts ringing at the end of my workday, I know I should ignore it again.

I've learned my lesson long ago.

But there's something that makes me duck into one of the single-use bathrooms and forces my fingers to swipe the screen of my phone.

I try to tell myself I'm answering because tomorrow is my birthday, and maybe this is simply a call to celebrate that. But I doubt Cecilia remembers the date I was born, even though she was there. And she's never bothered to celebrate my birthday in the past, so why start now?

No, I pick up the phone because I'm afraid.

There's a gnawing fear in my gut that she has an important piece of information I would regret missing. The anxiety is some lingering internal damage from the day that Josh called me and asked if he could come visit. Normally he didn't call. He would text his travel plans, and I would wait, excited for him to show up at my door.

When we did talk on the phone, it was never just a voice call. We would video chat.

So that time he called me was odd, but I didn't think about how strange the break in habit was until Josh arrived with a frantic look in his eye. Then the next morning, after going out and putting on a show of normalcy for my friends for a few hours, Josh sat on my couch and started crying. My brother was never shy with his emotions. But they tended to be excitement and enthusiasm, frustration and humor. I saw him tear up during movies or cute animal videos on the internet. But I never saw him sob with such a hopeless cast to his face.

That was the day that he told me about his diagnosis. It was so strange, the way that he had tears running down his face and fear in his eyes and yet he still tried to joke and make me laugh. I think he thought if *I* thought it was funny, what the doctors told him couldn't be serious.

So I joked back with him.

And now I hate phone calls.

But I also *need* to pick them up.

"Cecilia."

I may have referred to her as "Mom" at the funeral, but the moniker sounded wrong coming out of my lips. She never did much to earn the title. Josh was the one who took care of me. Mrs. Perry was the one who showed me what a mother's love should be like, even if I only ever got small doses. Just enough to keep me going.

"Darling," Cecilia greets me. "It's been too long since we caught up. You ran away from the funeral before I could introduce you to my friends."

Gross. Despite the circumstances of what had me leaving the funeral early, now I am glad that I did. The idea of having to directly speak to any of the people that were in attendance because they are associated with my mother makes me want to peel my skin off cell by cell.

"Darn. I'll catch them at the next funeral for your child."

"Of course," she agrees, and I don't know whether to laugh or hang up. While I'm deciding, she continues talking. "I wanted to talk to you about something."

"Is it an emergency?" Because that is the only reason I picked up this phone. Now, though, I'm having trouble contemplating what emergency I would care about that would be conveyed to me by my mother.

"It's very concerning, dear." If I were standing in front of my mother, I expect I would see a practiced pout on her lips. "Emilia mentioned that you are doing the most fascinating thing for your brother. Why didn't you tell me? It sounds like something from a movie. I think the world needs to know about it. They need to know how far his family would go to make sure that he is resting at peace."

Damn. I would have preferred if my mother didn't know about Josh's ashes and the letters. And I don't like where she's directing the conversation.

There was nothing in Josh's request about the world knowing. Sure, Josh took photographs that were world-renowned. But if he could've taken pictures and gotten paid and no one ever saw them other than friends and family, I think he would've been fine with that.

Josh and I aren't like our mother. We're not fame chasers.

I keep quiet, mainly to avoid saying something that will escalate this into a fight. Today was a long stretch in the office with my head buried in data and constant coworker distractions. I'm too tired and burnt out to go at it with my mother.

"Well?" she presses when I continue to say nothing. "Are you going to tell me?"

"Tell you what?" In the mirror I spy two dark circles under my eyes that scream at me to go home and sleep. "There's nothing to tell. I'm doing something Josh asked me to do. If he wanted you to do something, I'm sure it would've been in that letter he wrote you."

She huffs, and I try not to let curiosity push me into asking what he wrote her. His note to our mother could have contained anything. Forgiveness. Condemnation.

Despite Josh's loving personality, I suspect the latter.

He had little time for people who didn't at least *try* to be decent. Take our father, for example. The man left soon after I was born and never got in touch. Apparently, he sent childcare payments—though nowhere near enough if you ask Cecilia or Florence—and that was it. But when I was thirteen, I convinced myself that something was keeping him away. That Florence was wrong about me being the reason he left. That my father had wanted to be my dad all along but couldn't for some reason. Maybe our mother's uncaring personality had driven him away, or she was keeping us from him. Maybe he was so ashamed for leaving in the first place that he never thought we could forgive him. But I could. Thirteen-year-old Maddie was willing to do anything just to have one parent who cared about her.

I begged Josh to help me find him. Just a phone number. Just to call him and tell him that if he wanted back in my life, I'd welcome him.

At first, Josh tried to convince me not to bother. He didn't refuse outright—that harsh of a rejection was never Josh's way. But he did his best to gently redirect me. He asked what I wanted from a father and promised he'd do all of the things a dad would, if I just let go of the idea of the man who provided half my DNA.

But I was relentless, and eventually, Josh gave in.

After some internet sleuthing, he found a phone number and an address. On my fourteenth birthday, almost exactly thirteen years ago to the day, I called him. We sat in the front seat of Josh's car, my brother behind the wheel, fingers tapping an agitated rhythm and me clutching his cell phone because I didn't have one. The car stayed parked on the driveway because we weren't looking to go anywhere, I just wanted to keep Florence and Cecilia from interrupting.

Although, if our dad invited us to visit, I was ready to beg that we drive to New Jersey, where Josh said he lived.

When the call connected, I heard a voice that reminded me of my brother's, only a note deeper.

And it was so strange to hear the almost-Josh voice tell me he didn't want to see me. That he left us with Cecilia for a reason. That he started over and has a different life now. That we never knew each other in the first place.

What was even more jarring was my goofy, loving brother tearing the phone from my hand and snarling into the speaker that the man was a piece-of-shit scumbag who didn't deserve to know me and would never understand the amazing person he'd missed out on.

Josh hung up, started the car, and drove us to my favorite Italian-ice stand, where I forced myself to eat a cup of strawberry-flavored ice chips so my brother wouldn't be able to tell that my heart was a crumbled-up mess.

But he knew. Josh always knew.

He stopped at the supermarket, bought a twenty-four pack of bargain-brand toilet paper, then drove us to New Jersey, where we spent the rest of my birthday TPing our father's house. And when we stood back, admiring our handiwork, Josh wrapped an arm around my shoulders and held me tight against his chest.

"I know the world tells us that we need a mom and dad. But we don't, Magpie. We need each other. You have me. Always."

Those words held me together for a long time.

But they weren't true. Because it wasn't *always*, was it?

"I think your brother would love the idea of us doing this together." My mother's voice pulls me out of the painful tangle of memories back into my agonizing reality that *this* woman is left, and Josh is gone. "Where is the next trip? When are you going? I can meet you there anytime, anyplace."

Fuck, no.

I should've been expecting this phone call. Should've known it was coming and braced myself. Of course my mom is looking for a new angle. Something to write about on her blog and social feeds.

Her meal ticket is dead now.

But this? Spreading her son's ashes across the United States? That is a perfect story to milk. So many staged grieving images she could take in beautiful destinations. Even if she only wrote one article per state, that's eight right there. Publish one a month and that's most of a year covered. And I'm sure she could drag this out. The opportunities are limitless. I wouldn't be surprised if she tried to add on a few states just for dramatic value. Who gives a fuck what Josh wanted?

My eyes lock on my wrist.

Love, Josh

I did. I *do*. That's why this is my job.

Well, not mine alone.

"I've already got someone to do the task with." I don't know how those words made it out of my mouth with how hard my jaw is clenched. But I did it. I said something relatively mature, when all I wanna do is screech like a banshee and tell my mother to fuck off into the sun.

"I know, dear. You're doing this with Dom. His mother told me. Can you imagine how that made me feel? To find out from Emilia about what is being done with *my* son?" She lets out a dramatic sigh I expect is supposed to sound disappointed. "I know that Dom is an attractive man. And that he was friends with Josh. But I am his *blood*, Madeline. This is something that *I* should be doing." There's a pause, and then she adds, as if it's an afterthought, "With you, of course."

I want to stab something, but there's nothing stab-able in this bathroom. All I can do is grab a paper towel from the dispenser and crush it in my hands.

Not satisfying my violent urges in the least.

"You're *not* coming on these trips. Josh did not ask you to and so you are not coming."

I speak in a robot voice, attempting to emulate Dom's tone from whenever I frustrate him to the point of murder. Sometimes I find pretending to be Dominic Perry is the only way that I can talk to my mother. Not that it gets anything across to her. But it helps keep me from fighting, screeching, and drawing blood.

"I think this is what Josh would have wanted," she repeats.

I think a random person on the street would have a better idea of what Josh would've wanted than my mother does.

And the fact that Cecilia believes she has more of a right to Josh's final wishes than Dom does is baffling to me. He was in Josh's life daily. I bet all of the dirty secrets that my brother had, Dom knows. Hell, the guy might know more than I do. As much as it sucks to admit, Dom is probably the person who loves Josh almost as much as I do. Whenever I visited Josh in the hospital, likely as not I'd cross paths with Dom, or Rosaline would show up and I knew her husband wasn't far behind.

Ex-husband, I remind myself.

Dom is the one who showed up for Josh. And as frustrating as it is to have him on these trips with me, he's letting me grieve in the only way I can seem to manage: by spouting off a weird mixture of insults and sarcasm and truths before descending into intense silences and heavy, stuttered breathing.

My mother would never allow me the space to deal with the complex emotions of spreading my brother's ashes. Having Cecilia on even one of these trips would destroy something in me.

And that's not how it feels with Dom.

I thought it would. I thought spending one more moment in his presence would wreck me.

But—and I don't think I could ever admit this out loud—having Dom on each of these trips is . . . helpful.

I suck in a deep inhale through my nose, the stress of this phone call tightening my airways.

Then I stare at Josh's handwriting on my wrist. The love he left for Dom and me.

And only us.

"No, Cecilia. I'm doing this with Dom. He's the only one I need there with me."

Did I just say I need him?

"Now, Madeline, think about this." Her voice is tense, vibrating with anger she's trying to suppress. I guess I'm not the only one getting pissed off lately. "Think about how many people could benefit from this story. My writing helps people. People need to know about Josh."

"The people who matter *do* know about him," I snap, done with my Dom impression. "And it's clear that you're not one of them. I'm blocking your number. I can't do this anymore. Go back to pretending that you don't have a daughter. Because as far as I'm concerned, you don't."

I end the call and shove my phone into my bag, then crouch down in the public bathroom with my arms wrapped around my knees, and my forehead pressed against them, and I wait for the tears to come.

But they don't.

Happy fucking birthday.

Fall

CHAPTER
Seventeen

"That morbid son of a bitch."

Josh probably thought this was the funniest destination on his postmortem travel itinerary.

Dom and I just paid fifteen dollars each to enter Vulture City, Arizona. We both arrived in Phoenix a few hours ago, and because our flight times ended up being so close together, I reluctantly agreed to share a rental car with him. We checked into our rentals, got changed, and headed to the coordinates.

Which brought us here.

To a ghost town.

Dom huffs a dry laugh and leads the way through the wooden fence posts that signify the start of Vulture City.

Ironically, this dead civilization is rather lively. People wander around the dirt roads, some on their own like Dom and me, but others are led by guides dressed in Old West outfits. If Josh were here, he probably would have begged for a cowboy hat and sheriff's badge of his own.

Everything—not just Dom's humor—is dry here. Going from Seattle to the desert, my skin feels like brittle paper on the verge of cracking and crumbling away. I reach behind me to slip my water bottle out of the side pocket on my backpack. The container is slim, lightweight, and insufficient for this climate. I doubt it'll last me another twenty minutes from the way I guzzle half in one go.

I was not properly prepared. October is supposed to be cool, but here the temperatures have already crept to the high eighties and threaten to keep going. Even my SPF 60 sunscreen seems inadequate in the powerful sun. I pull the brim of my hat low over my face and hurry to catch up with Dom.

He's come to a stop in front of a building with a hand-painted sign that reads **BROTHEL**.

"Wow. Having trouble with the dating apps?" I ask. "Need some privacy in there?"

Dom tries to glare at me, but I spot the twitch at the corner of his firm mouth. "Looking for some shade to read his letter so you don't burst into flames halfway through."

"Was that your way of calling me a vampire? The sexiest of monsters? If so, I take it as a compliment."

Dom's lips curve further. "You've got the look. And the bite."

I scoff. Then I scurry up the wooden steps into the building like the sunlight-fearing creature he called me. It's not that I *hate* the sunshine. It's just that I know how painful overexposure can be. On sunny days, I like to enjoy the natural light from the cool shade of my condo while curled up in my armchair or sitting on my floor.

Not in the middle of a desert with zero cloud cover or conveniently placed awnings.

Dom's chuckle follows me through the door, and soon his feet do, too.

Then he flinches and mutters, "Hell," and clutches his chest.

I turn to see the shape of a looming figure and jump back before snorting when I realize we haven't found a ghost, but instead a mannequin dressed in period clothes. The fake person is the most modern thing in the room. Time has worn away the remnants of what the former inhabitants left behind. An aged piano sits pressed up against the wall, and a warped mirror hangs across from it. A sturdy black stove in the corner has a simple kind of beauty to it. Not that I'd want to see it lit in this sweltering heat. As I shuffle farther into the brothel, the floor gives—only slightly—under my feet. A reminder that the boards have lived far longer than I have and still remain.

Dust floats in the air and settles on my tongue. I pull out my water for another swig.

"Charming," I offer after my drink, tilting my head toward a creepy baby doll watching us from the next room. "What a place to spend an afterlife."

Dom's presence looms at my side. "You think this place is haunted?"

I let my eyes trail up to his face, trying to discern if there's any mockery in his expression. But Dom reveals nothing.

"If there *are* ghosts here, I'm not about to say there aren't and then piss them off. But if you would like to bring down some old-timey prostitute spectral wrath on your head, go for it." I wave toward a vanity with a cracked mirror.

Dom opens his mouth but pauses when I press my hands against his chest and give him a hearty shove toward the next room. "Over *there*. You can insult the dead once I'm not in the splatter zone."

Dom rolls his eyes but doesn't bother to hide his smile as he mutters, "Coward."

Before I can come back at him with a witty retort, he draws his backpack off and unzips a small pocket. From it, he produces one of Josh's letters.

"Want to read it?" he asks, extending the envelope to me.

I accept the offering, and as my fingers clutch the missive, my eyes flick between our wrists.

Love, Josh

My tattoo is visible, having healed nicely, with only some itching and soreness. Now the black lines are smoothly embedded in my skin. If I close my eyes and run a thumb over my wrist, I can't even feel them.

But I find myself tracing the letters all the time.

Ten months, and I still think about him every day. I'm not sure an hour has passed without a thought of Josh. A flash of his smile in my memory. The urge to text him about random things in my life.

As the envelope slides free of Dom's grip, I search his wrist. There, peeking out from under the wristband of his watch, are the edges of the same letters.

Suddenly self-conscious, I focus on opening Josh's letter, wanting to read it before another ghost-town visitor decides to stroll into the brothel. Excitement thrums through my veins in anticipation of getting one more piece of my brother. When I pull out the paper and see Josh's familiar scrawl, I can almost hear his voice in my head reading the letter aloud.

Dear Maddie & Dom,

Welcome to Arizona!

I've explored plenty of ruins in my travels, but never got around to any of these abandoned mining towns.

Is it spooky? Do you see any ghosts?

If I end up being a ghost, I hope I haunt someplace cool and not this hospital. Maybe you all should perform an exorcism here just in case, so I don't get stuck floating around for eternity in this backless gown. Though they are nice and breezy . . .

Sorry. Getting off topic.

Now, your task, should you choose to accept it (and you better accept it because I'm dead and I said so) is to have a Josh-story sharing fest. As you explore Vulture City, I want you to tell each other stories only you know about me. Yes, I'm that vain. And I give you permission to be brutally honest. Tell the funny ones, but also tell how I screwed up.

Because I did. I know I did.

Tell each other the things you regret not doing with me. Here, I'll go first.

Maddie, there's a town in Wales that's full of bookshops. I regret not taking you there and buying every story you wanted.

Dom, I regret not going to more Phillies games with you. I got so focused on always seeking out new experiences, I forgot how good a classic could be.

Maybe I'll haunt Citizen Bank Park and you can grab an extra beer for me next time you go.

Try not to have as many regrets as I do.

Spread me with the desert sand and take a picture with a cactus for me.

Love,
Josh

"Hell," Dom mutters, and I couldn't agree more.

I know these trips are entirely about Josh, but we haven't done much talking about my brother. The question I asked Dom a moment ago was a big step for me.

Now I'm supposed to spend the next however many hours sharing stories? Stories Dom doesn't already know?

Those pieces of Josh that have only ever been mine.

But he has to tell me things, too.

It's an exchange. And in the end, I'll have more of my brother than I did when this day started. It'll be like Josh lived a little longer.

"Let's walk. Explore." Dom doesn't use his commanding tone. Instead, he speaks carefully, with a questioning tilt of his head toward the open doorway.

"Yeah. Okay."

As we step over the threshold, I suddenly remember the phone call with my mother. How she wanted to come. How if I'd given in, she'd be here for whatever we both say next.

I could never have given up my Josh secrets to Cecilia Sanderson. Not to a woman who would use them to entertain strangers.

I turn abruptly to face Dom and stumble a step back when I come face-to-chest. He grabs my shoulders to keep me from tumbling off the porch.

"Sorry. I was walking too close," he says.

"Has my mom called you?" I blurt.

Dom's lips tighten, and I know the answer even before he gives a short nod.

"Did she ask to come on these trips?" I clarify.

"Cecilia doesn't *ask* to do anything."

Though accurate, I don't like how he phrased his answer. My stare swings toward where we parked, expecting to see her striding toward us in her designer bohemian wear, talking about how this reminds her of Burning Man.

"I told her no." Dom's low voice brings my attention back to him.

"You did?"

In that moment, I realize Dom still has his hands on me, and his thumbs are rubbing soothing circles against the bare skin my tank top reveals. As if coming to the same realization, Dom drops his hands and slips them in the pockets of his shorts.

"Did Josh ever tell you about the time we got your mom's car towed on purpose?"

I gape at the man I'd always thought of as Mr. Responsible. "No." I choke on the word and my disbelief.

Dom's lips tilt in a rueful smirk. "Josh showed up at school and I could tell he was pissed. And you know, he didn't get mad. I knew it was bad. He told me Cecilia had thrown out a bunch of your books when you weren't home. Books that meant a lot to you."

I remember that. One was a signed copy by my favorite author that I only had because Josh drove me to a bookstore in the city and stood in line with me for an hour so I could meet her.

Cecilia had apparently wanted the shelf to display her collection of healing crystals and didn't see the point in me keeping books I'd already read.

"After school, we went by your house, got the spare key to her car. Josh knew she was in a yoga class or something, so we found her car, parked it in a fire lane, then called the cops to report it."

"Oh my god." I gape at him. "You didn't."

"I did." Dom leans in close, until our foreheads almost touch, and holds my eyes with his. "I don't regret it. Never have. Never will. You both deserved better than her. Better than Florence, too."

I swallow hard and turn away, mind reeling as I think about the immature but also oddly sweet act Josh and Dom did for me.

"That . . ." I clear my throat, certain the dry air is what is making it so hard to speak. "That was a good one. Guess it's my turn to think of a story."

Dom grunts and steps around me, walking into the bright sunlight.

The glow of midday caresses his skin, soaking into his arms and neck like kisses from a lover. The sun adores the Perry family as much as it hates me. Still, just because Dom tans when I burn doesn't mean he's immune to an overabundance of UV rays.

"Sunscreen!" I call after him.

He pauses halfway across the narrow dirt road, turning back to me. With sunglasses over his eyes, I can't read his expression. But even if he's rolling his eyes in exasperation, I will not let up on this.

"Did you put on any sunscreen?" I ask as I jog up to him, pulling my backpack off so I can rummage in it for the bottle I bought at the airport gift shop.

"No. It's fine."

"It's fine," I mutter in a deep voice, mocking him. "Arms out."

Dom hesitates, then extends his mile-long arms. Luckily, I decided to buy the spray type. My lungs do weird fluttery clenches when I imagine rubbing lotion on every inch of exposed skin.

Spray allows me to keep my distance.

I apply a coating of protection to his arms, then his legs from the knees down. When I circle around his back, I encounter a problem.

"Has anyone ever told you that you're entirely too tall?"

He snorts. I poke him in the kidney.

"Squat. I need to get your neck."

"This is overkill," he argues even as he bends his knees.

"You'll be thanking me in twenty years when you don't have skin—" I choke on the final word I was about to say so flippantly.

Cancer.

That is the worst word to ever have existed.

Dom turns, and I cover up my painful misstep.

"Wrinkles. When you're not a wrinkly mess." Then I busy myself replacing the bottle in my bag.

"You're right," Dom speaks softly. "I don't want wrinkles. Thank you."

I humph and sling my backpack on. "Right. Okay." My eyes scan around the abandoned town and alight on a set of saloon doors. I point to them. "Let's look for ghosts in the bar. And did Josh ever tell you about the time he helped me look for a prom dress?"

The concerned creases around Dom's mouth ease as he smiles. "No."

The memory of that day blares like a bright butterfly of joy in my mind, coaxing a reluctant grin of my own. "Oh, really? He never shared how he decided to get involved? How he decided to try a few on himself?"

Dom's laughter booms loud, reverberating through the sun-soaked air.

Bringing life to a place that was once void of it.

For such a taciturn man, Dom is a talented storyteller. Each memory of Josh he shares is vivid with detail and emotion, to the point I can almost imagine myself living through the experiences with him.

But I didn't. Because I moved to the other side of the country.

Not for the first time, I wish I hadn't loved Dominic Perry so much. That affection I built up for him over my life, in those formative years, made his abandonment hurt so much more than if anyone else had done the same.

But I don't love him anymore, so I can move on from the past.

Right?

As he smiles and tells me about the time Josh challenged the Phillies' mascot to a dance battle, I start to believe it. That I can move on. Dom is a different person than the young man I fell in love with. And I'm a different woman.

I can be cautious around him, but maybe I can let some of the resentment go?

After sharing a few more anecdotes, our stories naturally trail off as we continue to explore the ghost town. We meander away from each other, then find our way back. The sun beats down, hot and heavy, and I duck into the shade of an old building whenever I can.

Unfortunately, while I planned to keep my skin safe from the sun, I didn't think about how quickly my water bottle would deplete. I upend it over my mouth, searching out the last drop for my sandpaper tongue.

"Here." Dom appears at my side, a small blue spout in his hand that connects to a tube. The other end disappears inside his backpack. "It's a CamelBak. I've got plenty of water. Have some."

After hesitating, I step in close to accept the mouthpiece and wrap my lips around it. When I suck, warm water fills my mouth, and while I'd prefer a tall glass full of ice, this is still nice.

But also, intimate. I have to stand close to Dom to sip the water, and I can smell sweat mixing with his cedar scent and feel the heat radiating off his body. After another long drag I hope will last me for a while, I hand back the spout.

My eyes flick up to meet a dark set, and even though we're both wearing sunglasses, I can *feel* Dom watching me as he sets the mouthpiece on his own lips for a drink. One that probably tastes like me.

I turn away fast and continue deeper into the town, Dom following.

A short while later the sound of Dom's stomach growling is so loud, I can't help a quick hiccup of laughter. The man tries to scowl at me. Doesn't work, though, when his lips tick up into a smile.

It's nice to know that as his hunger was growing, he was able to subdue his dickishness. One more sign he's not the boy he once was.

I'm about to offer Dom one of the snacks I have in my backpack— it's only fair when he's keeping me hydrated—but he's busy searching his own supplies. The man slips his pack off his back, reaches into a small zipper pocket, and pulls out a granola bar. As he peels back the reflective wrapping, I spot the way his mouth curves in a different direction. No longer suppressing a smile.

Dom gives the slightest involuntary grimace.

Abruptly, I'm flung back in time. My mind cycles through snippets from my younger years when I would watch Dominic Perry. So many times, I saw the guy choose carrots over chips, granola over donuts, peanuts over Sour Patch Kids. And during my Dom observations, I'd watch his mouth tighten in resignation as he masticated the one option while gazing longingly at the other.

I never understood why, only that for some reason he thought he had to deny himself.

The sight of his current distaste brings on an irrational fury, burning away my previous decision to set aside all my resentment.

Right when Dom is about to stick the snack in his mouth, I slap his hand, sending the granola bar flying. The food rockets through the air, eventually landing in the dirt a good distance away, next to a car without wheels. We watch as dirt and dust coat the now-inedible bar.

Dom turns a confused frown on me. "Why'd you do that?"

"Because it needed to be done," I snap. "And you weren't about to do it."

A muscle in Dom's jaw flexes, and I can see the irritation that normally comes along with his hunger rise to the surface.

Too bad. I got pissed first. I have dibs. "Here's the *thing* about you, Dom."

"What's the *thing* about me?" His voice is drier than the desert around us.

Well, he asked for it. So, I'm going to give it to him.

"The thing about you is that you know you eat a lot. You know you get hungry. And so, you pack yourself snacks." *Seems smart, right? Wrong.* "Healthy snacks. Gross snacks. Snacks that you don't want to eat." I step into his space, crowding him. So close I can see a droplet of sweat tracing down his neck. But I don't let that distract me. "And so, you *don't* eat them. Not until you're so hungry that your stomach is growling, and you're on the verge of—or already being—Dom the Dick." I jab his muscular chest with my finger. "You did it when we were younger, and you're still doing it *now*. If I had a dollar for every time I saw you practically gagging as you forced down an oat-based snack, I'd have enough capital to buy this town and turn it into a resort! Why do you do this to yourself?" I'm getting far angrier than this topic deserves, but I can't stop myself. "If you just packed something delicious and unhealthy, you would eat it the moment you start to feel even the slightest hunger pangs." I poke him again. "And then you would be happy. Or at least not a miserable sad sack." I glare into his bewildered gaze, and I soak in that raw emotion he hasn't hidden away, letting it fuel my righteous ranting. "But over and over again you refuse to pack yourself something that is tasty and not made of ground-up tree bark and dried fruits." I throw up my arms, as if begging some heavenly being to come down and save me from his frustrating nonsense. "Just admit that you don't like healthy food! Admit that you crave tasty things covered in salt and made of cheese. And then *eat* them. Stop making yourself hungry and just eat!"

I'm breathing hard now, bellowing breaths. But I don't feel an asthma attack coming on. My exhales are hot and powerful.

"That's the *thing* about you, Dom. That is your thing. You don't make choices based on what is going to make you happy. You choose the responsible thing. Then you're miserable while you're doing it. But it's not responsible to make yourself hungry because you don't like the food that you brought. It's responsible to be honest with yourself and to keep yourself well-fed." I yank off my backpack, plunge a hand into the side pocket, and pull out a familiar red bag. "So, eat the fucking Cheez-Its and be fucking happy for once in your responsible goddamn life!"

He catches the bag I chuck at him out of reflex, and I leave him standing there with the food he should have brought for himself while I go pick up the pathetically abandoned granola bar. Because even though this town isn't inhabited anymore, that doesn't mean I'm about to start littering here. Once it's tucked in my bag, I stomp toward the edge of town, realizing we've reached the end. And I try to ignore how I'm thirsty again, because I'm not about to ask Dom for a sip from his little backpack hose.

As I linger on the edge of a ghost town, gazing out at the desert, my temper transforms into embarrassment. Then regret.

My rant started about food but ended with too much of my inner pain revealed.

What was I even saying at the end there? Do I think I'm *the Cheez-Its?*

But that would mean I'm the one who would make Dom happy. Doubt that's the case when I spend half our time together insulting him. I've turned the man into my grief punching bag because he hurt me a long time ago. I'm supposed to be past this.

I'm supposed to be a lot of things.

Dom's unescapable presence appears at my side. I don't look up at him or acknowledge him in any way, too mixed up in my unmanageable emotions to speak.

Still, I hear the crunching.

We stand side by side, me brooding and him eating.

Eventually, Dom finishes his snack. Out of the corner of my eye, I watch him neatly fold up the empty bag and tuck it into his pocket.

"Thank you," he says.

I grunt.

He releases a sigh so deep I expect to see it stir the dust in front of us and send a tumbleweed rolling.

"I ate healthy stuff for the twins," Dom confesses. "Because I was responsible for feeding them most times. They never ate anything unless I ate it first. Mom and Dad wouldn't have liked if I was only ever feeding them junk food. I guess it became a habit."

And now I feel like a garbage person. Apparently, that bitch zombie virus is still pumping strong through my veins.

The Perry parents are kind and loving, but this isn't the first time I've thought they put too much responsibility on their eldest son's shoulders. Dom may be nine years older than Adam and Carter, but that still means he was only *nine* when they expected him to start helping out.

If it weren't for Josh and Rosaline nudging Dom out of his responsible shell, I'm not sure the guy would've gotten much of a childhood.

"I'm sorry." That was easier to say than I thought, so I keep going, sharing my thoughts in a normal volume instead of yelling like before. "That makes sense. And I shouldn't have shamed you about what you were eating. That was shitty of me. I just . . ." *I'm just projecting my insecurities onto you.* But I don't say that. "I just think you should make choices for yourself now. Do what makes you happy. Eat the food you like. Don't make yourself hungry."

Silence falls between us for a stretch, probably because Dom is so shocked that I willingly apologized to him. Maybe he's wondering if I'm experiencing heatstroke.

"Are you thirsty?" he asks. The question sounds like a peace offering.

I hold out my hand and a moment later he hands me the nozzle.

Once more, the lukewarm liquid hits the spot, and I make the mistake of peeking over the top of my sunglasses in time to spy Dom's smile. The expression almost looks satisfied.

Probably because he sees this as doing his duty for my brother. Making sure I don't perish on any of these postmortem missions.

Reminded of Josh's request, I slip my phone out of my back pocket, and I keep slurping Dom's water supply as I hold up the phone in selfie mode and snap a quick picture of us.

Happy, Josh? There's a cactus over my shoulder and we kind of look friend-adjacent in this one. Is that what you wanted?

I keep the snarky comments toward my brother to myself and give Dom back his hose.

"The letter said we should share regrets, too," I say.

All the stories we told so far were funny ones.

Dom's smile becomes subdued but doesn't disappear completely. "He did, didn't he?"

I nod. "I regret not . . ." The words I meant to say fade into silence, as if speaking them will reveal how terrible of a sister I was.

My silence lingers past the point of comfort.

"I regret not going with him when he asked."

Dom's admission pulls me out of my struggling thoughts. I stare up at him while he gazes out at the expanse of land littered with cacti.

"Going with him where?"

"Anywhere. Everywhere." Dom rubs a hand over the back of his neck in a rough gesture. I can feel the frustration and regret rolling off him. "He'd invite me on trips all the time. Told me the invitation was open. I never went. Work kept me busy, but I could've taken time off. I always thought . . ."

The pain in his voice guts me because it's a reflection of my own.

"You always thought there'd be more time." I finish the statement for him with the same reasoning I used myself whenever I turned down one of my brother's invites.

The future always seemed to stretch out in an unending road before me. Maybe Josh sensed the end of his life was closer than most others. And that's why he did as much as he could with the time he had.

More, I guess. If we count the ashes in my bag as him reaching farther than the limits of death.

"Exactly." Dom does a slow turn, taking in the town that also manages to live on after its demise.

When the silence goes on for longer than it needs to, I worry that Dom has fallen down a mental rabbit hole of despair. The same one I practically live in. It's a dark place that as few people as possible should have to deal with. Which is why I break the stale air with an inappropriate comment.

"Josh had terrible table manners."

Maybe it would have been fair to share a regret. To expose my pain the way Dom did.

But I want to laugh again.

It feels so good to joke about my brother instead of constantly reminding myself that he's gone.

Dom jerks, as if he forgot he wasn't alone in this ghost town.

I keep going. "He was a loud chewer, and his mouth was open half the time. Plus, he always stole food off my plate! More than once I thought about stabbing his sneaky hand with my fork."

Dom chuckles. "He did that with me, too. I used to guard my meals from him."

We turn in silent agreement and start walking through the town again. I tug my backpack off, unzip it, and root around until I find the Rubbermaid container with my brother's remains.

"And his singing," I say.

Dom groans. "So pitchy. Like he was constantly going through puberty."

The perfect description of my brother's wailing calls up vivid memories of me cringing through his caroling.

"Horrendous," I agree while my fingers pop off the lid. "He used it as a torture method to get me to do what he wanted."

"Or to make you smile," Dom adds. "When he sang to you on your birthday, you always had the biggest grin."

"I did, didn't I?" My soft response drifts away with the wind. I hold up the container of Josh, the small particles of him already catching in the breeze. Dancing to freedom and a new adventure.

"He was an atrocious dancer, too," I say as my hand tilts.

"The absolute worst," Dom agrees. "One time he accidentally gave me a black eye during the Electric Slide."

And as another piece of my brother leaves me, he departs to the sound of my laughter.

CHAPTER
Nineteen

The world finally cools off once the sun goes down. Enough that I'm willing to venture out from the small bungalow I booked for myself—Dom has his own—and wander down to the pool. Not that I plan on swimming. But sometimes I find the scent of chlorine soothing, and after today I need that.

Things were close to cordial between Dom and me before I went after him about his snack choices. My temper boiled hot and fast, something that it's been doing a lot in the months since Josh passed. I regret letting it spill out. My body refuses to expel tears, but harsh words flow easily.

The lap of water slows my steps, and as I slip through the gate, I realize the pool is occupied.

By Dom.

The man glides through the water with both power and grace. His freestyle shows off flexing biceps and tensing back muscles. Nothing like the gawky adolescents I used to see at the twins' swim meets.

Dom is a grown man, and my body is happy about it.

I pull my loosely knitted cardigan more securely around my shoulders to hide the way my hard nipples press against the thin material of my tank top. Briefly, I consider retreating.

But I'm tired of being in my room. Once we got back from Vulture City, I immediately logged into work and have been catching up on everything these past few hours. My fingers need a rest from typing, and forget about tears—my eyes will start bleeding if I have to search for another impossible-to-find error in another dataset.

I settle on one of the padded lounge chairs, reclining as I watch Dom continue to cut across the surface, his body lit by the blue glow of the pool lights.

After another few laps, he lets his hands hit the wall rather than performing a flip turn. The night goes quiet without the slap of his skin against water. A sky full of stars stretches above us, and I wait for Dom to realize he has an audience.

He doesn't. He simply lets his feet settle on the bottom of the pool, and stares straight ahead into the dark night.

I start to clap, slow and mocking, because I'm incapable of telling him that I found his skill legitimately impressive.

Dom whips around and tugs off his goggles. I try not to shiver when his attention lands and stays on me.

"Do the twins know you're trying to steal their sport? Last Adam said, they're Olympic hopefuls. Maybe you should stick to baseball."

Dom smirks and drifts through the water toward the side of the pool where I sit.

"Noted." His eyes drag over my reclined body in a heavy sweep that makes me shiver. "Can't sleep?"

I shrug. "Yeah. I was terrified when someone said they spotted a grotesque monster in the pool."

He snorts, and I give myself a point for earning his laughter. Dom does that more and more each trip. I guess we both needed time to adjust to each other. To learn what this dynamic would be.

Dom as the protector, and me his reluctant charge?

Yeah, not going to work.

Me mooning over him like a besotted teenager and stealing a drunken kiss?

Once again, a major mistake.

Enemies?

Impossible with Josh's words forcing us together. With his requirement for us to be vulnerable around each other.

Ever since my blowup at Dom earlier, I've been thinking about all the times that he's responsible—almost every minute of every day—and the few times I can recall him letting loose.

The latter mainly occurred when Josh pushed and needled him.

Who's going to do that now that my brother is gone?

Maybe including Dom in this task wasn't Josh assigning a babysitter to me. He must have known I'd do the trips, no matter how hard or ridiculous each one was. Josh would've known I didn't need Dom to force me.

That I didn't need Dom at all.

But maybe . . .

Maybe he thought that Dom might need *me.*

Does Josh want me to be Dom's friend?

I could see my brother worrying about that. See him growing concerned that his gruffly responsible friend who spends all his time working and taking care of his brothers might forget to socialize. Especially after finding out the man separated from his wife of seven years. From what I saw, Rosaline was the only one other than my brother who could get Dom to relax. Often Josh and she would team up to trick the taciturn man into having a good time.

My brother approached the end thinking his best friend would live on without that get-out-of-your-own-head force in his life. Josh knew Dom would need someone.

But it couldn't be just anyone. Josh had to pick someone Dom couldn't say no to.

His kid sister.

The sneaky machinations are so clear now, I'm tempted to laugh.

Josh left me more than the job of spreading his ashes.

He left me his best friend.

You better not think Dom is taking that title from Jeremy and Tula, I silently scold my brother.

Maybe I can handle some version of friendship. But "best" is taken.

I stand from my seat, traverse the few feet of concrete separating us, and settle cross-legged on the ground directly in front of Dom. He watches my approach with narrowed eyes, like an animal in a trap.

But he doesn't back up.

"How's work going?" I ask. A question I would pose to Jeremy or Tula. My friends. The people I check on because I care about them.

Can I do this? Be Dom's friend? Can I set aside the mess of our past and start over?

For Josh, I think I can do almost anything.

Confusion creases Dom's handsome face, but I don't explain my motives. He's too proud to accept my friendship knowing I was doing it as a favor to Josh.

"Fine," he offers eventually.

"Define 'fine,'" I press. "Use details. Examples. Maybe draw a chart. That's how you accountants communicate, right? With line graphs and spreadsheets?"

Dom's lips twitch, and he crosses his arms on the concrete in front of my shins.

"'Fine' means it pays well. And they know I'm worth every cent."

"Cocky." I brace my elbows on my knees and lean toward him, attempting to keep my eyes away from the water droplets tracing down his bare chest. "Sounds like it should be *great*. But you said it's *fine*. Why's it just fine?"

Dom stares at me for a stretch, and I hold his eye contact, suddenly determined to commit to this friendship. To accept this task left to me by my brother.

Don't worry, asshole. I will take care of Dom for you.

"It's the same place I've worked since college." He shrugs,

rippling the water with his movement. "Feels stagnant now, even though I get a raise every year. Also, my boss is a prick."

I snort at that last bit. "Are you applying to other firms?"

Dom shakes his head.

"Why not?"

"It's a good job. The office is close to my town house. I don't need to move on from it."

I reach out and flick his forehead. He scowls and grabs my wrist in his damp fingers before I can retreat.

"What was that for?"

"Punishment. For undervaluing yourself. You're worth more than a shitty boss and spending forty plus hours a week doing something that's just *fine*."

Dom continues to hold on to me as he studies my face. Then his gaze drops, and I watch his pupils dilate. Belatedly, I realize my cardigan has fallen open, revealing overexcited nipples that have yet to calm down.

"What am I worth, Maddie?" His voice rasps over my name.

Damn him and that deep voice.

"More," I mutter. "I'm not the accountant. You can figure out a way to quantify it yourself."

Dom's mouth tightens, then eases. "Do you like that cover-up?"

Confused by the change of subject, I glance down at my cardigan. "Uh, yeah? I guess. It doesn't have pockets, so it could be better." I roll my eyes, guessing where this is going. "Are you going to try to use some metaphor about not always wearing my favorite clothes as an excuse to stay in your boring-ass job?"

Dom gives a slow headshake. "I just wanted to make sure I didn't ruin something you loved."

His words make no sense, and his hot hand on my wrist makes it hard to decipher their underlying meaning. "What? Ruin it how?"

"By doing this." Dom tugs hard on my wrist, unbalancing me.

I faceplant in the water.

Luckily, I realized what was happening in enough time to hold my breath, but I'm still sputtering in indignation when I resurface.

Once I'm able to blink the water from my eyes, I realize Dom has retreated halfway across the pool. He wears a smug grin that is entirely too attractive on his face.

"You dick bag!" I screech, loud enough to wake the rest of the bungalow guests. "I'm going to kill you!"

"I'm terrified," he says in a flat tone, even as he continues to grin.

My soggy cardigan will only hold me back, so I shrug out of it, leaving the sad material drifting in the pool behind me like the leavings of a shipwreck. Then I lunge forward, not sure what my plan is other than revenge.

Dom chuckles and moves to dodge my assault. My fingers slip off the tight, warm skin of his hip.

"Gotta be faster than that," he taunts.

I growl and fake pounce. He believes my bluff, pushing off to the side. That's when I go for him. I manage to hook an arm around his neck and wrap my legs around his waist. Once I've fully octopused myself around his body, I latch my fingers on to Dom's nipple, pinching just hard enough for him to understand my threat. Panting, I lock his eyes with mine.

"Beg for forgiveness or prepare to fly home tomorrow with a bruised nipple."

Only when I pause for his response do I realize the position I've placed myself in. Soaking wet and plastered to Dom's hard body. My core, covered only by a soaked set of cotton sleep shorts, hovers inches from his package.

And a tank top that used to be white is now so see-through, Dom could sketch a portrait of my areolas.

"I—"

Whatever apology he was about to say comes too late. I attack out of self-preservation, pinching and twisting hard.

I expect a high-pitched yelp or a ripe curse.

Instead, Dom lets out a deep groan.

We stare at each other, eyes wide.

Looks like Dominic Perry just discovered a new kink.

How inconvenient.

I release my hold and shove away from him, water swirling around us as I retreat. Dom lifts a hand to rub his pec, and it takes everything in me not to watch the movement. Instead, I paddle until I find my water-logged cardigan, and drag it behind me as I swim toward the stairs in the shallow end. It feels like half the pool clings to my clothes when I climb into the cool night air. If I'd known I was going for a swim, I would've brought a towel.

"Maddie." Dom's voice dares me to leave without acknowledging him. Gritting my teeth, I turn to face the man I've decided to be friends with. For my brother's sake.

He stares up at me, hand still on his chest, obviously unsure what to say next.

And damn me, I take pity on him. Because there's something about seeing Dom step away from his must-be-responsible-at-all-times demeanor in an effort to be playful that softens my defenses. That has me wanting to let him know it's okay to joke and be silly and not be serious about every decision you make.

"You better hope I don't dump my drink on your crotch tomorrow," I warn, scrunching my face into a terrifying scowl. "Would make for a hell of an uncomfortable flight. And the perfect revenge."

His smile unfurls slowly, all the more beautiful for the reluctance.

"Sorry I got you wet," he taunts.

If only he knew.

Twenty

"We apologize for the delay as we wait for your plane to arrive."

A few people around me groan, but I merely sigh at the unfortunate but inevitable shit storm that is air travel. Hopefully, I can still catch my connecting flight once we make it to Dallas. Originally, I had a good three hours to meander my way through the Dallas airport to my gate. We'll see how much of that remains. This travel hiccup convinces me I was right to insist on combining the next two states into one trip, driving between them. It's the logical decision.

When we were comparing our schedules and researching the weather for the four remaining destinations, Dom and I realized the best time to meet again would be the spring. Next year.

Half a year without any new words from my brother. The only way I could stomach the wait was the idea of getting a double dose.

Dom signed on to my idea when I agreed we'd take one vehicle. Spending hours in a car with him doesn't seem as horrible as it used to. During this stretch of time apart, I plan to fully immerse my mind in the idea of being Dom's friend. If I successfully suppress my insecurities and resentment, the excursion might actually be pleasant.

As pleasant as spreading my dead brother's remains can be anyway.

"How's your connection looking?" I ask. We sit side by side in the terminal, both on this first flight from Phoenix. When Dom found out I'd booked myself a seat in coach, he immediately pushed me to upgrade to first class into the seat next to him and insisted I also upgrade for my next flight to Seattle. He pointed out Josh left us more than enough to cover the expense, but I still feel weird traveling in luxury on my brother's dime. The larger seat makes sense for Dom, who would have to fold his tall body into a painful shape to fit into a cheaper seat. But I'm more compact than him.

These arguments held no sway, so now I possess a first-class seat.

"I'll probably miss it," he says. "But there's two more to Philly later in the day. I'll grab one of those."

I nod and reach back to bundle the hood of my sweatshirt into a makeshift pillow. "Gonna nap. Wake me when our plane gets here." A thunderstorm in Dallas pushed back a morning flight to Phoenix, which means the plane we were supposed to be boarding in five minutes hasn't even landed in the airport yet. I expect a long wait, and I'd rather sleep through it. My body needs the rest after I spent half the night fidgeting and rolling around in my bed, trying to forget the way Dom's heat soaked into my thighs when I wrapped my legs around him in the pool. Or how the phantom touch of his hip lingers like hot sparks in my fingertips . . .

"Maddie." Someone says my name in a low, gentle voice, and a warm pressure brushes my cheek.

When I blink my eyes open, the world is a bright blur of colorful, unfamiliar shapes. I jerk upright, hands skittering over my face.

"I can't see!"

"Maddie." The same voice, though sterner this time, draws my attention to my side. Dom's there, close enough to be visible in my nearsighted range, and he holds out my glasses. I slip them on, remembering I'm in an airport terminal and I don't wear contacts when I'm traveling for exactly this reason—I tend to nap, and I don't want them gluing to my eyeballs.

"How long was I out for?" I slip my glasses off again and hold them up to the light. They seem cleaner than they were this morning. *Did Dom polish the lenses?*

"An hour. I forgot how you can sleep anywhere." He has his laptop open and looks to be sorting through an email inbox. "Our plane is here. They're going to start boarding in a minute." He glances at me and a hint of a smile tugs at his full lips.

"What?"

"Nothing."

"Bullshit. Did you write on my forehead while I was out?" I scrub my hand across my skin and look for traces of ink on my fingers.

Dom snorts. "That's Adam's move. I can't believe it took Josh an entire day to realize he had 'butt' on his face."

I chuckle at the memory. "I have my suspicions that he figured it out much earlier and just went with it."

Dom's half smile turns into an almost full curve of his lips. "He would. But you don't have an insult on your face. Just a crease on your cheek from my shirt."

"Your shirt . . ." That's when I realize my head was tilted to the side, not back, when I woke up. Unconscious Maddie decided to turn Dominic Perry into her personal pillow. I eye his cotton T-shirt, relieved there are no drool stains there.

Before I can decide if I want to apologize or fall back on my normal snark, an announcement comes over the intercom.

"Boarding will begin in five minutes, starting with Group A."

"That's us." He shuts his computer. "I'm going to use a normal-sized bathroom before we board."

Just the idea of Dom trying to tuck his wide shoulders into one of those closet-sized airplane bathrooms has me snorting.

"Can I check my email?" I gesture toward his laptop. "I don't feel like getting mine out."

"Lazy," he murmurs with another twitch at the corner of his mouth as he settles his computer in my lap. Dom stands with a stretch and a groan, and I try hard—but not hard enough—to avert my eyes from the stretch of skin that peeks out between his T-shirt and the waistband of his sweatpants. He drops his arms, the strip of his lower belly that haunts me disappears, and the man strides toward the bathroom. It takes me entirely too long to realize I'm staring at Dom's butt.

"Damn nice-fitting pants," I grumble as I tap the touch pad to bring the laptop screen to life.

The desktop background is a picture of the Perry family. The Perry family plus Josh and Rosaline. Adam and Carter wear graduation robes and huge grins, standing in the middle of the gathering.

I missed this.

Emilia had sent me the announcement, and I'd mailed the two graduates gift cards. But I could've been there. As awkward as I would have felt around Dom and Rosaline, everyone would have welcomed me.

The day could've been another memory with Josh.

My throat tightens, and I hurry to open the browser. Only, I pause again when one of the desktop files catches my attention. As if the computer knew who I was thinking about, the title blares up at me.

JOSH

Why does Dom have a file named after my brother?

Maybe these are photos of them together. More memories I missed.

The masochist in me double taps the folder.

But the files that pop up on the screen aren't tiny previews of Josh's grinning face. Instead, I find a collection of PDF files with academic-sounding names. As I scroll through, I realize they're research articles. There's over a hundred.

And all the titles mention a particular type of lung cancer.

The one that took Josh from me. From us.

It felt like a perverse cosmic joke that Josh's lungs were what failed him. For years *I* was the one who couldn't catch my breath.

My fingers scroll through the vast list until I come across a file with the title "Treatment Options." I click to open it. The document is a simple format with clear headings.

In the same way that I hear my brother's voice in my head when I read one of his letters, I could swear Dom is the one reading this to me. Every word clearly typed by his hand.

Josh's Current Treatment
Promising Treatment Options
Experimental Treatment Options
Experts in the Field—

"Any work emergencies?"

I flinch at the question, jerking my chin up to find Dom looming over me. From his vantage point, he can't see his screen, so I hurriedly close the documents and folder.

Would he be mad about my snooping?

"Nope." I hand over his laptop, then busy myself pulling out my ticket and turning my phone to airplane mode.

Meanwhile, my mind tries to make sense of what I just found.

As I follow Dom onto the plane, my eyes locked on his broad back, I imagine him compiling all that information. Reading those dense articles and teaching himself all the medical jargon so he could understand what was happening to Josh.

He was trying to find a way to fix it.

"Window or aisle?" We've made it to our cushy first-class seats—cushy compared to coach anyway—and Dom claims my carry-on, depressing the handle and easily lifting it into the overhead bin.

"Uh, window, I guess." My mind is still mostly on that file, but the corner I allot to his question reasons he can extend his legs into the aisle if he still needs more knee space. I shimmy past him and plop down into my seat, pushing my glasses back into place as they try to slip down my nose.

"Are you a nervous flier?" Dom sits down and turns to study me.

"No. Why?"

His eyes narrow, but after a pause he shakes his head. "No reason."

But there was a reason. If I had said yes—that going up in the air terrified me—he would have done something to help. Distracted me, gotten me a drink or sleeping pills. Demanded to speak to the pilot so he could tell the person in charge of the plane that this better be the smoothest flight we've ever experienced. And if none of that worked, he'd probably escort me off the plane, rent us a car, and drive me home to Seattle himself.

Because that's what Dom does. He takes control, and he fixes things.

That's what that folder was. Dom trying to grab hold of the situation. As if all he needed to do was learn enough, and then he would have found the solution.

What must it have been like to watch his best friend die slowly and not be able to do a thing to stop it?

For the man who controls everything, to have none.

The truth smashes into me, more solid than I've allowed it to be up until this point.

Dom lost his best friend.

More like he lost his brother.

Whenever I think about Josh passing and leaving us all behind, my grief outweighs my concern for anyone else's.

Josh was *my* brother. *I* loved him most. Therefore, surely, I hurt the most.

But with that folder in my mind, I'm finally able to untangle the idea of Dom's grief from mine, until his pain sits on its own, a gaping wound the man beside me is probably trying to hold shut with the mere force of his will.

I can imagine Dom talking to himself, growling in an unrelenting voice. *Stop hurting*, he'd say, as if it were that simple. There may have even been a moment when he looked Josh straight in the face and demanded, *Stop having cancer.*

He would do that. The arrogant asshole.

The idea has me choking on a horrified bubble of laughter.

"Maddie?" I face the man filling my thoughts to find him eyeing me with a concerned crease between his brows.

Damn. I want to hug him.

But I can't do that for a whole load of reasons, so I do the next best thing.

"Could you flag down a flight attendant when you see one? I want a gin and tonic."

A strain of tension eases from his face and he nods, a stern, determined movement. "Of course."

Stop it, I want to beg him. *Stop before you make me fall again.*

When he hands me my drink a minute later, I down half of it in a single gulp. But the dose of alcohol does nothing to ease the temptation to lean closer and ask him to take control of more arbitrary things if the responsibility soothes his pain.

To impose his stifling, infuriating, loving will upon me.

Don't do it, I remind myself.

Dom might think he needs to be in charge, be in control. That he needs to take care of everything and everyone around him.

But I think what he really needs is someone who reminds him to take care of himself.

Twenty-One

"Crap. I didn't want to spend the night here."

As our plane sits so close to the building, but not there yet, I watch the minutes on my phone tick away. Unlike with Dom's connection, there aren't any more flights to Seattle today.

Having to wait until tomorrow normally wouldn't be a problem, but there's an in-person staff meeting first thing in the morning. Pamela will go into panic mode if I'm not there, and I hate screwing up at work.

"You won't miss your flight." Dom has his phone out, and I see a map of the airport on his screen.

"It's on the other side of the airport. And boarding stops in"—I lean closer to see the time on his screen—"twenty minutes. They haven't even opened the doors yet."

Some people might be able to sprint the distance in time, but those people don't have chronic asthma, a heavy carry-on full of ghost town souvenirs for their needy friends, and two gin and tonics sloshing around in their stomachs.

I should've stopped after the first one, but I kept wanting to reach over and touch Dom in some soothing way. I needed to fill my hands and numb this sudden onslaught of affection.

Remember that time when hooking up with you was so bad, Dom proposed to another woman the next day?

But then he offered me his tiny bag of pretzels and my heart insisted that the salty treat solved everything and I should unbuckle, sit in his lap, and wrap my arms around him instead.

So, I drank. And now I'm in no state to make a mad dash dragging a suitcase while trying not to asphyxiate.

"They're about to." Dom points out the window and I see the walkway extending toward our plane. "We don't need to run. The distance is doable. I'll carry your suitcase. We'll walk at a quick pace, and you'll make it. Use your inhaler now."

Fuck. Why is Dom doling out instructions suddenly so fucking hot? Normally, I want to push back on everything he says to prove he has no control over me. But now I find myself pulling my backpack out from under the seat in front of me, shaking my inhaler, taking a puff, and getting ready to follow him even if he leads me straight off a cliff.

Shit. Reading that file was a mistake.

Now I can't avoid the knowledge that no matter how domineering Dominic gets, the control is always coming from a place of love. That the compulsion likely started when he was saddled with two baby brothers and given the task of being one of their primary caregivers.

Dom had a lot asked of him too early in life. Now he shows love by taking care of people.

And he's trying to take care of me.

The man in question stands in the aisle now that the seat belt light is off. He slings the straps of his two bags over his shoulders, then heaves my suitcase out of the overhead. Because we're in first class, there's only one row of passengers in front of us.

"We're catching a connection," Dom says, meeting the eyes of the four businessmen who by all rights should be allowed to get off before us. They stay seated, cowed by Dom's unrelenting stare.

This is when those six foot, too many extra inches come in handy.

There's a pop and slight change in the air pressure. A flight attendant waves us forward, and Dom steps back for me to scramble out in front of him.

"It's not a big deal," I say over my shoulder as we hurry off the plane and up the walkway. "I can get a hotel room and fly out tomorrow morning."

"I'm not leaving you here. Come on." Once in the airport, Dom maneuvers in front of me to take the lead, his imposing body parting the sea of travelers.

An unexpected comforting sensation radiates up my arm, and I realize that when switching positions, Dom grabbed my hand and laced our fingers together.

The man is carrying both his bags, one of mine, and guiding me forward with an easy yet unrelenting grip. Though his long legs eat up the ground, I can tell he's keeping to a pace I can manage. Accelerated, but I don't have to jog.

"The suitcase has wheels," I call to him over the crowd's chatter and blare of announcements.

He's still gripping my bag by the handle instead of dragging it at his side like everyone else around us.

"Wheels slow me down."

I scoff and try to ignore how that arrogant statement made my lower belly clench. "How do wheels slow you down? Are you a hover car from the future? Or a ghost?"

"Stop using your air for snark," he commands. "Use it for breathing."

Has a woman ever wanted to both strangle and fondle a man so much?

As I'm left no other option than to breathe and follow Dom, my eyes have plenty of time to latch on to his backside and stay there.

Admiring the accountant's bubble butt is a surprisingly pleasant way to race through a crowded airport.

And, of course, with exactly two minutes to spare, my gate comes into view.

"Last call for Madeline Sanderson." The announcement rings out.

"She's here," Dom booms, louder than the overhead speaker.

"Stop shouting before you get me arrested." I swat his back like the ungrateful troll person I am.

But he only tugs me toward the counter, holding up the hand clutching my bag so the attendant will spot us if his thunderous announcement didn't do the trick. His biceps strain at the move and I drool a little. The airline employee's eyes go wide at Dom's approach, and I watch her swallow hard.

From fear? From horniness? Who knows. Probably both.

When we come to a stop at the counter, Dom sets my bag down and faces me.

"Guess I shouldn't have doubted you," I say, reaching for the handle of my roller bag, but his thick thigh is in the way.

"You've got everything?" Dom asks as his eyes scan my body.

Then, without warning, his hands take the same route.

"Phone," he mutters, palming my right thigh pocket. "Plane ticket." He pats my hoodie pouch. "Wallet." Left thigh pocket. "Laptop is in your bag. Inhaler is in the side pocket. And you're wearing your glasses." He pushes the frames up the bridge of my nose as his brows dip in concentration. "Am I missing anything?"

That last question breaks something open inside me. I'm shattered by the desperate, concerned edge that reveals too much of this man who tries to maintain control of every element around him.

Am I missing anything?

I've heard that question from Dom before.

The same question he muttered to himself when the twins were leaving for camp.

The same question he whispered when sorting his mother's pain medications.

The same question he murmured the few times we crossed paths in Josh's hospital room.

Those words sound like a quick double check, but for Dom, they're a warning.

Don't miss anything, he's telling himself. *If you miss something, and this person gets hurt, it's your fault. You could've stopped it.*

I see it in his eyes. The fear.

How many hours did he spend poring over those medical articles and research studies with the same question berating him?

Am I missing anything?

Finally, Dom looks me in the eyes, his brusque check of my essentials complete.

Maybe I should be affronted that he's sending me off the way a loving mother would drop her toddler off at preschool. Instead, my heart skips and trips over knowing that he took the time to notice where I store all my essentials when traveling.

He missed one thing, though. Something that, in this moment, I've never needed more.

Don't do it! You've been burned too many times by this man! Stop sticking your hand in the fire!

But I can't help myself around Dom. This is why I moved across the country after that first rejection. Because like an immortal moth, I keep reviving my scorched heart and flying straight into the beautiful, deadly lantern that is Dominic Perry, ignoring that I'll probably get fried to a crisp.

"This is your fault," I grit out. His eyes widen as I lunge forward, wrapping my arms around his neck.

I kiss him hard.

This is what he gets for letting me nap on his shoulder and cleaning my glasses. This is what he gets for hauling my suitcase through a crowded airport at a fast yet manageable speed. This is what he gets for learning every detail of Josh's disease in hopes that he could save my brother's life.

This is what he gets for always being steady and caring.

This kiss is *his* fault.

Dom grunts, but he doesn't pull away. I don't give him time to. Almost as quick as I started the lip lock, I break it. Without sparing him another glance, I grab my bag, scan my ticket, and disappear into the safety of the boarding bridge, pressing my fingers against my lips to cling to the traces of him.

CHAPTER
twenty-two

Sender: Dominic Perry
Subject: Phone Number

Maddie,

Give me your phone number.

Sincerely,
Dom

· · · · · · · · · · ·

Sender: Maddie Sanderson
Subject: RE: Phone Number

New phone. Who dis?

I never claimed to be mature.

In fact, I am often extremely immature for my age. However, I also have a full-time job, pay all my bills on time, and schedule regular dentist appointments. So, I think that balances out my childish response to Dom. Especially after I attacked his face at the airport yesterday, despite him already rejecting my advances twice.

"I'm just going for the trifecta," I mutter as I pace around my condo while a comfort grilled cheese sandwich browns in the cast iron. "Can you even say you fucked up if you haven't done it three times in three different ways in three different states?"

My email pings again.

Sender: Dominic Perry
Subject: RE: RE: Phone Number

Maddie,

This is the man you are going to spend multiple days in a car with and who would like your phone number for emergency reasons.

Sincerely,
Just Give Me Your Goddamn Number Already

Two messages and no mention of the kiss. That's got to be good, right? Maybe he convinced himself it was an accident. I was in a hurry to board the plane and his mouth got in the way. Or we could blame alcohol. The gin made me do it!

To appease Dom, I could give him my phone number.

Or I could continue to evade his attempts to have a direct connection to me.

Email is safer. It's a boundary I need.

Sender: Maddie Sanderson
Subject: RE: RE: RE: Phone Number

What kind of emergencies? Are you planning on forgetting me at a rest stop? Because I think I could entertain myself with

snacks and nudey mags until you realized your error and
turned around.

Sincerely,
I Don't Give Scrubs My Number

Besides, I already have his digits saved in my contacts from that
first email he sent. If some terrible—unlikely—emergency arises, I
can call him. Until then, emails will have to suffice.

I need to maintain a sense of separation. Getting close to the
man scrambles my common sense. Every time I decide I have the
maturity to be around him, my hormones and needy emotions get in
the way. Some overly romantic corner of my brain decides the best
way to interact with Dom is a passionate embrace.

Why do I make the same mistake on an endless loop?

I've replayed that night on the porch swing far too many times,
and through those many dissections, I realized that I initiated
everything. I kissed him. I took off my shirt and kicked off my
shorts. I covered his hand with mine and nudged it between my legs.

Sure, Dom participated. "Like this, Maddie?" he would ask.
"You like it when I touch you like this?" And damn it, I did, moan-
ing his name.

Thank the universe my mouth was pressed against his shoulder
when I eventually came, because I'm pretty sure "I love you" wanted
to force its way out on that final wave of pleasure.

And I did. I loved him. He made it so easy.

And he left me easily, too.

I sink onto my couch, cradling my head in my hands as an ache
starts up a slow pounding in the base of my skull.

I was supposed to be establishing a platonic friendship with
Dom. Working on becoming the person who made sure he never
took life too seriously. Josh wanted me to look out for his friend, not
rediscover a pointless infatuation.

Too far. I went too far in the other direction.

My email pings.

Sender: Dominic Perry
Subject: RE: RE: RE: RE: Phone Number

Maddie,

I wasn't aware you enjoyed viewing porn in public gas stations. Is this a trip requirement? How many times will we need to stop to get you your fix?

Sincerely,
Not a Scrub, A Responsible Accountant

I bark out an unexpected laugh after reading Dom's response. I can hear the words spoken in his dry, sarcastic tone, while a smile twitches at the corner of his mouth. A lot of people who meet Dom assume the man is all serious scowls with no sense of humor.

But he just needs to be pushed. And prodded. And poked. And only then does he give himself permission to make a joke.

My fingers creep to the keyboard, the act of typing a response easing the pain in my skull.

Sender: Maddie Sanderson
Subject: Travel Budget

Dear Responsible Accountant,

What percentage of the funds that Josh left us do you believe he intended for the purchase of smutty magazines? 10%? 15%?

I hope you've budgeted for this.

Sincerely,
Never Settle For Cheap Smut

. . . .

Sender: Dominic Perry
Subject: RE: Travel Budget

Dear Expensive Smut,

I will add "Maddie's Gas Station Pornography" as a line item.
Please make sure to submit your receipts so you can be
properly reimbursed.

Or you could text me a picture of them. Using your phone.

Sincerely,
Give Me Your Phone Number And I'll Send You An
Embarrassing Picture Of Myself

Oh.
Oh no.
Now, *that* is a tempting offer.
My mind buzzes with the possibilities of what that picture could
be. What would Dom consider embarrassing? And why would he
keep the photo?
Dom seems like the kind of guy who would delete all possible
evidence of him ever making a mistake.
*Maybe giving him my number would be okay. It's not like I can spon-
taneously make out with him through the phone.*
I'm weak.

Sender: Maddie Sanderson
Subject: RE: RE: Travel Budget

(206) 555-6501

If the next message I receive does not have a mortifying image of Dominic Perry, I will block the number.

Try me.

Sincerely,

Show Me Your Shame

Perched on the edge of my couch, I wait for his response. On the tab of my browser, I see notifications for my work email, but I ignore them, too focused on whether I made a massive misstep.

My phone vibrates and I snatch it up. MR. RESPONSIBLE ASSHOLE flashes on the screen.

This is a mistake. I know that before I make it. Still, I swipe to open the message. At first, I don't know whether to be furious or thankful.

The asshole sent me a thirst trap.

In the image, a shirtless Dom lays on a beach towel, skin glowing with the start of a tan, beat-up baseball hat shielding his eyes from the sun, body on full display. My eager eyes trace the lines of muscle on his chest and the light coating of hair across his pecs. The column of his throat tempts me, that dip at the base tantalizing me.

What I wouldn't do to lick that V marking his hips.

Fuck you, Dominic Perry. This is the opposite of embarrassing.

But my frustration allows me to focus on the whole image, and I realize he's not the only one in the picture.

A dog stands beside the towel.

Leg lifted.

I'm admiring a photographic masterpiece that shows a sleeping, sunbathing Dom receiving a golden shower from a Doberman.

MR. RESPONSIBLE ASSHOLE: Josh
thought it was more important to get

a good shot than to shoo the dog
away.

I laugh.

I laugh so hard I roll off my couch, fall to the floor, and curl in the fetal position as my body shakes with giggles. The cackles are never-ending, so I grab my phone, swipe to start a voice message, and let Dom hear exactly what I think of my brother's choice.

MR. RESPONSIBLE ASSHOLE: Glad I
could amuse you.

Once the chuckles finally trail off and I wipe the tears of hilarity from the corners of my eyes, I decide not to let myself worry about giving Dom my number. As I said before, I can always block him.

This can be a good thing, I decide. The first true step in becoming friends. I can practice conversing with Dom on a regular basis without the distraction of his handsome face and all the memories attached to it. With the delay between typing new messages, I can apply a filter to my words. I can take a moment to rein in the harsher comments I've been throwing at him that he doesn't deserve.

Maybe this could work.

Winter

CHAPTER
Twenty-Three

I text Dom sometimes.

Usually when I think of Josh. Because when I think of my brother, my mind now turns to the friend he left behind for me to take care of.

> MADDIE: I saw a dog peeing on a very stern-looking tree and it reminded me of you

> DOM: I don't like the associations your brain makes.
> DOM: How does a tree look stern?

> MADDIE: It's just a vibe
> MADDIE: Trees have vibes
> MADDIE: And this one positively LOOMS over the sidewalk
> MADDIE: Classic Dom move

> DOM: What you call looming, I call standing and being tall.

MADDIE: I'm just warning you

MADDIE: Dom = tree vibes

MADDIE: It's a matter of time before you get peed on again!

DOM: You're ridiculous. I have a meeting.

MADDIE: I'm going to send you a picture of the tree

DOM: Don't

MADDIE: It's happening

The exchange makes my always-pleasant-at-work smile easier to wear for the rest of the day. Especially when I check my phone a few hours later and see another notification from him.

DOM: Apparently, it's not happening. I've yet to receive a single tree picture.

MADDIE: I didn't know you wanted it RIGHT NOW

DOM: I don't want it.
DOM: But you said you were going to send it.
DOM: So, I was checking.
DOM: I'm not curious in the slightest.

On my walk home from work I deviate into the nearby park where the Dom tree is, snap a picture, and send it to him. Then I send a version with arrows to emphasize the particularly looming nature of the branches.

DOM: That's an extremely handsome
tree.

At least once a week I initiate an exchange of nonsense text messages so I know that Dom has a small portion of his life where he's not required to be serious or responsible.

All he needs to do is text me back. And he does, every time.

I wonder if he regrets demanding my phone number?

Too bad. I don't stop.

In January, Pamela insists I accompany her to a conference in New York.

A massive gathering of businesspeople is not my idea of fun, but I don't try to slip out of the responsibility for three reasons.

Reason one: I want to stay in Pamela's good favor at all times.

Reason two: there's another event in New York at the same time I want to try to attend.

Reason three: I will do anything to distract myself from the fact that next week will mark a year since Josh died.

Tula and Jeremy already told me they're taking me to a spa for the day. Then in the evening, they plan to buy out the cheese section at the local grocery store, stock up on my favorite gin, and play some action-movie drinking game Tula swears will get me so drunk I'll forget my own name.

I hope their distraction techniques work, but I'm finding even the lead-up to the anniversary hurts my entire body. Like my innards are getting dragged against a cheese grater.

So I agree to New York, no questions asked.

The first day, I attend the workshops Pamela can't make and take copious notes for her. The second day, I end up manning The Redford Team's booth with two women from the marketing department. They shop our services to the crowd of CEOs and CFOs while I make sure no one steals company swag without first listening to their spiel.

My coworkers are nice. The event is an introvert's hell. But the conference leaves me no time to wallow, which is what I needed. And then there's the other New York event.

The day after the conference ends, the UPenn swim team has an away meet at Columbia. The Perry twins are competing in NYC, and I'm determined to go.

I don't inform Adam or Carter of my plan beforehand in case something goes wrong and I can't show up. But the morning of the meet, all my obligations are complete and my flight isn't until later in the day. I drive my rental to Columbia after wishing Pamela safe travels on her earlier departure.

After finding parking and locating the pool area, I make my way to the entrance. The chlorine smell in the humid air transports me back to the good days of that one summer.

The Perrys made it to a lot of Adam and Carter's meets when they were younger, but there were times when it was just me, pressing up against the rope they suspended around the pool to keep crowds back. Both of them had let their floppy Perry hair grow long, so it was my job to stretch their swim caps over their heads.

They could have helped each other, but Adam insisted that I did it best. Carter didn't argue, just held the bright blue head covering out to me.

I rub my sternum to sooth the ache of times gone.

My eyes alight on a helpful sign that proclaims **POOL** with an arrow pointing down the hall where a stream of people trickle through the doorway. I tug out my phone, flip the camera, then get a selfie with the sign. Navigating to my texts, I open the group chat I have with Adam and Carter.

MADDIE: I think I'm lost

A few minutes go by without an answer, and I reason they've probably stored their phones while they get ready for the meet. Just as I decide to head in and grab a seat, my phone buzzes.

ADAM: No way
ADAM: NO FUCKING WAY!!!!!!!
CARTER: Heading your way

I'm about to text back, scolding Adam for using irresponsible language, when a metal door swings inward and deposits two grinning Perrys.

"Maddie!" Adam bounds across the space dividing us and scoops me into a hug. Carter follows at a more sedate pace, his gaze jumping from his brother's back to meet my eyes. He rolls his, and we share a grin.

Adam sets me down and steps back, taking me in. "I can't believe you're here! Why didn't you tell us you were coming? We didn't think we'd have any family in the stands for this one."

Well, that answers my unasked question about whether I'd see Dom while I'm here. I refuse to examine the odd mixture of relief and disappointment in my gut.

"I flew in for a work thing and wasn't sure if I'd make it." Deliberately running my eyes over Adam's towering form, I let my mouth fall into an exaggerated pout. "Damn. I was expecting Speedos."

"Oh, don't worry. I've got you." Adam tugs his sweatshirt over his head and shoves it at Carter, revealing a six-pack I'm not sure it's legal for him to have. Then he fists the front of his pants and tears them off in one go like a veteran stripper, leaving him in a *very* small bathing suit.

Carter snorts. "I'm not helping you button those up again."

"Worth it." Adam grins down at me, then does a slow circle with his arms spread. "What d'ya think? Ryan Lochte's got nothing on me."

"You certainly have a bigger ego than him." I grin even as I tease him, happy I made it here, and not minding I'm about to sit for hours to only see these two swim a few times.

Like Adam said. *Worth it.*

A middle-aged white woman with hair that looks like it was bleached blond by chlorine sticks her head out of the locker-room door and points our way. "Adam. Carter. Get your asses back here. You can flirt *after* you break some records. Not before."

"Coming, Coach!" Adam sings back, not chastised in the slightest. He grabs my face in his massive hands and plants a loud kiss on my forehead. "I want to hear you cheering me on, Sanderson."

"Perrys!" The coach shouts again. Adam lets me go with a smirk and jogs away, his muscular body looking like the peak of athleticism as he goes.

"Thanks for showing up," Carter says. Then he leans in for a quick kiss on my cheek before following his brother.

My face feels warm after their affection. Pleasantly so. My cheeks ache because of my wide smile that I can't seem to diminish.

I find my way into the pool area and settle in my seat just as the UPenn swimmers take over the deck, the mass of them jumping into the water to start their warm-up laps. Adam's eyes find me in the stands, and he waves vigorously. I hold up my phone and point to Carter. He gets the message, grabbing his twin around the shoulders. When the other Perry realizes what's happening, he offers a small smile to Adam's generous grin. I snap a quick shot, then give them a thumbs-up.

A little while later, after watching them win their first relay event and screaming myself hoarse, I sneak out of the pool to swing by the snack bar. While waiting in line, I send the picture of Adam and Carter to Dom.

> MADDIE: Are these two naturally
> naked mole rats, or did they wax
> off all that Perry fuzz? The things
> men do for sports . . .

The person in front of me steps away from the counter with their snacks, and I immediately order nachos. At home I always have high-quality artisanal cheeses I get from a local shop, but today I'm about to indulge in the same terribly delicious not-sure-if-it's-real dairy I used to treat myself to at the twins' summer swim meets.

My phone buzzes with a message.

> DOM: How did you get that picture?

> MADDIE: Took it myself
> MADDIE: Josh didn't get all the
> photography genes!
> MADDIE: But only because I stole
> some of his talent when he
> passed out after too many
> mojitos one night

I'm proud of myself for making a joke about my brother that wasn't a morbid quip about his death. This seems like growth.

> DOM: You're on the East Coast?
> DOM: At the twins' meet?
> DOM: Right now?

> MADDIE: Yes x 3

Then I send him a selfie of me stuffing a chip covered in nacho cheese into my mouth with the door to the pool behind me.

Apparently, there's no eating in the pool area, so I plan to consume these in record time.

My phone vibrates.

DOM: Why didn't you tell me you
were going to be there?

Yeah, I guess that's what friends do. Maybe I should have. But I have the same excuse I gave the twins.

MADDIE: In New York for a work
thing. Wasn't sure I'd even get
away long enough for the swim
meet

The nacho cheese doesn't retain heat well and is already starting to lose some of its gooeyness. One more reason to scarf them down.

DOM: You should have told me
DOM: I'm driving up now

I suck in a breath, then cough to dislodge a chip that tried to sneak down my throat.

He's coming here?

The twins said their family probably wouldn't make this meet.

Maybe it was always Dom's plan to come, and he just couldn't make it to the first half. These things are *long*. This must be a surprise for Adam and Carter.

He's not coming for me.

MADDIE: Cool
MADDIE: I might not see you, I
can't stay the whole time

Then, horror of horror, my phone rings. I stare at Dom's name on my screen and consider ignoring it. But just like with my mom, I can't.

Besides, he's probably calling because he's driving, and texting isn't safe.

Also, my nachos are done, so I guess my mouth is technically free to talk.

Don't be mean to him. Don't hurt his feelings on purpose. He's your friend, I remind myself.

I swipe to accept the call as I toss out my trash.

"Dom," I say instead of hello. "Calling is for emergencies and extroverts. I consider this a form of harassment." I never promised to stop being sarcastic.

"Noted." His deep voice rumbles through the line, and I try to convince myself I shiver from the humidity that clings to my skin and not from the simple act of hearing him speak a single word to me. "How long can you stay at the meet?"

"You are an introvert and that's not an emergency question," I mutter as I pull my phone away from my ear so I can check the time. "Maybe two hours. But that would be pushing it. I'm not going to catch their last race."

"That should work. I'll text you when I'm there."

What should work? Does he want to make sure there's someone here the whole time cheering for them?

That's sweet.

"Cool. I'm heading back in. Drive safe. Don't speed."

"I never speed." He sounds affronted.

"Of course not. I forgot who I was talking to."

An hour and forty-five minutes later, my phone buzzes in my pocket.

DOM: I'm stuck in traffic. Can you
wait for me?

I mark my page in the book I've been reading in between Adam and Carter's events and tuck it into my bag. Then I pull up the map app on my phone and do the math of travel time plus dropping off my rental car and getting through security. Really, I should already be on the road. I send a quick goodbye and good luck text to the twins, then respond to Dom.

> MADDIE: I'm sorry. I've got to get to the airport
> MADDIE: The twins will be happy to see you!
> MADDIE: I mean not so happy that they'll rip their pants off for you
> MADDIE: That was just for me
> MADDIE: But I'm sure they'll give you a hug or something

DOM: What does that mean?
DOM: The thing about the pants?
DOM: Why were my brothers taking their pants off for you?
DOM: Traffic is moving

> MADDIE: It was only Adam
> MADDIE: I've really got to go
> MADDIE: I'll see you in a few months!

I make it to my gate just in time.

See? If I hung around longer, I would've missed it.

As I settle into my aisle seat—I always choose bathroom access over window view—I consider what missing my flight would have meant. Rescheduling, obviously. Would have probably had to stay overnight in New York, or maybe in Philly. Do Adam and Carter have an extra bed at their place? If they do, it's probably a gross college-boy futon. Booking a hotel room would've been a more sanitary option.

I would've had a whole evening with the Perry boys. That's never happened before. Just the three of them and me.

Would Dom have stayed the night, too? Maybe shared a hotel room with me?

An empty dip in my stomach that feels an awful lot like regret has me wishing I was still in a chlorine-scented room instead of listening to a flight safety speech about how my seat is a flotation device.

When I step off my cross-country flight, bleary-eyed and in need of my bed, I turn off airplane mode on my phone to see a few texts from the Perrys.

CARTER: Thanks for coming, it was
cool having you cheer us on like old
times
ADAM: Maddie!!!!! I won all of my
races for you!!! You're good luck!!!
DOM: I wish you'd told me you were
coming
DOM: Text me when you get home
safe

Once I've settled in the back seat of my rideshare, I send the twins a kissy face emoji.

But for Dom I wake myself up enough to type out a message.

MADDIE: Safe in Seattle
MADDIE: Sorry I missed you
buddy

DOM: Are you home?

MADDIE: In an Uber

DOM: That's not home safe.
DOM: What's the driver's rating?
DOM: Screen shot their profile to me.

MADDIE: I'm not doing that

DOM: Share your location with me.

MADDIE: Oh my god
MADDIE: I am at my building
MADDIE: I am in my building

DOM: Thank you.

MADDIE: I am in front of the
elevator
MADDIE: I am inside the elevator

DOM: I see what you're doing.

MADDIE: I am at floor 1
MADDIE: Floor 2

DOM: Got it.

MADDIE: Floor 3
MADDIE: Floor 4

DOM: What floor do you live on?

> MADDIE: Floor 5
>
> MADDIE: That's both where I live
> and where I am
>
> MADDIE: Halfway down the hall

DOM: Noted.

> MADDIE: In front of my door
>
> MADDIE: Key in the door

DOM: Maddie . . . are you talking dirty
to me?

I trip over my threshold and almost drop my phone. The sleepiness that fogged my brain since halfway through the flight evaporates in response to the heat roaring under my skin.

But I refuse to let Dom know he shook me.

> MADDIE: You caught me
>
> MADDIE: Hope it was good for
> you

The three dots appear and disappear on his screen multiple times, and I snort. Dominic Perry tried to make a naughty joke and now he can't follow through on it.

> MADDIE: Going to bed
>
> MADDIE: Tell the twins they were
> awesome and they're my favorite
> Perrys

DOM: I'm not doing that.

DOM: Good night.

DOM: Text me when you make it to
your bed safe.

MADDIE: You need help

I fall asleep smiling.

Spring

Twenty-Four

I survive six months without a new message from my brother and only long-distance correspondence with Dominic Perry. On the anniversary of Josh's death, I hid in a spa bathroom in a fuzzy robe and texted Dom, asking for pictures of the letters we had opened so far.

Less than five minutes later, the images came through, and I read them as eagerly as the first time.

Dom's name had then promptly lit up on my phone, calling me. I ignored it. Mainly because I was afraid all the grief in my chest would twist into anger like it tended to around him and I'd say something awful.

Before I left the bathroom, I texted him a type of apology.

> MADDIE: Can't talk now. Looking
> forward to our next trip.

The trip that we're on now. The views are breathtaking.
Literally.

The hike out here was hell on my lungs. I thought my tendency to walk to all my destinations in the city prepared me for this. But traversing a few blocks in Seattle is a lot different from trekking miles through the South Dakota backcountry, even if the website described it as "flat and easy to walk."

I rightly guessed that at least one of the destinations Josh sent us to involves physically exerting myself. He was a wilderness photographer after all. My brother would want to spend his afterlife in beautiful, remote places.

And that's exactly what the Badlands are. A national park full of prairies and jagged rock formations striped with lines of faded brown, rusty orange, and brick red, each layer designating another moment in time. The place is gorgeous and alien. Dom and I haven't passed another hiker in a while, and I could almost believe we're on another planet.

One full of chubby prairie dogs.

Last night we arrived late at the bed and breakfast I booked for us after my flight got delayed five hours and Dom waited around the whole time. Exhausted from the stress of almost ruining this trip, I mumbled "Good night" to my travel companion, stumbled into my bedroom, and fell into a deep sleep. But Dom made sure to knock on my door first thing this morning so we could get on the trail.

I'm glad I invested in a set of hiking boots. My sneakers would not have done well on some of the rocks we had to scramble over.

"Do you need your inhaler?" Dom asks, staring hard at me rather than the gorgeous vista surrounding us.

We've come to a stop at the exact halfway point of the five-mile trail. Roughly the spot where the coordinates sent us. I wave him off, then brace my hands on my knees and try to remember the breathing exercises a specialist taught me years ago.

Dom hovers a moment longer, then gives me the space I requested. Still, I can feel the concern radiating off him. The sensation isn't as bothersome as it once was. Not since I realized the reaction has more to do with his fear of losing control rather than believing me incapable. At least, I hope he doesn't think the latter.

"Why don't you—" I suck in another breath, the cold, dry air scraping against my lungs. But I power through. "Read the letter?" The hike might not have irritated my lungs so much if there was more humidity. That's the thing about my asthma. There are certain combinations that wreak havoc on my airways.

Confident that I'm not on the verge of passing out, I press my CamelBak mouthpiece past my lips and drink deep. I bought one of the water bladder bags after our ghost-town trip so Dom wouldn't be in charge of my hydration again.

Dom keeps his eyes on me as he slips off his backpack, unzips the outside pocket, and tugs out a familiar envelope.

South Dakota
43°45′50.9″ N
101°58′10.0″ W

But he doesn't immediately open it and start reading. Instead, he strides closer to a cluster of rocks and sets his ass down on a boulder. Then he pats the empty spot beside him.

The command is clear.

Sit.

Or maybe it was a request.

I roll my eyes but decide not to fight him on this. Besides, it is a nice spot to admire the view.

Only when I'm settled at his side does Dom slip a thumb under the fold of the envelope and tear. Instead of watching his fingers unearth the small piece of my brother, I keep my eyes forward on the lines of time marked on the landscape.

And I wait to hear Josh's words in Dom's voice.

Dear Maddie & Dom,

Welcome to South Dakota!
    You should be in the middle of the Badlands right now. That name is pretty awesome, right? And from what I've heard,

inaccurate. Because everyone who's told me about the place says it's a view like no other.

Take it in for me. And take a picture, of course.

Since I sent you on such a long trek, I'm confident you'll find the perfect spot to leave a piece of me behind. Make sure I have a good view. I want to see it all.

Dom pauses in his reading, and I glance over to watch his throat bob as he swallows.

I don't blame him for needing a break after only a few sentences. Even in our voices, all I hear is Josh when we read the letters. I hear his humor. His excitement. His hope.

And his regret.

Maddie.

It takes me a breath to realize Dom's started to read again.

I know the hike couldn't have been easy. But I'm glad you walked it. I hope you think it was worth it. Either way, you deserve a treat.

"Oh hell." I wheeze. "What does that mean?"

Did you know that Dom has a—

"Oh come on, Josh." The man in question groans my brother's name. I grin and bump my shoulder against his. "Keep reading."

Dom shoots me a glare without heat, then returns his attention to the letter and reads with obvious reluctance.

Did you know that Dom has a beautiful singing voice? And did you know that a part of hiking safety is to make plenty of noise to discourage bears from stumbling upon you?

On the return trip, consider Dominic Perry your personal
radio. And I want you to play all my favorite songs.
Enjoy yourself, Magpie.

Love,
Josh

I laugh so hard I start coughing. But the loss of breath is worth
it. And so is this hike if I get to force Dominic Perry to sing for me.

He scowls. "There aren't bears in the Badlands. This isn't fair."

"Oh, Dom, my boy." I pat his shoulder. "Life rarely is. Better you
learn early on. And you heard him. I *deserve* this. Now, what were a
few of Josh's favorites?"

He carefully folds the paper and slips it back into the envelope.
"I distinctly remember him saying he liked silence."

I snort. "Really? Because *I* distinctly remember him playing Paramore on a loop because he had a major crush on Hayley Williams."

Dom sighs. "I can't argue that."

Leaning back on my arms, I admire the prairie grass bending in
the strong wind while sorting through my mental list of Josh's favorite songs so I can be prepared for the hike back.

"Do you think this is the perfect spot?" Dom asks after a stretch.
"To leave him?"

Leave him. My heart beats in a heavy, painful pound.

But, after running my eyes over the beautiful expanse of wilderness, I nod. "Close to perfect as we can get."

I pull the South Dakota Rubbermaid out of my pack and pop the
lid. My knuckles are white from my tense grip, but Dom doesn't
comment on the hint of vulnerability. He's good about that. Letting
me feel how I feel in these hard moments, and simply staying by my
side through them.

I tilt the container so my brother pours out and mixes with the
wind. As the last particles are swept away, a hawk glides overhead,

and I take a small amount of comfort in the idea that Josh might encounter the bird.

Maybe he'll go on a few adventures with it.

"Happy travels," I murmur.

"Time for a picture." Dom slips his phone from his pocket.

I heave myself off the rock, and Dom rises to stand next to me. An idea pops into my head, and I scramble onto the boulder until I'm standing, which puts my head a few inches higher than Dom's.

"I'm going to be the tall one this time," I tell him while holding my hand out for his phone.

He narrows his eyes, but his tight lips fight a smile. And he passes his phone over.

At this elevated position, I easily drape an arm around Dom's broad shoulders, and even with my shorter arms, I manage to snap a selfie of the colorful hills behind us with both of our faces in the frame.

"Looks good. Send it to me when we get reception." I return his phone, then rub my hands together. When we were hiking, the constant movement kept my body plenty warm. But now the chill of the cloudy day seeps past my fleece pullover and into my skin.

"Are you ready to head back?" Dom stares up at me, and I can't help thinking how good he looks in his knitted hat.

"What's the rush?" Even with Josh in the wind, I'm reluctant to leave this spot, knowing that walking away will be the true goodbye.

Dom tilts his head south, and I stare into the distance where some ominous clouds lurk. "There's a chance of storms. Thought it wasn't until later tonight. But from the looks of that, the weather might hit faster than we expected." Tension tightens his voice.

Oof. I'm barely equipped to deal with the outdoors on a decent weather day. Storms and Maddie Sanderson do not mix.

Plus, we have a four-hour drive to North Dakota.

"Yep. Let's go. I'm feeling good." Which is the truth as far as my body is concerned. My breathing has calmed, and this return trip is flat just like the way out here.

I should be good.

I am *not* good.

Ahead of me, Dom hikes at a steady pace while singing "Misery Business." The moment he started "Still Into You," I was in heaven. Josh was right, Dom is a fantastic singer. And once he agrees to a bit, the man commits. The guy has been singing for half an hour. The lung capacity is impressive. As is the knowledge of Paramore's backlist.

This experience would be perfect if each inhale didn't feel like forcing honey through a straw wrapped in rubber bands.

"Break!" I wheeze out, settling on a relatively flat rock and trying to get as much air into my lungs as I can before Dom realizes how much I'm struggling. He appears before me, all broad shoulders and brooding. "I'm fine," I gasp.

"You would be. If we had time."

I jerk back in surprise. I fully expected Dom to say, *You're not fine, Maddie. You're a mess. You can't breathe. Where's your inhaler?*

"I've been pushing our pace." Dom glances toward the sky, and I follow his gaze to spy the dark clouds gathering directly above us. The wind has also picked up, grabbing at the hair that's fallen out of my ponytail.

A storm is coming, and with the harsh chill in the air—the same one drying out my throat—I'm betting we're about to get snowfall in the Badlands.

Dom crouches in front of me, his eyes worried. "On a nice day, I know you could hike this, Maddie. We could break when you needed and take our time, and I wouldn't try to take over. I swear. But I'm worried we'll get stuck here if we don't pick up the pace. Honestly,

I'm not sure we should drive to North Dakota today, either. Not if it starts snowing."

"I'm going as fast as I can." The words aren't defensive. They're hopeless.

This is my best, I'm saying. *If I push myself more, I'll be out of commission.*

Dom reaches for my hands. "Let me carry you. Please."

"What?" I shake my head. "You can't do that."

Dom's lips tilt up at the corner. "Wanna bet?"

His playful expression disarms me. "Yeah, actually. I do."

He shrugs. "Fine. What are your terms?"

Hmm. A game. That's always how Josh got me out of my shell, too.

An evil, playful urge rises in me.

"If you *can't* carry me all the way back to the car, then . . . I get your letterman jacket."

Dom barks out a laugh. "You came up with that fast. Deal. If I win . . ." His eyes drag over my body, then return to my face. "You have to let me stay the night at your place before we go to Idaho."

I gape. "You want to stay at *my* place? Why?"

His smile grows to a full grin. "I'll tell you when I win." Dom slips off the straps of his backpack and situates the bag to hang on the front of his body. Then he crouches, facing away from me in the universal sign of *Climb on, it's time for a piggyback ride.*

I heave off my rocky seat, wrap my arms around Dom's neck, and let him hook a grip under both of my legs. Then the man straightens, standing easily, as if my extra weight means nothing.

"Let me know if you need to stop," he says over his shoulder as he strikes out on the trail.

"Let me know when *you* need to set me down," I taunt back. "Hell, I'm gonna look so cool in that jacket. All the cheerleaders are going to be *so* jealous."

Dom snorts, and I feel the way his chest jumps with the abrupt exhale. In this position, there's not much about Dom I don't feel, even through my layers. The guy is like a walking, talking oven, toasting the front of my body where I'm mashed against his back. My boobs are flattened against the shifting muscles of his shoulders. Not that I'm complaining.

But I might need a distraction.

"Hey, Dom." As I speak into his ear, I spy goose bumps scattering along his strong neck.

He swallows. "Yeah?"

I rest my chin on my bicep and wonder if he can see my smirk out of the corner of his eye.

"This doesn't get you out of singing. Josh also had a crush on Avril Lavigne. Let's hear some 'Sk8ter Boi.'"

CHAPTER

Twenty-Five

Dom wins.

He carries me through the fucking snow. *Singing*. Only for the last quarter mile, but still.

"Damn," I mutter when he sets me down at the edge of the parking lot, my teeth clicking with shivers now that I don't have his delicious warmth pressed up against me. "I really wanted that jacket."

The man gives me a cocky smile and a deep chuckle as he scoops up my hand and draws me across the gravel toward our car. It's the last one left in the lot.

"Maybe I'll let you borrow it." Dom holds my door open for me, and once again I notice I don't instinctively prickle at the caretaking gesture.

Because we're friends. I'm being a good friend, like Josh wanted.

I should've known that even snow wouldn't be able to force Dom to lose control of a car. As we leave the trailhead, the flakes start to fall in heavy clumps, but he simply turns on the four-wheel drive and guides us through the storm.

A trip to North Dakota isn't going to happen today, and we decide to try our luck at the bed and breakfast I booked us last night. As I'm entering the address into Dom's phone's GPS, an incoming message pops up.

"You have a text from Adam."

"Read it to me." He keeps his focus on the road that's quickly turning white.

I dramatically clear my throat and try to sound like Dom's younger brother.

ADAM: I need some advice about an opportunity.

The message goes into detail about how some big-name artisanal furniture designer offered him a full-time paid gig working in his shop after graduation, but Adam is worried about giving up on swimming when it was always the plan to pursue the Olympics.

I've seen some of Adam's work when he posts pictures and videos on his socials, but I didn't realize woodworking was anything more than a hobby. Guilt scratches at my heart. I should have kept up with him all these years. Now Adam and Carter are practically strangers. There's so much to rebuild between us, so much I missed while hiding away on the other side of the country.

"What should I text back?" I ask.

Dom rests his left elbow on the car door and pinches his bottom lip, appearing thoughtful. And my traitorous body starts tingling and growing overly warm as I stare at the contemplating man.

"Tell him I'll call him tomorrow to talk it through."

"Got it." I start typing. "How many emojis should I use?"

"None."

"Three it is. The thoughtful face lets him know you're thinking deeply about what he asked. And then the smiling one with hearts tells him you appreciate that he came to you with such an important question. What should the third one be?"

"Maddie." His warning tone doesn't intimidate me.

"I'm a fan of the kissy face—"

"I'm pulling over."

"Fine! Fine, no emojis. But don't blame me if your message reads like nonsense without them."

Even as I teased Dom, I had already sent off his basic text and got a thumbs-up from Adam in response. I settle the phone back on the dashboard mount so Dom knows where to go, and hope we arrive before the snow picks up. After a handful of mile markers pass, I voice a question that's been nagging me.

"Why do you think Adam texted you, and not your parents? To ask about the apprenticeship?"

Mr. Perry might have a busy work schedule, but I know he loves his kids and makes time for them. And Emilia is one of the sweetest women I know. I bet she'd love to hear about Adam's job offer.

I never called Cecilia, because she never cared about my life.

I always called Josh.

Or I figured things out on my own.

I guess that second one is my only option now.

Dom tilts his head side to side, letting out a delicious joint crack with each movement. "Mom and Dad are supportive of whatever, but they also have this expectation that we figure things out on our own. Especially with the twins being adults now." He grimaces. "In theory, it might sound like a good parenting technique. Let your kids try, fail, learn, and make sure they take responsibility for their mistakes."

"You don't agree?"

Dom scratches the back of his neck. "To an extent. But I would've appreciated advice sometimes. From someone who'd lived life longer than me. From someone I trusted."

"And that's what you do for Adam and Carter?"

"When they let me."

Not for the first time, I think back on their family dynamic. The Perry parents were always fun, and buoyant, and happy to cheer whoever on. They were kind and loving.

But Mr. Perry also spent a lot of hours working at the hospital and Emilia's nonprofit demanded way more than a forty-hour work-week. Dom was the responsible one at home, taking on a parent-like role for his younger siblings.

"They look up to you," I say.

Dom huffs a laugh. "Maybe. Doesn't mean they listen to me."

"Sure they do." I keep going when Dom throws me a skeptical side-eye. "Okay, maybe not one hundred percent of the time. But they listen to you more than anyone else."

"Not more than you."

I open my mouth to argue, but all that comes out is "What?"

Dom keeps his eyes on the snowy road. "You're the one they listen to. You're the Perry twins whisperer." His lips tick up in a smirk that immediately fades as his fingers tighten on the steering wheel. "With everything that happened, I never got a chance to thank you. For how you helped us out. That summer."

That summer.

The one after my freshman year of college, when I saw Dom for the first time in months. He'd always had an air of responsibility, but the first few days of that summer, I was afraid he was going to combust from repressed anxiety.

His mother's car accident almost destroyed him.

I've always thought of it as the summer Dom discarded me. But it's also the summer when an illegal left turn plowed into the side of Mrs. Perry's Prius and sent the woman to the hospital. The same one where her husband worked.

How must that have felt, for Nathanial to learn his wife was a few floors down in the ER, battered, bruised, and bleeding?

I never talked with Dom's dad about it—we weren't close like that—but I do know he took off work for maybe the first time in his whole life. Emilia was laid up in bed for weeks, needing help with everything, then she had to go to PT. Dom was supposed to start a full-time internship, but Josh told me Mr. Perry wanted him to turn it down and take care of his brothers and help with his mom when the surgeon had to return to work.

Yes, I helped, but it was selfish, really. I wanted to escape my grandmother and spend more time around the Perrys. I wanted to pretend their family was mine as much as I could.

"I spent the summer poolside." I shrug. "Not a hardship."

"Just you being around made everything easier." He taps a random rhythm on the wheel with his thumbs. "Adam had a huge crush on you."

I snort. "You were a fan of your teenage brother lusting after me? Didn't seem so happy about it at the funeral."

Dom stares straight ahead, but I spy the corner quiver that tells me he's fighting against a smile.

"You know . . ." I adopt a contemplative tone. "Maybe I should be making these trips with Adam. Since I was so pivotal in his life."

"Not happening," Dom grumbles without an ounce of heat. He reaches over and claims my hand, his long fingers interlocking with mine.

For a moment, I sit motionless, trying to come to terms with the casually affectionate touch.

Is this what friends do? They hold hands?

Even if they do, I don't think the heat of a friend's palm is supposed to send achy flutters shooting through my body.

Still, I manage to breathe normally. No stutters or gasps to have Dom questioning the move.

He also tried to hold my hand on the glow worm trip. Maybe Dom just likes to grasp things.

"Let's get back to why Adam having a crush was a good thing," I press, resolving to ponder friendship hand-holding later. "In *your* opinion."

Dom sighs but relents. "He did anything you told him. If Mom or

Dad or I asked him to take out the garbage, it would've been fifteen minutes of complaining followed by a half-assed job." His eyes sweep over me before returning to the road. "You'd come over and say, 'Adam, stop being lazy and go take out the trash.' He *sprinted*. Chore done in record time. No complaints. Back again asking for more."

Now that I think about it, I do recall Emilia and Dom asking me to convey a lot of simple requests to Adam. At the time, I was happy to help in any way, even if that meant being a courier pigeon. But apparently, I was also acting as a buffer against teenage rebellion. The thought has me fighting another snort of laughter.

"Did you know Carter is dyslexic?" The random piece of information throws me out of my humorous mood.

"I-I . . . No. I didn't." Another detail I might have known if I hadn't disappeared from their lives.

The half of Dom's smile I can see looks pained. "None of us did for a while. What we did know was that he was smart but doing bad in school. Mom would let out these hopeless sighs whenever report cards came out. Dad would get so frustrated. I mean, the man was all about hands-free, figure it out, but then got aggravated when you *didn't* figure it out. Carter . . . he couldn't do anything. He didn't know what was wrong. He would just shut down." Dom rubs a thumb over my knuckles. "I think that's why Adam started acting out. To take the pressure off Carter. Yeah, maybe his grades were bad, but he didn't fill all the locker-room drains with bubble bath."

"What happened?" I feel like complete shit that I don't know any of this. All I know is that Carter was in that graduation photo alongside Adam, so something must have changed.

"The entire locker room exploded with suds after the homecoming football game."

"No. Not that. Though that sounds amazing, and I want to circle back later." *Adam, you evil genius.* "What happened with Carter?"

Dom squeezes my hand. A comforting pressure.

"You remember those graphic novels you were always checking out from the library for him?"

I nod. Sometimes Carter would sit under my umbrella with me and flip through them, lacking the daylong social stamina of Adam.

"He kept getting them. Even after you . . ." Dom clears his throat. "After you were gone. He read them all the time. Started sneaking them into class, reading them there, too. One of his teachers saw how he always had them and asked why he liked them so much. He told her that with the pictures he could read the story even when the words didn't make sense." Dom's voice is thick now. "She figured it out. Fourteen years old and no one else had. Some public school education. He could barely read and was going to get pushed straight through to high school. Guess it goes to show how clever he was, though, huh? That he still got by. Was able to hide how much he was struggling."

My heart aches for the quiet teenager I used to know. "But he's doing better now?"

"Once Mom and Dad knew, they talked to the school and set him up with a specialist tutor. He wants to be a writer now. Did you know that? Wants to tell stories. He's studying creative writing with a minor in design." His thumb strokes the length of mine. "One more way you helped that summer. The twins were obsessed with you. Mom adored you. Dad kept trying to give you money just so you'd stick around. And I . . ."

Silence descends in the car, and I try not to let resentment into my voice when I finally fill it.

"You were grateful for my help," I finish for him.

His grip tightens. "Not exactly."

"Then what, exactly?"

Dom's jaw firms, then relaxes. "When you helped me, I could breathe. When I could breathe, I could see you."

My stomach bottoms out as if we just tilted over the top of a roller coaster. But we're actually slowing down, turning into the parking lot for the B&B. The wild ride is all with this man at my side who I'm not sure I've ever truly known.

"And do you see me now?" I whisper, the sound more vulnerable than I ever thought I'd let myself be with Dominic Perry again.

He doesn't hesitate on his answer.

"You're all I see."

CHAPTER

Twenty-Six

If it weren't for the risk of getting entombed in the rental car by fast-falling snow, I would've sat in stunned silence for another hour.

"You're all I see."

That's what Dom said. About *me*.

Then he says, "Get out of the car, Maddie. You're not allowed to freeze to death."

Slightly less life-altering than the former statement.

Dom climbs out from behind the wheel, then circles around to my door, helping me from the car and holding my hand as we trudge through the steadily growing snowdrifts. If our hike had taken longer, I'm not sure even Dom could have driven us back here. We knock the clinging snow off our boots before pushing into the warm house. There's a real fire burning in the sitting room that I wish I could hurry over to and soak in the smoky heat.

But I follow Dom to the front desk instead.

"Oh goodness! Did you two get turned around by the storm?" Sandra, a gray-haired white woman with kind blue eyes, gazes at us with concern from her spot behind the desk. She co-owns the B&B with her husband, Alan, a soft-spoken Korean American man with hooded eyes and an easy smile.

"It did." Dom offers Sandra a rueful smile. "Would we be able to book our rooms for an extra night?"

"Oh, well, those rooms are already claimed, unfortunately."

My stomach dips as I meet Dom's eyes.

What are we going to do?

Even driving across town would be treacherous at this point.

"But," Sandra chirps, "don't you worry. We've got space for you all. The Morning Room—we call it that because it has the best light first thing in the morning—is open. You'll have to bunk together, but there's a queen bed and a daybed in there. Plenty of room. How's that sound?"

Dom and I meet stares again, only I can't read a single thought on his stoic face.

Together.

Sleeping together.

In a room *together*, I remind myself. *Not sleeping together, exactly.*

"Yeah." I croak the word when I realize Dom is waiting for my final say on the matter. I clear my throat. "That would be great."

It's not like we have any other choice.

I accept our key as Dom heads out to the car to grab our bags. Like a moth, I'm drawn toward the fire, standing in the radius of its glow. A moment later Dom joins me, his body giving off almost as much heat as the bare flames dancing near my fingers, despite his having just come in from the snow.

"We might not be able to make it to North Dakota tomorrow, either, if this keeps up," he murmurs.

I follow his gaze to the window, where the snow continues to fall in a white blur. Wind rattles the windows, and I soak in the ambiance of the place.

"We can see how it is in the morning. If it's still coming down, maybe Sandra will let us book the Morning Room for another night."

Another night sleeping in the same room as Dom.

You're all I see.

My skin flushes, but I easily blame the flames.

He nods and we stand beside each other for a stretch until Sandra peeks her head in the sitting area.

"Getting rough out there. Don't you worry, though. Alan is making sandwiches and I've got soup brewing. You come to the dining room once you get settled, and we'll feed you."

"Thank you, Sandra," Dom says, resting his hand low on my back to guide me away from the fire, as if he thinks I can't be trusted with it if he leaves the room.

Maybe I can't. I love fireplaces so much I want to curl up inside the crackling flames.

In our room, I take the bathroom first, turning on the hot water in the shower. My skin feels gross, covered in sweat from our hike that's now dried on my skin. I strip everything off and leave it in a pile in the corner. When I step under the hot water, I groan in relief. The soap is a delicious minty scent, and I suds up my whole body, then rinse off quick. I want to linger, but Dom still needs to take his turn. When I finish, I pat my body dry, then wrap my hair in a towel. Once I have on the complimentary robe, I scoop up my dirty clothes and head back to the bedroom. Dom slips past me the moment I step out, shutting the door between us with a definitive click.

While I wait for him to finish showering, I pull on a clean sweater and leggings, then towel my hair and examine the daybed. It looks plenty comfortable, covered in pillows and soft blankets. It sits under a window that shows the winter wonderland building outside. Overall, a perfectly cozy sleeping spot.

And yet, my eyes track to the four-poster bed. *That* looks like a mattress someone could sink into and not want to leave for days.

Especially if they're next to a certain man—

"Stop it," I mutter, shaking my head.

Dom has held my hand and given me a piggyback ride and said

sweet things that could mean more . . . but he hasn't mentioned the airport kiss.

We're pretending it never happened. We're moving past the wrongs in our past and becoming friends. That's what is important.

You're all I see. His words whisper to me. A statement that sounds more intimate than anything two friends share.

But I don't want to make the mistakes of the past. What if I'm misinterpreting? What if I'm misunderstanding?

I cannot make another move only to be rejected again.

I busy myself with finding a thick pair of wool socks and pull them on. Dom reappears with damp hair and a freshly washed look. He has on a different pair of jeans with a long-sleeved thermal.

"Let's go eat," I mutter, suddenly grumpy with how tempting the man is.

Maybe I could sleep on the fainting couch by the fire, so I don't have to think about him in a bed only feet from me.

In the dining room we find small tables arranged with individual place settings. Two are already occupied by the other house visitors. Dom and I claim one in the far corner near a large window. It's too dark outside to see far, but an exterior light reveals the flakes are still cascading down relentlessly.

"This is good sleeping weather," Sandra announces as she approaches our table with a wide smile. "But you'll want a full belly first. Now, we have chicken noodle soup, grilled cheese, and roast beef sandwiches. What can I get you two?"

After we give her our orders—I get the grilled cheese because that's the only correct choice—Sandra bustles off toward the kitchen, leaving us alone.

"That was some impressive snow driving you did," I offer. "Don't think we slid once."

Dom grunts and focuses on arranging his silverware just so. He's not looking at me.

I try again. "Guess since you won our bet, you'll be wanting to crash at my place when you come out my way. When did you want to do Idaho?"

"Not sure," he murmurs, his attention sliding from his utensils to the snowy window.

"Have you looked up the coordinates?"

"Yes." When he doesn't expand, I try not to grind my teeth in irritation.

"And?" I press.

"It's another hike." Dom glances around the room, eyeing the other patrons.

Apparently, I'm boring him. "A hike. Cool. I'll make sure I'm ready for that." *So you don't have to carry me again*, I silently add.

Dom nods and just then our food comes out. He's quiet for the rest of the meal, and so am I because I don't want my attempts at conversation to get shot down again. I seethe quietly, only forcing a smile when Sandra approaches our table again, this time carrying a tray of steaming mugs.

"This is Alan's special hot toddy. He's perfected the recipe. Just what you need on a snowy night. Would you like one?"

A drink to help distract me from the tension at this table? "Yes, please!" I hold my hands out for one of the warm mugs. Sandra grins wide, passes me the beverage, and heads off to the next table when Dom gives her a tight smile and shakes his head no.

I purse my lips to blow on the hot liquid, wanting a warm sip but not a scalding one.

A hand appears over the fragrant cocktail, blocking me from taking a taste.

"Wait." Dom stares at me, determination in his eyes. "Don't drink that."

"What's up with you?" I snap, my temper making a reappearance. I thought I'd started to get over the insecure irritation Dom inspires in me. But his statue act since arriving at the B&B is wearing on me.

I assume he regrets what he said in the car. That he knows I took it to mean more than he meant.

"Could you . . . just wait? Don't drink."

My cheeks heat. "Do you think I have a problem or something? I normally only have a drink one or two nights a week. I'm not guzzling gin to get through the day."

Plus, a hot toddy sounds *so* good right now. Warm lemon and honey with a touch of cloves and the sting of whiskey.

"It's not that." Dom retracts his hand, and when I don't immediately toss back my mug, he keeps talking in a rush. "Every time you've kissed me, it's been after you've had a few drinks." His jaw tenses, then relaxes. "And then you run away. I don't want it to become a pattern."

I jerk my head back.

He's not exactly wrong.

Still, it's not *all* my fault.

"What don't you want to be a pattern?" I ask. "Me kissing you? Me getting tipsy to do it?" I cross my arms and glare into his too-handsome face.

"I don't want it to be a pattern for you to kiss me while in a state where I'm not sure if you actually want to or not." He leans over the small table, dark eyes holding me immobile. "If you're inebriated, I'm not about to take advantage of you. No matter how badly I want to suck on that pouty lip you're sticking out right now."

Said pouty lip falls open along with my jaw. Then I splutter. "I haven't been drunk *every* time we kissed."

Dom raises a brow. "Gin on the plane. Beer, gin, and tequila in Delaware. And we were drinking that first time, too."

He's right. That summer night, I wanted to treat a stressed-out Dom to his favorite beer. I'd convinced a pool lifeguard to buy me a six-pack of Coors Light—Dom was twenty-one, I assume he has more refined taste now—and I split it with him. Two light beers did not equate to drunk for teenage me. More like just tipsy enough to be brave.

But from the anguish on Dom's face, the detail stuck with him.

"I've never, not once, had a sober kiss from you, Maddie. And it kills me."

I gape across the table at the man I thought I knew. My brother's best friend who I believed only ever saw me as an obligation. A responsibility. The pitiful little neighbor girl in need of a charity hookup that he immediately regretted.

Ever since Arizona, I've been trying my hardest to situate Dom into the friend category.

Trying my best not to resent him.

Trying my best not to fall in love with him.

Friendship. A simple, clear goal.

But he wants a kiss from me so bad it *kills* him?

"How are you kids doing?" Sandra arrives at our table, unaware of the tense weight of our conversation.

After a bracing breath, I offer her a smile. "Good, only I realized I'm pretty tired. If I drink this, it'll send me straight to sleep. Thank you, though." I slide the still-steaming mug toward our hostess.

"Maddie—" Dom starts.

"Oh, no problem. You both had an adventurous day. Remember there are extra blankets in your closet and breakfast is served at eight tomorrow morning. Have a good night." The innkeeper scoops up my drink and offers a wink only I can see before hustling away.

Across the small table I meet Dom's guarded eyes.

"Come on." Standing, I manage to speak with a relatively steady tone. "We're finishing this conversation upstairs."

Twenty-Seven

"I'm not going to kiss you."

Dom freezes facing the door he just finished closing. I've shocked him.

Maybe. I don't know.

And that's the problem with Dom. I never know. These past few hours, I've been trying to figure out if Dom is attracted to me.

When I stepped over the threshold to our room, I settled on an important realization.

It's not my job to figure it out.

It's Dom's.

Dom needs to decide if he's hot for me. Then it's his job to tell me that.

"You're not going to kiss me," he repeats. Dom faces me, expression unreadable. As usual.

"Nope. To clarify, I *will* participate if kissing occurs."

His brows dip. "How does that clarify things?"

I plop onto the daybed, bouncing on the squeaky springs. "Here. I'll simplify it even more." From across the room, I hold his gaze with mine. I do not cower or shy away. I do not rely on alcohol to make me brave. I do not guess or hope. I simply ask, "Dom, do you want to fuck me?"

Shit. I meant to say "kiss."

Really, I did. I swear!

But also, I would like the answer to the question I asked, too.

Dom's thick brows creep up and there's a touch of slackness around his mouth.

There's also silence.

Maybe it's a count of five. Maybe it's a count of fifty. There are no accurate or inaccurate clocks in my eyeline for me to measure the passage of time.

All I know is I reach the point where his silence becomes an answer.

"Got it." I veer my stare toward the window, focusing on the snow and wishing we had separate rooms.

"Maddie." The mattress dips as Dom settles at my side, which is annoying because he could easily *not* put his tempting body right next to mine as he rejects me.

Again.

What's this, number four? Will I ever learn?

"Dom." I mock his low voice because I will never be a fully mature adult.

"Look at me."

"Nah. I'm good."

Lies. I'm not good at all. Even when I'm trying to keep an emotional wall between Dom and me, I still find a way to leave myself vulnerable to his rejection. When the lights go out, I'm definitely sneaking downstairs to sleep on the couch.

"Maddie—"

"Stop saying my name!" I whirl and glare at him. "I'm the only person in this room! Who else would you be talking to? Just *say* what you want to say."

The fucking asshole has the nerve to grin at me. Then he cups the back of my neck in a gentle, yet firm hold and pulls my face to his, pausing when only a breath divides us.

"If I tell you I want to fuck you"—he speaks the words so close our lips brush—"can I kiss you, too?"

Oh.

My pulse thunders, and Dom has to feel my rapid heartbeat with his hand almost fully wrapped around my neck in a possessive, erotic, and yet somehow comforting gesture.

"Well, if you insist that there's a certain order to these things." My sarcastic comment comes out breathless. "Keep in mind, we can shuffle what people might label as the traditional sequence of events."

"Maddie Sanderson." This time Dom growls my name, and I shiver at the sound of it. "How dare you suggest I do things out of order? I might malfunction."

I'm in the middle of a laugh when Dom kisses me.

He kisses *me.*

Finally.

And as I might have expected with Dom, he takes full control of the action. His mouth claims mine as his thumb presses against my chin, tilting my head into position with a single finger. My lip that he labeled as "pouty" gets thoroughly chastised with a tonguing and reprimanding bite.

What's more, he doesn't suffocate me with his kisses. There have been so many times I had to stop a make-out session because my lungs protested the depleted oxygen. But not with Dom. He ravishes my mouth for a moment, then allows me uninterrupted inhales as he focuses on my cheeks, the edge of my jaw, the soft spot just below my ear. Then he comes back for another round of ravishment before letting me breathe again.

Dom is so good with only his mouth that wetness gathers between my legs. I press my thighs together to heighten the sensation.

Somehow, he knows.

A heavy hand lands on my thigh, then sinks between them. Dom cups me over my leggings as his mouth continues to explore and demand. His touch is a weighty, all-encompassing pressure that I rock against. I go so far as to grab his forearm, wrapping my hands around the muscled limb and grinding like he's a stripper pole.

"Hell," Dom groans into my open mouth. "You're soaked. I can feel it." His hand presses hard, and his tongue drags along mine. "I want to feel more."

When Dom slides his hold out from between my legs, I let out a pathetic whine. But a second later his fingers slip past my waistband and delve through my curls, a hot demanding touch against my sensitive folds.

At first, it's amazing.

Everything I could ever want.

His strong fingers approach where I ache, promising pleasure only he can give me.

But then everything about this moment becomes a little too familiar.

Suddenly, I'm back on the swing on the Perry's porch, Dom kissing me slow, his hand going where only mine had been before. The way he'd touched me that summer was world-altering. He stroked and explored until my body fell apart for him.

And as I trembled in his arms, Dom tucked me close, kissed my neck, and told me I did good.

Then the next day he chose someone else.

Slamming back into the present moment, I shove Dom's hand away, rip my mouth from his, and scramble off the bed.

Distance. I need space.

But standing, seeing his lips swollen from kisses and his cheeks flushed and his eyes hungry, does nothing to ease the amount I crave him. Or the way I fear what he could do to me if I let him in again.

"Maddie?"

"I can't do that," I blurt, and Dom stiffens.

His face begins to shutter, all the wanting he showed me getting forcefully repressed.

My gut clenches, regret clawing at my insides.

"You don't have to," he says. "You don't have to do anything you don't want to."

"I know," I growl, frustrated with him and myself. This was going so well a moment ago. "And I still want to do things. Just . . . can you not finger me?"

Dom pauses his emotional withdrawal, tilting his head to study me. "You don't like it?"

Physically, I love it. Mentally, it's tied up with some shit I thought I got over.

Even if he fingers me tonight, it doesn't mean he'll leave me for Rosaline tomorrow, I lecture myself.

Still, I just can't. It's too close to repeating the past.

"I want to do something else," I say instead of answering his question.

"Whatever you want, Maddie. If you want to cuddle, we can do that." He spreads his arms. "This doesn't have to be sexual."

Great. Mr. Responsible Asshole strolled his way into the building to remind me that orgasming with a man I hated not too long ago—and live on the opposite side of the country from—may not be the smartest idea.

"Could you shut up and take your pants off?" I snap.

Back off, phone sex operators, Maddie Sanderson is coming for your job.

Dom's brows dip as he stares at me, and I wait for him to refuse. To insist we change course. To *talk*.

Then his long-fingered hands settle at his waistband, where his thermal has ridden up a few inches. I spy that stretch of skin on his lower belly that I want to suck on like sour candy. Dom rubs the fabric, and that's when I see the decent-sized bulge pressing against his jeans.

"These pants?" Dom asks, as if he needs guidance.

I gape.

The asshole is *taunting* me. I can see it in the way his lips firm, pressing away a smile.

I click my mouth shut before I accidentally grin. "Yes, Dom. Those pants." I try to sound unaffected. "Take them off."

"Why?" He drags a thumb under the waistband, but even though we can both see his arousal through the material, he doesn't follow my order.

"Because I want to see if you stuffed a bunch of socks in there for a confidence boost, obviously."

As Dom barks a surprised laugh, I stalk back over to the daybed. Then I stand between his spread knees and loom over him as much as I can manage, glaring into his melty brown eyes.

"I want you to take your pants off, because I want to make you come."

Because he's had one of my orgasms for years, and now I need a return. To be balanced.

To prove this isn't some pity hookup.

I need Dominic Perry to fall apart at *my* hands. Because it seems like I'm the only one ever crumbling to pieces in this pair.

"What if *I* want to make *you* come?" he asks, reaching out to palm my thigh before dragging his hand upward until his touch is under my sweater and caressing the overheated skin of my waist.

I'm going to need these clothes off soon so I don't pass out from heatstroke. Maybe we should crack the window and let some of that snowstorm in.

But first, his question requires an answer.

"Dominic Perry. I'm offering to lick and suck your cock until you come in my mouth. That is a high-quality orgasm offer. I don't hand them out to just anyone." Leaning in, I place a gentle kiss on his lips and enjoy the ragged way he exhales. "Now, do you want me to retract my offer, or do you want to take your pants off?"

Leaving him to what I hope is an easy decision, I step back, cross my arms, and raise a single eyebrow in challenge.

Dom's chest rises and falls in slow, heavy breaths.

And finally, the man undoes the button on his jeans and tugs down the zipper. But since he is a man of order, Dom reroutes, pulling his shirt over his head in one smooth move.

I bite my lip to keep from groaning at the sight of his bare chest. Plenty of nights over these past months, I've lain in bed thinking of the time when he pulled me into the pool and I ended up wrapped around him. I would imagine dragging my nails down over his taut skin as he tugged my sleep shorts to the side and slipped inside me while the water cradled us.

But I don't need to imagine tonight, because he's reclined in front of me, toeing off his shoes and shoving down his pants and briefs. In the quiet room, I hear the slap of his erection popping free and hitting his stomach. Dom's tip is ruddy, and I wonder if there's any pain mixed in with his pleasure. If he's so hard that he's desperate for me to ease him.

The idea has me licking my lips. But before I approach, I return the favor and take off my clothes, too. Quickly, because I'm not in a teasing mood.

Bare, I fall to my knees in front of him.

"Hell," Dom mutters, and I love the irresponsible words I make him say.

As I grip his base firmly with one hand, I let the other slide down my body. As I set the head on my bottom lip, I part my intimate folds. As I lick the precum off his tip, I find my needy clit. As I draw him in with deep, wet sucks, I press and rub myself.

He tastes heady, not like any food, only like sex and wanting and years of need. From the corner of my eye, I watch the way his fingers fist the soft comforter, knuckles turning white.

My clitoris hums with a pulse of its own as I stroke. Moans spill from my throat and vibrate against Dom's cock as I suck him down slow and breathe deep through my nose.

"Maddie." He says my name with disbelief. "Are you . . . Fuck. You're fingering yourself right now?" He chokes on his question when I spread my legs wider so he can see. "Goddamn it!"

That's just the start of his irresponsible language. Apparently, when Dom gets turned on, he transforms into a sailor. He can't seem to help his foul mouth as I swallow him as deep as I can and massage my clit just how I like.

Dom's hips rock once with a particularly hard pull, then he stills himself, muscles quivering with the effort to hold back.

A sense of power mixes in with my pleasure, and I briefly understand Dom's need for control in all things.

"I need to fucking touch you," he growls even as his one hand fists my loose hair into a ponytail and the other cradles the back of my neck. Again, he doesn't try to take over the rhythm—only holds on as I work him at my pace.

The raw craving in Dom's words spikes my own arousal, and I let his cock slip from my mouth, the length slapping wetly against his stomach. Meanwhile, I dig my teeth into the salty-with-sweat skin of his hip bone as my sudden orgasm rocks through me. I gasp and whimper and try to remember to breathe.

"Fuck, Maddie. Let me feel."

As the pleasure rolls and clenches through my nerves, Dom hauls me off the floor and across his chest. Then he shoves a hand between my legs like he did earlier, his large hot palm engulfing my vulva. His scorching, reverent touch lengthens the tail of the pleasure, and my hips writhe.

Dom doesn't penetrate me or even try to stroke my clit. He just revels in the way my body shudders through the orgasm.

Once I settle into a shivering post-orgasm recovery, I realize my mistake.

Damn it. This wasn't the plan.

"You were supposed to come first." I grit the words out, pissed at myself for falling into this pattern again.

"How about I come next?" Dom asks, his face buried against my neck. "And then we stop keeping score and just do what feels good?"

Easy for him to say. He's winning.

I wriggle out of his embrace and settle beside him on the smaller bed. His erection lays heavy against his stomach, the skin still wet from my mouth. When I grasp him, Dom's body jerks and he grunts.

"Use my hand on yourself," I tell him.

"What?"

"Jerk yourself off. With my hand."

I've always thought masturbation was an intimate act. Getting to know exactly what your partner needs from a sexual experience.

I want Dom to be vulnerable with me. Crack open this part of himself so I know. So I have some kind of ownership over even this small portion of his pleasure.

The way he's always had a claim to a portion of mine.

Dom's hand engulfs my hold. I expect him to start to slide my grip down his shaft, then back up. Instead, his thumb nudges mine, guiding it to the tip. There he shows me how to draw small, firm circles until precum seeps out. My fingers grow slick.

"How am I doing?" I ask, my voice unnaturally husky.

"Perfect. You're fucking perfect," he mutters, then clenches his teeth against a groan as he finally starts to stroke himself, pressing my fingers into a harder grasp than I would have guessed. The hold almost feels angry. Punishing.

I love it.

Sitting up for better leverage, I brace my free hand against Dom's chest and continue to work his shaft. His heart pounds hard and fast and I find myself timing my strokes to the beat.

"Maddie . . . God . . . Fucking Maddie." Dom moans the words between pants, and when I meet his eyes, I find heavy lids and a dark gaze locked on my face.

"Come on, Dom." I squeeze hard at his base. "Show me how you come."

He says my name again as his abdomen tenses, then his cock jerks in my hand and streams of cum jut out to coat our clasped fingers and his stomach.

Finally.

I don't bother fighting my grin as Dom lays in the frilly daybed, covered in his release, still clutching my hand. Seeing him wrung out like this is a special kind of beautiful.

Eventually he sits up, presses a quick kiss to my mouth, then disappears into the bathroom. I bite my lip to keep from giggling when I spot the tattoo on his ass.

Jelly butt.

Dom reappears a moment later with a damp washcloth for me, and I wipe the sticky proof of his pleasure off my fingers before climbing into the bigger bed.

A small spike of anxiety sets off a sharp pain in my chest.

What now? Will he retreat again? Tell me this was a mistake?

Dom strolls out of the bathroom again, chest clean, and crouches over his duffle bag. The man's naked body is glorious and aggravating. My fear of what happens next starts to transform into defensive anger.

A biting comment rests on my tongue, ready to cut, when Dom finally faces me and tosses an item on the bedspread.

A condom.

"You still want me?" he asks, and I swear I hear a hint of the same vulnerability that was stirring up the insecurities in my own mind these past few moments.

To cover up how I almost imploded this special moment, I snatch up the condom and tear the foil pack open. "Someone thinks he has a fast recovery time."

Dom plucks the rubber out of my hands, and I watch with wide eyes as he rolls it onto an already-hard dick.

"It's you, Maddie. I need you more than once. A lot more."

He looms over me, climbing onto the bed, his large body threatening to overwhelm mine. And while I might like this position in theory, in practice I know it's a bad idea.

"Sorry, big guy." I pat his shoulder. "You are not going on top. Learned that the hard way."

He freezes. "What do you mean?"

I scoot out from under his imposing form. "I mean I was having sex with a guy on top, and I started having an asthma attack."

"What happened?" He watches my retreat with narrow eyes.

I shrug. "Like I said. I had an asthma attack. Used my emergency inhaler. He freaked out and left."

"He left you in the middle of an attack?" The muscle of Dom's jaw turns white as he clenches his teeth.

I wonder if he has to wear a mouth guard to keep from grinding them at night.

"Well, it's kind of freaky when the person you're fucking starts gasping for breath, I guess."

"That means you stop," he snaps. "Not that you *leave*. Why are you not more pissed about this?"

The sexy vibes start to fade in the presence of his protective instincts. But I'm not in the mood to be coddled.

"I don't know, Dom." My voice is all bitter sarcasm. "Maybe because I'm used to people leaving me."

Realizing how vulnerable that statement was after I said it, I try to roll away from him.

Dom doesn't let me. He hooks his arms around my hips and drags my body back, settling me on his lap so I straddle him. His large palm wraps around my thigh as his lips press against my ear.

"I didn't mean to yell."

He begins to stroke me, his hand creeping toward my center. I grab his wrist before he can start fingering me, a spike of panic shuddering through me again.

"It can't just be me," I rasp. "We both need to be in it. I need you inside me. I can't be on my own."

Dom holds my gaze for a stretch, his thick brows furrowing, but eventually he nods. "Tell me what position works best for you."

Truthfully, the best position is us both on our sides with him behind me. But I can't stand the idea of penetration without looking into Dom's eyes. I need to know that he is feeling everything that I am.

"Standing. Slow, steady thrusting. You using those vanity muscles to do most of the work."

"Done." Dom scoops me up easily and finds a free spot on the wall where I can brace my shoulders. His large hands support my legs wrapped around his hips, and I feel the press of him at my entrance. "Good?"

"Wow. Uh, fast. You did that fast." Words fail me as I fully grasp that Dominic Perry is about to be inside me.

"Don't worry. We'll take this next part slow." Angling his hips, Dom offers a gentle, shallow thrust that has him dipping just past my sensitive lips.

My body stretches around him, and my lower belly flutters and clenches until I'm sure this man could get me to come a second time with only the tip of his dick.

"And Maddie?" When he says my name in that deep, soothing voice, I drag my eyes away from where our bodies join and meet his stare.

"Yeah?" I whisper, worried a loud noise will shatter this dream of a moment.

"You should know"—he sinks deeper—"they're not vanity muscles." Another thrust and his hips meet my thighs as he buries himself fully. "I play in *two* rec baseball leagues."

Then, holding my gaze, the man has the audacity to smirk.

Dom is teasing me as he fucks me, and nothing could be more perfect.

"You're such an asshole." I laugh, then groan as my giggles make my abdomen tense and somehow draw him deeper while forcing me to feel how entirely full I am.

"Hell, Maddie." Dom's fingers press hard into my ass, and I wonder if he'll leave bruises.

I hope he does.

"You're going to come to one of my games, right?" He slides almost all the way out, then returns to me with a grunt. "Cheer me on. Tell everyone the pitcher is your guy?"

"Oh god," I moan. In part because he's insufferable, but mostly because he feels *so* good. "You're going to wear the letterman jacket when we fuck at some point, aren't you?"

Dom grins and shakes his head, dark hair flopping into his face and sticking to his sweat-damp forehead. Color collects high on his cheeks as he works himself into me over and over. Then he leans forward enough to press a kiss below my ear before whispering, "No. I'm gonna fuck my girl while *she* wears it."

That's when Dominic Perry claims one more of my orgasms.

But who's counting?

Twenty-Eight

"Can I have a hot toddy tonight and you still trust that I'm hot for you, too?" These are the first words I speak to Dom the next morning. The question I use to wake him up.

I've been up for a solid twenty minutes, lying in our messy sheets, memorizing the way Dom holds me to him. This isn't a classic spooning situation, not with our fronts pressed together. Nor is it a classic tucked-into-the-chest embrace. At some point, as we were sinking into sleep last night, he snaked his arm between my legs and tugged me to him with a solid grip on my thigh. My head settled higher than his on the pillows, and Dom's face found a new home pressed against my boobs. He still hugs my leg like my limb is his teddy bear, and I've utilized my position to finger-comb his silky hair while occasionally sniffing said hair because I like the way his cedar shampoo mixes with the salty tang of his sweat.

As much as I enjoy this half-asleep petting session, I figured it was time he reentered the world of the living.

Dom makes a grumble in the back of his throat that sends shivers over my bare skin. "Prove it."

"Prove that I'm hot for you?" I trace the curve of his ear with my fingertip and smile at the goose bumps that prickle down his strong neck. "Our sex marathon didn't do it?"

He grunts and rubs his nose along the underside of my breast. "I need more evidence."

"You're insatiable. I knew we should've picked you up some gas station porn." But even as I feign exasperation, I wiggle out of his hold and proceed to kiss my way down Dom's expansive body. When I get low enough, I palm his half-hard cock—half that is quickly transitioning into fully.

Dom lays sprawled on his back now, jaw slack, hazy gaze fixated on where my mouth licks and nips his hip bone. There's something about this spot I can't get enough of. I'm addicted to the way it twitches and heats under my ministrations.

I decide I want to mark it. Leave a signature, not as permanent as the one on his wrist, but something that will last for a short while. Proof that Dom was mine for however long.

Gently, I tug the skin that stretches over his hip bone into my mouth. I suck and tease, use tongue and teeth, knowing he'll have a little bruise right here, in my favorite spot.

Dom's jaw clicks shut and his nostrils flare. The man breathes heavy as he watches me, and his hips give a subtle, involuntary rock.

Marking done, I release the delicate part of him, pressing an apology kiss to the abused skin.

Sorry, not sorry.

Dom's panting picks up pace and his hips rock again.

I grip the base of his shaft, meeting his dark eyes over the heave of his chest. "Is this what you need?" My tongue drags along the thick vein running up his engorged cock and collects the salty pre-cum leaking from the tip. "Is this how I prove I want you?"

"Maddie," he grunts. "Hell. You don't have to."

Dom pushes to sit up, as if he might stop me. As if this is some trial for me and not a fantasy I've had since I was fifteen years old and first learned what a blow job was.

Before he can decide stopping now is the responsible thing to do,

I suck him past my lips, nestling Dom in the slick heat of my mouth. Not too far back, but just enough.

The big man groans and collapses against the pillows in defeat. *That's right. I'm in charge now.*

As I work him in and out of my mouth, Dom's hips give gentle thrusts, silent pleas to plunge deep in my throat. Unfortunately, gagging on a dick is an asthma risk, so I stick to shallow, torturous dips. Then I make up for my evil ways with a firm suck on his sensitive crown.

Dom mutters a string of irresponsible language, his heels pressing hard into the bed, his lower belly muscles going taut.

"Damn it. I'm gonna come. Fuck, Maddie. Fuck."

Letting him pop free, I sit up and work Dom with one hand, stroking him in rough jerks like he showed me, while my other palm gently cradles his balls, giving him careful, teasing tugs. From my vantage point, I get to watch the normally put-together man fall to pieces. His massive hands reach back to grip the headboard, biceps straining. He pants in great bellows, as his back bows off the mattress.

Then his cock jerks in my hand, spilling his pleasure over my fingers and across his bare chest.

I love every moment.

Dom's arms fall lax beside his head as he sucks in ragged inhales and stares at me with an unfathomable expression. When I release his shaft, Dom lets out a hiss that sounds almost angry. Slowly, I crawl up his body, hovering over him, naked and on all fours. My hair falls in a light brown curtain around his face, enclosing us in an intimate space.

"How was that evidence?" I keep my voice casual.

He hooks his arms around my torso, pulling me flush against his chest as he claims my mouth in a searing kiss.

Meanwhile I laugh and moan. "No!" I wail when he finally moves his kisses to my chin and neck. "You made us a cum sandwich! The evidence is smashed all over me now!"

"I want the evidence on your tits," he mumbles against my pounding pulse.

And damn the man, he gets his wish.

Eventually we shower—together—and find lunch in the kitchen—together—and settle in the sitting room by the fire. The snow is too heavy to even consider making a run at North Dakota today. Sandra says we can book our room for another night, and we take her up on the offer.

Unfortunately, this isn't technically a vacation for me. I get comfy on the floor with my laptop and an old bird-themed puzzle Sandra dug out for me. I log into my work email and try not to balk at the number I have waiting for me. *For every five I answer, I get to put a piece in the puzzle,* I promise myself.

I spread the pieces on the coffee table, then get to clearing out my inbox. Dom sits behind me on the fainting couch, his legs on either side of my body, with yesterday's newspaper loosely held in hands that I now know much better—but refuse to think about because I might accidentally type dirty thoughts into a response to the marketing department.

Dom isn't helping matters, doing what has been widely established as one of the sluttiest things a man can do: wearing gray sweatpants. I can't stop listing to the side to lean against his calf, reveling in the warm, soft fabric. Every time I do, his muscle tenses, then relaxes, and I swear I feel a featherlight tug on my hair.

When my email Everest is temporarily summited and the puzzle is done, I help Dom figure out the last few answers to the crossword in the paper before we sneak back upstairs. Dom asks what other positions are best for my breathing and generously practices every one of them with me.

In between rounds of decadent sex, we talk about small things that don't matter but make us smile. My fantasy fan fiction. His baseball leagues. The thrift stores where I find the best sweaters. The pigeon that stares at him whenever he grills on his back porch.

I tease him and kiss him and promise myself I won't fall for him again.

It's perfect.

But it's also fragile. Neither of us brings up the past, as if worried this new development might shatter under the weight of memories. We make a silent pact to live in our snowy sex bubble and forget the rest of the world for as long as we can.

Twenty-Nine

"Maddie, did you hear anything I just said?"

I stare at Pamela's face on my computer screen and realize that at some point in the last ten minutes, my brain automatically tuned my boss out. Not that what she was saying wasn't important. I honestly have no idea if it was or if she was reciting her grocery list. The problem is, I've been having trouble concentrating ever since getting back from South Dakota last week.

"I'm sorry. My internet seems spotty today. Your audio and video are going in and out." Okay, yeah, so I'm a liar. But to be honest, I would say seventy-five percent of the information that she tells me in these meetings could have been written in a single email.

"Fine." Pamela sighs. "I guess I'll send it to you in an email."

And my point is proven.

"Thank you so much. And I'll be sure to follow up on the market dashboards we talked about. "

"Oh good. Yes, that needs to happen. And can you also consolidate the team's quarterly performance reviews?"

"Sure. I'm on it."

I shouldn't have said that. Shouldn't have agreed to take on extra tasks that aren't in my job description. Sometimes there's so much additional work I feel like I have another full-time job.

But the idea of saying no to Pamela gives me hives.

She appreciates my work. Considers me an invaluable part of the company. And I got an impressive holiday bonus, plus a raise.

Do not ruin a good thing!

We log off our meeting and for a stretch I just stare at my blank screen and hype myself up to do my job. Normally, it's not like this. Normally, I am in work mode practically twenty-four seven.

But other things have been crowding my mind.

Mainly the mental image of a naked Dom.

Followed closely by the words we spoke to each other right before parting ways.

"Are you seeing anyone?" Dom had asked me when we were fifteen minutes away from the airport. "In Seattle?"

"Way to ask me that *after* our two-day sex marathon."

He'd glared at me, and I'd rolled my eyes. "No. I'm not seeing anyone. Currently, I am sleeping with you. And only you. Are you currently sleeping with me, and only me?"

That earned a reluctant smile from his stern mouth. "Yes. You and only you."

"Cool. If that changes, please let me know." And I was proud I didn't even hint at what happened that summer.

"It's not going to change."

I liked how he said that. Kind of with a warning growl.

"Awesome. But if it does, give me a heads-up."

"Maddie." He sighed my name like I was the most exasperating woman in the world, which for Dom, I probably am.

But then he reached over the center console and held my hand until we arrived at the rental car return. Then he stood close to me in the security line and walked with me to my gate—even though it was the opposite direction of his—and watched my stuff while I used the bathroom. When they called my boarding group, he did the same check of my items he'd performed at the Dallas airport, only this time he kissed me when his checklist was complete.

"Come to the twins' graduation," he said the moment our lips parted.

I told him I'd think about it.

A week later I'm still thinking about it.

And about him.

And about whatever the hell we're doing.

What is happening between us?

It feels so much like that time when I was nineteen that it scares me. But it also feels deeper. It feels like more. Like all the barriers I put in place have cracks in them and Dom is finding his way through to the center of me. And having him here, so close to my heart, is wonderful and terrible. Because I don't know how to trust it. How to trust him.

Maybe we're just . . . bang buddies. Ash-spreading bang buddies.

Though I doubt this is what Josh had in mind when he left me the task of watching over his friend.

Shoving up from my desk, I pace around my apartment, my feet leaving imprints in my newly vacuumed carpet. Sometimes I stress clean. Luckily, I have plenty of framed puzzles to dust. I pluck my Swiffer from the closet and get to work, starting with the puzzled-together image of a redwood forest that hangs above my bed.

I know what Josh is trying to do with these letters. He's forcing me to have adventures. Part of me loves him for it. But another part of me hates how he continues to force me out of my comfort zone. How this request takes away my safety. Not so much physically, although there is that risk every time I pull out my inhaler because my breath is short. But Josh unknowingly is forcing me to risk my heart. Because it's impossible to spend any amount of time around Dom and not give him pieces of it.

He hurt me in the past. He wrecked me.

Would I survive if he did it again?

Rain pounds against the windows in my apartment, reflecting the storm in my mind.

If I keep it simple, I can keep my heart safe. If Dom and I just hook up when we're together, but don't plan or ask for more.

That was the problem when I was younger. I thought I was at the beginning of an epic love story. If I know this is simply a release for us both, one that will end when the trips do, then there's no reason for my heart to break.

"I wish you were still here so I could yell at you about this." I say the words to the pirate trunk that holds the rest of Josh's remains, imagining that my brother can hear me. "You always wanted me to be brave like you. But I'm not like you. Honestly, I think I'm a coward. And it's not fair that you can go and die and leave me with this task that forces me to be uncomfortable around your sexy best friend and I can't even argue with you about it."

I laugh in exasperation.

And then I think of the graduation.

I should be pumped about the idea of supporting Adam and Carter on their big day, and I am. But my mind also does the math that adding this trip means instead of three more Dom meetups, I'll have four.

Graduation, North Dakota, Idaho, and Alaska.

The tangle of emotions in my brain and chest intensifies. I am eager for the next adventure. The next time that I see Dom and I can touch him and kiss him and he'll hold me and we'll open an envelope together and we'll do or say whatever Josh asked us and . . .

And I'll have to say one more goodbye. And then I'll only have two left.

Which brings on guilt.

Guilt that I've pushed for these trips to happen as soon as we could manage. Guilt that I want to charge into these adventures even more now because I'll get to see Dom again. Guilt because in my eagerness, I've chipped away the final pieces of my brother.

Now that Josh's correspondence is dwindling, I want to wait

forever to read the rest of the words. I want them now. And I don't ever want them to end.

What do I do after Alaska?

What will happen when I don't have anything left from my brother?

When I have to figure out a way to be brave on my own, will I be the Maddie that I've always been? Will I take something from this time of bravery with me?

Will I take Dom?

His friendship. That's a precious thing I should try to hold on to. We can go back to being texting friends from afar. After the last trip, I doubt we'll see each other again. Not for a while anyway.

But I want to see him now as something more than friends. And I want to see him without the countdown of Josh's final goodbye hanging over us. A bonus trip.

Having made a decision, I settle back at my laptop and force myself to concentrate on work till five p.m. Like usual, I actually end up logging off somewhere closer to seven.

Then I pour myself a drink, smirking at the memory of Dom asking me to hold off on my hot toddy because he wasn't sure if I actually wanted him.

> MADDIE: What should I bring the
> twins for their graduation?

Barely five minutes pass before I get a response in the form of rapid-fire buzzes.

> DOM: You're coming?
> DOM: When does your flight get in?
> Are you flying into Philly?
> DOM: I'll pick you up.
> DOM: You'll stay at my place.

I press my glass against my mouth to cool my grin.

> MADDIE: I haven't booked a flight
> yet
> MADDIE: And that's presumptuous

DOM: I have a big comfortable bed.

> MADDIE: I'm more interested in
> the snack situation

DOM: I plan to eat your pussy.

Gin sprays across my kitchen as I choke on a gasping laugh. As I sop up my mess with one hand, I text him back with the other.

> MADDIE: That's lovely for you, but
> what will I eat?

I prepare for Dom to respond with some version of *How about my dick?* But I should have known better. He's not that guy.

DOM: Sour Patch Kids, Cheez-Its, and
all the lavender lattes your heart
desires.

Damn him.

> MADDIE: You know how to woo a
> lady. I'm in

CHAPTER

Thirty

Dom pulls his car up to the arrivals pickup at the Philadelphia airport and immediately jumps out of his SUV to help me with a bag I'm perfectly able to lift on my own. Which I tell him as I shoulder check him away from my suitcase.

He doesn't fight me over loading it into the trunk, but when he closes the door, Dom immediately crowds me against the bumper. His hands cup my face, fingers digging into my lopsided I-just-spent-hours-on-an-airplane messy bun, and he tilts my chin up only to press a kiss on my nose rather than my mouth.

"You came," he mutters, pressing another kiss just below my ear, unleashing a riot of goose bumps to overwhelm my body.

I cross my arms over my chest so he won't see how hard my nipples are through my bralette. Dom's eyes flick down to the defensive pose, then back up to meet my eyes. He frowns but doesn't let me go.

"Something change?" he asks.

Oh. He thinks I'm not horny for his handsome jelly-tattooed ass?

"You want to have your snack, then you better take me back to your place."

His eyes darken, his mouth curls, and a pleased rumble sounds in the back of his throat, which doesn't help the nipple situation.

"You're the boss."

Then Dom steps back from me, and I straighten my glasses while pretending I don't feel the loss of his looming presence. On the drive from the airport to Dom's town house, he holds my hand and tells me about the schedule for the next day, which involves an earlier departure time to hopefully beat some of the commencement ceremony traffic. His parents are going to be there, and the twins, too, obviously.

I know we need to talk about how we'll act around each other when we're with the group, but I'd rather do that when I don't smell like airplane food.

"I'm showering first thing when I get to your place," I tell him.

Dom nods as he flicks on the turn signal. "I put extra towels in the master bathroom for you."

That sounds like the bathroom connected to his room.

"You know you don't have to share your bed with me. If you've got an extra room, I can stay there."

The half of Dom's face I can see frowns. "No."

"No, you don't have an extra room?" A "town house" sounds like it would have at least one guest bedroom.

"There's an extra room," he admits, voice full of reluctance. "But . . . it's broken."

"The room is broken?"

He nods. I fight a smile and manage a serious tone.

"An entire room in your house just . . . broke?"

He nods again as his thumb rubs my knuckles.

"Ah. Hate when that happens."

Dom grunts as he parallel parks on a residential street, maneuvering the wheel one-handed, his forearm flexing in a visual display that I would label as porn. Dirty, lick-able, X-rated arm pornography.

A half hour later, after I've gotten the quick tour of the two-story home—which isn't as minimalist as I expected, with its dark wood bookshelves and cushy sectional—I pop my contacts in and enjoy a shower in Dom's massive bathroom. Clean and wrapped in a too-large robe he left me, I wander back into the bedroom to grab an outfit from my bag. While I have my suitcase open, I pull out the dress I plan to wear tomorrow and open Dom's closet, hoping that hanging the fabric overnight will get rid of some of the travel wrinkles. When I have it situated on a hanger next to all of Dom's crisp dress shirts, I notice something I should have expected to find here.

On the floor of his closet, tucked back in the corner, I spy a small safe with a number keypad.

The safe.

Dom never sent me a message about changing the combination. I settle cross-legged in front of it, under the cedar-scented shirts, feeling for a moment like I'm about to rifle through his private things. But then I remind myself they're *my* things, too.

Reaching out, I type in four numbers.

0–7–1–8

The handle clicks and when I grasp it, I'm able to swing the door open.

My birthday. Why is it my birthday?

Inside there's Dom's passport and other documents I don't care about. My attention is all for a stack of envelopes, most of them with ragged edges from where we tore them to get at Josh's words.

"Hey, Josh," I whisper, reaching out to tap the missives as if they were my brother's shoulder and I only wanted to get his attention.

"You looking to rob me?"

I jump, then glance behind me to find Dom leaning a shoulder against the doorway, wearing a half smile as he watches me snoop.

"Of course." I swing the safe shut, waiting until I hear the click of the lock before I turn fully around to face him. "But a good cat burglar always seduces her prey first." I tug on the robe's belt until it gapes open, then spread my knees in invitation.

Dom's lids lower as he drags his gaze over my bare body. "You *are* good." He stalks across the room, switching our roles until I feel like the prey. In a smooth move, Dom lifts me off the floor and drops me on the edge of his bed. A breath later his face finds a home between my thighs, and I focus on my controlled breathing as he eats the snack I promised him while my fingers tangle in his silky dark hair.

For the rest of the night Dom and I reacquaint ourselves with each other's bodies, only pausing when a pizza delivery arrives, and then again when he announces that we need to get some sleep. I pretend as though I plan to walk down the hall to the "broken" guest room, but only because I love the way Dom growls and hooks me around the hips to tug me back into bed beside him.

When I wake up in the morning to Dom's irritating alarm, my sleep shirt feels overly tight and I realize it's because his hand is fisted in the material, the guy maintaining an unrelenting grip even as he sleeps, which is both annoying and endearing.

Dom takes me in the shower with my hands pressed against the slick tiles and his hips pressing against my ass. I keep my breathing steady by inhaling in time with his slow thrusts, and when I come first, he promises to follow me, praising how I take him so well.

Our shower goes longer than planned, which fucks with Dom's schedule. But he only smiles and continues to touch me after I towel off until I have to laughingly swat his hands away so I can put on my dress without interference.

My outfit is a simple sundress, just some flowy green fabric with burnt orange flowers. But Dom seems fascinated with the bows that hold up the straps, his fingers smoothing over them as I try to wrangle my hair into a braid crown.

Dom looks handsome enough to model whatever his secret cedar cologne is, of course. His gray pants fit him indecently well, and he's paired them with a short-sleeve white button-up that brings out the subtle tan notes in his skin.

The whole morning and process of getting ready together felt flirty and fun.

The mood changes on our drive to the campus when I ask a simple yet obvious question.

"What should we say to your family?"

Dom's fingers tighten on my hand that he's claimed once more.

"What do you want to tell them?" He keeps his eyes on the road.

I smooth my skirt over my legs. "I'm not super interested in explaining the concept of hookup buddies to the rest of the Perrys."

Dom doesn't respond, but he's also switching lanes in heavy traffic, so I don't blame his divided focus.

I clear my throat and say what I brainstormed on the cross-country flight. "We'll just say we're friends. Friendly. That we've learned how to get along while traveling together. And you offered me your broken guest room when I said I wanted to come to the graduation." I throw a teasing smile at Dom, but I can't read his stoic face.

"If that's what you want," Dom says after taking our exit.

I nod. "Less questions and weirdness this way."

Less of the Perrys wondering why Dom would choose me. Less of me being compared to the date he brought to the twins' last graduation.

I've spent enough of my younger years using the perfect example of Rosaline to pick myself apart. I don't want to see the look in people's eyes as they do the same and find me wanting.

I turn to stare out the window and try to ignore the queasy feeling in my gut.

Dom doesn't let go of my hand until he parks in the designated parking garage. He doesn't try to reclaim it as we make our way toward the stadium. Not that he should.

Friends don't walk around holding hands.

We find the Perry parents and they both claim hugs from me,

thanking me for coming so far. I shrug, guilty, telling them I regret missing the twins' high school graduation.

The one Josh attended.

My phone buzzes in my pocket, and a quick check shows me Pamela's name. I ignore it, but a second later, the phone starts ringing again.

Shit. Shit shit shit.

I told her about this trip, but said I'd be available if needed.

Why? Why didn't I just say I'd be out for two days?

"I'm going to go to the bathroom real quick." I throw a thumb over my shoulder and Emilia promises they'll wait for me. Dom's eyes drop to my buzzing pocket, and I turn before he sees the mortified flush that overtakes my face. I feel like he knows I'm sneaking off to the bathroom to take a work call.

He was the one to find me in the janitor's closet.

That feels like forever ago. But also, kind of like it was yesterday.

Josh has been gone for over a year.

I press my hand against my twisting stomach and try to think about why Pamela would be calling me instead.

Ten minutes later, after sitting in a not particularly clean bathroom stall and talking my boss through where a certain dataset was stored, I jog back to where I split off from the Perrys, worried I took too long and they left to find seats without me.

A sigh of relief gusts out of me when I spot Dom's handsome head above the crowd, but then the people in front of me part and I tense up.

Another person has joined the group in my absence.

Rosaline smiles up at Dom as he says something to her. The woman looks stunning in a flowing blue dress that brushes the tops of her knees. Her russet hair falls in beautiful silky waves down her back, and with a set of heeled sandals, she's the perfect height for Dom to not have to crane his neck to talk to her.

She chuckles at something he says, and I close my eyes briefly because, damn it, even her laughter is stunning.

How could he not love this woman anymore?

After dragging in a deep breath and blinking my eyes open again, I approach the group, feeling like my footsteps clomp loudly on the cement floor.

"Maddie!" Emilia says. "There you are. Thought we'd lost you."

"Sorry. Long line." I give a vague wave toward the bathroom.

Dom's mom chuckles in understanding. "Well, now we're all here. Thank you both again for coming." She shares a smile between Rosaline and me. "After everything . . ." Emilia clears her throat, eyes glassy. "Well, I just don't want us to pass out of each other's lives."

My throat is thick as I try to swallow. Her sentiment is genuine, and I wish there wasn't a twisted part of me that is unhappy to find out that despite the divorce, Dom's ex still gets along with her in-laws.

Are they just waiting for the two of them to patch things up?

I might need to go back to the bathroom and vomit.

"Hi, Maddie. I love your dress." Rosaline stares down at me with a small smile, her eyes wide and sincere.

And that's one of the many problems with her.

Rosaline is kind. And decent. And smart.

And has never done anything to earn my ill will other than love, and be loved by, Dominic Perry.

"Hi," I croak. "Yours is really pretty, too." *Good job. That was nice. Maybe I can keep from turning into a jealous troll person.*

"Let's go grab seats. I don't want to sit in the nosebleeds." Mr. Perry ushers us toward the entrance of the stadium and I'm thankful I don't have to formulate any more small talk when I really have one question.

Are you here because you're still in love with Dom and you want him back?

Damn it. I'm fucking hopeless.

But all I want is to beg Rosaline to wait a little longer to make her move.

Give me till Alaska. Please. I know you're the perfect choice for him. But just let me have him a little while longer.

We end up sitting in a row, Mr. Perry, Mrs. Perry, Rosaline, Dom, and me on the end. The add-on that could easily be done away with. To keep from sliding too far into my hopeless spiral, I search the crowd of graduates in their square hats, looking for two familiar faces.

"The section closest to our side," Dom murmurs in my ear, making me jump. "Four rows from the back, eight chairs in."

Following his directions, I spot Adam and Carter. The former is chatting with the guy seated behind him and the latter is on his phone.

"I see them." And I keep my eyes on them.

At least I do until I feel a brush on my thigh. Glancing down, I realize Dom has a small bit of my dress pinched between his fingers. He fiddles with the material in an idle gesture, as if he doesn't know what he's doing. But when I raise my gaze to his face, I find him staring intently at his hand.

Mr. Perry is focused on recording the start of the ceremony, and Emilia is telling Rosaline about some new branch of the nonprofit she works for. No one notices what Dom is doing. Only me.

Soon enough we're cheering for Adam and Carter as they walk across the stage, then filing out of our seats with the rest of the crowd, off to find our graduates.

The twins grin wide when they locate us. Everyone hugs. Adam picks me up off the ground for a quick twirl, and when he sets me down, I wobble until Dom steadies me with warm hands on my exposed shoulders. He runs his thumbs over the bows of my dress straps before letting his hands drop.

Our group goes to lunch at a Mexican restaurant—a real one, not

Taco Bell—and I wonder if I feel like an odd interloper on their family outing. They have Rosaline—why would they need me? There's clearly no lingering tension from the divorce. Almost like the split never even happened.

I'm grateful when Adam sits beside me and leans in close, insisting I describe to him, in detail, what would make a perfect puzzle table. By the time the food is gone, he has a sketch on his napkin that sounds like a dream piece of furniture, but I still insist he doesn't need to make it for me.

"Hey." Carter knocks Adam's shoulder. "The team is texting."

"Crap. I forgot." He straightens, tucking the napkin into the pocket of his shirt. "Mom, Dad, some of the swim team was gonna meet up for drinks. A last hurrah. You mind if we go?"

The Perry parents exchange quick commiserating smiles. "You have fun," Emilia says. "But you promised to be at Sunday breakfast. Don't forget."

"Yes, Mom," the twins say in unison, pushing their chairs back. Carter waves at the table, but Adam takes a moment to hug his dad around the neck, kiss his mom's cheek, and blow a raspberry against Rosaline's shoulder that has her shrieking a giggle. The silly man clasps the sides of his older brother's head and plants a loud smacking kiss right on his crown. Dom huffs an aggravated sigh at the antics, but I see a smile peek through his put-upon grumpy expression. But he frowns for real when Adam kneels beside my chair, takes my hand, and presses a lingering kiss to the back of it.

"Maddie Sanderson. My queen. My autumn rose. My purple bathing suit—"

"No," Dom says, reaching across my lap and extracting my hand from his little brother's grip. "Go away."

Adam clutches his chest dramatically, sends me a wink, then launches to his feet and jogs after Carter, who's already halfway to the door.

Under the table, Dom keeps his fingers wrapped around my wrist.

"It's still early, and I've got the day off," Mr. Perry announces with a grin. "Let's do something fun."

Apparently fun means wandering around the UPenn campus and listening to Nathanial and Emilia's college days anecdotes. Admittedly, they have some funny stories, and Mr. Perry's charming attitude reminds me a lot of Adam's. Emilia is more reserved, like Dom and Carter, but when she opens up, her humor is dry and witty.

Rosaline and Dom share some memories, too, both UPenn alumni as well. Josh attended Drexel, another Philly university close enough that he appears in a few of their stories.

When my brother's name comes up, I lean closer, desperate for another piece of him.

But when Dom and Rosaline exchange smiles at shared recollections, I try to find something else to look at.

Eventually, we end up at a rooftop bar, Mr. Perry opening a tab and telling us to order whatever we want before pulling his wife onto the dance floor.

But all I want is a moment to practice some breathing exercises because my throat feels tight with an emotion I refuse to dig into. I order a soda water with lime and mentally list off the work tasks I need to complete tomorrow on the flight back to Seattle.

Dom excuses himself to the bathroom, and when Rosaline leans over the bar to order her drink, I mutter a quick "Going to get some air" and slip away to a glass door that leads to an open viewing deck.

Alone, finally, I hold my drink in one hand and place the other on my belly, practicing my diaphragmatic breathing. One technique of a handful my breathing specialist has coached me in for addressing my asthma with more than just medication. I scheduled a series of appointments with her in the lead-up to our Idaho trip.

"Hey, Maddie." Rosaline appears beside me at the railing, and I try not to flinch away. "How are you doing?"

"Uh, fine." I drop my hand, pretty sure I look weird during my exercises. "Good. Just, yeah. Fine and good." When I speak to her, the ease of childhood familiarity is missing. She was close with Josh and Dom, but not me.

I can't remove my cordial mask and show her my petty temper or even my snarky teasing side. Talking with Rosaline is like meeting with a helpful coworker who is better qualified for my job and likely to get it simply by existing.

Rosaline smiles, her eyes soft, and I can swear she sees right through me. "Okay." She glances out over the city, then back at me. "If you ever want to talk, I'm here." A little blush gives her face the perfect amount of color. "I know we don't do that. Talk. But we could. If you want. Talk about J-Josh." She stumbles over my brother's name, and I clutch the cold glass of my drink, wishing I'd opted for booze. "It was nice today. Talking about him. We could do that." Her manicured nails fiddle with the stem of her wineglass. "Tell stories about him or something. If that helps. To remember him."

"Oh. Uh, thank you." I swallow hard and breathe through my nose. "That's . . . a kind offer."

And it is. So fucking kind. Because that's what Rosaline is. Kind and gracious and caring.

Which is one of the many reasons I find it so hard to be around her. Because with every sweet, thoughtful gesture she makes, I'm reminded of the surly, sarcastic troll person I am at my core.

Just the thought of reminiscing with her about my brother makes me queasy because I know most of her recollections will involve Dom, too. It was the three of them for years, best friends.

What good would those walks down memory lane do?

Remind me of all the times I didn't see my brother?

Remind her of all the happy moments she spent with Josh and her ex-husband?

Maybe the diagnosis fractured something in their marriage, but I can't get past the idea that one day, Rosaline will realize her mistake like she did that summer, show up on Dom's doorstep, and he will take her back.

Excuse me if I don't want to witness the moment she has that revelation.

"Hey, Maddie." Dom's voice pulls me out of my dark thoughts, and I turn to see him standing at the patio door. "I'm beat. You ready to head out?"

"Yes." I try not to sound desperate, setting my drink down on an empty table and hurrying his way.

"Bye, Ros." Dom nods to his ex-wife, using his cute nickname for her.

"See you, Dom," she replies with warm affection in her voice. "Bye, Maddie. Please call me. If you want to talk."

I nod and force a smile her way without meeting her eyes. Then I dodge around Dom, heading toward the exit. He catches up to me in two steps, placing his hand on my lower back.

"Are you alright?" he asks once we're in his car. Dom makes no move to start driving, only waits for my response.

"Yep. Just tired." I manage a yawn that I think is pretty convincing.

But then Dom continues to stare at me, and I know I didn't fool him.

"Maddie," he says, voice deep on my name, and I hear the hidden command to tell him what has me in a self-esteem nosedive.

"Dominic." I mock him with an equally low delivery, trying to use snark to avoid what I cannot say.

Something shifts in the air between us, his attention more intense as he leans toward me. "I did not invite Rosaline," Dom says, the words heavy between us. "My mom did. Because she knows even though we're divorced, we still get along. There's no betrayal or animosity. There's friendship."

"That's good," I grit out because logically I know it is. "That's healthy."

I'm the messed-up one. The dramatic, needy, insecure one.

Strong fingers cradle my chin, forcing our eyes to meet and hold.

"When you're in the room," he says, "you're all I see."

The repeated words from our South Dakota trip soften my rigid defenses, and suddenly I'm not thinking of anyone else. Just the two of us and how scared I am to let myself want Dominic Perry again.

How scared I am to believe him when he says he wants me.

"You're all I see, too," I admit.

Triumph flares in his eyes, and he claims my mouth with a stern kiss, almost a reprimand for doubting him. When we're back at his house, in his bed, Dom's body spoons me from behind. My leg is draped over his hip as he thrusts deep and groans my name into the back of my neck.

And I wonder if letting him into my heart again would be the ultimate act of bravery, or a desperate woman repeating the same mistakes of the past.

Summer

Thirty-One

The stair-climber taunts me.

"You can use the treadmill." Jeremy hovers at my side, ever the supportive friend. But I don't need support at the moment. I need someone to kick my ass. And someone to hand me my emergency inhaler if I overdo it.

"I've used the treadmill the past two weeks. But this one is a hike in the mountains. That means going up." I hear the reluctance in my own voice. "The treadmill only tilts so much."

In three weeks, Dom and I are heading to Idaho. Ever prepared, he searched the coordinates beforehand.

Josh is sending us to Alpine Lake.

This one is a seven-and-a-half-mile hike, with over a thousand feet in elevation.

After my abysmal showing in South Dakota, I'm determined not to make Dom my pack mule again.

Even if I did enjoy the way his back muscles felt pressed against my boobs.

Maybe I'll get strong enough to handle the first ninety percent of the hike, then make him carry me the last ten percent.

That seems fair.

"Well, don't force it." Jeremy eyes me with concern. "Take it slow. Don't choke on your own lungs."

I roll my eyes and try not to hate my friend for his fit form. The guy runs full marathons. For fun.

Fucking weird, if you ask me.

"You're in charge of this." I wave my inhaler under his nose, then set it in the cupholder of the treadmill next to the stair-climber, knowing that Jeremy plans to go on a too-many-miles-to-contemplate run while I find out how many flights of stairs I have in me.

A half hour later, I'm gushing sweat from every pore in my body and cursing every piece of land that dares to rise above sea level as my legs shake on the final step. Meanwhile, Jeremy continues to jog while laughing at my colorful cursing as if he has a separate set of lungs.

Amazingly, I haven't had to utilize my inhaler. True, I've taken frequent breaks whenever I felt myself start to wheeze. But each time I go through the breathing exercises the specialist taught me, my body eventually calms down enough for me to remount the torture device. I can also give credit for my improved lung function to spending a portion of my days wearing a high-altitude mask to strengthen my airways. The thing fits over my nose and mouth, restricting my airflow while making me look like Bane from *The Dark Knight Rises*. I tend to wear it while I'm responding to annoying emails, pretending I'm going to demolish Gotham City instead of answering the same mind-numbing question for the fiftieth time. Last week I accidentally kept the mask on when answering a Zoom call from Pamela, and she screamed.

I apologized, but I'm not sorry for being able to breathe better.

Still, I've officially reached the stopping point. For today, at least.

I think Dom would be proud. I'd send him a success selfie if I didn't feel like a swamp monster from a sweaty lagoon. Plus, Jeremy would probably ask who I'm texting.

I still haven't told him and Tula about my travel buddy.

At first, I simply didn't want to acknowledge Dom's existence. If they knew I was making the trips with Josh's best friend, they'd ask about him every time I got back. It was easier to distract them with souvenirs and descriptions of the destinations.

Then, when I realized how much Dom still affected me, I didn't want to bring him up to Jeremy and Tula because I'd have to give them the whole backstory. A tale that at its core is just a naive nineteen-year-old falling for the wrong guy. They'd be sympathetic, but in the end they would have advised me to find a way to move on from him.

I *knew* that already.

Or maybe they would have told me I had every right to be pissed off, which also seemed terrible because then I'd have to admit what Dom did was truly horrendous.

I didn't want to be told what I felt was wrong, but I also didn't want to be told what I felt was right.

I just . . . didn't want to think about him.

Now, though, I don't know how to talk about Dom after keeping him a secret for so long.

How do I tell my amazing friends I've been lying to them since the day my brother died?

The Maddie solution: I don't.

Real fucking mature.

But as hot as things currently burn between me and Dom, I figure they will snuff out when the fuel of our shared task is done. We'll help each other through these final trips, and then after Alaska we'll move on from my brother's death, and we'll move on from each other. I'll send Dom the occasional check-in text the way Josh would have wanted, and it'll be good.

All good. I'm *so* good.

But also, currently, I'm dying on the gym floor.

"You're doing great, Maddie! Now, why don't you run a few miles and call it a day," Jeremy hollers over the repetitive slap of his sneakers on the belt.

"Fuck you," I whimper, offering my mature response as I sprawl like a starfish on the floor of our condo's gym. "If I do any more, I'll have to crawl to my apartment." I may have to anyway. My legs no longer have muscles in them. Only the insubstantial ghosts of what used to be.

"Fine." My friend points to the space near the entrance that's clear of machines and weights and has extra padding on the ground. "Go through your stretches so you don't cramp up tomorrow. I'll be off in ten."

I groan my response, then decide to logroll my way to the stretching mat instead of forcing myself to stand. Who cares if I look like a human-sized slug? Jeremy and I have the place to ourselves.

"That doesn't look like stretching," Jeremy scolds ten minutes later when he finds me in the same position.

"It's corpse pose."

"You're going to be a corpse if you don't let me or Tula come on this hike with you," he mutters, while scooping up one of my heels and helping me stretch my leg.

"I'll be fine," I gasp as I try to relax my tight glutes. "It's a well-hiked path. Other people will be around." Including Mr. Overly Protective and Always Prepared.

"So, you'll let strangers rescue you, but not your best friends?" Jeremy gives my other leg the same treatment.

I scowl. "Maybe I don't want to hike with someone who thinks I need saving." The words come out in a harsh snap I immediately regret. "Sorry. I didn't mean—"

"No," Jeremy cuts me off. "You're right. I shouldn't baby you. Or try to push my way onto your trip." He resettles my leg on the ground, then sits cross-legged beside me. "I just want you to ask for help if you need it."

I exhale deeply, trying to force my unreasonable animosity out with the air. "You are helping. That's why I asked you to come with me today." I wave around the gym.

"I'm glad you did. We can make it a regular thing."

I let out a pathetic groan that earns a chuckle.

"How's your life?" I press, trying to get the focus off me and my upcoming trip.

Jeremy narrows his eyes, clearly seeing my topic change for what it is. But he's kind enough to let me get away with it. Jeremy leads me through a series of stretches as he chats about the website redesign committee he's been assigned to at his job and the Caribbean cruise he plans to surprise his boyfriend with for their anniversary.

Dom and I won't be together long enough to celebrate an anniversary.

I force the thought away, ignoring how it feels like a sharp needle jab to the heart.

And as my friend talks, I realize how I've let distance settle between us. Not just the Dom secret, but also these simple life plans. Before Josh got sick, I would have been helping Jeremy plan the cruise, researching the most luxurious ships with him and seeking out the best deals. In the past, we'd text throughout the day, and I'd already have a mental map of all the relationships and drama going down with his work committee.

We still hang out all the time, watching movies and shows together in my condo.

But I sit quietly beside him, letting my brain zone out. Like a form of self-preservation to guard me from the pain of Josh and the guilt of my Dom secret.

I blink when Jeremy's hand appears in front of my face. "Let's go. Time for you to shower, smelly."

When I glance up to meet my friend's eyes, I see his normal teasing nature, but also a flash of worry. And I acknowledge that he has a reason to be concerned. I would worry, too, if he started folding into himself the way I have been.

I slip my hand into his.

"I'm running out of books," I announce once I'm standing.

Jeremy laughs. "I doubt that very much."

"Fine." I offer him a cheeky smile. "I'm running out of *new* books. What do you say to you, me, and Tula going to happy hour tomorrow, then some tipsy bookstore shopping?"

The relieved grin that spreads over his face from the simple suggestion tells me all I need to know.

It's time to start living my life again.

Two months after the twins' graduation, I prepare for Dom to arrive.

In Seattle.

In my condo.

In my life.

If I didn't have to work, I would've picked him up from the airport. But there was a deadline, and he said he was fine getting a rideshare. Now I'm pacing my kitchen, done with my tasks for the day, staring at my phone screen as I wait for updates and reread the ones he's already sent.

DOM: Landed

DOM: Off the plane

DOM: On my way. Can't wait to see you.

Tingles vibrate throughout my body, and I do a giggle dance, then swear to never repeat the move because it was creepy and weird. After another five minutes, I decide waiting five floors up is a waste of time. I shove my feet into some worn sneakers and abandon my condo.

On the first floor is a small sitting area, the gym, and our mailboxes. Unable to sit down, I fiddle with my key in my mailbox, eyes on my hands. It's either this or press my face to the glass and wait for him to appear.

There's a whoosh of a door opening, a heavy footstep, and the sensation of eyes on the back of my neck.

"Maddie."

I don't remember how the kiss started, only that it doesn't stop even as we stumble into the elevator and travel up five floors.

"I've missed you." He whispers the words on a hot, harsh breath against my neck.

I let out a whimper just as the metal doors slide open. Luckily, to an empty hallway. Dom steps back and gestures for me to lead the way. On not-so-steady legs, I show him the door to my apartment, feeling his looming presence at my back as I unlock the door.

When Dom steps into my home, I brace for him to start kissing me again. Immediately. I mean, that elevator ride left so much heat lingering between us I half expect my smoke detectors to start wailing.

But Dom sets his bag inside the door, steps past me, and wanders around my home. His sharp eyes flick around the space, and I can imagine what he sees. My half-finished puzzle and knickknacks and throw pillows are all useless clutter. No clear organization to the bookshelves. His books were arranged alphabetically by the author's last name, which theoretically is good practice for finding things, but in practice seems like too much work when I could spend the time reading. Everything here is too soft, like my underbelly that he's about to gut if he insults my randomly cultivated home.

"This feels like you," he says.

I release a breath I didn't realize I was holding.

"Feels like me?" I repeat, not sure how to take his comment.

Dom finishes circling the main living area that butts up with an open–floor plan kitchen.

"Cozy. Warm. Comforting."

"You think I'm those things?"

Dom rests his hands on my hips. "You are to me." He leans in to press a line of kisses down my neck. "I'm hungry."

Knowing Dom was coming, I prepared for this. "I have lots of snacks. Most of them involve cheese. Not a granola bar in sight. You can have whatever you want."

His lips smile against my skin and shivers roll through my body. "Not for food. I want you. Want to taste you again. I'm starving, Maddie."

As he speaks, Dom's hand flattens on my lower belly, then slips down until he's cupping my core with only my shorts between his flesh and mine.

"Oh," I half gasp, half groan. "Well, I told you to eat whatever you want. If that happens to be me, it's my own fault for encouraging you."

Dom's laugh is a deep rumble in his throat, the sound so deliciously distracting I don't realize his intention until my shoulder blades meet the wall and Dom's knees hit the floor. I have to tangle my fingers in his silky hair to keep my balance as he drags the cotton shorts down my legs along with a set of cute lacy underwear that I wore in hopes he'd want to see. But Dom is more focused on what lies beneath, setting his thumbs at either side of my entrance and pulling apart my folds until I'm fully exposed.

"Oh god," I groan, not sure if I'm more embarrassed or turned on.

"Don't bother praying," he mutters. "Just say my name."

Then he swipes a long, slow lick over my sensitive center, and I spend the next however many minutes trying to breathe and keep my knees locked as Dom eases his appetite.

Thirty-Three

I thought when Dom arrived in Seattle he'd want to go out. Want to see the city. Be eager to explore.

But the man is more interested in visiting every possible destination on my body.

He got here an hour and three orgasms ago. But who's counting? His enthusiastic approach eases any past insecurity until I don't feel the need to check in that he's enjoying himself.

Dom makes that clear every moment his body touches mine.

Like right now, with me bracing my hands on the cushy back of my couch as I stand with legs splayed wide, Dom slowly sinking into my soaking, tender pussy. His muscular thighs press against the back of mine with every thrust and his fingers dig into my hips, keeping me in place for his leisurely strokes.

"So good," he grunts low, as if talking to himself. "Can't get enough."

Luckily, I've been training for endurance exercise, though I'd had mountains in mind, not sex marathons. Truly a lack of creative thinking on my part.

I'd probably grin if my face hadn't melted with pleasure. My whole body is overly hot like I have a fever. Tender to the touch.

Which is Dom's fault because he insisted on taking his time. On exploring all the positions that feel divine and don't compress my lungs. And he insisted on earning one of my orgasms in each one.

As if this is a training session for my pleasure. And damn it if his organized approach doesn't make me even hotter.

But now I want him to lose control.

Reaching down, I find his wrists and grab hold, then drag his rough palms up to cup my boobs. Then I use his fingers to massage and pinch my nipples. When his pace falters, then speeds up, triumph has my body clenching down on him.

"Maddie." Dom hisses my name with warning and need.

I let go of my hold, happy when he keeps his hands where I set them. Straightening as much as I can, I reach back and twine my arms around Dom's neck until the hair on his chest teases the bare skin of my back.

In this position, each of his penetrations sends me up on my toes, and I love the powerful drive.

"You're gonna make me come." He growls the words against my ears as he thumbs my nipples.

"I could never make you do anything." As breathless as my voice is, I still manage to taunt him.

The man moans, deep in his chest, and reaches down to press the heel of his hand against my clit, knowing I'm too sensitive for a direct touch. My pussy clenches in the shadow of an earlier orgasm, and that paired with an hour of erotic play finally sends Dom over the edge. He plunges deep before going rigid, gasping my name while his heavy hands hold me close.

As Dom comes down from the high, he whispers my name between kisses on my neck, his voice reverent.

It's intoxicating.

And scary.

But I ignore the fear as Dom slips out of me. After tossing the condom and cleaning up, we start to discuss real food. Only, our conversation is interrupted by an insistent, familiar pounding on my door.

"Maddie, I miss you!" The words sound clear even through the door. "I'm feeling needy. Pay attention to me!"

Fuck.

"Who is that?" Dom's heavy eyes stay on me rather than glancing in the direction of the voice.

"Oh, that's just my downstairs neighbor. Jeremy." I slide off my stool, shivering at the leftover tenderness from Dom's enthusiastic greeting.

"Maddie!" Jeremy wails dramatically, playing a game he refers to as "the scorned lover," oblivious to the fact that I have company. Because I still haven't told him about Dom. "We were so good together! We're soulmates!"

Dom raises a single eyebrow, and I try not to cringe.

He's joking. No reason to feel guilty. "He's a really good friend," I explain, wavering between admitting Jeremy and pretending I'm not home.

"Maddie, let me in. *Please.* I know I was vanilla when we were together, but I'll go kinky for you. I will do anything in bed that you want me to. Anything at all!"

This time I can't help the cringe, and once again err on the side of honesty. "Also, technically my ex. But he's *joking.*"

Too late. Dom is across the kitchen and wrenching open the door before I can explain the odd friendship dynamic Jeremy and I share.

"Maddie! When did you turn into a hot man?" My friend sounds perturbed on the other side of Dom's wall of a body. "If I'd known you could do this, we would've lasted *so* much longer."

I hurry to shove myself between Dom and my best friend, who is asking for a throwdown, whether he knows it or not.

"Hey, Jeremy. This is Dominic Perry. My, uh . . ." *Crap, we haven't talked about this. What is he? My death trip fuck buddy? Yeah, no . . .*

"My brother's friend. Josh's best friend." Shit. From the way Dom tenses out of the corner of my eye, I get the sense he would've applied a different label. But which one? Is there any label in existence for what we are to each other?

Ignoring the way Jeremy's eyes go comically wide, I continue the introduction. "Dom." I reach behind me to pat his stomach in what I hope is a reassuring gesture. "This is Jeremy. One of my best friends."

"You never mentioned him," Dom says, voice noticeably emotionless.

With my eyes on Jeremy, I catch the flash of hurt in his face. But he covers it quickly with a jovial smile. "Not surprised. Maddie is a closed book until you earn her trust." He steps in close and slings an arm around my shoulders before pressing a kiss against the side of my head.

A gesture Dom might not think is platonic.

This is getting out of hand. Why didn't I just tell everyone about everyone beforehand?

Oh yeah, because I didn't want my friends to know I was still messed up over a guy I liked as a teenager, and I didn't want Dom to know about my life because up until North Dakota I fully expected him to walk out of it.

I back into my apartment, dragging Jeremy with me as I scramble for a way to fix this. When I turn to face Dom, I find his expression a cold mask.

"Jeremy lives downstairs. With his partner, Carlisle. We haven't slept together in years because we're *just* friends." Not sure if it'll help, I add, "Also the sex wasn't very good when we did have it."

Jeremy gasps and narrows his eyes at me. "How dare you tell the hot man I'm lackluster in bed. At least say I was a decent lay."

Dom offers a stiff nod. "Good to meet you, Jeremy."

"And you, Dominic." Jeremy lets his hold slip from my shoulders as he tilts his head, studying the man in my kitchen. When he speaks next, the teasing note is gone, replaced with hesitant sincerity. "I'm sorry about Josh. I only met him a handful of times, but he was one of the good ones."

Something in Dom's posture eases slightly. Meanwhile, I suck in a deep breath through my nose, suddenly sure there's less oxygen in this room than there was before. When I feel my friend's gaze searching my face, I duck into the kitchen. "Are you here for food? I was going to make nachos." I call over my shoulder.

A weighty pause, then, "I wouldn't say no to them."

As I dig through my fridge, deciding to cut up toppings rather than just dumping salsa on top of cheese and chips, Jeremy settles on a stool at my butcher block island and Dom leans against the counter near where I've set up my cutting board.

He's not in the way, exactly. But he *is* looming.

I preheat the oven and ignore the ever-thickening silence.

Jeremy, of course, is the one to break it.

"Are you here to talk Maddie out of this wild plan to climb an Idaho mountain by herself?"

"The hike is *in* a mountain range," I correct him, not for the first time. "But I'm not hiking an entire mountain."

"I'm going with her."

Shit.

That sends Jeremy into a long enough silence that I turn around to check on him.

"*You're* going to Idaho? With Maddie?" Jeremy glances between the both of us. "Is this a new plan?"

"No," Dom says. "Been planning for a few months now."

Damn it. I clench my teeth to hold back a groan.

Jeremy is a smart guy, even if he likes to play the silly, helpless flirt. His brow wrinkles as he keeps his attention on me but speaks to Dom. "And did you happen to go to South Dakota with Maddie?"

Dom doesn't hesitate. "Yes."

"Kansas?"

"Yes."

Jeremy knows all the states. I told him and Tula that night they converged on my condo after I got back from Josh's funeral. He could list off the rest, but he doesn't need to in order to know I've gone with Dom to every one so far.

To know that Dom isn't the only one I've kept things from.

Pain flashes in Jeremy's eyes before he tucks the expression away behind a broad smile.

"Well, good. I'm glad Maddie had someone she trusts to share the trips with."

Ouch. That may have sounded kind, and there's a genuine note in Jeremy's words, but I also pick up on the underlying context.

Jeremy thinks I don't trust him. Not enough to tell him the full truth anyway.

Well, he's right, isn't he?

I've had over a year to explain to him and Tula the full extent of my brother's final wishes. To reveal that the task wasn't for me alone, but a joint venture.

But I knew if I told him, he'd ask about Dom.

And if he asked, Jeremy would hear in my voice there was something more, and he would joke and cajole and dig and pry. He would be a loving sort of relentless until I laid out everything.

I didn't trust Jeremy with that vulnerable piece of me, and now he knows.

A thickness gathers in my throat, feeling like guilty tears. But my cheeks stay dry. As I pretend to be fully engaged in the creation of nachos, Jeremy asks Dom surface questions about his trip and what it's like to live in Philadelphia.

He stays away from the meaningful stuff, where with my actions I've made it clear I don't want him to go.

After an awkward half hour, Jeremy makes an excuse about needing to meet up with Carlisle, which is BS because he only comes scrounging for food when his partner is out of town or working late.

Before slipping out the door, my friend sets his hands on my shoulders and presses a kiss to my forehead.

"You'll do great on your hike. Alone or with him. I'm proud of you."

He squeezes my shoulders and is gone before I can find my voice to say *thank you*. Or maybe to say *sorry*.

Jeremy deserves a better friend than me. Honestly, I'm surprised he still spends time with me. Maybe this will be what makes him leave me behind.

"Maddie?" A warm finger under my chin tilts my head upward until all I can see is a dark set of eyes. "How are you doing?"

I shrug. "Fine."

When Dom continues to stare at me like he doesn't believe me, anger stirs deep in my belly. I glare at him.

Dom smiles. "I have a gift for you."

That reroutes my temper, morphing it into surprised curiosity. "A gift? What is it?"

His smile widens to a grin. "Greedy little Magpie." Dom releases my chin and leaves me in the kitchen, reeling from his words.

Josh would call me that sometimes, especially when I showed him some random treasure I found or bought for myself. Magpie.

But I can't help it. I like things. Cute, beautiful, cool things.

I wouldn't consider myself a hoarder. My condo is plenty easy to navigate, and I make regular trips to Goodwill with the items that lost their immediate appeal and don't feel like treasures anymore.

But I could never be described as a minimalist.

And the things that never go in the donation bin are gifts. Thoughtful items someone else chose for me. I have so few of them. They mean so much more.

Dom comes out of my bedroom, where he tossed his bag earlier, carrying a folded clothing item. He holds it up so I can see.

A letterman jacket.

"Oh my god, you brought it with you?" Without another thought,

I'm in front of him, my hands fisted in the dark blue wool under his company's name.

Dom watches my eagerness with a teasing glint in his eyes. "Gotta make sure everyone in the school knows you're my girl."

High school Maddie is squealing and passing out right now.

Thirty-Four

Without the stair-stepper, I would've been done in the first twenty minutes. The Idaho hike is no joke.

Our destination is close to four miles into the Sawtooth Mountain Range. For the first part of the hike, I get overly confident, lulled by the cool morning and gradual incline into thinking myself a badass. But then the sun rises higher, and the elevation increases. As we navigate the trail through towering pines and up switchbacks, my lungs begin to lodge protests.

I focus on inhaling through my nose and exhaling with control like I've practiced with my Bane mask.

"Let's take a pause." Dom slips his backpack off his shoulders and settles on a flat rock, stretching out his long legs, looking like his limbs need the respite.

They don't. He could go for miles more and barely be winded.

Meanwhile, I collapse next to him as if I've been heaving boulders up this mountainside for the past two hours we've been hiking.

"Need your inhaler?" he asks.

I almost shake my head no, but I remind myself not to be proud. *Be honest, and maybe I'll get through this.*

"Yes," I wheeze. As far as I can tell, I'm not about to have an attack, but breathing isn't comfortable at the moment. The inhaler can be preemptive instead of responsive.

Dom digs it out of the side pocket of the backpack I'm still wearing, so I don't have to bend my arm at a weird angle. He also finds the spacer, which I brought with me. I attach the two pieces and take a puff.

After allowing the medication to ease my airways and resting for a stretch, I'm ready to go again. A few chipmunks scurry away when I heave off the rock. I stand tall, hands braced on the lightweight trekking poles Dom gifted me on our arrival at the trailhead.

"Let's get back to it."

To Dom's credit, he doesn't argue with me or push that we rest for longer. He trusts me to tell him my limits, and I appreciate that. Even when I wobble while trying to balance on a loose collection of logs laid over a stream, he doesn't swoop in and scoop me up.

Though his face does look pale, jaw tense, when I reach the other side and turn back to check on him.

Dom makes the crossing with annoyingly perfect grace. The hiking pants stretch over his muscular thighs, and I'm suddenly thankful for the rising temperature, because he's already stripped off his jacket. I chew on my lower lip as my eyes trace the way his sleeves strain over his biceps.

As if he can tell what has me distracted, Dom smirks.

"Come on, Maddie. You're holding up the line."

I snort but turn back to the trail. He's not *entirely* wrong.

Josh might send us to remote places, but they aren't without people. We've already crossed paths with a handful of other day hikers like us, and I bet if this were a weekend, we'd see a lot more. If my brother were here, he probably would have made friends with half the people we passed by now. Dom and I, introverts that we are, tend to offer nods and smiles and "Good day for a hike." And leave it at that.

We're loners.

Loners together.

Maybe Josh was worried about both *of us.*

Finally, after more breaks than I'd like but the amount I needed, the sparkle of water flashes through the trees. Another minute and we come upon a lake plucked from a fairy tale.

Alpine Lake. The water is so clear I can see straight to the bottom, which is a cluttered tapestry of stones and logs. Mountains surround the crystal water, their rocky peaks still holding on to small swaths of snow even in the middle of summer.

"Good choice, Josh," Dom murmurs as he stops by my side. The heat of his body so close to mine should bother me since I'm already sweaty and running hot from the exertion of the climb out here. But having Dom at my side is soothing and has been for a while.

Gone are the days where his presence brought discomfort and bad memories. Around him, the world feels better.

"Ready to read it?" He asks, voice low as if speaking too loudly might disturb the tranquil scene.

I nod and let my trekking pole dangle from my wrist as I open my hand to accept the envelope, hungry eyes on the familiar handwriting.

Idaho
44°03'53.6" N
115°01'21.7" W

Dear Maddie & Dom,

Welcome to Idaho!

Oh, Idaho, how did I overlook you? So many mountains. So much deep powder to ski down. And those views . . .

You see one now, right? I hope you do. Maddie, if you made the hike to the coordinates I left, I'm so proud of you. I know it's far, but I also knew you could do it.

And if you didn't, I'm still fucking proud of you because you don't have to climb a mountain to be amazing. But one day I hope you do because you deserve to see all the beautiful places in the world.

Assuming that you've both made it to Alpine Lake, it's time for my dreaded task! Don't worry, I've already made you hike miles, so I'll keep this one easy.

Tell each other what you hope your future looks like. What do you dream for yourself?

This is one of the things that made my diagnosis suck so much in the beginning. I lost my will to hope.

I found it again, and now my future isn't a faraway thing. It's tomorrow and the next day. Next week and maybe next month if I'm lucky.

But I still have dreams for those futures. Still have hopes.

And they're coming true. Mostly because I speak up now. I ask for what I want.

So, tell each other your perfect futures. Say them out loud. And help each other make them come true.

Love,
Josh

P.S. Don't forget to take a picture for me and leave me among the trees.

I huff a frustrated laugh. What is it with Josh wanting me to crack myself open time and time again. Isn't it enough that I have to deal with knowing each read letter is a step closer to his final words?

Dom clears his throat and I glance up at the tall man, framed in sunlight that sets the few lighter strands on his head to blazing.

"I can go first," he offers. "If you need time to think."

Truthfully? I do. If I want to say something other than . . .

My perfect future has my brother in it, but that's not going to happen, so I guess the rest of my life is shit.

"Go for it."

My body leans toward his, as if my cells want to know his answer. To melt this secret piece of Dom knowledge into the very makeup of my being.

He nods, gazing out over the pristine water before turning back to me.

"My perfect future has you in it." Dom's eyes hold mine, and I lose my breath again, but not because of the climb. The intensity of his stare holds me transfixed. Then his hands cup my face, and he tilts my chin at the perfect angle to deliver a soft kiss. "Happy birthday, Maddie."

I should've known he would remember. He has the day programmed as the lock on his safe, after all.

Today is my birthday. A day that my brother always sought to make special for me even if all he could afford was my favorite bag of candy from the local gas station. This day, a year ago, I was in a dark pit of misery that was only growing deeper after I cut off contact with my mother.

But today? This day is special again.

Because of my brother and his best friend.

I fully face Dom and press up on my toes, fisting my fingers in his moisture-wicking shirt to drag him down to me. Our mouths meet with a slow burning that ends with tangled tongues and both of us breathing heavy on each other's air. Eventually, I break away only so I don't have to take another dose of my inhaler to survive this man. Still, we hold on to each other, and I finally fulfill the requirements.

"My perfect future has more birthdays like this," I murmur, and Dom's lips twitch into a barely-there smile.

But I see it. And as his words and pleased expression play on repeat in my mind for the return journey, I can't help remembering how we only have two states left.

At the start of this, I wanted everything to go by faster. Get to the next destination quick, so I could hear from Josh and get Dominic Perry out of my life for good.

But now?

Now I think I'm ready for life to slow down.

Fall

Thirty-Five

The **OUT OF ORDER** sign on the elevator has me groaning.

"Sorry about that," Simon calls out to me from his desk. "Forgot to mention they're doing maintenance this morning. Should be good to go by the afternoon. Everyone coming in today is in for a morning workout." He chuckles and points toward the door leading to the stairs.

If only it were as simple as that. Walking up twelve flights of stairs might be annoying for the average person, but it's a breathing hellscape for me. Even after my Idaho training. I haven't taken many trips to the gym since getting back two months ago. My Bane mask is collecting dust on my shelf. My fitness level is questionable once more.

And I don't have Dom to give me a piggyback ride this time if I get too winded.

Which I will. Because it's *twelve* freaking flights.

And I've got a meeting at the top of those stairs in a half hour.

"Fuck," I mutter under my breath.

Walking farther down the hallway, I tug my phone out of my pocket and pull up Pamela's number. She answers on the second ring.

"Maddie! Are you almost here? We're getting set up in Conference Room B."

"Hey, Pamela. About that. How imperative is it that I attend in person?" My apartment is a fifteen-minute walk from here. A flat walk that ends with a functional elevator. I could get home and situated faster than I could get up these steps. I try not to dwell on how one technical malfunction has pretty much ruined my day. But I can still salvage things if—

"Oh no, Maddie. We need you here! You have the slides for the logistics team. And Francine even flew in this morning." She names the CEO of the company, and I barely keep a curse to myself. Francine likes me. We've had good interactions. But she's also old-school and big into the work-at-work mentality. If I try to video conference in, no matter how good the connection is, she'll be irritated.

Enough to consider replacing me?

I breathe with my diaphragm, hand on my belly, knowing panic won't help this situation. For a brief moment, I consider reminding Pamela about my asthma. She knows in a general sense that I have asthma. She's seen my inhaler. But I've never had to use it in front of her because the most I've exerted myself around her is hauling my laptop bag from room to room.

Still, what would telling her help? I need to attend this meeting, and she can't get the elevators turned on for me.

"Okay. Yes. Of course. I'll be there."

"Good. I'll save you a seat."

When we hang up, I stare at my phone screen, then switch my eyes back to the door of the stairwell. Better start now if I have a hope of making it up to the twelfth floor in time.

I really wish Dom were here.

And not just so he could carry me, although that would be nice.

What I need now is a distraction from how shitty this climb is about to be, and no one is better at claiming my attention than Dominic Perry.

On a wild hope, I pop in an earbud and dial his number.

He picks up after the first ring.

"Maddie?" Through the phone, I hear the smile in his voice.

"Hey." I sigh in relief from the simple fact that I was able to reach him so quickly.

"What's up? Is something wrong?"

Yes.

"No. I just have to do something tedious and annoying"—and potentially dangerous—"for the next twenty minutes or so. Are you busy? Could you entertain me?"

He chuckles, and I luxuriate in the sound. "Sure. I've got twenty minutes. How am I supposed to entertain you?" There's the sound of a door closing on his end, then Dom's voice lowers an octave. "Do you want me to describe what I'd do to you if I was with you right now?"

My heartbeat spikes and my breathing with it. Not a good idea.

"Sorry, that's a little *too* entertaining." I pull open the stairwell door and grimace at the cement steps. "Could you sing?"

"Maddie." He groans my name and even though it's in exasperation, I still love the sound.

"Come on," I plead. "We both know you have a rock star voice. I won't even set the playlist. Sing whatever you want."

"Hmm. Whatever I want?" He pauses. "Fine. When should I start?"

I stare up at the steep stairs and set my foot on the first. "Now, please. And I'm not going to be able to talk while I'm doing my tedious task, so you just keep going until I tell you I'm done." I mute myself, so he doesn't hear me when the inevitable panting starts.

"This sounds like a prank. But I'm trusting you, Sanderson." Dom clears his throat. Then the amazing man starts singing "Death of a Bachelor."

Of course. Josh loved the angry punk girl music, but Dom always leaned into the emo boy bands. In high school, he tried to comb his dark hair over his forehead and eyes like Brendon Urie and Gerard Way, but the strands constantly curled in a charming swoop.

I guess he continued to listen to his favorite band throughout the years.

I start my climb with a smile.

But inevitably it melts to a grimace, and eventually my mouth merely sags open as I pant. Dom's voice helps take my mind off the tightening in my chest, but no matter how amazing his serenading is, he can't sing breath into my lungs.

On the seventh floor, I'm forced to sit down and take a puff of my inhaler. As I give my lungs a break and listen to Dom sing more Panic! At the Disco, a guy in a suit literally jogs up the stairs, passing me by with barely a glance.

His ease taunts me, but I push my envy to the side as I rise to my feet again.

Fifteen minutes until my meeting and five more flights.

Dom moves on to "High Hopes," and it's like he knows exactly the boost I need.

When I reach the floor The Redford Team offices live on, I'm gasping but still breathing, and I've got five minutes to try and regain my composure before walking into the conference room. Before exiting the staircase, I unmute my phone.

"Hey," I wheeze, my throat expelling words like a punctured balloon. I wince at the tell, and Dom's abrupt change in tone.

"Maddie?" No more playful singing. "You sound out of breath."

I cough out a chuckle, glad he's not here to see how flushed and damp my face is. Good thing I wore black today, because I can feel sweat pooling in my pits.

"I'm fine." My voice sounds a touch better. Not much, though, and Dom can tell.

"What did you just do?"

"It's okay. Just, the elevator is broken at my office. I had to climb some steps." Look at that. Managing multiple sentences. I'm basically good as new. I check the time on my phone. Three minutes till the meeting. "Thank you—"

"How many floors?" His voice is ice. No more of the humor and crooning beauty of his singing.

"Not too many." I hold the phone away as I drag in another ragged breath, then press it back to my ear. "I've got to get to a meeting. You were great. Thank you."

"Maddie—"

"Love you! Bye!"

Only once I hang up do I realize what I just yelled at Dom to hurry him off the phone.

Oh god. Oh no.

Did I just tell Dom that I love him?

The panicked thought sticks with me as I hustle through the Redford workspace to Conference Room B. Luckily, someone decided to get this catered, and most everyone is too busy pouring themselves coffee and spreading cream cheese on bagels to notice I arrived with less than a minute to spare, looking like death dragged me up the stairs.

He won't think I meant it. He can't. It wasn't a real confession of love. Just a casual sign-off.

"Maddie," Pamela calls from across the room as she adds her third packet of sugar to her coffee. "Why don't you hook your computer up to the monitor so we can start this off with a look at the numbers?"

I nod and reach for the projector remote, both annoyed at my boss for mandating that I be here and grateful that she's given me something to focus on other than the words I accidentally spoke to a man who takes everything in life extremely seriously.

The meeting drags on all morning. It's not a pointless gathering, but the length could have been halved if my coworkers didn't enjoy hearing themselves talk so much. After my boss's boss says the same thing in a different way for the tenth time, I'm ready to toss him out the twelfth-story window and make him hike up all those stairs in hopes he'll be too winded to keep filling this conference room with his coffee breath and self-important chatter.

But I can't defenestrate a man just because he's annoying. I can't even sarcastically mock him the way I would Dom or Jeremy or Tula if they were bothering me this much. No, at work I must maintain my cheerful, helpful persona. The version of Maddie that has a smile for everyone and is a team player. The one who laughs at jokes even if the person has no idea what comedic timing is. The Maddie who quietly listens to coworkers complain about the most mundane things they could fix in five minutes.

The people at Redford call me sweet, and charming, and helpful. They also say I'm necessary, and a lifesaver, and irreplaceable.

Without the first list of adjectives, I doubt I'd hang on to the second. And without the second, my job security would be shaky.

So I keep my little annoyances to myself. Like having to climb up twelve flights of stairs when I have chronic asthma.

Finally, just before noon, my superiors land on a solution to the issue, and we're able to disperse. After collapsing into the chair at a free cubical, I slip my phone out of the pocket of my pants, which look like they're made of a dressy material but are just fitted sweatpants in disguise. Throughout the meeting my phone buzzed a few times, and I read over my text messages now.

> DOM: Call me when you get out of
> your meeting.
> DOM: Or if you get taken to the
> hospital after climbing twelve flights
> of stairs.
> DOM: And don't try lying about the
> number. I went to Redford's website,
> and it says what floor you're on.
> ADAM: Hey! I'm at lunch with Dom
> and he's being a growly dick! Food
> isn't helping!!! He keeps glaring at

his phone. Did something happen on
your last trip?

I sigh and tap Dom's name. Then I press my fingers against my lips, trying to smooth away the smile that automatically spreads at the thought of hearing his voice.

"Maddie." He says my name with a chiding growl when he picks up.

"Dominic." I deepen my voice, mocking his tone, and enjoy the relief at this quick moment of being myself after a morning of false smiles.

"How are you doing?" His tone has less censure this time, and I bet if I were in front of him, I'd catch the hint of a smile.

I hum a nonsense noise and press my chair into a slow spin. "Ready for lunch."

"I meant your breathing."

"Been doing it all morning. Don't plan to stop now."

"You shouldn't have had to climb all those stairs. It's bullshit."

The curse makes me smile wider. "Adam was right. You *are* growly today."

"You two talk about me?" Now he sounds extra grumpy, which just has me wanting to tease him more.

"Only *all* the time. Dom this, Dom that. We have no lives outside of our Dominic Perry fan club. Adam is arranging our annual conference in your honor. I'm in charge of the swag. I'm thinking shirtless blow-up dolls that look like you."

"Maddie," he huffs. "You can't say stuff like that."

"Why not? Saying stuff like that is ninety percent of my personality."

"Because when you go on nonsense tangents at my expense, I want to kiss you. Then fuck you until all you can say is my name."

"Dom!" I gasp.

"Just like that." He grunts. "And now I'm hard at my desk."

"That is entirely your fault. And here's your boner killer. What do I say to Adam?"

"What do you mean?"

My gut churns, and I have a flashback to that motel in Delaware where I threw up what felt like my entire soul when Dom rebuffed me after I kissed him.

"He asked if something happened on our last trip. And we both know some*thing* happened." *You said you wanted me in your perfect future.* "I just want to know what we're telling people."

And I need you to be the one to pick the words.

There's a pause on the other end of the line and dread liquifies my bones until I slip out of my chair and settle under my desk. I really wish I weren't in a cubical right now. Luckily, the office has mostly emptied out for the lunch hour.

Finally, Dom speaks. "I want you, Maddie. In every way I can have you. As your boyfriend. Your partner. Whatever you want to call us. But it needs to be just you and me. Monogamous. I'm yours. Only yours." His inhale is heavy and audible. "Are you mine?"

Warmth starts in my chest, then spreads through every one of my limbs, regrowing all my bones until I'm ready to get up and start dancing. Or at least crawl out from under my desk.

"Uh, yes. Okay. Sure," I say, starting to frown at my inability to speak like a mature adult. "I mean, I've got to say yes, right? I'd lose my membership to the Dominic Perry fan club if I didn't."

His laugh is a ragged growl. "You're adorable. And frustrating."

"I think what you meant to say was gorgeous and intriguing."

"Cute and aggravating."

"Effervescent and captivating."

"All those," he relents. "Plus, sexy as fuck."

The way he speaks the irresponsible word in his deep, tantalizing voice is too much for midday on a Monday. Plus, I just agreed to be *his*, and my mind is struggling to come to terms with that fact.

And trying not to panic.

I need a moment without his sinful voice in my ear to process these last five minutes of conversation.

"Glad we agree," I chirp. "Love you! Bye!"

I hang up.

Then gape at my phone.

I said it again. We went through that whole conversation without acknowledging my slipup, and then I said it. Again.

With a groan, I toss my phone across my desk before burying my head in my arms.

Thirty-Six

One week until I see Dom in person again, and I'm frantically working. Trying to make sure there's nothing that will come up while I'm gone and interrupt our North Dakota trip. I'm in the zone, knocking items off my to-do list left and right, which is why I barely suppress a growl when the phone in my shared cubicle rings.

I loathe unscheduled work calls. But it might be Pamela, and I'm not about to piss her off when I'm on the edge of a vacation.

A vacation with my boyfriend.

The thought of Dom brings a smile to my face and eases the tension in my shoulders. A little over a month has passed since he sang to me as I trekked up all those stairs to this floor, then said he was mine. We've video-chatted almost every night since, usually while I'm working on a puzzle. Unless it's a sexy Zoom call. We play other games during those.

And even though Dom isn't the most talkative person, he makes an effort for me. Or maybe it's not an effort. Maybe his dry retorts to my teasing trip easily off his lips. He's always on time for our chats. Always the one texting me in the morning asking what time I'm free to talk.

As if sensing my tendency to doubt, Dom hasn't given me a moment to question his commitment. He didn't just say he's in this with me. He's showing up.

And hell, it feels good to rely on him.

I pick up the phone, wishing I'll hear a deep voice on the other end saying, "Maddie."

Instead I get Toby, our reception desk attendant, with his rapid-fire nasally voice. "Maddie. Hi. You have a visitor here. I don't have approval to send them back. Could you come grab them?"

"A visitor?" Could he . . . No. Dom wouldn't have shown up early.

Or would he? Maybe dating me is pushing him to be a little spontaneous.

"Yes. Sorry. I have calls coming in." Toby's end of the line clicks dead, but I'm already hanging up on my end and shoving out of my chair.

Did he take the week off? Will I get seven more days of him?

Already I'm tired of the distance between us, but I haven't figured out a solution. The idea of moving back to Philadelphia gives me stress hives. That's where my toxic childhood home is, and I have a string of memories of Josh in a hospital bed.

Does it say something about me that I don't think I could move there for Dom?

But how could I ask him to relocate here? Leave his job. Leave his family. Leave his home.

This is all too early. You're moving too fast.

I may have more confidence in us, but we haven't been together long enough to broach that topic. Not yet.

Trying not to look like I'm sprinting, I hurry through The Redford Team workspace toward the front desk, searching for a familiar head of dark hair and set of striking eyes.

But when I reach reception, I stumble to a halt, faced with a familiar figure that is not the man I hoped to see.

"Surprise!" Cecilia Sanderson chirps while tucking her phone into her purse.

"What the hell?" I mutter, which makes my mother's smile take on a strained note.

"Is that any way to greet your mother?"

I don't bother answering the question because, honestly, I don't know the correct way to acknowledge the woman I haven't spoken to in over a year. I meant it when I said I was blocking her number, and I went ahead and blocked my grandmother, too. Not that I expected Florence to reach out to me, but just in case.

"What are you doing here?" A quick glance to the side shows a once-busy Toby is now watching this exchange with curious eyes.

"It's been so long—"

"Let's get lunch," I interrupt her. Whatever this unexpected visit is about, I don't want our mother-daughter catch-up happening in my workspace. Everyone at The Redford Team sees me as a reliable, levelheaded worker. If anyone can have me ruining my reputation, it's my mother.

She grins wide. "I would love that." There's an air of sincerity to her words that sends my mind reeling as I hasten back to my desk to grab my bag.

Does Cecilia actually want to have a meal with me? To catch up with me?

Maybe in the same way that this time since Josh's death has seen me set aside old grudges, she also experienced some shifts in her outlook on life.

Don't hope for too much.

But maybe I could hope for something.

The autumn weather is brisk as we walk a block to a trendy vegan restaurant I know my mother will prefer. I'll silently suffer through their lack of cheese. The chill temperature has me thinking of North Dakota and all the layers I plan to pack. But I can also rely on Dom and his body to keep me warm. The thought almost brings a smile to my face.

Then we sit down, and Cecilia immediately starts talking. "I think we can both admit I've given you long enough for this tantrum to pass. It's time for you to start thinking of someone other than yourself. You're not the only one who lost Josh." She flicks a napkin and settles it on her lap as I gape at her, feeling like I've been slapped.

"I-I know that." I stutter, though to be fair I was very self-focused at the funeral. But since then I've grasped how I'm not the only one grieving my brother. Dom sits prominent in my mind.

"Good." She offers me a sweet smile that looks wrong to me. "I'm looking forward to reading the letters he left you."

I jerk back so hard my chair almost topples over, and I think I scare our waitress. While Cecilia's words solidify in my brain, she orders for us, which I don't entirely mind because I can't comprehend the idea of eating at the moment.

"What do you mean you're looking forward to reading his letters? *My* letters?" I haven't even read all of them yet.

She huffs a breath and gives me a disappointed look. "Come now, Maddie. I miss my son. I deserve to read what he wrote."

Already I'm shaking my head. "The notes aren't for you." A wave of righteous aggression has me leaning forward with a glare. "Are you going to show me the letter he wrote *you*?"

For the first time a true emotion breaks through her motherly act. Discomfort. She clears her throat and smooths a hand down her linen shirt. "That was a personal correspondence. I'm his mother. It's different."

"The only thing different is I don't want to read what Josh wrote to you." And I realize as I say the words, they're the truth. I'm rabid to read the final two letters from him, even as I'm reluctant to run out of words. But I don't have the urge to track down the Perry parents to read their note. I haven't asked Adam or Carter to share theirs. Josh's words to someone else aren't what I want. What I need.

What I crave more than anything are the words he left for me.

Me and Dom. But I don't mind sharing with him. Not anymore.

My mother's whole face is pinched now, and I'm sure she'd be horrified if her followers saw her like this. "I thought you might have grown up by now. But you're still doing what you've always done." She shuts her mouth as our salads are delivered.

"And what's that?" I ask once the waitress is gone. "Respecting Josh's wishes?"

"Clinging to Josh," Cecilia snaps, voice low and harsh. "So much so you never bothered to *do* anything with your life." I flinch and she rolls her eyes, like my pain only annoys her. "To think I believed having another child might entice your father to stay. But you only drove him away faster. Watching you grow up, I don't know that I blame him." She aggressively stabs her lettuce. "Your brother had promise. He was popular and talented, even in high school. And as surly as that Dominic Perry was, he was just as impressive as your brother with all his sports and clubs." Cecilia sets her fork down with a clank without taking a bite. "And they were always bringing Rosaline around. Beautiful, charismatic, intelligent Rosaline. Do you know what it was like to come home and see her, the perfect daughter?" She goes back to salad stabbing. "Meanwhile, you followed the three of them everywhere. And when you weren't annoying your brother and his friends, you just sat there with your books. Reading about make-believe worlds instead of living in the real one."

As my mother goes into what sounds like a prerehearsed speech about how much of an utter disappointment I am, I sit completely still. I'm worried if I move, the jagged spikes of her vitriol will work deeper under my skin. Only by not moving can I avoid fatal internal bleeding.

All my life she's thrown dismissive, hurtful comments my way, but this is the first time I'm getting a full lecture. As if she came here with the sole intention of breaking me down. Wearing away any bit of self-confidence I've built for myself.

What would I have turned into if Cecilia was all I'd ever had?

Without Josh, I'm not sure I would have survived.

"My mother always said if it weren't for you, your father would have come back." Cecilia glares at me, and I'm shocked to see the glimmer of tears in her eyes. "But he never did. I lost my husband. And I lost my son. First to travel—probably to get some distance from you—and then to cancer." Finally, she puts food in her mouth, briefly stemming the flow of her condemnation.

"That's . . ." I rasp. "That's not . . . I didn't *make* them leave."

At least, I don't think I did.

She swallows and stares at me like I'm a dead fly she found in her food. "Well, you weren't worth sticking around for, either, were you?"

The statement rings like a too-loud gong in my mind.

This would be an optimal time to cry—when the woman who is supposed to love me unconditionally is pointing out how I drive people away.

This is what she does, I try to remind myself. *Acts the saint until she doesn't get her way.*

But when I was growing up, her retaliation wasn't like this. She was dismissive and would disappear on a random trip. Florence was the one to berate me with harsh words. I wonder if mother and daughter have been spending more time together.

This clarifies something I always had trouble understanding: Florence's clear dislike for me. But I guess if my grandmother blamed me for the dissolution of her daughter's marriage, the harsh words she always flung at me make more sense.

But that doesn't make them right.

And I don't have to listen to this.

With a jerky move, I stand from my chair.

"Don't contact me again," I tell her. "If you do, I will post online all of the horrible things you just said to me. I doubt your followers will be very impressed that you bully your daughter."

She gasps, but I don't stay around to hear whatever convoluted defense she comes up with for herself.

And as I walk on shaky legs back to my job, I try not to internalize her criticism. But I can't hear my voice in my own head. Only hers. I need something to drown out the toxic noise.

I know it's the middle of his workday, but I still dial Dom's number as I hide out in the stairwell. I don't plan on climbing them, but I figure with the elevator working this is likely as much privacy as I can hope for.

The phone rings four times before going to his voicemail. Not wanting to worry him, I leave a quick message. "Hey! Just wanted to say hi. Feel free to ignore this. I'm sure we'll talk later." I hang up.

"You followed the three of them everywhere . . . annoying your brother and his friends . . ."

But I don't annoy Dom. He said . . . In Idaho he said . . .

I grit my teeth as I try to pull up the beautiful memory, but I only see Dom and Rosaline pulling into the driveway of my childhood home, and Josh sprinting out the front door to hop in the back seat of the car. They drove away, and I hid in my bedroom, wishing I could go with them. The three of them were best friends.

I don't need to cling to them. My thumb shakes as I swipe through my contacts and find another number.

Jeremy picks up on the second ring. "Thank god you called. My eyes are going to start bleeding if I stare at my screen any longer."

The greeting immediately relaxes an unforgiving band I hadn't realized was tightening around my lungs. I breathe easier and manage a not-too-strained voice. "How did I know you needed me? We must have a psychic connection."

"I've always thought so. What am I thinking now?"

More tension in my body loosens as I lean against the cold concrete wall. "Hmm. You're thinking that you want to binge a new K-drama and eat too much Gouda tonight with me."

"Amazing. You should have your own circus act with skills like that." I can hear the smile in my friend's voice and find comfort in how quickly he signs on to spending time with me.

"You need to pull your weight, sir," I mock scold him. "Dessert duty."

"Of course. I'm feeling cannoli. I'm also feeling . . ." He pauses, and I try not to read into the hesitation. "I'm feeling like you're upset about something."

Damn him. Why does he have to be so perceptive?

I clutch the front of my sweater to try to stop the shaking in my hand. Briefly, I consider lying to him. But after the awkward meeting between him and Dom, I've been trying to be more honest. Even about uncomfortable things.

"It's just some drama with my mom. Stuff I'd rather not dwell on."

Jeremy's voice is gentle this time. "Okay. I get that. We don't have to talk about it." He clears his throat. "But we can," he offers. "If you want to."

"I don't." I want to forget. "But thank you."

Jeremy doesn't take offense to my dismissal, and we set up a time for him to arrive at my place.

Later, when I'm at my desk trying to find the laser focus I had before, my phone rings with Dom's name. I ignore the call in favor of texting him that I'm trying to finish up my work for the day and I won't be able to chat later because of my plans with Jeremy.

No reason to feel guilty, I assure myself. *I'll see him in a week.*

Everything will be better then.

Thirty-Seven

For the North Dakota trip, I find another bed and breakfast. This one is bird-themed, and I cannot wait to see Dom's face when he walks into the peacock room I booked for us. Alone for now, I collapse on the bed giggling as I take in all the peacock-themed decor, including a headboard resplendent with feathers fanned out, mimicking the look of a peacock tail.

"I'm going to say 'cock' so many times," I mutter in glee.

Eager to finally see Dom in person after months of being apart, I shove off the cushy bed and search for my purse, digging through it until I unearth my phone. This device has been my main connection to him. But soon I'll have my hands on Dom, then my mouth, then my tongue. And after I go sex wild on him, I'll get to slow down and take my time. Run my fingers through his silky hair. Feel his chest vibrate with a chuckle when I make a snarky comment. Coax him into singing so I can hear his deep voice and watch his lips spread in a smile I'll get to kiss the corners of.

As I search my phone's screen for a notification from Dom, I realize I never turned off airplane mode. My rental car had a navigation system I used to get to this small North Dakota town, and Dom's flight isn't supposed to arrive for another half hour, so I wasn't expecting any messages.

Which is why I'm surprised when my phone starts chiming immediately upon connecting to data.

Multiple messages and missed calls from Dom.

I dial him right away instead of reading his texts.

"Maddie." Dom sighs my name, picking up on the first ring. A knot of anxiety in my chest eases at the sound of his voice.

"Hey. Sorry, I left my phone in airplane mode, and I just got to the B&B. Did your flight get in early?" Regret pinches me. If I'd turned on my phone and checked his flight, I would have realized and hung around the airport so we could share a car and an extra few hours together.

"I missed my flight."

A spike of worry stabs into my chest. "What happened? Are you alright?"

"I'm fine," he assures me, and I breathe easier. "I couldn't get to the airport in time. A pipe burst in our house—Rosaline's house."

The air expels from my lungs so fast I'm sure someone just punched me in the gut.

Our house.

That slip shuts something down inside me.

A part of my brain keeps track of the conversation enough to hear him explain how there was a foot of water in the basement and in their scramble to save her belongings he lost track of time, got on the road too late, and missed his flight.

But while that information registers on the outermost layer of my consciousness, I'm locked deeper in my mind. In a dark place I thought—hoped—I'd never return to again. The place that compares me to another woman and finds all the ways I'm lacking.

She's more beautiful than me.

She's smarter than me.

She's friendlier than me.

She's kinder than me.

When she needs him, he goes to her.

He goes to their house.

She was his first.

She'll be his last.

He'll leave me for her. Just like he did last time.

"Now there's a storm grounding the planes." Dom's voice is low and tense with frustration. "Nothing is going out. I'm sorry, Maddie. I'll get there as soon as I can."

He's only coming because he feels responsible for me.

Because Josh thought I needed someone to hold my hand, and Dom's instinct is to care for people.

I've been fooling myself this whole time, lying to myself that Josh thought I could take care of Dom. That he'd leave the responsibility of his best friend's well-being to me. That my brother thought I had enough strength to be strong for someone else.

But Josh knew me best. He knew how weak I was.

How weak I *am*.

Not like Rosaline.

"Do you know what it was like to come home and see her, the perfect daughter?"

Rosaline was so amazing even my mother wanted her as a daughter.

"You weren't worth sticking around for, were you?"

I guess I'm also not worth making a flight for.

Not when his ex-wife needs him to help fix something in the home they used to share.

How long before he goes back?

The painful doubts prick at me until I'm flinching back into reality and armoring myself with anger to protect my ravaged underbelly.

"Don't bother," I say into the phone I still clutch to my ear.

"What?"

"You're busy. Don't inconvenience yourself." Shoving off the bed, I kneel by my suitcase and unzip the large pocket. Pushing aside my cutest sweaters and a new silk nighty I feel like a fool for buying, I unearth Josh. "I'm here. I have the ashes. I'll go to the coordinates and spread them myself."

"Maddie." Dom's voice tightens. He almost sounds hurt. "We're supposed to do this together."

"I know that. *I'm* the one who's here," I snap. He has no right to feel pain over this decision. I'm the one alone in North Dakota.

"And I'll be there soon." He keeps his voice calm and careful. "With the letter."

The letter. Josh's words.

I was supposed to be only a short drive away from hearing Josh speak to me again. And even if he did pity me, his homebody sister, that doesn't change the fact that I love him. That I need him.

In this moment more than ever.

I still can hear from him. I don't need Dom to be here with me.

"I'll call you when I'm at the destination. You can read it to me."

Ignoring the sounds of his protest, I hang up my phone and switch it back to airplane mode.

With fingers that shake, I grab the rental keys and the room key that has a tiny peacock key chain I don't find so charming anymore. When I'm in the car, I start the engine and point the wheels toward the next destination.

North Dakota's Enchanted Highway.

This time I did my research, wanting to know how much physical training I'd need to reach the coordinates Josh left. But there's no hiking this time around. This visit clearly arose from my brother's fascination with roadside oddities.

When I set out, my intention was to head directly to the coordinates.

But the Enchanted Highway has multiple massive sculptures along the route, and when I spy the first one, my hands turn the wheel to pull over and park without conscious thought.

Geese in Flight. I recall the name from my online search, and I spend a good long time staring at the geese formed from scrap metal.

Eventually, I start the car again and keep driving, only to pull over at the next one. *Deer Crossing.*

When I stop at the third—*Grasshoppers in the Field*—I realize I'm avoiding the end. The end of this, the second to last trip.

Avoiding the man who's been with me at every other step of this journey.

When I reach the coordinates, I'll have to call Dom. I'll have to listen to his excuses that don't change the fact that he's *not here.*

I want to reach the coordinates and call Dom so he'll read Josh's words to me.

I don't want to reach them, because I'll call Dom and he'll read the letter to me.

Then that'll be it.

That piece will be done.

One more remnant of my brother will be gone.

My eyes flick to my passenger seat where Dom should be sitting. Where one eighth of Josh sits instead.

"Why did you make me do this with him?" I ask Josh, hopelessness and anger a tangle in my voice. "You were wrong if you thought he needed me." My fingers grip the steering wheel tight. "And you were wrong if you thought *I* needed *him.*"

Ahead, I spy the next sculpture. The one the coordinates lead to.

I park and stare out my windshield at the gigantic birds.

Pheasants on the Prairie.

"You would've loved this." I laugh, though the noise sounds more panicked than humorous. Needing to breathe fresh air and to avoid the sense of being trapped, I climb out of my car with Josh in my arms and approach the forty-foot-tall metal rooster.

With fingers that I swear aren't shaking, I power my phone on. Multiple missed calls and texts and voicemail notifications pop up, but I don't bother to look or listen. I simply click on the number I've called daily since my birthday.

A few months of letting myself live in a fantasy.

But I never should've relied on him. He's the most responsible man I've ever known, and he still abandoned me.

It's me. I've always known I was easy to set aside.

He picks up on the first ring.

"Maddie! Goddamn it. Are you alright? It's been two hours."

"I'm aware." The snark in my voice covers up my pain. "And I managed to survive them without you. Impressive, huh?"

Dom ignores my sarcasm the same way he did at Josh's funeral when I threw verbal barbs at him from a collapsed box of toilet paper.

"I've been studying the storm system," he says. "It should be clearing out by midnight. I can get on a flight first thing in the morning and be there by afternoon tomorrow."

"Like I said before, don't bother." The wind plucks at my loose hair and I clutch Josh tight against my chest as if his remains will warm me. "I'm changing my flight to leave in the morning. I'm at the coordinates now. Just open the letter and read it."

Despite the chill of the day, my hands are sweaty against the glass Rubbermaid.

"I don't think—"

"Open the letter and read it," I grit out. "Or I'll hang up and spread the ashes without you even listening in."

"Can't we just—"

"This is your final warning."

"Fine." Dom's voice has a ragged edge. "I'm opening it."

I expect relief to flood my chest at his words, but all I feel is anxiety. And loneliness.

I'm not lonely. I have Josh. Josh's words are all I need.

There's the sound of tearing over the line, and a moment later Dom clears his throat. "I'm going to start reading. Ready?"

"Yes."

Dear Maddie and Dom,

Welcome to North Dakota.

If it's anything like the other letters, there should be an exclamation mark there. But Dom speaks in a monotone. And I struggle to hear my brother's voice through his.

You should be standing near, or under, a giant bird right about now.

"What does that mean?"

It takes me a moment to realize the question was from Dom, not the letter. I'm tempted to say that if he wanted to know, he should've showed up himself. But that won't get him to keep reading.

"It's a metal sculpture. The Enchanted Highway. Keep reading."

Take a picture for me. Now, let's get to what I want you both to do here in my memory . . .

Dom's voice cuts off, and I check my phone to see if the call dropped. Nope, still going strong.

"Keep reading," I tell him. "Out loud." Maybe Dom didn't realize he'd stopped speaking.

There's a throat clearing on the other end of the line, which reassures me the call is still connected.

"Maddie," he says. "We should be together when I read this."

No! I need my brother now. Right now. "Just finish the letter."

"We can reschedule North Dakota," he offers, "if staying an extra day doesn't work for you."

Panic and anger pulse through my veins in a headache-inducing toxic sludge.

"You know what would work for me, Dom? If you read the god-damn letter my brother left!" *And read it* right *so all I hear is him and not you!*

My outburst results in a long pause on his end, so all I'm left listening to is the wind and my heavy breathing.

Then . . .

"I can't. We need to be together to do this."

Fury scalds the inside of my body until every part of me is pain-fully tender.

"No. We don't." I bite off each word. "I don't need *you*, Dom." My fingers clutch my phone too hard, and my other hand presses the container of Josh's remains into my chest. "You know what? Fuck you. Fuck you very much. I'll spread the ashes on my own."

I end the call and shut my phone down again so he can't pester me with more calls and messages. Then I pace and rage at the man.

How dare he?

How dare he not show up?

How dare he refuse to read my brother's last words to me?

How dare he trick me to counting on him only to abandon me again?

With slippery fingers, I wrench the airtight lid off the container of ashes. Only, in my haste to open the Rubbermaid, the whole thing flies from my hands, whirls through the air, and lands lid-off and upside-down on the dusty ground.

"Josh!" I cry out, falling to my knees beside the overturned con-tainer. Unrelenting wind swirls the grit on the ground, mixing in with the precious pieces of my brother until I can't see where he is anymore.

Until he's gone, and I don't even have his written words to com-fort me.

A dry sob chokes out of my throat. No tears come, but I start coughing and wheezing, struggling to inhale through my grief and loneliness and fury.

How dare Dom keep Josh from me?

As the sharp ache of unfulfilled breaths stabs at my chest, I scramble for my inhaler.

Even though my hands shake, I manage to spray the medication into my airways. But recovery is slow and painful. Especially with no one here to distract me or comfort me or simply reassure me that I'm not alone.

But that's exactly what I am. What I always seem to be.

Alone.

Thirty-Eight

I arrived home from North Dakota a week ago and haven't gone much of anywhere since, other than my bed and my couch. When Pamela texted me to come into work, I replied that I was sick. I'm still working, though. Doing the bare minimum needed to keep the company from collapsing in on itself.

If I had trained someone on my job, I could take time off to mourn.

The mocking thought fills my stomach with sickening guilt. What is wrong with me? I'm more seriously considering a break from work due to Dom and me imploding than I did when my brother passed away.

I'm a mess. A wreck. And I still haven't cried.

With all the aimless drifting my mind and body take part in, I might as well be a ghost living in Vulture City.

A pounding knock on my door jerks me from a half-sleep state. I unearth myself from the mound of blankets I entombed myself in sometime after finishing my last work task. Submitting data reports drains me in a way it didn't used to.

All I want is to sleep and not dream.

The knock comes again, and I glance at the oven clock, which tells me it's just past seven. I slept for two hours. This has become a habit lately. Spending my evenings either asleep or in a groggy half-conscious state. Waking up just enough to go eat something, go through my nightly routine, then tuck myself into my bed and attempt to sleep some more.

Another knock.

"Coming," I shout, my voice croaky.

Jeremy is going to want fancy cheese. As I push to my feet, I try to remember the last time I went to the store. I'm not sure I even have a basic cheddar.

I'll need to distract him before he asks. He'll know something is wrong if he finds out I don't have cheese. Then he'll pry. Jeremy will find a way to make me admit what I did. That I blew up at the guy I kept secret from my friends. That I tore into the man I was falling in love with—again—the minute he messed up.

I'll have to say it all out loud.

Have to face what I knew from the start but tried to forget: Dom and I will never work.

Maybe I can convince Jeremy we're better off ordering takeout.

"I don't . . ." I start speaking the moment I pull open the door, but my words trail off when I realize the person on the other side isn't my dairy-mooching friend.

Adam Perry stares at me, concern creasing his forehead as his eyes take me in. "Hell, Maddie. You look like—"

A sharp cough cuts him off, and I realize both twins are on my doorstep. Carter slips around Adam and offers a soft smile. "Hey, Maddie. You look tired. Did we wake you up?"

"Uh . . . yeah." Dazed, I flick my eyes between the two Perry boys and wonder if I'm still dreaming. "You're here. In Seattle." Look at me, stating the obvious. But a part of me wonders if I did fall asleep in my blanket pile and I'm living out an odd dream.

"We wanted to see you," Adam explains.

"Can we come in?" Carter asks. "Or take you out for food?"

As much as I don't want to leave my condo, or do much of anything really, I also can't stand the idea of these two men poking around my place when I haven't even run my robot vacuum in days. Plus, I can't feed them here.

"Food sounds good." I glance down at myself and realize I'm wearing the same shirt I fell asleep in last night. "Let me change."

Carter, who I always thought was the more perceptive of the two, slaps a hand onto his brother's shoulder, guiding Adam toward the elevator. "We'll sit in the car. Green Honda parked half a block to the right of the front door."

I nod, shut my door, and suck in a shaky breath that barely fills my lungs.

"Get changed. Get food. Thank them for coming. Send them home." Having the simple list of tasks helps me focus and get my feet moving. In my closet, I realize I've neglected laundry along with everything else. I pull on a sweatshirt with no shirt and no bra underneath, and a neon pink pair of athletic leggings I bought for my gym training with Jeremy.

Not runway ready, but at least both items smell clean.

I find the car easily and reach for the door to the back seat, only for the passenger side to open.

"Come on, Maddie!" Adam calls from behind the wheel. "You're riding shotgun."

I smooth away a grimace. So much for my hope to quietly fade into the background while the twins talk to each other. This will put me right in the middle of the group.

Surprisingly, once I'm settled and strapped in, Adam doesn't immediately start with jokes or probing questions. Instead, he pulls on to the road and types in a familiar business into his GPS.

Taco Bell

I almost smile. Almost.

But the expression feels like a muscle movement I don't know how to accomplish. Like I've forgotten.

We drive to the food chain in silence. Adam orders for us at the drive-through, getting the same selections we'd always choose all those years ago.

It's strange how I can feel so empty, yet also have this uncomfortable pressure in my chest.

I got dressed. We got food. Now I just thank them for coming and send them home.

My throat clearing sounds overly loud in the small car.

"Thank you for visiting, but—"

"You stopped answering my texts." Adam speaks over me, cutting off my attempt to create distance.

A guilty blush infuses my face. In my defense, I stopped answering most everyone's texts. Communicating about anything not related to work just seemed so . . . insurmountable.

Especially with Dom's name continuing to appear on my phone.

"I'm sorry. I'll do better." *Will I, though?*

"Maddie." Adam taps his thumb on the steering wheel. "This isn't the first time you've ghosted me."

At this rate, I'm not sure I'll be able to eat anything, guilt twisting my insides into an indigestible tangle. I never let myself think about the effect my permanent departure had on the twins, I was so focused on my own heartache.

"I know. That was a shitty thing to do." But apparently on brand. Because I'm a shitty person who blows up at a man I care about and drops her brother's ashes in the dirt and can't cry even though the most important person in her life is dead.

"I think it was self-preservation," he says.

I blink at Adam, not sure I heard him properly.

"What?"

But I don't get my answer right away, because he takes a large bite of his burrito and chews slowly. Only once the guy swallows does he clarify.

"I panicked," he says. "After that summer, when you stopped

answering our texts. I thought something happened to you. I begged Dom to drive me out to Seattle when I found out you moved there, so I could check on you."

"You did?" My throat tightens, and I palm my inhaler in my sweatshirt pocket. I don't trust my lungs to function in emotional situations.

He throws me a rueful smile. "In case it wasn't obvious, I used to be slightly obsessed with you, Maddie Sanderson." He grimaces. "A Perry trait, turns out." Before I can think of a response to that, Adam shakes his head and continues. "But when Dom realized how serious I was, he sat me down and told me it was his fault you left. That he pissed you off and did something unforgivable, and you didn't want to be around him." Adam rubs his thumb over his bottom lip in an agitated gesture. "I was livid. I didn't speak to him for a month. But I never blamed you."

My whole body aches at his admission. "You should have. Even if I was mad at Dom, I shouldn't have cut you both out, too. I shouldn't have left . . ." I trip over the realization as I say it but keep speaking anyway. "I shouldn't have left you."

Fucking hell. I left.

I did to Adam and Carter what everyone in my life had always done to me.

Adam reaches over to take my hand, giving my fingers a gentle squeeze. "Dom never told us what he did to piss you off, but I can guess. And he did it again, didn't he?"

He chose Rosaline over me.

At least, that's how it felt when I was standing in the peacock bedroom all alone and he said her name. Said he wasn't coming, and it was because Rosaline needed him at *their* house.

"I'll answer your calls," I say instead of answering Adam's question. "And your texts. I swear. And I'll visit you. I want to come see your workshop." He told me about the studio space he's renting, and I bet it's full of amazing creations and smells like freshly cut wood.

Adam squeezes my hand again. "Cool. I'd like that. And you can come with me to cheer on *his* slow ass at his next swim competition." Adam throws a thumb toward his twin in the back seat. "But we're talking about you."

I flick my eyes to the rearview mirror and meet Carter's gaze. Sometimes he's so quiet I could forget he's back there.

But I never do.

"How's life, Carter?"

The corners of his eyes crinkle in a knowing smile. My attempted subject change was kind of obvious.

"Okay. Trying to figure out if Adam and I need to Saran Wrap Dom's car."

I groan and let my head drop to the dashboard, bombarded with bittersweet memories of the Perry prank antics.

"Don't do that. Dom technically didn't do anything wrong. Not this time anyway. I just . . ." I suck in a shuddering sigh. "We were starting something. And I realized it's a bad idea."

"Why?" Adam asks, the question slightly garbled because the temptation of Taco Bell was too much, and he's taken another bite of his burrito.

I shrug. "We don't work. For a lot of reasons." Mainly mine. I'm the problem.

"Does being with Dom make you happy?" Adam asks, like that's the simplest question to answer.

"Being with Dom makes me . . ." So many different things.

Happy. Aggravated. Exhilarated. Angry. Giddy.

But mostly . . . terrified.

"Spending time with Dom made it clear we won't work," I finally land on. "And that's okay." *Please let me be okay. Let me survive this.* "But that's between your brother and me. It doesn't affect how I feel about you two. It shouldn't have back then. And I won't let it now."

I make sure to meet both their eyes in turn. "Thank you for coming. Really. Thank you for not giving up on me."

Adam reaches over to squeeze my knee. Carter does the same to my shoulder, then leans forward, shoving his shoulders between our seats and pressing buttons on the screen until he connects his phone to the car Bluetooth.

"Since Adam picked the food, we pick the music."

It's an old refrain that has my heart clenching in nostalgic joy. A moment later, the *Wicked* soundtrack starts up and Carter cranks the volume. Adam groans at first, but it's not long before he's belting out about defying gravity along with us.

As we eat greasy food and pretend we're Broadway stars, the pressure in my chest eases, and the emptiness . . . Well, it doesn't disappear.

But the gaping hole of sadness lessens. Just a touch.

Because in this moment, I'm not alone. Not only did the twins not abandon me, but they also both sought me out when *I* left them. They held on to me.

And in this moment, they feel a lot like brothers.

CHAPTER

Thirty-Nine

"I'll get it!" Adam shouts when there's a knock on my door. I cringe, expecting it's my downstairs neighbor coming to scold us for being too loud. But it's hard to keep things down with not only Adam and Carter in my apartment, but Jeremy and Tula, too. My friends showed up this morning with croissants and a determination to excavate me from my blanket pile of sadness, unaware that the Perry twins had beaten them by a day.

Of course, my friends didn't just say "Looks like they've got it covered" and leave. No, they invited themselves into my condo and started peppering the guys with questions about a younger Maddie, all while cooking breakfast in *my* kitchen. After a good hour of this, I couldn't ignore how much of myself I'd kept from Jeremy and Tula. How little I talked about my past.

This was different, though. Hearing about younger me from Adam and Carter's perspective. They told stories about me like I was this cool chick they were lucky to know. I'm still processing the unfathomable perspective.

At one point, Jeremy disappeared and returned with his partner, Carlisle, and an armful of board games. That's when things really started to get rowdy. It's like they think the more boisterous they are, the less time I'll have to slip back into despair.

Which, to be fair, seems to be working.

Well, that and my reignited competitive nature. I'd just finished yelling a series of Pictionary guesses at Carter, who is a fantastic singer but terrible artist, when the knock sounded.

If Ms. Boyd from downstairs is here to berate me for hollering "In *what* fucking universe is *that* a fairy godmother?!" then I deserve it.

"Wait, Adam," I call after him as I stand, not wanting anyone to get tongue-lashed in my stead. "I'll get it."

But the guy is too quick, already at my front door with a charming grin on his face. When he turns the knob and swings it open, I watch his welcoming expression morph into surprise, then, of all things, nervousness.

"Adam?" The deep voice is unmistakable and stops my feet so fast, my fuzzy socks have me sliding on the hardwood floor.

"Dom!" Adam lets out a strained laugh. "Hey, bro! What a coincidence, am I right? Had no idea you were coming."

And there he is. The man I most want to see, while also the one I most want to hide from under an avalanche of blankets.

Seeing Dom now, a crush of recent memories makes me gasp in my next few breaths.

Him wrapping his arms around me on the shores of Alpine Lake.

His voice saying I was a part of his perfect future.

His hot kiss in the airport after swearing to see me soon.

His voice on the phone telling me he wouldn't make it.

Him saying Rosaline's name and *our* house.

His refusal to read Josh's letter to me when I was alone and needed my brother.

I'm too mixed up in the good and the terrible associated with him to figure out how to respond to his sudden appearance.

Plus, he's put together much better than I was twenty-four hours ago when the twins discovered me. Dom wears a perfectly fitted button-up with ironed slacks and polished loafers. His hair is styled, and his face is shaved.

This is accountant Dom. He stands on my threshold looking as devastating as ever. All broad shoulders and dark eyes and looming presence.

Luckily, Adam Perry exists in the world.

"Come on in. Join the party. You know the gang, right?" Adam claps a hand on Dom's shoulder and draws his brother into my home. Then he shuts the door, trapping us all inside together.

And I try not to cringe at the added awkwardness of Dom actually not knowing everyone. After the unexpected encounter with Jeremy, I planned to find a time to officially introduce Dom to Tula and Carlisle. But this is the first time he's been back in Seattle since the Idaho trip.

Dom's sharp gaze scans the room, giving Jeremy, Tula, and Carlisle curt nods of acknowledgment. His eyes narrow when they land on Carter.

When Dom looks at me, I see the betrayal on his normally unreadable face.

"You're keeping in touch with my brothers."

Guilt twists in my gut, but then consternation fueled by anger unwinds it. "No. Actually, they took my radio silence as an invitation to show up. Which you did, too, it would seem. Can't a girl properly ghost people these days? Next time I'll buy a van and go off-grid."

Ah, discomfort covered by sarcasm. My old friend.

Dom's lips tighten, then relax. "We need to talk."

"I have guests over." A protective barrier of friends that are currently keeping me from tearing into Dominic Perry.

Or kissing his face off.

Or climbing out my window and down my fire escape.

I don't know what I want to do more, but it's probably not healthy that I have such an equally strong urge for all three.

"Hey, guys!" Jeremy jumps up from his cross-legged seat on the ground and captures the attention of the room. "You want to see a condo with the exact same layout as this one but is three floors closer to the ground?"

"You know I do!" Adam responds with equal enthusiasm, and I wonder if the reason I gravitated toward Jeremy in the first place was that he reminded me of a certain Perry.

"You know, I think I forget what your place even looks like," Tula says to Carlisle.

"Yes. And I left the stove on," Carlisle adds. "Silly of me. Must go turn that off. Immediately."

Carter merely shrugs. "Sure. Let's go."

I gape as my buffer network promptly abandons me. And I'm on my own.

With Dominic Perry.

The man steps forward, and I suddenly feel like prey in my own home. Stalked by him and his intense stare and impeccably dressed body. I tear my eyes from his and point at the couch.

"Sit. You're looming. I don't abide looming in my home. It's strictly against the rules."

He doesn't follow my command. Instead, Dom strides until he's standing directly in front of me.

Looming dialed up to a thousand.

He's so close I can smell his cedar scent and see the twitching vein in his forehead.

"You know what I *don't abide*? Is you letting me have a taste of life with you, then disappearing the moment things don't go exactly as you planned," he growls.

I gape at the man. Guess we're not playacting niceties.

Fury burns through me, fueling my next scathing words.

"So what? You're saying I should get used to you abandoning me? If you shut me out, I should shut my mouth and deal with it?"

"No—"

"*You* didn't show. *You* refused to read Josh's letter to me." I jab him in the chest with a finger, emphasizing my hissed accusations. "*I'm* not the reason we're over. *You* are."

"Over?" Dom rasps the question.

I guess this is the problem with ghosting. You never properly clarify that things have ended.

"We never should've started in the first place." Crossing my arms over my chest, I hope I look intimidating rather than like I'm protecting my vital organs. "It was a mistake we made because of grief. Or loneliness. Or whatever."

"No," he growls. "It wasn't. And I'm going to read you the letter now because I didn't want to talk about this on the phone. I needed to see your face even if you won't meet my eyes."

Dom pulls a familiar envelope out of his back pocket, and my heart hurts to see the ragged edge of where it's already been torn open.

He slips the letter free and starts reading before I can decide if I want to hear it.

Dear Maddie and Dom,

Welcome to North Dakota!

You should be standing near, or under, a giant bird right about now. Take a picture for me.

Now, let's get to what I want you both to do here in my memory.

This is a big one. First off, Maddie, your job is to listen. That's it. Just listen. Let Dom speak before you decide anything.

Secondly, Dom, your job is to tell my sister why we didn't speak for a stretch of time this past year.

And hey, maybe this request is immaterial. Maybe you've already told her everything. But if I know you, Dom, which I think I still do, you haven't. And let me give you a piece of advice.

Tell Maddie everything. Always. Don't hold back.
I wish I hadn't.

Love,
Josh

"What does that mean?" My agitated fingers fist in my sweater, trying to find comfort in the knitted material. "About you not talking to Josh?"

Dom refolds the paper, then extends his arm so I can take it from him. I do, unfolding and scanning the letter. Everything is as he just read it.

"He meant exactly what he said. Josh refused to talk to me for a month." Dom straightens his shoulders, bracing himself for whatever comes next. "He kept pushing me about the divorce. Saying that when he was gone, Rosaline and I would need each other. That whatever happened between us we should forgive and forget and rebuild our marriage. One day, I snapped." Dom's entire body is tense as he speaks. "I told him that Ros and I never should've gotten married in the first place. That I knew it was a mistake even when I spoke my vows."

I jerk my head back, blinking fast. "You . . . What?"

Dom leans toward me, his earnest gaze holding mine. "I told Josh we got married because Rosaline was pregnant."

Those last three words play on repeat in my head, looping over and over again as my memory takes me back to that morning when I watched as Dom proposed. She'd had tears in her eyes, glittering like delicate jewels on her lashes.

I'd thought they were happy tears.

I'd thought a lot of things.

"But"—I gasp, my airways tight—"you don't have a kid." That's something I would know, no matter how much I tried to cut out all reminders of Dom from my life.

His gaze falls to his shiny shoes, and I hear a thickness in his voice when he next speaks.

"A miscarriage. A month after we got married."

My first thought comes with an unexpected wave of pain.

Josh is not the first one Dom lost.

The man is a planner. Fatherhood may have been a surprise, but he'd immediately dive into the role. Pick names, paint the bedroom, research the safest car seat. Hell, he probably started a college fund for his unborn child.

And then there was no kid.

One more shitty thing in life that Dom couldn't control. A loss that probably wrecked him. Maybe left scars.

Wounds that Josh's diagnosis might have reopened.

My urge is to hug him, but I wrap my arms around myself instead. "I'm sorry. I didn't know. I . . ." I dig my fingers into my sides and try to shove away the anger that still smolders alongside my sadness. "I was mad at you. But I never wanted something like that to happen. I'm sorry, Dom. I really, truly am."

He dips his chin to his chest. "I shouldn't have let things go on as long as they did with Rosaline. After the miscarriage, I think we just stayed together because it was comfortable. We both wanted something stable. It wasn't until Josh told us he was dying that we truly looked at our marriage."

Did they really look at it? Or did they make a rash decision to shake up their lives when reminded of their inevitable mortality?

"I knew I ruined things between us," he confesses. "When you blocked my number and moved away. Knew you found out about the proposal before I could tell you."

"I didn't find out about it. I *heard* it."

Horror washes over Dom's face. "You what?"

"I went over to your house that morning. Because . . . Never mind. It doesn't matter." My sympathy for his loss and grief doesn't ease the bitterness in my voice. "Hearing you propose to someone else or having you tell me later, it doesn't matter."

"Of course it matters."

"No, Dom. It doesn't. What would have changed?" Furious, hurt words spill from my soul as I realize a clearer view of the past still ends with the same conclusion. "You didn't hesitate. Didn't pause a moment to come up with any other ideas. Didn't wait a single day to at least tell the girl you gave her first orgasm the *night before*, 'Hey, this can't go anywhere because I decided that I live in the nineteen-fifties when finding out my high school sweetheart is knocked up requires a proposal.'" I'm panting now, my cheeks flushed with humiliation I'd convinced myself I'd moved past.

Dom stares at me, eyes wide. "Your first—"

"Me not being your priority with a baby on the way would've made sense, you know," I speak over him. "Things would've been messy and awkward, but if you'd talked to me *at all* before you made that decision, I would've at least known you cared. That I meant *something* to you, even if we couldn't have been what I wanted." My arms are in a vise grip around my waist, holding myself together as best I can. "But you didn't just choose being a father over starting something with me. You chose being Rosaline's *husband*. Rosaline needed you. And you forgot about me. You left me. Just for a different reason than I thought." I shake my head, almost tempted to laugh. "Not for love. For responsibility." My heart wants to stop talking, but my mouth keeps spitting words, seeping my pain like an infected wound refusing to close. "I was so upset, I couldn't even remember if you enjoyed what we did." I turn away from him, pacing around my kitchen. Dom watches every movement I make. "It's not like you got off. It was just me. You did a favor for the girl who helped your family out."

"Tell me you didn't think that." He says the command quietly. Carefully.

"I still do," I volley back. "I was your best friend's little sister with a silly crush. You gave me one amazing night as a thank-you for helping your family." Whirling to face him, I plan on glaring into his eyes but only make it to the hollow of his throat because I'm a coward. "You took care of me. That's what you do. But . . . fucking hell." My eyes feel gritty as if I've been crying, and yet even now the tears don't come. "When you leave me in the end, it all just feels like pity."

"It wasn't pity. It was perfection!" Dom thunders. "Touching you like that was perfection." His body gives off too much heat as he moves into my space again. "And *that's* why Josh refused to talk to me for weeks. He was furious because I told him I married Rosaline because of the pregnancy and not because of love. That I couldn't feel that way about her. Not after falling in love with you."

The world goes wonky on me, and I grab the kitchen counter to keep myself steady.

"You loved me?" That's big enough on its own, but add in the other part? "You told Josh you were in love with me?"

Fucking hell.

I thought I knew what Josh wanted. What these trips were all about. Have his best friend take care of his little sister. Or maybe have me show his taciturn buddy that life isn't all schedules and to-do lists.

But what if my brother had a different goal?

Josh knew that Dom loved me.

"Did you know he was planning these trips?" I throw the accusation at Dom. He'd seemed surprised at the funeral, or so I thought. That was a mess of a day for me, and I don't know what to believe anymore. "Was all of this some kind of . . . matchmaking from the grave?"

Dom shakes his head. "I don't know what Josh was thinking. Don't know what he wanted. And no, he didn't tell me about the trips. All I know is after going radio silent on me, he suddenly called me one day a couple months later. He apologized for getting angry. He said . . ." Dom clears his throat. "He said he could never be mad at someone for loving you. And I do, Maddie. I love you. I did then, too."

The words from our car ride through South Dakota come back to me.

"When I could breathe, I could see you."

So what? That summer Dom finally saw me and then fell for me?

There's no relief at his revelation. No sense of peace or vindication.

There's only panic.

"That's not the flex you think it is," I snap, shuffling away, seeking distance from his intensity that refuses to dial down a single notch. "You fell for me? So what? Is that supposed to make me feel better? Because all I'm hearing is that you thought you loved me, and you still left me. Whatever you felt for me wasn't enough."

"I made the wrong choice." His jaw is rigid as he grits his teeth. "Leaving you was a mistake."

"Well, what's there to keep you from making it again? What's to keep you from realizing your divorce was some strange grief reaction to Josh's diagnosis, and you and Rosaline actually belong together? You're still in each other's lives. She's still probably the loveliest fucking human being on the planet." My voice goes shrill, and my back digs into the counter because I've retreated as far as I can from him. "Meanwhile I'm the weird girl who spends most nights doing puzzles and talking to her dead brother and only smiles when I think my boss might see me. You are responsible, and caring, and loyal, and entirely too good-looking." I gesture to him in all his beauty, then to me in my old sweater that now has a hole in the sleeve because I tugged a loose thread too much. "You being with me doesn't make sense." I wave around my tiny condo that he takes up too much room in. "I live here, you live on the other side of the country. We only see each other when we're spreading ashes. Aka, emotionally fucked up. And those trips are done after this last one." A jagged pain wrenches through my stomach at the thought.

One more message from Josh.

One last goodbye to my brother.

One more guaranteed time to see Dom.

But that's only if he shows, of course.

"The two of us together is not the responsible choice. *I'm* not the responsible choice. So how can I trust that you would make it? Because you can't just do it once. You have to make the choice to be with me every single day. And I can't deal with knowing that one day you might choose to go another way." I force the words past my internal pain.

Then he'll leave like everyone else does.

Dom's expression waivers between emotions, making it impossible for me to decipher what he's feeling. As if I ever could.

"You are weird," he finally says, and I flinch. But he's not done. "You're so fucking weird, Maddie Sanderson. And I love it." He runs an agitated hand through his hair, messing up the careful styling. "I love that half of your personality is puzzles and the other half is giving me shit. I love that you're quiet sometimes, but your laugh is huge. I love that in spite of your mother and grandmother, you are kind. I love that there are times you let me take care of you even though you're strong enough to stand on your own. All these years, I've never stopped loving you." Dom takes a step toward me, then rocks back on his heels. "But I knew I'd ruined us. That even if Rosaline and I split, you were gone because I messed up. You're right. Since I couldn't be with the woman I wanted, I tried to do the responsible thing. To take care of Rosaline while we grieved what we lost. To commit to my marriage. But then Josh would mention your name, and I was done. He'd tell me one small thing about your life, and I'd fall all over again. You want to know why your birthday is the combination to my safe?" His eyes try to catch mine, but I stare at the framed puzzle of the Rocky Mountains over his shoulder instead, even as my body wants to lean toward his to better hear the answer. "Because I tried to literally lock thoughts of you away, too. It never worked. How I feel about you isn't going away."

My heart beats so hard it takes up precious space my lungs need.

Dom loves me.

I want it to be enough. But I know it's not.

"I don't trust you. I don't trust anyone. I'm not built for this."

"Built for what?" Dom gentles his harsh tone.

"Relationships. Loving someone. Relying on them." I've found another loose thread and feel a kinship with this sweater. We're both unraveling. "I don't trust anymore. If I were with you, I would be afraid all the time. Love is so inconsequential now. People can love you and leave you. They do it every day." I shake my head. "I can't go through that again. I can't worry about that every day."

My whole life I've had to live through people turning away from me.

My father.

Cecilia.

Florence.

Dom.

"Maddie—"

"No. It's not enough. Nothing is enough for me. I am broken."

I don't know when it happened. Maybe I've been breaking every day of my life. Little fractures that have slowly built into the shattering, and now I am simply pieces of a person that I have to hold together with my own will. Without the help of anyone else. Because how can I trust that their hold will remain? How can I trust anyone else to keep the pieces of me together? *I* can't even keep the pieces of me together.

Dom stares at me with something like devastation.

I can't meet his eyes anymore. I can't be around him anymore. I can't have the temptation of his love mixing with the toxic fear that is my constant distrust. I need him gone from my life. I need to sever this connection. I need to free Dom from me and myself from him.

"Alaska. I'll start the planning. We'll do the final state. We'll say goodbye to Josh." I suck in a deep breath. "And we'll say goodbye to each other."

"No."

I ignore him. "This will fade when we're not around each other anymore. When you don't feel responsible for me. You'll realize you want something different." And I won't be collateral damage when he does.

"No," Dom repeats. "*I'm* not the reason we're over," he says, reusing my earlier words. "I'm not going anywhere. Not now and not after Alaska. Plan it, or don't. These trips aren't the reason I'm still obsessed with you." He stalks across the room toward me. "This distance between us is you pushing me away. Trying to make me leave you." He looms once more, voice deep with warning. "Get this straight, Maddie. I won't go."

Anxiety transforms into defensiveness and makes me snap back.

"So, what? You're squatting in my condo now?" I glare up at him. "Adam and Carter may be your brothers, but if I ask them to carry you out of here bodily, what do you want to bet they'll do it?"

Dom smirks. "They can try." Then he reaches out to tuck a strand of hair behind my ear. "We don't have to test your theory, though. I won't force my way into your home."

"Good," I mutter, longing for him to walk out already so I can entomb myself in a pile of quilts. "Have a safe flight back to Philly. I hope you sit beside a chatty creep with a crying baby."

Instead of scowling at me, Dom's expression stretches into a mischievous smile I'm more used to seeing on his brothers' faces.

"I said I wouldn't stay in your home." The asshole cups my chin, his thumb tracing the curve of my cheek, and I accidentally let him keep doing it. "But I didn't say I'd leave your city."

"What?"

"Don't you want to know why it took me a week to seek you out?" A shadow crosses his expression. "I didn't want to wait. After you hung up on me, I booked a ticket to come the moment the storm let up."

"Yeah, well, you didn't." My voice is breathless instead of sharp, the way I need it to be.

"No," he agrees. "I didn't. Because I realized that this time, I didn't want to book a round-trip ticket."

Time stutters, and I wonder if this is what happened in our Alabama Airbnb. If someone said something so shocking that all the clocks ceased to function properly.

"You . . ."

Dom backs up, giving me space, and I try to use it to breathe. But as he keeps talking, I have trouble focusing on anything other than his words.

"I found a town house. Not too far from here. You can walk to it when you're ready. And this morning?" He smooths a hand over his perfectly ironed button-up. "I had my final meet and greet in the interview process. Not to sound too cocky, but they were quite impressed with me. I expect to get an offer in the next few days."

A horrifying suspicion arises. "Interviewing where?"

He holds my eyes. "The Redford Team."

"Fuck you," I whisper.

Dom's smile is hard this time, his stare piercing. "Tell me you don't love me. And I'll turn it down."

"Fuck you," I say louder this time.

My irresponsible language doesn't faze him.

Dom's eyes drag over me, his stare possessive, and then he gives a curt nod. "That's what I thought."

He turns on his heel and strides toward the door, pausing with his fingers wrapped around the knob. "I'm leaving your home, but I'm not leaving you. I'm not going anywhere." Dom gives his speech to the molding, and I'm grateful because I don't know if I could survive the next words paired with the weight of his gaze. "I messed up. I will again. You had me on a pedestal, and I hurt you when I fell off it. I can't promise you perfection, much as I want to be that man for you. What I can swear is that I will never be the one to leave. I'm yours, Maddie Sanderson. And I'm ready to wait, as long as it takes."

Then he's gone.

But if what he told me is true, he hasn't gone far.

Winter

CHAPTER

Forty

Two years ago today, my brother died.

And on this anniversary of the worst day in my life, I sit alone in my apartment lit only by the glow of my laptop screen as I manually finish a data report because a glitch in the preprogramed steps caused it to quit running seventy-five percent of the way through.

My eyes itch. My lower back aches. The knuckles in my fingers have started popping in weird ways because of the repetitive movement.

But none of that compares to the squeezing splinter-covered hand that grips my heart.

Josh is gone.

I'm alone.

The reminders come with every painful beat.

And I'm angry at the universe for insisting I still hurt this way even though it's technically been years since my brother died.

Why does it feel like I held his cold hand in the hospital yesterday? Why can I remember the rattling sound of his machine-assisted breathing at the end better than I can recall his laugh?

I lunge for my phone, hands shaking as I swipe it open and desperately scroll through videos until I find one from just over three years ago.

Josh grins up at me from the screen, and I press play.

"Hey, Magpie! Look what I found." The screen pans around a clothing shop, every surface covered in thick knit sweaters. *"Can you guess where I am?"* The camera is back on his face. *"Don't worry, even if you guess wrong, I'll still bring a jumper back for you. Extra large just like you like."* He chuckles.

That's it.

That's what it sounds like.

Clutching the phone to my chest, I leave my laptop on my coffee table and shuffle through my condo until I'm in my closet. There, hanging with a collection of other warm clothes, is the emerald green sweater Josh brought me back from Ireland. I pull off the sweatshirt I'm wearing, then tug the gift over my head, eased by the way it swallows me.

Before I leave the closet, another garment catches my attention.

The letterman jacket.

The silly company gift Dom gave me. A company he doesn't even work at anymore now that he's part of The Redford Team. A star member apparently, from the way my coworkers talk about him.

Though Dom's natural state is akin to a stoic, looming tree, he knows how to turn on the charm at work. He's only been in Seattle for a few months and half the company wants to be his best friend. Most of the others want to date him.

I dread the day I hear about Dom with someone else through the Redford gossip churn.

Not that I have any claim on him.

Still, there's the text message he sent me after his first day on the job.

DOM: This is a reminder that I'm not
going anywhere. But I also won't
badger you. I'm giving up control.
What happens next is up to you. I'm

a patient man, and you're worth
waiting for.

He hasn't texted me since, and I never responded.

I didn't know what to say. I didn't know what to feel.

Today, though, I know. Everything is pain.

Without thinking, I slide the letterman jacket off the hanger and slip it on over the sweater. I should probably turn the heat down if I'm going to wear all these layers.

This isn't the first time I've worn Dom's jacket. But usually, it happens after a few drinks and when I make the mistake of scrolling through the pictures we took on our trips. I don't examine why I needed to put it on now. I simply fold my arms around my torso and settle in front of my laptop again, sitting cross-legged on the floor.

Sometime later there's a knock on my front door. I blink and rub my eyes, realizing a pounding has sprung up at the base of my temple to go along with all my other pains. With a groan, I push to my feet and try to remember if I ordered myself food.

But when I pull the door open, I find Tula and Jeremy on my threshold.

Their eyes widen in sync when they take me in. That's when I remember that I shimmied off my leggings at some point to deal with the heat of my many layers. Now I stand barefoot in a cable-knit sweater falling midthigh and a letterman jacket, probably with dark circles under my eyes since I don't sleep well these days.

"When's the last time you ate?" Tula maneuvers past me, carrying a pizza box with her.

"Uh, earlier." I wasn't keeping track. "You didn't need to bring me food."

She sets the box on my butcher block island, then glares across the room at my still-open laptop. "It's eight. In the evening. And you're still working."

Self-consciously I tug on the edge of my sweater and scurry over to my laptop, saving everything before I close it. Jeremy shuts the apartment door and watches me with a wary expression, like he thinks I'm a timid animal easily frightened.

"What?" I snap. Then I silently berate myself for letting my anger spew onto my friends.

If you do that, they'll leave you.

"Sorry," I mumble. "I didn't expect to have people over."

"We figured," Tula says, her voice gentle, "but we hoped you would. That you'd reach out to us today."

My head snaps up. "What?"

Jeremey leans a hip on the counter, tucks his hands in his pockets, and watches me as he speaks. "We remember what today is. That it's the day Josh—"

"Don't." I slice my hand through the air, cutting him off midsentence and drawing sadness into his eyes. "I'm fine," I lie.

"You let us support you last time," Tula presses.

I try to meld my expression into something socially acceptable. "It's been two years." *Two short years. Two long years.* "You don't need to worry about me. I'm doing fine."

Jeremy drops his chin to his chest, then raises it in a defiant tilt. "The guy I dated before you, Maddie . . . He would hit me sometimes."

Air leaves me in a rush, and I press my hand against my stomach to help guide it back in. "What?" I wheeze. "He . . . What?"

Jeremy nods, solemn. "Not all the time. But once was enough. I should've left. I say that now. But I didn't. I lived with him for a year. Told myself I loved him, and he loved me. Until he broke my arm." My friend, the joyful, funny, flirtatious man I love like family, rubs his forearm as if the limb aches. "That's when I left. I never told anyone. Not until Carlisle." Jeremy grimaces, his focus on his feet. "I was ashamed. Thought that people would think less of me for staying so long. That *you* might, even though you're the first person I learned to trust after him." He offers me an apologetic smile. "But I didn't trust you enough then, I guess. Didn't trust you to understand. To stay."

To stay. The words batter my chest. "You're telling me now."

Jeremey holds my eyes this time when he speaks. "I trust you. I want you to trust me. To know you're my best friend, and that's not about to change." He leans forward, but still stays by the counter, giving me space. "Even if you open up and show me, show us"—he nods toward Tula, who's been quietly letting him speak—"the less flattering parts of your past and present. Even if you get mad and snap at us. Even if we argue. We're not leaving."

I swallow hard.

The idea of being open with them both—truly open, holding nothing back—is terrifying. How many times have I allowed someone else access to my heart, only for them to hurt me?

Then again, how many of those people deserved the chance?

My mother, Florence, and my father didn't.

But then there are people like Josh, who tried his hardest to make me happy. Adam and Carter, who sought me out when I drifted away.

And Dom, who makes me want to believe I can trust someone. That not everyone I dare to love will hurt me.

My hands clutch at the long sleeves of Dom's jacket, fisting in the smooth leather.

It seems like I've tried to trust so many times before. But maybe, like the footsteps on a hike, when my lungs feel shredded and my muscles protest and ache, I should take another step forward.

Keep going. Keep trying.

Keep trusting.

Even when it hurts, let yourself heal, then try again.

Keep loving.

"My mom wasn't around much, and when she was, she wasn't really *there*," I start. And then, as if all I needed to do was chisel one crack in the wall around my emotions, suddenly they spill out. As

Tula puts pizza on a plate for me, I tell them about my dad leaving before I knew him. Between bites, I describe the strained childhood I had in Florence's home, with Josh as my only supportive bright light. I explain the respite of the Perrys' house, and the boy I had a crush on. While wiping my fingers, I tell them about Dom and Rosaline, and being jealous of a girl who was nothing but kind to me. And as I sink onto the couch, feeling much better than I had before I ate, I tell them about falling for that boy, having him for a moment, then watching him walk into another woman's arms.

And how I fell for him all over again these past two years, and I'm terrified of him walking away from me again.

My hands, needing something to do during this verbal vomit, reach for my laptop and open it to click on a familiar icon.

"What are you doing?" Tula's voice is sharper than I'm used to, and only that tone is what gets me to turn my head. My friend wears a scowl as she eyes my screen.

"It's just my email," I explain, not sure what has her so pissed off.

"It's your *work* email. It's late and you were telling us some heavy stuff, Maddie."

I shrug. "Work doesn't ever really stop for me."

"It does if you have a proper work-life balance."

Doesn't she know I don't like my life right now? I'd rather give it as little time on the scale as possible.

"I'm just checking some things."

"You need to take a day off. Hell, you need to take a week. A month even," she presses.

"Impossible. No one else can do what I do."

She scoffs. "Come on, Maddie. Yes, they can. They don't need you."

They don't need you. Her words scorch through me, igniting my temper.

"Actually, yes, they do. Literally no one else in the company does my job. No one else knows how to. Not even my boss. When certain things go wrong, I'm the only one who can fix them. So yes, they do *need* me!"

The apartment rings with the echoing aftermath of my heated outburst, and I cringe when I realize that I'd just yelled at Tula.

Tula circles the couch and carefully picks up my laptop before setting it aside so she can settle herself on the table in front of me.

"Honey," she speaks carefully, as if I'm a bomb with a touch trigger. "Why doesn't anyone else know how to do your job?"

"Because they don't need to," I snap. *Why am I still snapping?* Tula isn't arguing with me. She's just asking questions. But I just laid out my childhood of pain and now it feels like she's digging her sharp acrylics into a tender spot at the center of me. "I get it done. The workload only requires one person and that's me."

"Still, they could train someone else—"

"Why? Why would they do that? Why would *I* do that? Train my replacement? Make it easier for them to fire me if they felt like it? I'm not the CEO, but I'm *necessary*. I hold important parts of the company together and everyone knows that. They know I'm necessary. If they need me, then they can't leave me!" I choke after that last sentence, the panic steeling my breath and my fingers scrambling against the couch cushions, on the verge of reaching for my inhaler.

Jeremy perches at my side, rubbing a soothing hand over my back.

Tula's eyes widen with every statement, and her perfectly shaped brows rise until they meet her hairline. "Leave you?"

I try to suppress a cringe. "I meant fire me. Of course a whole company doesn't *leave* a person."

But that's what it would feel like. If The Redford Team handed me my notice, it would be one more abandonment in my life.

I'm not letting that happen again.

"Oh, Maddie," Tula whispers, sounding so heartbroken I can't meet her gaze. She settles on my free side, the cushion dipping with her weight until I'm leaning my shoulder against hers, Jeremy's hand still on my back.

I close my eyes and breathe, focusing on calming my spiked heart rate.

"I'm sorry for yelling at you," I say eventually, wondering how long until they both get up and leave. Wondering how much damage I've done and if this is the beginning of the end.

"You know we're forever, right?" Jeremy whispers before pressing a gentle kiss against my hair.

I gasp a little and squeeze my eyes shut tighter. But Tula speaks next.

"You, me, and Jeremy. Forever." Her fingers squeeze mine. "You'd have to do some fucked-up shit just for me to even *consider* not talking to you again. I'm talking 'sleep with my boyfriend, murder my dog' level shit."

I huff out a stunned laugh. "You don't have a boyfriend. Or a dog."

The soothing caress of her hand runs over my hair, comforting me. "Not yet. But you get what I'm saying. You don't have to earn our friendship to keep us around. It's yours. We're not going anywhere."

"My job—"

"Your job is a *job*, Maddie. You do your best within reason. Work normal hours, be a team player, show them your passion, and then trust them to realize what an amazing employee they have. And if they don't, that's on them. Not a judgment of you. Jobs come and go. Don't let it overwhelm your life. Don't base your self-worth in the same place you get a paycheck. And give yourself a goddamn day off when someone you love dies."

Thinking back over the year when Josh was sick, I see I worked extra hard not because of the joy of it but because of the distraction.

Why did I let myself do that? Why do Pamela and Redford expect me to take on so much?

Don't be ungrateful.

But shouldn't I be? Just a little bit?

I like my company. I like the people that I work with. But Tula is right. For a long time, I've let work take too much of me for fear of losing the comforting safety of a position I'm familiar with and confident performing.

But lately, all I am is my job. Tula and Jeremy had to show up here unannounced because I've made no effort to meet up with them.

Not since Dom moved to Seattle and I've hid myself away as much as I could.

I brace my elbows on my knees and bury my face in my hands.

"If you need to cry," Tula whispers, "you can."

"I haven't cried since Josh told me about his diagnosis," I admit, the confession muffled by my palms.

Jeremy stiffens at my side, but Tula goes back to stroking my hair, leaning her cheek on the crown of my head.

"Everyone grieves differently. Tears are a symptom of sadness, not the feeling itself. You can be sad with your eyes dry. Your pain is valid in whatever form it comes."

As I let her words soak in, trying to draw them inside myself and believe their truth, we three sit quietly.

"I'm sorry I didn't tell you about Dom," I murmur after a while. "At first, I just didn't want to talk about him. But then things started to be different between us. Better. And I liked him again. More than that. He . . . made the pain of losing Josh easier. Because he loves my brother like I do. And I thought if I told you about him then, I'd have to tell you everything. The way he hurt me in the past. The way he left me."

"Something else changed, didn't it?" Tula asks.

I nod, feeling so close to crying. But my eyes stay dry.

"I fell in love with him again. But I . . . I still thought he'd end things after a while. So I wanted to keep him separate from you. Like"—I groan in self-disgust as I articulate my irrational fear—"leaving me is contagious."

When I hazard a glance at my friends, Jeremy's mouth is in a hard line and Tula gapes. She snaps her mouth shut and shakes her head, but before she can speak, Jeremy leans in and captures my eyes.

"You're not as easy to give up as you think, Maddie Sanderson. I hope you figure that out one day."

As I sit in stunned silence, absorbing Jeremy's words, I thank the universe that my bag full of cheeses spilled in the lobby the day he was walking through it.

Maybe an important part of keeping someone in my life is knowing who is worth hanging on to.

I watch as my two friends share a heavy glance, then face me simultaneously.

"We brought you something," Tula says.

"It's nonreturnable," Jeremy adds.

They got me a death day gift? Weird, but I guess it's on brand for them.

"Okay." I glance around the condo, wondering where this thing might be.

They each grab one of my wrists and pull me to my feet and toward the door.

"I'd like it noted," Jeremy says as they guide me, "that I am still very pro this present even after everything you shared."

Tula nods. "Agreed."

"Wha—"

Jeremy lets go of my wrist and pulls open the door. In the hallway, leaning against the opposite wall, arms crossed, head bowed, is Dominic Perry.

Damn it, he looks good.

I haven't been able to avoid him entirely these last few months. We're in the occasional meeting together, and his name pops up in my deployment emails all the time. A ghost haunting me.

I'd prefer a real ghost.

But now he's here, in my space, looking slightly disheveled and super tempting in a well-fitting pair of gray sweatpants and loose sweatshirt.

Dom's chin jerks up at our appearance, his dark gaze dragging over my body until his eyes stay directed at my chest. For a brief second, I wonder if Dom turned into a pervy boob guy at some point in these last few months. But then I remember what I'm wearing.

His letterman jacket. Over the sweater Josh gave me.

Which brings back the reason I wrapped myself in these comforting clothes.

"Happy Death Day," I announce to the awkwardly quiet gathering, once again falling into my penchant for morbid humor in uncomfortable situations.

Dom's mouth tightens into something like a smile. "Happy Death Day, Maddie."

"You both are weird," Jeremy says. Then he slips past me, along with Tula. "You alright? Is our gift acceptable?"

"Well, you said it's nonreturnable so . . ." I give them a little shooing gesture. "Thank you. I'm good."

Tula lifts a brow, and I roll my eyes. "Okay, not good. But better. I'm better."

And it's the truth. Finally, being honest with them eased something inside me. Lightened a strain I didn't realize was wound so tight.

Tula nods, and my friends leave me alone with Dom. I cross my arms to mirror his pose and lean a shoulder against the doorjamb. "So. You're here."

"I'm here."

"My friends brought you."

"They like me." He shrugs. "And they know I love you."

I swallow hard at that, all snarky comebacks smothered under the weight of his honesty.

Dom continues to watch me. "I'm not here to plead my case."

"Oh." I swear I don't feel disappointment.

He unfolds his arms and spreads them wide. The hallway light reflects off my brother's watch, and I feel my pulse trip in my wrist, under my tattoo.

"I'm here because I miss you. And I miss Josh. I'm here because this day is brutal. And I . . ." His voice is gravelly and dry like a road leading to a ghost town. "I could use a hug."

A hug. He's not demanding my love or my trust or even my forgiveness.

Just a moment of holding someone who hurts the way he does, as if pressing our bodies together might lessen the never-ending ache of loss.

And the asshole is wearing a hoodie.

It's impossible for me to do anything other than step forward and slip my arms around his waist. To fist my fingers in the cotton and press my cheek to the warm, soft fabric.

Dom doesn't immediately return the embrace. Maybe he thought I'd refuse. That I'd kick him out with a goodbye *fuck you* like I did the last time he was here.

But something about my conversation with Jeremy and Tula left me extra vulnerable. But also, oddly, hopeful. I told them about my childhood and my mistakes with my heart and the way I cling to my work. They listened. They told me I was worth sticking around for.

And I think I might believe them.

Dom hugs me in return. He clutches me against his chest, and I pretend I never have to leave this glorious spot.

But eventually we break apart, and I haven't been cured of my perpetual melancholy.

"I think we should go to Alaska this summer," I say to the pouch pocket on Dom's sweatshirt. "When it warms up."

Maybe once my pirate chest doesn't have any more of my brother's remains, I'll be able to move on. We both will.

"Okay."

"And I think . . ." I straighten my shoulders and meet his

searching gaze. "I need to work on some things. About myself. Before then."

"Can I help?"

I shake my head.

He rubs a rough hand against the back of his neck. "Can I do anything?"

Such a Dom thing to ask. *You can't fix me*, I want to say.

But also . . . *Stay. Don't leave me.* The words are there, on the back of my tongue, ready, yet unwilling to come out. Just like my tears have been and still are.

So, I say the only thing I can manage. The only request I *need* him to fulfill.

"Just keep living."

Summer

CHAPTER

Forty-One

I still see Dom. Not every day, or even every week, but we work for the same company. Our paths cross, and he greets me like a co-worker with a polite smile and a "Hello, Maddie." But my name sounds like irresponsible language in his deep voice and his intense stare holds mine, promising more the moment I ask.

Also, Dom was right about his town house being walkable from my apartment.

I may have walked by it.

More than once.

But I never knock on the door.

And even though I give him nothing more than a death day hug for over half a year, he doesn't leave.

The man stays.

Maybe I should break through the wall I've placed between us and tell him how much that means to me. But I don't.

I told Dom I need to figure some things out on my own, and I meant it. After visiting three different therapists, I finally find a middle-aged woman with a kind face and a way of asking me questions that doesn't have me pasting on my customer service smile or snapping back with sarcastic humor.

Mary hasn't fixed my life or my emotions—that's a lot to expect from a person, even a paid professional—but it's surprisingly nice to talk to someone who has absolutely no investment in what I choose to do.

But even finding a good therapist doesn't take away the sick anxiety curdling in my gut as I clutch my backpack to my chest and step onto this final leg of my brother's journey.

The flight to Pika Glacier.

Josh's coordinates put us squarely in the Alaskan wilderness, on a stretch of frozen land reachable only by airplanes. It's June, five months since the day Dom showed up at my condo asking for a hug. After he left, I started planning. Researched the coordinates, booked our flights, and found a small cabin for us to stay in. Two bedrooms.

The whole way out here, he's been cordial to me, as if we're at work.

I don't know if I appreciate his approach or not. Part of me wants Dom to keep his distance, as my entire being feels made of cracked glass, ready to fracture at even the slightest touch.

But then there's what's just past that fragile shell. I miss Dom so bad, sometimes I forget why he's not waking up in my bed. And when I try to stitch together the arguments I made against being with him, they are flimsier each time. The excuses slip further from my grip the more I meet with Mary and articulate my fears of intimacy and work through where they originated.

At our last meeting I made what felt like a breakthrough.

I told Mary I *want* to trust Dom.

That may be a far step from actually trusting him, but it's a step nonetheless.

But here we are, on an airplane headed into Denali National Park, and all my hard-won confidence and self-assurance is crumbling under the hefty fear of what this day is.

There are about sixteen seats in the aircraft, and we're all snug together with only a thin aisle between seats—one on each side. As we board, I worry Dom might get lodged in the tight space like he did in Dismals Canyon. But he maneuvers his wide shoulders at just the right angle to slip into his seat. The other passengers load on the same time as us, the family of six claiming the seats farther back and leaving me across the narrow aisle from Dom.

And I find I want him there. Inches from me. So close I swear I can feel his body heat even through my layers of clothes. Close enough that I can smell his cedar scent and see the grain of his facial hair that he shaved off before we left the cabin this morning.

As the pilot buckles in behind the controls, I clutch my backpack hard against my chest, feeling the small round container that contains the final piece of my brother.

That last bit of Josh.

Multiple times on the way out here, I noticed Dom rubbing his chest, and I wondered if the man might have heartburn. But then his coat parted when he crouched to retie his shoe, and I saw the flash of a corner of an envelope.

The final one.

My brother's last words living close to his chest.

The plane's engine roars to life, and Dom's body goes rigid beside me. I wonder what it's like being a control freak and yet having to put your life in someone else's hands whenever you board a plane. The reality must be hard to ignore in an aircraft this small.

As the plane slowly rattles over the asphalt to a runway, my hand loosens on its own accord, fingers peeling away from the fabric of my backpack. Like a snake, my hand creeps across the less than a foot of space between us and settles over the back of Dom's where his tendons stand out like tight guitar strings.

Unable to acknowledge what I'm doing, I choose to stare out the window at the Alaskan landscape. Only this touch connects me to him.

Against my palm, I feel Dom's tense grip slacken. Then he flips his hand and laces our fingers together.

We hold on without a word as the plane lifts into the air, and we keep a firm grasp on each other for the forty-five minutes it takes to fly to the last destination Josh left for us.

We're going to say goodbye.

The thought tightens like a cluster of rubber bands around my lungs. I utilize the breathing exercises my doctor gave me, and turn my mind to other comforting things.

Like Mary telling me I'm strong for wanting to take this step in the process of dealing with my grief.

Like how I successfully trained both my boss and a backup on how to perform the necessary tasks of my job. Training started slow, but now they can do it, and I can take time off.

Like the engagement ring Carlisle asked Tula's and my opinions on.

Like the puzzle table that Adam planned to surprise me with next month for my birthday but was too excited about to wait. He and Carter are road-tripping out to visit in a few weeks to deliver it.

Like Dom's hand. The feel of his familiar fingers in mine. How I can still remember exactly how his touch felt against all the intimate parts of me even though it's been close to a year since we were last together that way.

He's what comforts me. Better than anything or anyone else. His gentle thumb brushing over my knuckles. A solid presence beside me when this plane seems so insubstantial. The one that will stand steady beside me for this moment that is sure to be all kinds of painful.

Don't think about it. Not yet.

But all that can keep my mind off my brother is his best friend. The man I fell in love with twice.

Was it a mistake both times? Will he hurt me again?

Will the pain be worse than it is now, living without him?

Focusing on my missteps in life scratches at my airways and threatens my oxygen, so I go back to distractions.

Holding my hand out in a dark cave lit by glow worms and watching Dom's long fingers twine with mine.

Admiring the sunlight filtering through a snowy window and how it fell across his skin.

Burrowing into a soft sweatshirt hug and knowing the heat on the other side of the material was his broad chest.

My stomach dips, and I realize we're landing, the plane approaching a massive white expanse that must be the glacier. The pilot has been speaking to us through our headsets this whole time, but I haven't heard a word. Dom's hand tightens on mine, and I grip him back just as hard as I resume my breathing exercises.

Last goodbye.

Don't think about it.

Last of Josh.

Don't think about it.

The plane lands without issue and the other passengers start chattering in excitement.

This is fun for them. Of course it is. This place is gorgeous. A once-in-a-lifetime experience.

And Josh's life ended without him seeing it.

On wobbly knees, I climb out of the airplane. Dom keeps his hand on my elbow, as if sensing my unsteadiness.

"How are you doing?" he asks, and I realize it's the first thing he's said to me all day. We've barely exchanged a handful of words on this trip.

"I . . ." No more words come. I'm terrified to even try naming how I feel in this moment. There's a fragile shell of numbness that's keeping me together. A delicate surface that could fracture at any moment. I must move carefully to keep from falling apart.

Dom gives a curt nod, as if he understands.

Maybe he does.

"Let's go for a walk," he says. "We have some time."

Not forever, though. The guide directed us to return to the plane in twenty minutes.

Twenty minutes, then it's all over.

Twenty minutes until my brother is gone forever.

Dom helps me slip my backpack onto my shoulders. I didn't realize I was still clinging to it. Clutching Josh close while I have him.

Last goodbye. This is the last goodbye.

The air is cold here. Dry. It makes the inside of my nostrils raw as I suck in deep breaths that do little to soothe me.

As we walk away from the group, I keep my eyes on the toes of my boots. I should raise my head. Gaze around to admire the beauty of this place.

But a part of me is terrified that the moment I fully take this in, this last place my brother wanted to visit, everything that mattered about Josh will be over.

Dom stops walking, and so I do, too. He sets heavy hands on my shoulders, turning me to face him.

"Look at me, Maddie."

With more effort than it should require, I force my head up as far as his nose. It's all I can manage. He doesn't push for more.

"Do you want to read the letter?"

I shake my head. I can barely breathe, let alone read.

"Okay." He rubs my shoulders. "Do you want me to read it?"

Yes! I want more of Josh!

No! We must keep him forever!

Yes . . . no . . . yes . . . no . . .

The internal argument goes on and on until I give a quick jerk of my head that's almost a nod. Enough of one that Dom slips his hand into his jacket and pulls out the envelope. The tearing sounds overly loud on the vast landscape.

He clears his throat.

I try to inhale but only manage a thin stream of air.

Dear Maddie and Dom,

This is the goodbye letter.

Pain. Sharp and jagged. A rusty serrated knife piercing my heart and lungs all in one go.

I think you two were meant for each other.

Dom stumbles over the words, seemingly shocked by them. I might have been, too, if all my capacity for feeling wasn't overwhelmed by panic.

He clears his throat again.

Don't give up on that.

> *Love you both forever,*
> *Josh*

He stops reading.
No. He doesn't *stop*.
He *finishes*.
He's done.
That was all.
My brother is gone.
Forever.
Gone.
I stop breathing.
"Maddie!" Dom's roar is barely louder than the pounding of my own heartbeat in my ears. My eyesight flickers from glorious white to black.

There's the familiar press of my inhaler against my lips and the slightly sweet taste of the medication as it passes my tongue on the way to my lungs. I'm not the one spraying, so the timing doesn't line up quite right for me to breathe it all in. But my hands are too busy clutching my brother's remains to my chest to take over.

"Breathe," Dom demands as if he plans to reach into my chest and work my lungs for me if I don't. "In. Out. In. Out. Nod when you need another dose."

I nod. Dom, whose lap I realize I rest in, brings the inhaler to my lips again. "Pressing in three . . . two . . . one."

This time we get it right, but it's still a good five minutes and another spray before I'm not gasping like a dying fish.

"Ashes," I wheeze, knowing we have to get on the plane soon, though my episode might have bought us some time. I don't want to look over Dom's shoulder to see if we have an audience.

"Fuck the ashes. Fuck this," Dom snarls, holding me closer, while careful not to compress my rib cage. "I'm not going to have you dying of an anxiety-induced asthma attack to keep to some arbitrary schedule."

I blink up at him and spy a scowl that others might interpret as furious.

But I can see the fear.

Look at that. I can finally read his face again.

And I know he wants to control this. But he can't. All he can do is hold me.

When our eyes meet, Dom gentles his voice while remaining firm. "We can come back here every year for fifty years, if that's what you need. If that's how long it takes to do this without it tearing your heart out. You keep that piece of Josh as long as you want. Hell, keep him forever. Leave your own will directing some other asshole to trek up here and spread you two together. But that's not going to happen for a long while, because you will keep breathing, and you will not give up on me, Maddie Sanderson. Do you understand? You told me to just keep living. And I did. Without you. And I'll live as long as you tell me to. But you've got to live, too. For me. For you. For Josh, who didn't get to. Just keep living."

Dom holds my gaze and cradles my body so close I can feel him shaking.

I stare into his terrified eyes.

And I start crying.

We don't spread the ashes.

The pilot stretches out our departure another fifteen minutes until I'm breathing at a normal rate. The guy seems mildly concerned, but not overly surprised. Maybe I'm not the only person who's gone through a panic attack on one of his flights. Dom sets us up in the back row of the airplane, so I don't have to deal with curious looks from the strangers who wonder what's up with the weird girl who passed out on the glacier.

When we get back to town, Dom asks if I want to head to our cabin.

But I can't fathom sitting for the rest of the day, clutching my brother as my mind threatens to sink back into a dark place that makes it hard to breathe.

I shake my head.

"Okay." Dom pulls our rental car into a parking spot on the main street in town. "Let's walk around."

My fingers fumble with the door handle, my nerve endings numb. All of me is numb at this point, and not from the cold. Too many feelings overwhelmed me on the glacier that something in my brain short-circuited. I can feel all that turmoil lingering on the periphery, waiting for the protective numbness to dissipate so it can descend again.

I make it out of the car and onto the cracked sidewalk. After declaring we wouldn't be spreading Josh's remains on this trip, Dom tucked the final container of ashes back into my backpack, which I now wear on the front of my body, arms wrapped around the bag protectively. Dom appears at my side, and when I make no move to choose a direction, he pries one of my hands free, laces our fingers together, and leads me in a slow meander down the street.

"Are you hungry?" he asks.

I shake my head, nauseous at the idea of food.

He doesn't push, only keeps us moving, but not with any expediency, which is probably odd for a man who always has a goal, destination, or purpose. Probably he's wondering how he can fix whatever broke inside me up on that glacier.

But there's no cure. No glue that works on a soul.

After a half hour of directionless wandering, Dom sits me down on a bench, then settles at my side. "Should we take a picture?"

The question registers in my brain on a delay, as if it has to fight its way through the cloud of grief I live in.

"Why?" I ask, my voice monotone. "The letter didn't say to." A spark of emotion burns through the grief. Anger. "That fucking letter."

"What about it?"

"That's it?" I snap. "That's *all* that's left? Three sentences?" I bark a sharp laugh with zero humor. "Thanks a lot, Josh."

"Were you hoping he'd say something he didn't?" Dom asks, his voice careful, as if worried another asthma attack might be on the horizon.

Maybe it is, but I'm more focused on my increasing vehemence than on my breathing.

"No. He didn't need to say anything in particular. All he needed to do was keep writing!" I shove up from the bench and slam my backpack onto the seat beside Dom, my glare bouncing between the two of them. "Eight letters? That's all I get. Now they're read. Now he's . . ." I dig my fingers into my hair, tugging at the roots, and making an inarticulate noise of fury.

"Maddie—"

"He's gone!" I snarl. "He left me! He left me *forever*!" I pant and rage, pacing on the public street and not caring because no one in this world matters like the man who's no longer in it. Tears begin to stream down my cheeks again, but instead of bringing relief, they itch on my skin and stuff up my nose. "People have left me before— they leave me all the time—but never like *this*." I swipe the wetness from beneath my eyes and storm up to Dom, looming over him and the backpack. "I tell myself that's part of him." My finger jabs toward the bag. "But it's just dust. Those letters were more him than the ashes ever were. And they're done. And I *hate* him, Dom. I hate him for leaving me. And I know he didn't do it on purpose. I know he would have stayed if he could have. I know I'm the worst sister because I hate my brother for dying. But I do. And I don't think I can forgive him."

My inhales are painful, my exhales are ragged, and my selfish heart lays in a bloody mess on the concrete at Dom's feet.

Quiet falls between us as his dark eyes hold mine. Then the man has the audacity to reach out, circle his arms around my waist, and tug me close until I settle on his lap. I curl into a ball, my head tucked under his chin, and I focus on breathing through my anger and devastation. And Dom holds me close, like he doesn't care that I'm a grenade with the pin pulled, liable to go off and decimate everything in a twenty-foot radius.

No, the ridiculous man presses a kiss against my hair, then speaks to me in a low soothing voice.

"I hate him for leaving, too."

That surprises a laugh out of me. A hollow "we're a pair of horrible people" chuckle.

Dom rests his chin on my head and while we wait for my breathing to regulate, he hums angry emo girl songs to me.

And I love him so much I think it's a mortal wound.

I love him so much, and I try to distract myself by cataloging everything about our surroundings just to keep from thinking about my inescapable infatuation with Dominic Perry.

In the process of reading the signs above each storefront, I pause on one in particular. Something about it sparks a memory, but I don't know why.

NORTH POLE PAPER & PICTURES

I mouth the name, trying to place where I might have heard it before. But my mind brings nothing to the surface.

And yet the sign feels familiar.

That's when my eyes land on the logo.

"The compass," I mutter, staring at the four-pointed star with a smaller burst behind it and a fancy *N* resting above the top point.

"What was that?" Dom asks.

I lift my head to meet his eyes, then point to the store across the street. "Do you recognize that compass logo?"

Dom's thick brows dip, then rise slowly as he comes to the same realization I did. He slips his hand between us to tug Josh's last letter from his coat pocket. With his arms around me, Dom slips the piece of paper from the envelope and unfolds it.

At the top of the parchment is a stylized compass, just like the one across the street.

"What the hell?" Dom mutters.

"Josh, you fucking scavenger hunt–loving asshole." Annoyance and anticipation collide in my chest as my heart rate picks up. "It's a clue." I slip off Dom's lap, snatch up my backpack, and barely take a moment to check for oncoming traffic before jogging across the street, closely shadowed by my brother's best friend.

When we enter the shop, a small bell rings and a middle-aged white man with rosy cheeks and thinning hair smiles at us from behind a counter. "Welcome to the North Pole. We have any office supplies you might need as well as a varied selection of cameras if you're on a trip and looking to memorialize the moments." The guy gives the spiel with no pause for breath, as if he says the speech as often as he slips on a pair of his favorite shoes. "My name is Harold. How can I help you?"

Not sure what to ask, I stare around the shop, searching for a sign of my brother or another clue he might have left me.

"Do you sell this stationery?" Dom approaches Harold and shows the man Josh's letter.

"You bet. It's our signature stock." He gestures to a shelf at the end of the closest aisle, and I see a stack of blank sheets, all sporting the same compass as Josh's letters.

How did he get it if he's never been here?

Thinking along the same lines as me, Dom asks a follow-up question. "Do you know a Josh Sanderson?"

I switch my attention to Harold in time to see the shop owner's eyes light up with true excitement. "Of course I knew Josh. He took all these."

The man points to the walls, and I realize almost every inch has a framed photo of some beautiful wildlife image.

Probably all taken in this state.

"Josh Sanderson took these photographs?" I speak the words slowly, my mind struggling to catch up with this shift in my reality.

Harold grins and gives a deep nod. Then the expression flickers, a trace of sadness chasing over his features.

"Oh. You must be . . ."

"Maddie Sanderson. His sister."

Harold's eyes soften. "Ah. I see. Well, he did tell me you'd come."

"I don't know why. None of his letters told me to."

"He said you'd figure it out. Especially with Broken Spines across the street."

"Broken . . ." I trail off as I glance out the window and realize the bench Dom and I paused on sits outside a bookshop.

"I have something for you."

My head whips back to Harold. "You do?"

He nods, big grin back in place. "Kept it in the safe in the back. You wait right here."

Harold shouldn't be concerned about me running off. Any correspondence from my brother could keep me waiting in a single spot for centuries.

The shop owner reappears holding a ziplock bag. Through the gallon-sized plastic, I see something amazing.

Puzzle pieces.

"Josh mailed this to me a few years back. Said if you ever made your way into my shop, I should give it to you." He walks up to me and offers the bag, which I accept gingerly. Then he ushers us toward the door. "There's a coffee shop a block down to the right. They've got big tables and tasty drinks. You go put that together and see what your brother left for you. Make sure you stop back in before you leave town. I'll give you a ream of stationery on the house."

In a daze, I let myself be directed. Ten minutes later, Dom and I have claimed a booth in the back of the shop Harold suggested. After thoroughly cleaning and drying the worn wooden surface, we spread out the pieces and get to work.

When the image turns into something recognizable, my hands pause, and my mouth falls open in disbelief.

Then my eyes seek out Dom's.

"Did you know?"

I knock on the door and wait, trying not to shift on my feet. The warm presence at my back helps keep me calm. Holds me steady.

The door opens to reveal Rosaline dressed in a pair of ratty sweats that still look amazing on her. And I'm happy to realize I don't resent her attractiveness.

Is this what people call progress? Go me, I guess.

The woman stares at me, eyes wide, knuckles going white on the doorknob. "Maddie. I'm sorry. I didn't know you were coming. Dom said . . ." She glances over my shoulder. "Dom said he wanted to talk."

And again, I'm pleasantly surprised that their shared glance, which probably communicated more than her words did, elicits no negative reactions in me. No suspicion or resentment or hopelessness. The reminder of their past together doesn't feel like an attack on what Dom and I might be building between us.

For this emotional growth, I can probably thank the combination of therapy and the gift I brought.

"We're going to drink." I hold up the bottle of gin I'm clutching, and Dom has a cloth bag with three types of wine because he said that's what Rosaline prefers. "And we're going to do this puzzle." I show her the glass Rubbermaid container full of jigsaw pieces.

Only the best container for my brother's final gift to me.

"Okay." Rosaline steps back to let us into her house. Her home—which is how I can think of it now instead of *their* home—is quaint in a way I didn't expect. Not the shabby hobbit librarian decor of my apartment, but kind of plant maiden cottagecore. I could spend some time here and not be mad about it. When I wander into her living room, Rosaline's decoration choices notch up even further in my opinion.

"This is a quality puzzling table." I place the container in the middle of a golden wood-grain masterpiece that's almost as large as mine.

"Thanks," she murmurs. "Adam made it for me."

Dom checks over the table, assessing his brother's work, then nods with a pleased grunt before setting out the bottles of wine. He disappears into another room that must be the kitchen, because he comes back a moment later with some stemless wineglasses—one full of ice for me—and a bottle opener.

"I'll leave you to it." He brushes a hand over my lower back as he steps away from the table.

"You're leaving?" Rosaline sounds lost as she glances between us.

"He's going to entertain himself in the other room," I assure her. "He's mainly here as my DD. Have fun." I pat his taught stomach, then settle cross-legged by the table and reach for the container. "Get to pouring, Ros. That wine isn't going to drink itself."

Dom squeezes her shoulder before strolling out of the room, and soon I hear the sound of a chair groan as he settles himself elsewhere.

After another prolonged pause, Rosaline pops the cork from a bottle of wine and pours herself a generous glass. Then she kindly unscrews the cap on the gin and gives me a healthy dose of the good stuff. Then she grabs two throw pillows off the nearby couch, hands one to me, and settles another across the way from where I'm sitting.

Even as I sort through the pieces, focused on finding the edges first, most of my concentration is on the redhead. I've always thought of Rosaline as utterly confident and secure. A league above me. A goddess to my mere mortal.

But now she moves as if waiting for me to jump at her. I don't think she's scared of me, but there's an element of caution. Of anticipation.

"Maddie, I'm not sure why you're here." Her voice carries a question. An invitation to explain my sudden game night invasion when most of my life I've shied away from her.

"The puzzle will reveal all," I say in the voice of a carnival fortune teller.

There's a snort from the other room, and I'm glad one person here finds me entertaining.

Rosaline blinks at me, looking suddenly stunned, and her shock is enough to have me pausing. "What? Did I spill on myself?" I examine my white tank top for wet spots.

"No. It's just . . . you sounded exactly like him. Just then. The way you said that."

We both know who "him" is.

Josh.

"Yeah, well, flare for the dramatic must be in the blood." I nod toward the scattering of pieces in front of her. "You going to help?"

She shakes her head, but not in a *no*. More like clearing the specter of my brother from her mind. "You're saying when the puzzle is done, you'll tell me why you're visiting me?"

"Correct. Now get to working. We've got a thousand pieces to sort out."

That may sound like a lot to a puzzle amateur, but I've been jigsawing for decades. And Rosaline ends up having a knack for finding those tricky solid-color pieces that look the same as twenty others. We settle into a mostly comfortable silence, sipping our drinks and slipping missing pieces into place.

Almost an hour has gone by when something in her demeanor

shifts. Rosaline finds the right spot for a piece she's been clutching for five minutes, settling it with a triumphant "Ha!"

Then she freezes.

I don't react, continuing to work on the corner I've claimed.

"Is . . ." She doesn't finish the question, letting her voice trail off with a quiver. After a prolonged pause she reaches for another piece with fingers that shake.

Another half hour, and we have the entire puzzle done. Sprawled across Rosaline's coffee table is a clear picture of a couple standing on the glacier in Denali, both in puffy jackets with their arms wrapped around each other. The woman smiles at the camera. The man gazes down at his companion with so much love on his face, it's hard to look at for long.

My brother left me a picture of himself.

And Rosaline.

"Tell me about your time with Josh," I say.

One important thing I've learned on these many trips with Dom is that I only know a portion of my brother. We were close, but there were pieces we kept to ourselves, or gave to others. Josh gave parts of himself to his best friend.

And he gave others to the woman he loved.

I want all of him I can have, even if the pieces are secondhand.

"We . . ." She clears her throat. "We loved each other."

I nod, not wanting to interrupt.

"N-nothing happened for years. Not while Dom and I were to-gether. I never would have. Josh wouldn't have. It wasn't until we separated."

My heart hurts when the timeline clarifies in my mind.

"After Josh's diagnosis, then," I say. "You were together for a year. Less."

Rosaline reaches out, her finger tracing Josh's face on the puzzle. "Yes. A year." Her smile is small and sad. "It seems both longer than that, and much shorter. I was the one who went to him. Showed up at his place, stared him in the eyes, and told him the rest of his days were mine." She chuckles. "Then I lost my nerve, apologized, and asked if he still loved me." Rosaline presses her fingers against her lips, appearing lost in a memory. "He told me he did. That he never stopped."

"Never stopped?" I ask.

Her face flushes a rosy color. "When we were twenty-one—the summer after we graduated college. Dom and I broke up. I had an internship in New York, same as Josh. And we just . . . clicked. Two months in love. Then . . ." She pauses again, and I realize this must be hard for her to talk about. To speak of the romance now that he's gone. "I found out I was pregnant. And timing-wise, it had to be Dom's. I was too far along. But the thing is, I also didn't want it to be Josh's."

"Why not?"

She traces the indents of the puzzle's pieces. "Because I was scared."

"Scared of what?" I press because I'm desperate and pushy.

Rosaline, still wearing her sad smile, keeps talking.

"Scared of how free your brother was. With life. With everything. He wanted to travel the world. I knew he loved me. But I was scared if I told him about the pregnancy, that it was Dom's, he'd leave. Or that he'd set aside all his dreams and stay. And I wondered, if he did stay, could he handle the responsibility? Every angle I studied it, I couldn't picture a way forward with Josh. And, well, you may remember my parents. How they raised me . . . Not having the baby didn't register as an option. So, I ended things with Josh. I came home. And I told Dom. About the pregnancy, not about your brother." She sends a pained grimace toward the doorway, as if she can see her ex-husband in the next room. "I panicked. And I knew Dom would keep me steady. That he was safe." She sighs, combing a rough hand through her hair. "I wish I had slowed down. That I had taken more time to think. That summer. It changed everything."

Yeah. For all of us.

"So, you loved Josh then," I say. "But that was years ago. You knew his chances of survival were low. How could you put yourself through loving someone, knowing you'd likely lose them so soon?"

Rosaline stares at her hands, turning a silver ring on her middle finger.

"One day," she says.

"One day, you'll what?"

"No. I'm saying if I'd had one day—*only one*—it would've been worth it. To be with Josh, loving him like I'd always wanted, a single day would have been a gift. And I got a year." She smiles wide, her eyes full of tears that slowly overflow and spill down her cheeks. "Yeah, I wish I'd had a lifetime. And yeah, it hurts more than I can describe. Two years, six months, three days, and I still miss him every day. But it would've been worse if I'd never had him at all."

One day.

My mind plays out the rest of my life in that moment. Me living a long, safe life to one hundred years old.

Without a single day more of Dominic Perry.

I think I'd rather leave this world the day after tomorrow and spend a solid twenty-four hours with him.

All I wish is that I'd been living the past ten years with him as well.

"Why didn't you two say anything? How did I miss it?" Since finishing the puzzle the first time, I've been racking my brain for memories of that last year. Josh was able to manage the pain well enough to keep traveling for a while—to Alaska apparently. He managed well enough that he didn't let on how bad things were until close to the end. But the final few weeks, I was in the hospital with him as much as I could be.

"That was something Josh asked for. To keep us just for us." Rosaline sighs. "I think he was worried what people would say about me when he was gone. Leaving his best friend for him. I told him I didn't care. But it worried him, and I didn't want to give him more things to stress over."

There's a weighty presence at my back, and I glance over my shoulder to find Dom leaning against the doorway, a grimace of regret on his face. "My family would've understood. They *will* understand, if you decide to tell them."

The Perrys. I think I get it now. Josh knew Rosaline would need people after the end, and her strict parents aren't the most comforting bunch. No wonder she was at Adam and Carter's graduation. They're the ones she turned to when she lost the love of her life, though no one really knew.

Rosaline huffs a sad laugh. "I just might. A bit of honesty would have done us all some good."

"Did you know about the letters he left us?" I ask. The puzzle was obviously a surprise.

Now her expression turns wistful. "Not exactly. Only that he was plotting something. I saw him writing a few, but when I asked, he gave me that mischievous smile of his and said he was figuring out how to fit two puzzle pieces together."

I snort and blink away tears. At the end of his life, my brother was trying to mastermind my love story.

I wish he and Rosaline hadn't had to wait so long for their own.

"Are you mad at Dom? For asking you to marry him?" The questions tumble out before I consider them.

Rosaline blinks at me, then she flicks her eyes over my shoulder, then back to me.

"Dom didn't ask. I did."

"What?" I yelp. "Wait. Wait wait wait. I was *there*. I heard Dom say, 'We'll get married.' When you two were sitting on the porch swing." I glance behind me and spy Dom rubbing a rough hand over his face.

"Yeah," Rosaline speaks slowly. "In response to me asking him. Begging him, more like."

"You"—I point an aggravated finger at him—"never clarified that. I thought the marriage was your idea."

Dom crosses the room to crouch beside me. "It might as well have been. I didn't turn her down. I prioritized what I thought I was supposed to do over what I should have done to make us both happy."

My breath leaves me in a huff. "I'm just saying, I would've been slightly less pissed at you. I think. Maybe not. I'm kind of petty."

Rosaline reaches across the puzzle to place her hand over mine.

"We were young fools. The two of us. I never should've asked him. And he never should have said yes. We should've chosen the people we loved, not the ones we felt safest with or responsible for. We both should've fought harder for the Sandersons."

I squeeze her hand back. "I'm glad you were brave. That Josh had you in the end."

And suddenly she's around the table, or maybe I went to her. Either way, I find myself hugging tight to the only other woman who loved Josh as much as I did.

As Rosaline's arms tighten around me, I breathe in the scent of lavender.

Forty-Four

After we leave Rosaline's, Dom drives me to his parents' house. His parents are out of town on an anniversary trip, so we don't go inside. Instead, we settle on the swinging bench on their back porch. Dom stretches out on his back until his feet hang off one edge.

After a questioning tug on my hand, I lay down beside him, throwing an arm over his torso and a leg over his hips.

My brain has a lot to process, and I hold on tight to the man I love as I file away the new information about my brother and the woman who loved him. Mentally, I revisit the moments in the hospital near the end when Rosaline would appear. I was so focused on avoiding her and Dom that I never took the time to ponder why Josh's smile was so much wider. I was too set on keeping my distance when they were around to realize the two of them rarely visited Josh together.

I always thought I left before the other showed up. Never realizing Rosaline was there to visit Josh all on her own. To spend as many moments with the man she loved as she could.

Because his final day was coming, and she knew that. But she wanted one more day for as long as she could have them.

"One day," I murmur against Dom's chest. "That would've been a good question for Josh to leave us. What would we do if we only had one day? If our futures were limited like his was?"

Dom's hand slides up to cup the back of my neck, but he doesn't make me look at him, only strokes my hairline with his thumb.

"If I only had one day," he says, "I wouldn't let you continue to stand outside my town house, never coming in."

I still against his chest. "I don't do that."

He grunts, but the noise suspiciously sounds amused.

"I don't do that . . . a lot," I concede. "And it's just a quick glance. When I happen to be in the neighborhood. You're probably mistaking someone else for me."

"You have a bright red raincoat and puzzle-patterned rain boots. It's hard to mistake those."

Damn. "That's an extremely popular look."

Dom's chests shakes with a chuckle, and I smile in response. He lets out a soul-deep sigh. His free hand finds one of mine, tangling our fingers together. "If I have one day left, or thousands, I want you to be in every one of them."

Rosaline's face comes to my mind, her mixture of sadness and contentment when she spoke about Josh.

"I'm not afraid of the days with you in them," I whisper. "I'm afraid of the ones I might have without you."

"Because you think I might leave?" he asks.

"Or die." The confession is so quiet, I'm surprised he hears it, but from the way his breath hitches, I know he did.

"I can't promise not to die, Maddie. But I can swear that while I'm living, I will always be loving you. And I think you'd enjoy being loved by me. If you let me do it up close."

I choke out a laugh. Propping myself up so my arms are braced on his chest, I gaze down at Dom.

"How close?" I ask in a nonchalant voice. Sliding my body fully on top of his, I ease up until our faces are inches away from each other. "This close?"

Dom's eyes are hot as he smirks. "Closer."

"Closer?" I ease my body forward until my nose presses against his and our lips are a breath apart. "This close?"

"Mm," Dom hums deep in his chest, and I can feel the rumble through the front of my body. He palms my ass, then presses me against him. "Closer."

"Any closer and you're going to be inside me." I'd intended a teasing tone, but my voice is so breathless I may need a puff from my inhaler. It's been too long since I was this tangled up in Dominic Perry. And I realize that if he were to slip his strong fingers between my legs in this moment, there would be no panic. No fear. Because in my bones, I know Dom would be touching me because he wants to. Because he loves me.

"Soon," he mutters, then releases his hold on my ass to wrap his arms in an iron hold around my waist. "Give me one day."

I blink. "What?"

"Give me one day. Tomorrow. To love you. And at the end of the day, you can decide if you want to give me one more."

I realize what he's doing. Taking the uncertainty onto his shoulders. Offering me the cautious approach to love he thinks I need.

Which makes my answer easy.

"No."

He scowls and the expression has me smiling and leaning in to kiss his nose. "I love you. I don't want just one day. I want them all."

His body stiffens, a statue under me. "Maddie?" My name is a raspy question in his throat.

I make a production of rolling my eyes. "Stop saying my name. I'm the only one on this porch. Who else would you be talking to? Just say what you want to say."

Dom mixes a chuckle with a groan. "I love you. And I accept. All your days are mine." Finally, he drags my head to his for a crushing kiss. When he pulls away, his hands cradle my face. "You're crying."

"Am I?" Reaching up, I touch my cheeks to realize they're damp. Rubbing my thumb and forefinger together, I smile at the moisture. Then I let my hand drop and grin down at the man I love. "Happy tears."

A Few
Summers
Later

Epilogue

We take the people Josh loved everywhere.

Swimming at Rehoboth.

Through a canyon of glowing larva.

To Ink Ever After—we all have Josh's love on our wrists now.

To fields of lavender.

Exploring a ghost town in the desert.

We road-trip through both the Dakotas in a rented van, making the entire trip this time. I manage the trek through the Badlands on my own legs, enjoying the views while only panting a little bit.

And on the Enchanted Highway, I get to remedy my mistake. Because I have more than one day, which means there's time for second chances.

The second time hiking in Idaho is as hard as the first, but no one complains about my slower pace, and whenever Adam offers to give me a piggyback ride, Dom whips a snowball at his brother's head.

And this time, when we board a plane to fly into Denali National Park, every seat is filled by someone who loves Josh Sanderson.

Except for the pilot—we don't know that guy.

Rosaline, Adam, and Carter join Dom and me as we return to all the coordinates. We read them the letters. We cry together. We laugh together.

We say hello to my brother.

And goodbye.

Every trip we take new pictures, and the best shots become puzzles framed on our walls, just like the collection Dom and I took on our original trips. I don't mind the awkward expressions in the first few because now I know he loved me in each one. And I admit that a part of me still loved him, too.

With my newfound intention of allowing the people in my life to claim second chances, before the first trip, I call my mother. I offer to tell her about one of the places I spread Josh's ashes, but only if she promises never to post about it. To never use the information in any way for her media career.

She agrees. Too fast in my opinion.

A week later, Jeremy—my mom-blog buffer—tells me softly there is an Instagram picture of her standing on a beach in Delaware staring out toward the ocean. The caption talks about her son's ashes living forever in the sea.

I thought knowing that she'd likely lie to me would lessen the hurt. And yet, I still curl up in my bed that evening, gutted by one more betrayal. When Dom arrives home from work—early, at Jeremy's directive—he bounds up the stairs of what was his town house, but is now ours, and lies beside me. He pulls my body into his, and he keeps my pieces together.

Cecilia Sanderson does not get an invite to any of the trips.

Which is why the group on this glacier consists of Dom, Rosaline, Adam, Carter, and me.

Tula, Jeremy, and Carlisle came to Alaska with us, but wait back in the town, knowing this last leg is something we need to do as a family.

"Here." I hand Rosaline the container of Josh. The Rubbermaid that's gone with us on every trip this second time around.

Another thing I'm working on, as encouraged by my therapist, is sharing my grief, and acknowledging the pain others might be experiencing. Surprisingly, I've found Rosaline to be one of the easiest people to empathize with.

Maybe that's because I have Dom now. I know what it's like to fear losing the love of my life. A fear that came true for her.

And I realized that while my brother's ashes mean a great deal to me, they might mean even more to her in some ways. I've gotten to deliver seven pieces of him to his requested destinations so far. This last responsibility, the final step, feels like it should be hers.

Rosaline stands still on the icy tundra, staring at the group of us, wide-eyed as she clutches what remains of the man she loved to her chest.

"I . . ." she starts, then stops, her eyes going glassy. "I don't think . . ."

We all hear the rest without her having to say the words.

I don't think I can.

Or maybe, *I don't think I'm ready.*

No doubt I wore a similar expression last time I was here before panic robbed me of breath.

I don't want Rosaline to grapple with the same panic. Luckily, Dom taught me exactly what this situation needs.

I step up to Rosaline, holding her eyes with mine as I cradle her wrists. "That's okay, Ros. You don't have to. You don't have to say goodbye yet."

I know she's where I was, horrified at the thought that this is the last of him. That after this, there's no more of Josh to hang on to. To plan for. To imagine still living beside her.

Her nod is jerky, and she tries to pass my brother back to me.

I don't take him. Not yet.

"We don't have to say goodbye. But, how about we let a little of him go?" I tap the lid. "Just a pinch."

Her eyes drop to the remains. "Not all of the ashes?"

"That's right. And maybe a few years from now we can come back. Try again. Sound good?"

Now her nod is slow, measured, and her smile is full of relief.
"That sounds good."

"I'm in!" Adam offers.

"Me, too," Carter adds.

Dom appears at my side, his arm going around my waist and pulling me close as he sets a comforting hand on Rosaline's shoulder.

"It's a plan."

She shares her beautiful smile between us, then pops off the airtight lid.

"Here." Adam shuffles forward and holds out a crisp business card with **PERRY'S FINE FURNITURE** printed in bold letters across the front. "You can use that to scoop a little bit of him up."

"Thank you," she murmurs, and with the stiff edge of the card stock, she draws up a pinch worth of the remains. The wind immediately plucks them from the card and sends the gray dust spiraling away. Rosaline hurriedly replaces the lid, securing the rest of Josh inside.

Maybe one day she'll come to the same realization that I did. That those particles aren't my brother. Not really.

He's the memories I have. The memories we all have. And the best way to keep him alive is to remember him. Silently in our minds, but also out loud with one another.

"What was it like when you two came here together?" I ask Rosaline.

Her smile is small, and wistful. "Amazing. Romantic. And . . ." She chuckles, her cheeks flushing from more than just the cold.

"What?" I press.

"When we were walking back to the plane, he slipped and fell on his ass." Rosaline grins wide now, her eyes sparkling more from humor than tears at this point. "He had a bruise right on his tattoo. It was huge! He kept—" She dissolves into giggles, tears of laughter streaming from the corners of her eyes. "He kept asking me to kiss his peanut butter to make it better," she forces out through her gasping laughs.

We all join her, our group cackling at the new anecdote.

And I can feel him. Josh, in the middle of us, binding our group together. Our little family.

A finger under my chin tilts my head up, and I meet Dom's loving gaze. He presses a kiss to my cheek, his lips claiming a single tear.

Because of Josh, I'm not alone. And I don't think I ever will be again.

ACKNOWLEDGMENTS

Always number one on my thank-you list: Mom and Dad. This book wouldn't exist without your love, support, and willingness to walk my grumpy dog when I work late.

This book hinged on the love Maddie has for her brother, so of course I have to thank Brendan and Devin, my own brothers. I appreciate your willingness to answer random questions when I give you the vague explanation that it's "for a book." I'm grateful for the times we spend together, especially since we live far apart. Don't you go dying on me!

And thank you, Rachel, for loving Brendan enough to answer my random research questions as well. Sorry, it's a requirement for being a Connolly.

The first spark of this idea came from a true story of powerful love. Thank you, Debra and Brave Joe, for that inspiration. *PS: I Hate You* came to life because of you.

A team of people turned my sloppy draft into this beautiful book, and I want to applaud everyone at Berkley who took part in this magic, especially Liz, my amazing editor. Thank you for taking a chance on Maddie and Dom!

Lesley, my agent, is a wonderful human being who has supported me throughout the years. When I send a manuscript her way, I know it is in good hands.

Special thanks to all my friends who helped get the word out about my story! Allyson, Jocelyn, and MC, you've been my cheerleaders throughout this process, and it means the world.

Lastly, I want to thank every reader who picked up this book. That you spent even one day living in the love I built for Maddie and Dom is amazing to me. Writing and sharing my stories brings me joy, and I'm grateful to each and every one of you for helping me live my dream.

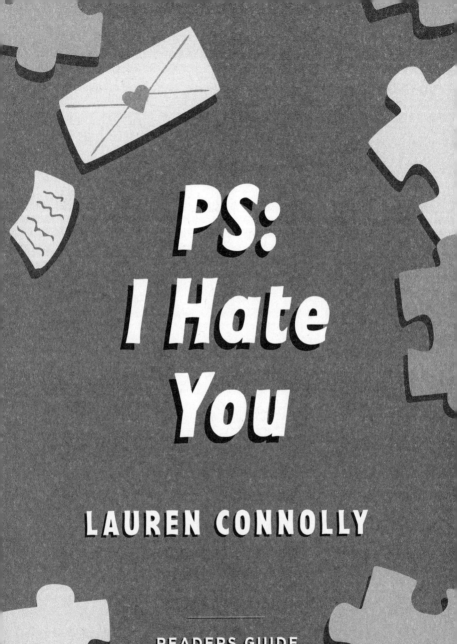

PS:
I Hate
You

LAUREN CONNOLLY

READERS GUIDE

MADDIE'S TRAVEL PLAYLIST

HATE/LOVE-YOUR-DEAD-BROTHER'S-BEST-FRIEND VIBES

1. "traitor" by Olivia Rodrigo

2. "Ghost Of You" by 5 Seconds of Summer

3. "Wishful Drinking" by Ingrid Andress (with Sam Hunt)

4. "How To Be Lonely" by Rita Ora

5. "Trying Not To" by Alana Springsteen (feat. Roman Alexander)

6. "Still into You" by Paramore

7. "Me Myself and Why" by Alana Springsteen

8. "Long Haul" by Ian Munsick

9. "it's been a year" by Ashley Cooke

10. "Death of a Bachelor" by Panic! At The Disco

11. "aftermath" by vaultboy

12. "Try Losing One" by Tyler Braden

13. "All You Had To Do Was Stay (Taylor's Version)" by Taylor Swift

14. "Twice" by Canaan Cox (feat. Shaylen)

15. "Locksmith" by Sadie Jean

16. "Homesick" by Alana Springsteen

17. "Love Is a Wild Thing" by Kacey Musgraves

18. "Ghost" by Justin Bieber

DISCUSSION QUESTIONS

1. Maddie loves cheese. She bakes Brie for her friends, reminisces about grilled cheese sandwiches Josh made her when they were growing up, and carries bags of Cheez-Its for Dom. What is your go-to comfort food?

2. How do you think the story would have turned out if Maddie and Dom had visited the states in a different order? If they'd had to share their perfect futures with each other on the second trip? If the secret-revealing North Dakota letter had been read earlier in the adventure rather than later?

3. Throughout the book, Maddie believes there's something wrong with the fact that she can't cry about losing Josh. She finds that her grief often morphs into anger and sarcasm, which she largely directs at Dom. How do you think her continued exposure to Dom affects her grief over her brother? What experiences do you have with large emotions (sadness, joy, anger, etc.) manifesting in odd behaviors that may not be viewed as "normal"?

4. Maddie is lovingly nudged (read: dared) into getting a tattoo during her visit to Kansas. Though the letter doesn't ask for the tattoo to be related to her brother, she chooses to get Josh's

signature on her wrist. If you were going to get a tattoo honoring a loved one, what would it be?

5. When Maddie realizes Josh has left letters, at first she is ecstatic that there is more of her brother—that he might not be truly gone. But soon her urge to read them battles her fear of eventually running out of his words. Do you think leaving a task for loved ones after someone passes affects the grieving process? If so, in what ways?

6. When Maddie and Dom are hiking in the Badlands of South Dakota, the letter requires Dom to sing some of Josh's favorite songs. If your best friends were to put together a playlist for you, what songs do you think they'd include?

7. Josh knew about Dom's feelings toward Maddie before he passed away but made no attempt to reconcile his sister and his friend while he was alive. Why do you think he waited? Why did Josh rely on his letters? What do you think would have happened if Josh had chosen to tell everyone's truths before he was gone?

8. Maddie and Dom were tasked with spreading Josh's ashes in interesting and beautiful places he never got the chance to visit. Is there a place in the world where you have gone or that you wish to visit that you think would be a pleasant eternal resting place?

9. By the end of the book, Maddie has gathered a family around herself made up of people she is not related to. How do you think this affected her mental health? How do you feel about the additional chance she gave Cecilia? What are your thoughts on blood relatives versus found families?

Photo by Evermore Photo Co. / Sara Wooten

Lauren Connolly is an award-winning author of contemporary and paranormal romance stories. She's lived among mountains, next to lakes, and in imaginary worlds. Lauren can never seem to stay in one place for too long, but trust that wherever she's residing, there is a dog who thinks he's a troll, twin cats hiding in the couch, and bookshelves bursting with stories written by the authors she loves.

VISIT LAUREN CONNOLLY ONLINE

LaurenConnollyRomance.com
𝕏 LaurenAliciaCon
⃝ LaurenConnollyRomance
⃝ LaurenConnollyRomance

Ready to find
your next great read?

Let us help.

Visit prh.com/nextread